1971

REPRISAL

BY

ARTHUR GORDON

SIMON AND SCHUSTER · NEW YORK

For
—and with—
Pamela

Note

The tragedy *at Morgan's Creek, as described in this story, is based on fact. However, the town of Hainesville, its inhabitants, and its law-enforcement agencies are completely imaginary. All the characters in this book are fictional; they are not intended to represent any actual persons, living or dead.*

A. G.

Princeton, 1950

CHAPTER 1

AFTER THE FURNACE glare of the street, the drugstore was dark as a cave. He went up to the cash register with his rocking terrier gait. "Change, please," he said. "Phone call."

While he waited, he leaned on his elbows and massaged his face with his hands. He was a compact little man in his mid-thirties with steel-wool hair and bright sardonic eyes. The skin of his face was loose and humor-wrinkled. It went out of shape when he pushed at it and took its time about crawling back.

When he had his change, he went into the phone booth and placed his call. It was like stepping into a sweatbox. He tried loosening his tie and pulling his collar open. When that did no good he came out of the booth, holding the receiver to his ear. When New York answered, he went back inside and closed the door.

"Let me speak to Cunningham, please." Cunningham's office would be dry and cool; air-conditioned, like its occupant. He did not like Cunningham; nobody did. But he was a good editor.

"Mr. Cunningham's office," said a starched, secretarial voice.

"Melady calling," he said impatiently. "Joe Melady."

The sweat was soaking through his shirt front, now. He could feel it running down the groove in his chest. He wished suddenly that he had never handed himself this assignment, that he had never come to Hainesville. Still, there was one consolation. The unexpected always annoyed Cunningham, so he would be annoyed by this. Good.

"Yes?" said Cunningham's precise whisper.

"Thought I'd better check in with you," Melady said. "The Atlanta job is finished. I air-mailed the story night before last. You get it?"

"Yes. Where are you? I thought you'd be back by now."

The little bastard, Melady thought; he might have said whether he liked the story or not. Aloud he said, "I'm in a red-hot phone booth about ninety miles from Atlanta. I'm covering a trial."

"Trial? What trial?"

Melady took out a limp handkerchief and mopped his face. The mouthpiece of the telephone had a stale, fetid odor. He draped the handkerchief over it. "Remember a little incident about a year ago that came to be known as the Hainesville Massacre?"

Silence for a moment, then Cunningham said, "Sure, I remember. A messy business; we ran a story on it. Mob down there killed four Negroes—two men and two women. Wasn't that it?"

"That was it," Melady said. "And I'm in Hainesville."

"Why, for God's sake? They haven't broken the case, have they?"

"No," Melady said, "they haven't broken it. But a little crack has appeared in it. I heard about it in Atlanta yesterday, hired a car, and drove down here."

Cunningham sounded suddenly interested. "You mean they finally identified some members of the mob?"

[2]

"Not exactly. Here's the story. They had a grand jury investigation of the lynching, remember? The grand jury listened to a lot of secret testimony, but never did get enough evidence to indict anybody. Or so they said. But apparently one of the witnesses they called, a colored boy who worked at the local icehouse, told of seeing three white men cleaning guns there the night of the lynching. Are you with me?"

"So far," said Cunningham.

"Well, the story leaked out, and not long ago the same three men paid a visit to the icehouse. They beat the living daylights out of the black boy—damn near killed him. So now they've got these three white men on trial in the Federal court here, charged with assault and intimidation of a Federal witness."

"Trial still going on?"

"It's almost over. Jury's out now."

"Think they'll convict 'em?"

"I doubt it. The Judge practically demanded a conviction, but after all, it's a white jury."

"Well," Cunningham said querulously, "if they're acquitted where's your story?"

"Hell, man," Melady cried, "the story is the town itself. Don't you see? The town's guilty, regardless of what the jury says. It's got blood on its hands, and a stinker of a guilty conscience. *That's* your story: the town that committed murder and got away with it. This trial is just a peg to hang it on."

"Um." Cunningham sounded thoughtful. "How much time would you need?"

"I don't know. Maybe a week. Maybe less, if I can find some stenographic help."

"I wanted you to cover something else."

"Give that assignment to one of your other slaves. I think I've got something here."

"Oh, all right," Cunningham said rather sulkily. "If you're on the spot you might as well stay there. But if you're going to tackle the race problem—which has been hammered almost to death lately—try to write about the Negroes as *people*, will you? Not symbols of suffering humanity or shuffling clowns. If you can make 'em *people*, with fairly coherent thoughts and reactions and emotions, you'll have done something no other feature writer has done yet—far as I know."

"I'll do what I can," Melady said shortly. He hated being given advice. Especially when it was good.

"Where are you staying?"

"Something they call the Eagle Hotel. It's not exactly the Ritz. Hang up, will you, for God's sake? I'm dying in this box."

"All right," Cunningham said. "Get on back to your trial. Keep your eyes and ears open."

Melady snorted. "How do you think I usually absorb information—by Braille?"

He hung up and came out of the phone booth. He stood under the overhead fan, letting the coolness flow over him like water. Through the hot yellow rectangle of the open door he could see the trees in the square, the sunburned grass, the heat waves quivering over the rows of parked cars. He pushed open the screen door and went out. A couple of loungers standing under the awning watched him with pale, hostile eyes. He stared at them contemptuously for a moment. Then he started back to the courthouse.

ii

THE courtroom was on the top floor. In summer the windows were always open, and the dry idiotic rasping of the insects in the trees outside came through and blended with the hum of the fans. Ordinarily the big ugly room was half empty. Today it was jammed.

Melady shoved through one of the doors and twisted down

[4]

the crowded aisle toward the space reserved for the press. People moved out of his way sluggishly, as if stupefied by the heat of their own bodies. Some of the faces were familiar to him; he had spent the morning studying them. The majority were countrymen: farmers in faded khaki or blue overalls, their skins burnt a dull brick color, their eyes light and expressionless. Some had brought their wives: tired plain women with babies on their laps. There were also businessmen in seersucker suits, avid housewives, teen-age boys in sweat-stained T-shirts, giggling bobby-soxers. In the gallery that clung to the wall a handful of Negroes sat, motionless. At the long table in front of the Judge's bench, flanked by their lawyers, the three defendants made a little triangle of tension.

The chairs in the press box were all taken; Melady had to stand behind a journalist with a shock of white hair who put his knuckles to his nose from time to time and sniffed loudly. He watched the shifting sea of faces, listening to the soft slurred voices. One girl in a mint-colored dress held his attention. He had noticed her before; she did not seem to belong there. She sat leaning forward, managing somehow, even in the crowded room, to look alone. She had dark hair pulled back from features that were too clear to be pretty. She would have made a handsome boy. Her eyes were either gray or green—sea-water color. Her mouth interested Melady; she held her lower lip thrust forward a little bit. It gave her a look of anxiety and anticipation. He decided her lipstick was a shade too dark.

Abruptly the courtroom was called to order. The Judge reappeared and summoned the jury. The twelve men filed back into the jury box, heads bowed, faces grave. The foreman stood up in response to the question from the bench. The room grew still and breathless, as if the ceiling had been raised suddenly, creating a vacuum. Everyone stared at the foreman.

He was a solid man with peevish bloodhound eyes. There were fresh razor nicks in the folds of his cheeks and his colorless hair was slicked down as if he had wanted to look his best for this moment.

The other jurymen sat staring at nothing.

The foreman put his knuckles on the railing of the jury box. He said softly, "We find the defendants . . ." and paused, prolonging his moment.

"Yes?" said the Judge impatiently. He leaned forward, a restless sparrow hawk of a man. His robe looked too large for him; the bench looked too high. But the yellowish eyes were hard and bright; above the freckled forehead the once-red hair still grew thick and aggressive.

The foreman, disconcerted, mumbled, "We find them not guilty," and sat down. He thrust out his lower jaw and stared defiantly at the Judge. There was a sharp sound as one of the defendants slapped another hard on the shoulder. Instantly a storm of whistles and high-pitched yelps burst from the spectators. Near the door, an overalled man sailed a black wide-brimmed hat into the air and caught it as it fell. In the front row, a barelegged girl in a calico dress stood up, tossed her brassy hair, and cried, "Nice goin', Bubber!"

The gavel slammed down. The applause died; the girl shrank back in her seat. The Judge gripped the edge of the bench with both hands. "Marshal!" A lean finger pointed. "Before he leaves, collect five dollars from the man who threw that hat!"

Silence again, except for the drone of the insects and the burr of the fans. Someone moved his foot so that it struck one of the brass spittoons. It chimed delicately, like a bell.

"Gentlemen of the jury," the Judge said with a faint, contemptuous accent on the first word, "you have acted in accordance with a long and miserable tradition. I trust you are pleased with yourselves."

[6]

The foreman of the jury thrust his head forward, looked down, spat noisily into the receptacle at his feet. Melady could see the dull red creep into his face. He settled back, raising angry eyes to the bench. The Judge stared him down. It took perhaps ten seconds. Then the tight mouth unclamped itself:

"These defendants were charged with assaulting and intimidating a Federal witness. You saw photographs taken of the colored boy shortly after the injuries were inflicted. You heard one of the defendants—the one known as Bubber Aycock—admit that he administered the beating. Witnesses testified that these men announced their intention of going to the icehouse where the Negro worked to beat him because—to use their own words—'he talked too much and needed to have his black mouth shut.'"

The Judge drew a handkerchief from his sleeve and dabbed at his face. In the jury box the twelve men sat stolidly. Their faces did not change, but on some foreheads little drops of perspiration began to appear. The spectators listened in hostile silence. In the gallery, the brown and black masks remained blank and submissive.

"You heard the evidence," the Judge continued. "You preferred to base your verdict on the contention of the defendants that they acted in self-defense." The thin nostrils flared. "A story without a shred of plausibility."

One of the defendants, a hulking giant with sand-colored hair, pressed the back of his fist against his mouth and yawned audibly. The yellow eyes flicked over him, then returned to the jurymen. "There are some cases in which the court takes pleasure in thanking the jury for a job well done. In this case"—the Judge sank his head into his narrow shoulders—"the court will have your names stricken from the jury list in this district. You have disgraced yourselves and this court. You will not be called upon to serve again, *gentlemen.*"

The gavel fell. The Judge stood up, gathering his too-big robe about him, and walked toward the door that led to his chambers. Instantly the crowd poured through the gate that had separated them from the defendants. Hands slapped backs; voices sputtered in the dry air.

The girl in the calico dress trotted around the ring of men until she found an opening. She put her head down and pushed through, her dress straining around her hips, the muscles tight in her bare calves, until she stood in front of the tallest of the three defendants. She gave an ecstatic squeal, flung her arms around his neck, and smeared his mouth with her lipstick.

Bubber Aycock gave her a playful smack on her calico bottom. "God's sake, Louella," he said, "stop shamin' yore uncle before all these people. They'll fergit I'm a re-spectable married man."

He gave a wheezing chuckle and his shoulders shook. His eyes swept the circle of faces to make sure his humor was appreciated. It was. Neal Aycock's scar-straight mouth cracked a trifle, and Bilsy Shoup, the sallow little hunchback who had been the third defendant, came sidling up and plucked at the girl's elbow with a hand that was like a claw. "If Bubber's bashful," he said in his high voice, "jest remember I ain't!" The crowd laughed again, the shrill laughter of a group released from nervous tension. A deputy marshal, lounging near the railing, said in a jeering voice, "That's tellin' her, Bilsy."

The jury box was empty, now, except for the foreman, who had not moved. One of the lawyers for the defense, a thin young man with long pale hands, hovered over him anxiously.

"Reckon I'm one of the biggest landholders in this yere county," the foreman was saying sullenly. "Reckon I pay more taxes than most. All I say is, he had no call to talk to us that-a-way. Judge or no judge. Give 'em a little a'thaw'ty an' some folks git to actin' mighty biggity."

[8]

"You did a fine job, Mr. Buckhalter," the young man said. He kept fluttering his fingers. "A mighty fine job. We appreciate your efforts, Mr. Buckhalter. We do indeed."

Buckhalter leaned forward and spat. "Mighty biggity," he repeated. "Some folks git to actin' mighty biggity."

Melady stood quietly, watching it all. When he looked again for the girl in the green dress, she was gone.

iii

UNITY CANTRELL left the courtroom, head bowed, elbowing her way through the crowd. She walked rapidly, almost running, down the hall until she came to an exit that led to a fire escape. She pushed blindly and went out into the tawny sunshine. Anger always sickened her.

Through the grating under her feet she could see the square below. It looked green and unsteady and too far away. She felt dizzy and closed her eyes. A breeze touched the wetness at the roots of her hair and stirred the skirt of her mint-colored dress. She waited until the fury was nothing but an acrid taste in her mouth and a tightness below her breastbone.

It hadn't been the verdict; she had expected that. But when the cheering began, when the girl in the calico dress smeared her lipstick over Bubber Aycock's meaty face . . .

She gripped the iron railing, staring down at the dusty magnolias, at the live oaks and the crape myrtles heavy with blooms the color of strawberry ice cream. Hainesville. She had lived here almost two years, she worked here, for all she knew she might die here, but Hainesville could never be her town.

It was not a big place. It lay spread out before her, streets blurred by trees, steeples placid in the lazy air. Farther out she could see rich red farmland beginning, and the railroad tracks glittering like dissected steel nerves in the waning sun, and the highway coming down from Atlanta in a merciless concrete arrow. It looked like a town full of good humor and an easy tempo of living. Pleasant, honest, decent, like any other American town.

You're guilty, she said to it in her mind; you're guilty. Today proves it.

She turned her back on the clear amber light. She went inside and joined the knot of people waiting for the elevator. When it came, she let herself be pushed to a corner in the rear. A soft, apologetic body nudged hers. Turning her head, she saw that it was Pop Halliday, the round, inoffensive little man who owned the Palace Drugstore across the street. His hairless face was beaming at her like a sweaty moon; his little paws were holding a stiff and yellowed straw hat in dangerous proximity to his own throat.

"Enjoy the trial?" he asked politely, over the hat.

Unity felt the elevator begin its slow, disembodied drop. She stared at the saw-toothed edge of the hat, repressing an almost uncontrollable desire to jostle the fat elbows so that the straw hat would bite into the flabby neck. Hurtfully. Suddenly. She said, "It made me sick."

The moist eyes widened in a look of injury and surprise. At the front of the car a couple of heads turned curiously, peered, then in accordance with the iron law of elevators swung front again. The motion stopped; the doors opened.

"Well," said Pop Halliday helplessly. "Well!" He settled the straw hat firmly on his head. "Gotta get back to business. Suppose you're through for the day?"

"No," Unity said. "I have to go back to the office for a while."

She walked away from Pop Halliday, down the steps of the courthouse, into the street. The worst of the heat was gone from the day, but the air over the baked sidewalks was still thick and lifeless. She lengthened her stride, trying to create her own breeze. She passed the Palace Drugstore, ignoring the pair of loungers who raked her lazily with their eyes.

"Nice," said one of these connoisseurs.

His companion spat delicately. "Not bad, if you like 'em rangy and stacked high. Not bad."

"Look," said the first. "Like I told you: some of it is good, and some of it is better. But none of it is bad."

The second connoisseur took out a knife and attacked his nails. "Reckon maybe you're right," he said.

iv

IN THE gallery of the courtroom, when the Judge had finished speaking, the Negroes got up quietly and moved toward the door. They filed out until only two were left, a squarish, chocolate-colored man holding a sheaf of yellow copy paper in his hand, and a slender, lighter-skinned Negro with a sharp, intelligent face and gold-rimmed glasses. The squarish man was a reporter from the *Blade*, a Negro daily in Atlanta. The other was Yancey Brown, colored undertaker in Hainesville. They stood there for a moment, listening to the tumult from the floor below.

Yancey said finally, "Get enough for a story, Howard?"

The other nodded slowly. "I can use some of what the Judge said."

"Some? Why not all?"

The sheaf of yellow papers slapped the stocky leg. "It'd sound too strong in print. They'd say we were inciting race hatred again."

"Who'd say so?"

"The *Bulletin*, probably. That's what they said when we ran the pictures of those corpses on the slabs in your undertaking parlor."

"Well, they weren't pretty."

"No, they weren't pretty; that's why we ran 'em."

"Do you have to do what the *Bulletin* says?"

"The *Bulletin's* a big paper for white folks. We're a little paper for colored folks. But we get our newsprint from the same source. We'd have a tough time if our supply was cut off."

"I see." Yancey made a wry face and glanced over his shoulder. The noise below was subsiding. "We'd better move along, Howard. No use runnin' into that crowd on the way out." His forehead wrinkled. "We may have trouble with 'em anyway, if they stay in town and get liquored up tonight."

The reporter put his notes into a coat pocket. "I don't see how you do it, Yancey."

"Do what?"

"Live out here in a town like this where you can't get away from it. In Atlanta, now, sometimes I go for days without ever speaking to a white man. Just do my job and keep out of their way. But here it's too small. You can't have a world of your own. You have to live in their world. As much of it as they'll give you."

Yancey shrugged. "I got a business here. Got to make a livin', like everyone else." He looked over his shoulder again. "What say we go now?"

Howard nodded. "Sooner I get out of this place the happier I'll be. Give you a ride home?"

"No, thanks," Yancey said. "I got to stop down the street and send a telegram. Promised somebody I'd let 'em know how the trial came out."

Howard grunted. "What damn fool needed to be told that?"

Yancey did not answer. They walked down the hall behind the gallery that led to the stairs. The elevator was not specifically reserved for whites. But they both knew that this was no time for them to use it.

IN THE dim, paneled room that had served many judges before him, Miles Winter took off the too-big robe and hung it in the musty closet. There was a mirror on the back of the closet door, and he peered at himself critically, smoothing his rust-colored hair with the flat of his hand. Across the room, standing in a patch of sunlight, young Saunders watched his chief admiringly. To his duties as law clerk to the Judge he had willingly added—in the five weeks since his graduation from law school—most of the functions of a body servant and a hero worship bordering on idolatry.

"You sure poured it on those jurors, Judge," he said. "You sure poured it on."

The Judge flung himself down on the sagging leather couch. "Think I overdid it?"

Saunders tried hard to look judicial. "I don't think they liked it much."

The Judge locked his hands behind his head. "What do you think, now, of trial by jury, Saunders?"

Saunders' smooth face looked startled. "Well, sir," he said cautiously, "we've always been taught that trial by jury is one of . . ."

"One of the priceless heritages of a free people. Quite so, quite so. They should also teach you that the law never quite catches up to the society it's supposed to regulate. It's always about a century behind. Now get the hell out of here for about an hour, will you, and let me get some sleep? I lost a lot of money at poker last night, and tonight by God I'm going to win it back. But I need one hour of . . ."

There was a knock at the door, a gentle, respectful knock.

"If that's Buckhalter," yawned the Judge, "leading a mob of

enraged jurymen, tell 'em I categorically refuse to be lynched until I've had my nap."

Saunders went to the door, opened it a crack. There was a whispered consultation, then he tiptoed back to the leather couch. "It's Lester Crowe. You know, editor of the paper here. Says he'd like a word with you."

The Judge sat up and ran a hand over his face as if to smooth the irritation out of it. "Oh, God," he said. "All right. Two good rules to follow, Saunders, if you want to get ahead in the world. Never draw to an inside straight. And never antagonize the press, even when it's an anemic little sheet like the *Courier*."

"Yes, sir," said Saunders.

Lester Crowe came in, carrying his soiled panama in one hand. He was a tall, stooped man in his middle fifties, with thick white hair, bloodshot blue eyes, and a voice that held a note of apology for its owner's failure to be the things he might have been. "Hello, Judge," he said. "Hope I'm not intruding." He tossed his hat on the table, ran the fingers of one hand through his splendid hair, pressed the knuckles of his other hand against his nose, and gave a loud sniff. It was a curious mannerism designed to reduce ear pressure caused by a chronic sinus infection. Even when they knew the reason, people often found it disconcerting.

The Judge came forward, holding out his hand. "Not at all; always glad to see you." He gestured toward a chair. "Drink?"

Lester's face brightened. "If it's handy." He collapsed slowly into a chair and sniffed again, less violently. "Nothing on my mind, really. I was in the courtroom just now, covering the case. Thought I'd stick my head in and tell you I admire your guts. Figured nobody else would bother."

The Judge gave a hoot of laughter and poured two shots of rye from the bottle that Saunders produced. "Easy to be brave when you've got nothing to lose by it. If my job depended on votes, now, I'd probably be a little less heroic." He held out one

[14]

of the glasses. "Going to put my immortal words in your newspaper?"

Lester took the glass, gestured with it, poured some of the rye onto his tongue, and swallowed slowly. "I may say that you seemed dissatisfied with the verdict. But that's all. When people read things they don't like in the newspaper, they get mad with the paper, regardless of who said 'em. Found that out a long time ago." He finished his drink in one long gulp.

The Judge beckoned to Saunders, who looked blank for a moment, then came forward and refilled the editor's glass.

Lester regarded the law clerk fondly. "Thank you kindly, son." The knuckles of his right hand made their swift automatic trip to his nose. He looked at the Judge, his eyes china-blue in their network of red veins. "You didn't really expect to get a conviction, did you?"

"I didn't expect it, no. But that jury was so smug and self-righteous that I got a little sore. Hell's-fire! Those countrymen practically admitted they were part of the lynch mob when they took the trouble to beat that black boy. It just naturally riled me to think of 'em adding assault and battery to murder, and then walking off scot-free. That hunchback doesn't count for much—he's just a hanger-on. But those Aycock brothers . . ." The Judge shook his head.

Lester rolled the rye on his tongue and narrowed his eyes with bliss. "Well, that's the end of it, I suppose. *Your* conscience should be clear, anyhow." He stood up. "Thanks for the refreshment. And thanks for the time."

"Not at all," the Judge murmured. He waited until Saunders had ushered the visitor out and closed the door. Then he loosened his collar and lay down again on the couch. He raised his right foot, pulled the laces on one of his narrow black shoes, eased it off, and let it drop. "Conscience. He talks about conscience. What would you recommend, Saunders, in cases where the normal processes of justice are blocked as they were today?

Would you say that the injured party had the right to avenge himself? Would that be preferable to letting the wicked go unpunished?"

"Well, sir," Saunders ventured, "that would involve breaking the law twice, and I can't see that two wrongs . . ."

"Oh, quite," said the Judge. "Quite." He pulled off the other shoe and held it in his hand. "If I had a black skin, though, I think I'd be tempted to do something about it. Very tempted." He weighed the shoe and let it drop. "But the thought of reprisal never seems to occur to them. They just sit and take it. So maybe I would too, if I had a black skin." He sighed and rolled over. "Call me in an hour, please, Saunders."

In less than a minute, he was asleep.

vi

YANCEY BROWN walked west on Blanchard, the principal business street in Hainesville. Behind his glasses his eyes made quick appraisal of each face as it came toward him. It was after five; offices were emptying themselves. Most of the faces, therefore, were white. Yancey knew many of them by sight, and some knew him. When an unfamiliar figure came toward him, Yancey noted the type of dress. For a business suit, or any form of city attire, he did not alter his course. For the dusty khaki or the faded blue overalls or the wide-brimmed black hat of the countryman, he veered to one side or the other, leaving a six-foot margin. A year ago he would not have thought it necessary to take this precaution.

He passed the gold-and-crimson front of the dime store, came to the corner, and waited for the light to change. A black-and-white car of the State Highway Patrol was parked at the curb. The patrolman, lithe and resplendent in whipcord breeches and black puttees, was chewing gum and talking to Pat Daly, deputy chief of the Haines County Police. Daly was an Irishman, fat and good-natured. The late sun reddened his amiable, rather stupid face.

He caught Yancey's eye and flipped a hand in recognition. Then suddenly he beckoned. Yancey did not hesitate. He walked up to the two men and stopped. "Yes, Lieutenant?"

"Been at the courthouse, Yancey?"

Yancey nodded. "Just came from there."

"Well, might be a good idea if you told your people to stay indoors tonight. Just stay off the street, then they'll be all right."

Yancey looked at him steadily. "I'll tell them, Lieutenant."

Daly hitched at his pistol belt and rubbed the chafed area fretfully. "No use borrowin' trouble, hey?"

"No," Yancey said, "we've had enough trouble." He glanced once into the glacial eyes of the highway patrolman, then back to Daly. "Thanks, Lieutenant."

"Take it easy, Yancey."

The two policemen watched the slight figure cross the street.

"Smartest coon in town," Daly said.

"Kind of uppity, ain't he?"

"Oh, Yancey's all right. He's a good nigger."

The patrolman said nothing. He took out a fresh stick of gum, unwrapped it, and began to chew it with his beautiful white teeth.

Yancey went on, past the movie-house, past the bank, past the dry-cleaning place owned by a colored man named Huggins that was doing the largest business in town. He went past the barbershop, past the shoeshine parlor where a man could be an emperor for a dime with a throne of his own and slaves bowing at his feet. At least, a white man could. He went on until he came to the white-and-blue sign that marked the telegraph office.

Inside, he picked up a pencil dangling from its little chain, thought a moment, then wrote a message and handed it to the bored blonde behind the high counter. She read it, counting the words and contemptuously adding a "t" to the word "acquitted," where Yancey had had only one. "Full rate or night letter?"

Yancey put his hand into his pocket and clenched his fist. The disdainful little flick of the pencil, correcting his spelling, had done something Daly's voice and the eyes of the patrolman had failed to do. No armor was proof against everything.

"Whatever's quickest," he said. He knew that a full-rate telegram was not necessary. He knew that it was more expensive. But the little bubble of resentment in the back of his mind was getting too big. He had to prick it before it got any bigger, and he did it the only way he could. He did it by sending a full-rate telegram where a slow one would do just as well. By taking the best he scored an obscure and pathetic triumph over the white girl who expected him to take second best. She could not know it, she would never know, but something inside Yancey knew it, and the bubble was pricked, and he felt better.

"Dollar thirty-five," the girl said indifferently.

He unclenched his fist slowly and took out his money and paid her. It was worth it, he thought. It was worth it because a telegram sent by a black man went just as fast as one sent by a white man. It was worth it because a telegram went by electricity, and electricity was like the eye of God, in Whose sight all colors are of equal value.

vii

IN FRONT of the courthouse the owners of half a dozen mud-stained cars were making certain preparations. Bubber

Aycock had hauled a bedraggled scarecrow from the trunk of an old Pontiac and was tying a rope around its neck. A placard was already pinned to the faded shirt. "Nigger-lover," the crude lettering said. Bilsy Shoup, using Louella's lipstick for a crayon, was working on another cardboard sign. "White Supremacy" he had printed, in letters a foot high. He tied it to the radiator of another car and stood back to judge the effect, his protruding chest and spindly legs giving him a sandpiper look. Around him the chorus swelled derisively.

"Who taught you them there big words, Bilsy?"

"Didn't know you could read, let alone write!"

"Aw, neh min' the decorations. Let's drive through Nigger Town an' show 'em. . . ."

"I know one great big winder right there on Blanchard Street jes' achin' for a brick. . . ."

"Keerful, now. Judge Winter'll put you right smack in jail if you talk that-a-way!"

"I de-clare, it's gittin' to where a man can't hardly do nothin' no more without the law jumpin' on him."

Louella hopped excitedly from one foot to the other. "I wanna ride with Bubber. I mean, right up in front with Bubber!"

A wispy old man in a black wool hat spat a stream of tobacco juice on the ground. "Louella, you sho' can talk mighty biggity for a fifteen-year-old."

Louella gave him a sulky look and turned her back. "I'm gonna sit right next to Bubber," she chanted. "Right up front next to Bubber!"

Fifty yards down the street in front of the Eagle Hotel, the bell captain in the frayed green uniform watched them, his chocolate face carefully wiped clean of all expression. A city policeman sauntered past. "Better get on back to the farm, boys," he said good-naturedly. "We don't want no more rough stuff." Nobody answered him.

[19]

In front of the Palace Drugstore one of the two loungers flicked his cigarette ashes with nervous, stained fingers. "Bastuds," he said. "Ignorant wool-hat bastuds!"

The other snapped his knife shut and made an easy prophecy. "They'll raise some hell in Nigger Town tonight," he said.

viii

THE building that housed the Hainesville *Courier* was old and narrow and roach-haunted. A worn flight of stairs led directly from the street to the editorial offices on the second floor. Into this unappetizing tunnel Unity Cantrell turned.

She climbed into the familiar atmosphere, an indescribable mixture of ink and stale tobacco, newsprint and paste, inertia and boredom. Pip the office boy was seated at his table, his porcupine head barricaded behind a comic book. Otherwise, the big untidy room was deserted. The *Courier* was run on a leisurely basis. It was a morning paper, but since it had no competitor in Hainesville it could afford to go to bed early. Most of the work was done by five o'clock. Lester Crowe usually stayed at his desk until nine or ten. If news broke after that, it had to wait until the following day.

Pip looked up as Unity appeared and his mouth worked soundlessly in the series of false starts that always preceded any statement. He did not stammer badly once he got past this initial hurdle, but the first utterance was always a struggle. Unity waited patiently until it was over. "Phone call for you, Miss C-Cantrell. Miss Fagan took the m-message."

"Thanks, Pip," Unity said. "Hester still here?"

Pip jerked his thumb over his shoulder and sank like a drowning man into the comic book.

Unity walked to the glassed-in corner office and pushed

open the door marked *Private*. The chair behind Lester Crowe's desk was empty, but Hester Fagan, the editor's secretary and general assistant, was standing at the washstand in the corner, drying her hands. Out of long habit, she held her face rigidly in profile until she recognized Unity.

"No sign of the boss," she said in her hoarse, pleasing voice. "But I'm going home anyway. If he wants me, he can damn well phone me."

She hung up the towel and put on her hat, pulling the brim well down over her right eye. "Another day, another inflated dollar."

She swung around, facing Unity, letting the terrible birthmark come into view. It lay like a slab of liver across the right side of her face from hairline to chin, discoloring even a corner of the mouth. It was so hideous and compelling that all the other attributes of the woman—the clear profile, the fine hands, the long classic legs—these things were rendered insignificant. Unity had worked in the same office with Hester for more than six months; the sight of the birthmark still jarred her like a blow in the stomach.

Hester gave her a searching look. "What's the matter? You look sort of peaked."

"I went to the trial," Unity said. Some instinct warned her that Hester would neither understand nor sympathize with her reaction to the verdict. "The courtroom was terribly hot," she added lamely.

"This dump isn't exactly air-conditioned either." Hester tugged automatically at her hat brim. "What happened? Turn 'em loose?"

Unity nodded.

"That's good," Hester said indifferently. She indicated some typed sheets on the desk. "Story's all written. Be a helluva bore if I had to change it."

"You wrote the story in advance?"

"Sure."

Anger made Unity forget her caution. "I think it stinks!"

Hester looked astonished. "What, the story?"

"No, the verdict."

Hester crossed over to the editor's desk and sat down on a corner of it. She put her long slender hands on her knees and swung her legs slowly. "How old are you, Unity?"

"Twenty-three."

"When you're thirty-three, like me, you won't be troubled by that surplus indignation."

"No?"

"No. What the world does to other people won't bother you so much. You'll be too busy worrying about what it's doing to you."

"I hope you're wrong," Unity said. It was easy, she thought, to discount bitterness when the source was so obvious. She said, changing the subject, "Pip mumbled something about a phone call for me."

"Oh, yes." Hester stopped swinging her legs. "Shep Townsend phoned." She sat very still, staring at her hands.

"Well?"

"He said he'd pick you up at six o'clock."

"Oh. That's a bit earlier than we'd planned. But I guess I can make it."

Hester had picked up a paperweight and was tossing it from one hand to the other. "You going out to his cabin?"

"I suppose so. He said something about a swim."

"Alone?"

Unity felt a prickle of annoyance. "No. My sister and another boy are coming."

Hester kept her eyes on the paperweight. "Do you know Shep very well?"

"Is that any business of yours?"

Hester made a gesture of apology. "I'm sorry. I used to work for Shep's father, did you know that? Two, three years ago, before the old man died. I suppose anything the Townsends do still interests me, that's all."

"Oh," said Unity. "Well, I haven't known him very long. I met him at some party a couple of months ago." She hesitated. "I've seen quite a lot of him since."

"Yes," Hester murmured. "I can imagine."

Something in her tone made Unity feel uncomfortable. She said, for lack of something better to say, "Was he popular at the lumber company?"

Hester put the paperweight down. "Well, there was some jealousy. People were bound to say he was spoiled. You know: the boss's son, only child, plenty of money, expensive cars, boats, and what not. Some of the men thought he was arrogant. But the women liked him."

"Did you?" asked Unity bluntly. If Hester could pry, so could she.

"Me?" Hester's mouth twisted sardonically. "Sure. The desire of the moth for the flame, and all that." She picked up her handbag. "He's a ruthless young man," she said. "He takes what he wants and doesn't care who gets trampled in the process. I admire him for it. In a way." She opened the door. "You might keep that in mind. So long."

The door closed. Unity sat down in the editor's swivel chair and glanced nervously at the wall clock. It was after five-thirty. She would be late for Shep if she waited much longer, and she did not want to be late for him. But she had made up her mind to see Lester Crowe before the day ended. If she put it off, she might lose her nerve. She wanted to ask him for a raise.

She took a copy of the *Courier* from the desk and began to mark items that had originated with her, or to which she had made some contribution. She had been hired originally to bring some order out of the newspaper's chaotic files. For half a year, now, her duties had been expanding. Her salary had not. It was the first paid job she had ever had; she was diffident about asking for a raise. But she felt she had earned it.

When she heard the slow familiar step on the stairs, she got up quickly from behind the desk and stood by the window. A moment later Lester came in.

"Well, Unity," he said with a surprised look. "Thought you'd be home by now. I saw Shep Townsend on the street. Said he was taking you out in the country for a swim."

"He is," Unity said, "but I wanted to see you." She hesitated, her carefully rehearsed speech failing her.

"Care to join me?" Lester said mildly. He opened the bottom drawer of his desk, took out a bottle and a glass. "Paper cups over by the water cooler."

Unity shook her head. "No, thanks."

Lester poured himself a generous drink. "I stopped in to see Judge Winter after the trial. Old boy didn't like the verdict. They were acquitted."

"I know," said Unity. "I was there."

"Really? Then you heard what he said to the jury. Pretty rough." Lester shook his head and waved his glass at Unity. "Your very good health, Missy. Yes, pretty rough. I don't think the learned Judge bothered to put himself in the jury's place. Ah-h-h, that's good." He took out a somewhat unclean handkerchief and wiped his mouth. "I know if I'd been on that jury I'd have thought twice before voting for anything but acquittal. If I wanted to sleep well nights, that is."

"Oh, Lester," Unity cried. "Don't *talk* like that!" She paced up and down, gripping her elbows.

The editor looked aggrieved. "How do you want me to talk? I'm just telling you the truth. What can I do? What can any one person do against a whole social system?"

"You've got the *Courier*, haven't you? Why don't you write an editorial denouncing trial by jury, if that's the sort of justice it gives us?"

[24]

Lester smiled and reached again for the bottle. "I did, once, when I was younger. Not here; in Carolina, that was. The editorial got picked up by the New York *Times*. We got a brick through the plate-glass window, and wrapped around the brick was a note saying the next mistake we made they'd burn us down. They would have, too."

"What you're saying is that you're afraid to do anything."

"Afraid?" Lester hunched his shoulders and sniffed. "I guess you could call it that. Or maybe when you pass forty, or even thirty-five, you stop trying to reform the world. God made it, after all. Why not leave it to Him?"

"God works through people," Unity said. "It's one of the limitations He placed on Himself—God knows why."

"That's a pretty good answer," Lester said. "I forget sometimes that your father was a preacher. But you weren't planning to give up your date with Shep Townsend just to discuss theology with me, were you?"

"No," said Unity. "It's not God I wanted to talk about—it's Mammon."

Lester looked up, a sudden wariness in his bloodshot eyes. "Mammon? You mean you want more money?"

"That's right." Her voice fluttered a little despite her efforts to control it. She indicated the ringed items in the newspaper. "I think I've earned a raise. I do all sorts of things now that are useful, things I wasn't really hired to do. I think you'll admit that. Besides . . ."

"Of course I admit it," Lester said impatiently. "You've developed tremendously. You're indispensable, really. But that's one of the traditions of this newspaper game: you take some of your pay in the form of experience. Why, I remember when I was your age I thought myself lucky to . . ."

"Please!" Unity stopped him. "Tell me, yes or no. Can I get more money here? If not, I've got to look for another job, that's all."

[25]

Lester put his knuckles to his nose and sniffed thoughtfully. "I'm not the owner of this sheet," he said. "You know that. All raises have to be cleared with Tarleton, and he's as tight as new shoes. I don't make enough myself to keep my wife decently dressed." He saw Unity's glance flicker toward the bottle. "Oh, all right. Have it your own way. I drink most of it. *And* consider it well spent. But I'll tell you this: the only way to get more money around this shop is by bringing more in." He eyed her speculatively. "Think you could talk Shep Townsend into increasing the amount of advertising space his lumber company buys? If you could, there'd be a raise in it for you. I can guarantee you that."

Something in his eyes, some faintly suggestive and ironic gleam, made her mouth go dry with anger. But she said, calmly enough, "That's a job for the business department, isn't it?"

Lester shrugged. He had long since discovered that after two or more drinks he could read almost any woman's mind. "Don't be angry with *me*, Missy," he said. "You're asking for more money. I'm simply telling you how to get it." He put the bottle back in the drawer and stood up. "Come on; I'll drive you home. Then you won't be late for your appointment. How's that?"

She smiled a little; Lester could be very disarming when he chose. "Fair enough," she said resignedly. "I'm ready."

"Let me take a quick look at my first draft of the Aycock story." Long ago Lester had succeeded in convincing himself that anything written by Hester must, somehow, be his own product. "I've saved a column on the back page. It's really only worth half a column, but there's a lot of interest in it." He ran his eye over the typescript. "That'll do, I guess." He picked up his panama. "Ready? Let's go."

They went out into the quiet street together. The sun was almost down, brushing the church steeples with coppery light. Lester's tired-looking coupé stood at the curb. He drove it slowly through the gilded streets. The whisky was working comfortably inside him; he felt mellow and unhurried. He let his shoulder touch Unity's lightly. She did not even notice the contact, but some obscure and dormant little beast inside Lester flexed its claws and was faintly gratified.

Unity stared blankly ahead of her. "You know, Lester, I try not to think about this Aycock business, but I just can't get it out of my mind. Do you suppose things will ever be any different where that—that sort of thing is concerned? Will these incidents go on happening, and people never care? Why should I worry, when nobody else gets excited? Am I queer, or something?"

Lester sat hunched over the steering wheel like some ancient white-thatched raven. "No, you're not queer. But remember, you weren't born in Hainesville, and you weren't brought up here. You're an outsider, like me. Things look different to you."

"I was born less than two hundred miles from here. The same state."

"Yes, but down on the coast things are different. It's an older part of the country, more settled, more mature. This is half frontier still. That's why they still have frontier law."

"Jungle law, you mean."

"Maybe so."

They drove for several blocks in silence. At last Unity said, "Do you think they'll ever catch and punish any of those—any of the lynchers?"

Lester slowed to avoid a disdainful cat. "I doubt it."

"But the trial today almost proved that the Aycock boys and Bilsy Shoup were part of the mob!"

"Almost isn't enough." Lester eased the car to a stop. "Here you are, Missy." He watched her get out. "Have a nice swim. Stop thinking so much." He gave a final sniff and drove away.

YANCEY BROWN's funeral parlor stood at the end of Primrose Street in the Negro section of Hainesville. It was a small frame building instantly identifiable by a show window in which an empty coffin rested on wooden trestles against a background of black crepe paper. Yancey, his wife Alma, and their small son lived on the second floor. The embalming room was in the basement.

Yancey let himself in quietly. He went through a parlor converted into a small chapel with folding chairs and vases full of artificial flowers. He climbed the stairs, and Alma met him at the top. She was a comfortable-looking woman with a gentle voice. She knew Yancey better than he knew himself. "What's wrong, honey?" she said.

The room was cool and restful after the heat of the street. Yancey sat down in the big chair that was his and took off his glasses. "Nothin', really." He rubbed his eyes. "I went to the trial, that's all."

Alma said nothing. He would talk it out, she knew.

"I didn't want to go much," Yancey said. "But Howard was down from Atlanta. He *had* to go, so I went with him."

"They let 'em go." It was more a statement than a question.

"Yeah, they turned 'em loose. The Judge was mad, but there wasn't much he could do about it."

Alma scraped with her foot at a spot on the linoleum. "Not much anybody can do about it."

"I sent a telegram to Nathan," Yancey said slowly.

Alma gave him a startled glance. "Nathan? Why?"

"He wanted to know how the trial came out. He sent me the money for the telegram."

[28]

Alma shook her head. "You shouldn't have done it. Just get him all stirred up, that's all."

"What's the difference? He'd have heard about it sooner or later."

Alma crossed the room slowly and straightened a picture on the faded wallpaper. "How you reckon he'll take it?"

Yancey shrugged. "How would you take it if I was murdered, and the law got three of the murderers in its hands and then let 'em go?"

"It's been almost a year. Maybe Nathan's got him another girl. Maybe he's begun to forget."

Yancey shook his head. "Nathan ain't the kind to forget."

"You think he might come back here?"

"Well, he knows now who three of 'em were. Up till they beat up that colored feller in the icehouse, wasn't no way in the world to tell for sure who was in that mob. But now . . ."

They were silent for a moment.

"I know what you're thinkin'," Yancey said. "I know what you're askin' yourself. And the answer is yes. Yes, he might."

"He better not come," Alma said. "Wouldn't do no good. Things been bad enough, but they could be worse. He better forget it. We all better forget it."

Yancey stood up. "How's Albert?"

For the first time Alma smiled. "Sleepin'."

"Let's go see him."

They walked together into the bedroom and looked down at the sleeping child, sprawled in three-year-old abandon across his cot. Alma bent down to straighten the sheet, then raised her head. "What's that?"

A braying of horns, starting as a confused clamor in the distance, was coming nearer. It grew steadily louder, an ugly, menacing dissonance. Yancey looked at Alma. "It's them."

"Them?"

"The Aycocks and their friends. They were fixin' to do this. You better keep away from the windows."

"Why?"

"Because they'll throw a brick if they see your head. They'll probably throw one anyway."

"They'll wake the baby!" Alma cried angrily. She pulled her husband out of the bedroom and closed the door. She went and stood defiantly at the window. "Look at 'em," she said, above the screeching of the horns. "Look at 'em!"

The motorcade swept past. Yancey moved to pull Alma away. He had a confused impression of sunburned faces, of open mouths contorted with yelling, of men in blue overalls or faded khaki, some sitting on fenders brandishing bottles. A stone arched from the rear of the last car. It was aimed at the show window below but missed it, striking the side of the house. The driver, turning his head to watch the flight of the stone, ran into the curb on the far side of the street with a jolt that dislodged one of the fender riders and sent him sprawling in the street. A liver-and-white hound, loping after the motorcade, bayed hysterically at the fallen figure, who stood up, brushed himself off, and ran shouting after the disappearing cars. From farther down the street there came the crash and tinkle of broken glass. The horns howled, diminishing in the distance.

Alma's face was rigid in the gray light. "They're gone."

"They'll be back," Yancey said.

"Can't we phone and ask the cops to stop 'em?"

"We can phone. Won't do no good."

They stood there for a while. Finally Alma turned away. "I'd better go fix some supper," she said.

THE house where the Cantrells lived sat back from the street with a faintly apologetic air. An uneven brick path led from the gate in the picket fence to the high porch, which, like the rest of the house, badly needed paint. In the rear was a garage. It was empty; the Cantrells had no car. Hattie, the colored cook, lived above the garage. She had been a fixture ever since the Cantrells moved to Hainesville.

Unity's father had bought the house not long before he died, but Unity never thought of it as home. It didn't smell like home. She missed the blend of coal dust and pipe tobacco, of leather chairs and furniture polish that had pervaded the old house in Savannah.

Sitting now in front of her dressing table in the bedroom she shared with her sister, she heard a car's door slam and then steps on the path outside. The bedroom door flew open and Helen's flushed face appeared.

She was a dynamic nineteen, still too busy discovering new sensations to be much concerned with anything else. She worked in Hainesville's only bookstore, a job which paid little but gave her plenty of time for daydreaming. She was prettier than Unity—always had been. Her hair had gold glints in it; her body already had a lushness that Unity's would never have. Unity felt a tolerant affection for her sister, shot through with faint surprise that she did not know her better. She consoled herself with the thought that nobody else knew Helen very well either.

"*Do* hurry, Unity!" Helen said in her light breathless voice. "They're *here*."

"Never hurts to keep 'em waiting," Unity told her cheerfully. "Mother home yet?"

"No. She and Aunt Guley are still down at the parish house. Please hurry, Unity." She closed the door. Her heels clicked on the uncarpeted stairs.

Unity arranged and rearranged her hair. She changed her lipstick because it seemed to clash with the pink of her blouse. Finally she touched her eyelashes with the mascara that she sometimes used, to the scandal of her Aunt Guley.

Hattie came in during this ritual and began to turn down the beds. She was a small, middle-aged woman with a flat, upturned nose, sherry-colored eyes, and the husky, good-humored voice of a semireformed dipsomaniac. Unity's father had literally picked her out of the gutter and had given her a job, disregarding the dire warnings of all her former employers. Hattie had rewarded this trust by remaining scrupulously sober during working hours. Her occasional lapses on her own time were more than balanced by her ferocious devotion to all the Cantrells. She moved around the bed now on spindly legs, covertly watching Unity.

"Sho' is fixin' herself up," she muttered, apparently to herself. "Sho' is prettifyin' herself fo' somebody. Wonder who it could be? Um, *um!*"

Unity stood up and made a face at Hattie. "As if you didn't know." She put her bathing suit and towel in a small overnight bag, looked at herself once more in the mirror, and went downstairs.

The two men were sitting on the sofa with Helen between them. John Haddon saw Unity first, and rose stiffly. He was a taciturn young man with a brown, thin-lipped face, very black hair, and wary blue eyes. He was the latest in a series of men who were beginning to be attracted by Helen's oddly provocative combination of invitation and innocence. He was older than most of the others. This intrigued Helen, as did the fact that he had lost a foot in the war. His limp was barely notice-

[32]

able, but he was hypersensitive about it. The injury was never mentioned. He ran his own tire and rubber company in Hainesville. He and Shep Townsend had known each other casually since childhood.

Shep got up with a powerful push of his arms. He went to the foot of the stairs and watched Unity descend. She came down slowly until her eyes were on a level with his stiff tan hair. She knew his features by heart, now; the slate-gray eyes, slanting a little bit, the high cheekbones, the heavy eyebrows much darker than his hair, the little white scar on his upper lip that broke the straight line of his mouth.

It was an uncompromising mouth, with no gentleness in it, and not much humor. But it had great strength, or the appearance of strength. She had thought a lot about Shep's mouth. She had wondered, with an urgency and abandon that startled her, what it would be like to have that mouth on her own, or seeking out the secret places of her body. So far, he had not touched her.

She was in love with this man; she was honest enough to admit that to herself. She wanted him for her own, but she wanted more than that. She wanted to challenge him, to shake that self-assurance, to *move* him somehow. And perversely, on a deeper level, she wanted ultimately to fail, to be unable to move him, to be crushed by him.

"I made it a little earlier," Shep was saying. "Thought we might try some aquaplaning if the light lasts. Ever try it?"

"Yes," Unity told him. "Once or twice."

Shep's convertible stood in front of the house, top down, chromium gleaming. The light was beginning to fade. A nighthawk, insect hunting, swooped down with a flash of white-barred wings, soared up again, and vanished. Helen and John climbed into the rear seat; Unity sat beside Shep. The engine purred; the car moved smoothly away from the curb.

"You're not very talkative," Shep observed after a while.

"I'm sorry," Unity said. "I had an unpleasant afternoon. It's still on my mind."

"Unpleasant?"

"I went to the Aycock trial."

"Oh, that. Have to cover it for the paper?"

"No, I just went."

Shep looked at her tolerantly. "You have strange hobbies."

"It's not a hobby. It's an—an obsession I've had ever since the lynching last year. I don't see how everybody can be so calm about it. It's as if—as if the town had cancer, and nobody cared."

"Nobody likes it very much."

"Apparently nobody dislikes it enough to do anything about it."

Shep shrugged his big shoulders. "It's unfortunate, I grant you, but it's nothing new. There's always been a layer of semi-educated whites, especially in the country districts, who hate the Negroes. I know the Aycocks slightly; they're typical. When life kicks them, they have to kick somebody, and the black man is handy."

"Furthermore," Unity said, "he can't kick back."

"They're afraid he will someday; a lot of the cruelty is based on that. The rest comes from ignorance, resentment, frustration—but hell"—he looked sideways at her—"most Southerners treat the Negroes pretty decently."

"I used to think so," Unity said.

Shep pressed his foot down and the car jumped forward. "Let's swim first and reform the world afterward, shall we?"

A sandy road carpeted with pine needles led from the highway to the cabin. It stood solidly against the sentinel pines, overlooking the river. At the foot of the bluff a boathouse jutted blackly into the steel-colored water.

"Best thing about this place," Shep said, unlocking the door,

[34]

"is the feeling of isolation. It's only three miles from town, but it might just as well be three hundred."

They went into the long living room. Guns and fishing tackle were racked on the walls. There was a stone fireplace at one end of the room, silver cups on the mantel. At the other end was a bar. In between, chairs and divans were scattered. A bunkroom was in the rear, and a small kitchen with kerosene stove. There was no electricity, no telephone.

"You girls can dress in the bunkroom," Shep said. "I'll use the kitchen. John, warm up the boat for us, will you? Keys are over there."

Haddon moved forward with his slightly off-balance stride, took the keys from their hook beside the mantelpiece, and went out. Unity had wondered if he would swim. Evidently not. How strange, she thought, to be self-conscious about an injury that was a badge of courage and patriotism. And yet, perhaps it was not so strange. People might react with pity—or revulsion. John Haddon looked as if he might resent one as much as the other.

In the bunkroom they changed quickly. Helen tugged at the zipper of her skin-tight black suit. It was fairly new. She watched distastefully as Unity put on her red halter and matching trunks.

"You really need a new suit, Unity," she said.

"Oh, sure," Unity agreed. "I'll just take that raise I asked for today and run right out and buy one."

"A raise?" Helen cried. "You got a raise?"

"I said I asked for it. I didn't say I got it."

Shep was waiting for them by the fireplace when they came out, his body brown and hard over his faded trunks. He glanced once at Unity, let his eyes shift briefly to Helen, who stood artlessly tucking her hair under her white cap. "This is the best part of the day," he said. "Let's not waste any of it."

He led the way out onto the porch, down the path to the

river. Haddon had the speedboat backed out, its engine throbbing. There was no wind. A bank of orange light hung in the western sky, dyeing the calm water. Behind the cabin a single star gleamed.

"Ready?" Shep asked.

John Haddon raised his head, stared at Helen, then bent over the engine again. He closed the hatch. "All set, I reckon."

The speedboat slid silently into the middle of the river, Haddon at the wheel, Helen beside him. Shep and Unity stood in the cockpit behind them. Unity looked up at him suddenly. "You could do a lot, you know. You've got the position and the opportunity and the—the strength. You might not cure the cancer, but you could make a start."

Shep had picked up the aquaplane. He stood holding the slender board slantwise across his body, the muscles of his chest and arms all planes and angles in the steely light.

"Would it please you if I did?"

"Yes. Yes, it would. More than you can possibly realize."

"Well, then," Shep said, "maybe I'll give it some thought."

xi

THE motorcade had shrunk to three cars: the car with the sign on the radiator, the car towing the scarecrow, and a third. When they came to a crossroad about two miles from town the lead car stopped suddenly and the other two pulled alongside, their combined headlights blasting a tunnel of light through the dark. In one angle of the crossroads was a filling station. Across from it was a country store.

The store was a whitewashed frame building armor-plated with tin signs. Its interior was lighted by naked bulbs dangling from wires. A woman came to the screen door, a bulky silhouette against the light. She listened to the chorus of drunken shouts, then raised one finger and hooked the latch.

The driver of the second car leaned out and cried angrily, "Whatcha stoppin' here for?"

Someone in the third car put his hand on the horn and held it there until someone else pushed it off. A bottle flew and smashed itself on the concrete. Voices rasped in the damp air.

The driver of the second car raced his engine suddenly, swung around, and headed back toward town, the scarecrow jumping like a live thing at the end of its rope. The third car backed uncertainly for a moment, then turned and followed. In the lead car an argument raged, then subsided when Bubber Aycock grew magnanimous. "We'll take Neal home like he wants," he announced, "an' then we'll take Bilsy to my house an' let him sleep it off. An' *then* by God I'll come back to this here store an' ain't *nobody* gonna stop me!"

The driver of the car gave a dry chuckle. "Less'n it's Nora. Well, I warned you about redheads, di'n' I, before you ever married her. I said . . ."

Bubber Aycock's hand came down on the seat like a pile driver. "Shut up!" he roared. "You talk too Godamighty much. Drive the car, an' shut up, Pa!"

The wispy man in the wide hat smiled furtively, as if he enjoyed goading the giant. He ground the gears badly, but he turned the car into the red dirt side road. In the back seat Bilsy Shoup lay with his head in Louella's lap, his twisted body inert and grotesque. Louella sat with her eyes shut and a look of incipient nausea on her face. Neal Aycock sat beside her. He held a bottle on his knee; every few seconds he hiccuped.

They followed the red road for half a mile, then turned off onto a dirt track. The headlights wavered across fields black and deserted. The road dipped suddenly. The lights picked up a swirl of muddy water and what seemed to be the skeleton of a bridge. The driver slowed almost to a stop, shifted gears groaningly, then crept forward. The bridge was little more than a trestle with flat strips of iron to fit a car's wheels. It trembled and swayed as the weight descended on it. From the close-packed vegetation on either side of the creek the tree toads whirred a steady chorus.

Bubber Aycock lit a cigarette. The spurt of yellow light burst against the massive structure of his face, then vanished. "Drive steady, Pa. Don't let no ghosts twist the wheel on you."

In the back seat Louella's eyes flew open. "Don't you talk like that! It ain't funny!"

Bubber's thick shoulders quivered. "If this place ain't haunted, then I reckon every nigger in the county is a liar. You won't find one who'll cross this bridge after dark."

The car hit the dirt on the other side of the creek and lurched up the hill. Pa Aycock gave his whinnying laugh. "Can't say as I blame 'em, all things considered. How 'bout it, Neal? Your house is closest. You see any ghosts down here, or hear any?"

Neal belched derisively. Louella flinched. "Hurry up, Gran'pa," she said in a disgusted voice.

The car topped the rise, turned off into a yard enclosed by a wire fence, and stopped in front of a small farmhouse. A little knot of dogs burst from under the house, barking hysterically. Neal got out, the bottle still in his hand, and made his way unsteadily to the steps that led to the porch. The occupants of the car watched while he let himself and the dogs into the house. The door slammed.

Bubber Aycock shook his head. "Jesus, what a way to live! All by yourself with some mangy dogs. No family, no woman, no nothin'."

Pa Aycock eased the car back onto the road. "He farms good, though," he said defensively.

"Yeah, but what good does it do him? He don't spend no

money, or have no fun. He don't even like likker. An' likker don't like him. The more he drinks, the meaner he gits."

"He farms good, though," the old man said.

xii

INSIDE the farmhouse Neal Aycock lit the electric lamp with the fringed shade that stood on the table and put the bottle beside it. He pulled down the shades and stared around the room. It was surgically clean and entirely colorless except for three scarlet cushions on a horsehair sofa backed stiffly against the wall. Some dust had settled on the wooden arms of the sofa, and he wiped it off. He picked up one of the cushions and smoothed it, holding it against his chest with one hand, stroking it with the other. The rag rug in front of the fireplace was crooked; he straightened it. One of a series of farm journals lying on the table was out of line; he put it back.

While he did these things, two of the dogs moved restlessly around the room behind him. One was a small mongrel bitch named Nellie. The other was a sad-faced coon hound of standard variety. The third dog was a powerful creature, half shepherd, half airedale. It lay motionless, its yellow eyes watching Neal. Its name was Rex.

Neal sat down in the chair by the table and picked up the bottle. About two inches of colorless liquid remained. He uncorked it and took a long gulp. He gasped and bared his teeth. Nellie crawled across the floor toward him, wagging her rump. He put out his foot and shoved her away.

He raised the bottle again and emptied it. He stood up and went into the kitchen, where he put the empty bottle on a shelf. Then he came back through the living room, went into his bedroom and turned on the light. The room was furnished with a bed, a chest of drawers, a mirror, and a washstand. Nothing else.

Neal undressed slowly, hanging his clothes carefully in the closet. When he was naked he stood for a moment in the center of the room, swaying a little. He blinked, as if trying to make up his mind about something. Then he bent down. From the bottom drawer of the chest of drawers he took a pair of pajamas still in their cellophane package. Red silk; new. He tore off the cellophane and crumpled it. He picked out the pins in the cool, heavy material and let it unfold with a faint slithering sound. He put on the trousers first, then the jacket. He buttoned it up to his chin, moving his shoulders sinuously. He smoothed the red silk over his arms, looking at himself in the mirror.

Finally he went back into the living room. His fingers were extended toward the fringed lamp when Nellie touched his foot. She sniffed once or twice and then began to lick his toes. Her tongue made a rhythmic lapping sound in the quiet room.

Neal turned out the lamp and stood very still. From the bedroom a block of yellow light fell across the floor. He reached down slowly and closed his hand on Nellie's nose. The licking stopped, but her muzzle remained in his hand, pulling gently against the pressure. His fingers closed tighter, crushing the soft lips against the teeth. Nellie whined; her feet made scrabbling noises on the bare boards. Rex slunk into a corner. The hound trotted up behind Nellie and gave a short anxious bark.

Neal let go of Nellie and all in the same motion caught the hound. He rolled it on its back, cuffing it lightly from side to side, slowly at first, then faster and faster. The animal squirmed onto its feet. Neal caught it and tossed it against the wall. Not too hard. It bounced and fell on its back, but was up instantly. It made a pathetic little ducking gesture with its head, as if it hoped this were only a game, a game it would be glad to play if it could. Neal slapped it across the muzzle— a thick, wet sound. He struck it again, so hard that it yelped. It made a desperate dash sideways into the corner where Rex was crouching. Neal lunged after it, ignoring Rex. The big dog snarled; its teeth clashed. There was a harsh tearing sound and Neal straightened up, holding his arm. The crimson sleeve was ripped from shoulder to wrist. On the forearm a red gash in the skin began to ooze slowly.

Neal backed away, his eyes on the dog. Rex glided across the floor and clawed frantically at the door. Neal pinched the torn fabric together, then let go and groped behind him. When he brought his hand forward again it held a stick of lightwood from the box beside the fireplace. He began to move forward holding the stick like a club. Rex flattened himself on the floor in front of the door, hair bristling, his yellow eyes wild.

Neal kept inching forward, the club held ready. "You hadn't orta done that, Rex," he said. "You hadn't orta tore 'em."

xiii

WHEN the car stopped again, Bubber said, "Come on in for a minute, Pa."

The gray-faced man shook his head. "Not me. I doan' want Nora to go blamin' all this on *me*."

"All what?"

Pa Aycock glanced over his shoulder at the limp figure of Bilsy Shoup, then at the farmhouse squatting dark and silent under a gigantic live-oak tree. "All this drinkin' an' such. You know how Nora carries on about drinkin'."

"Godamighty," Bubber said. "Way you talk, might think Nora was boss around here." He opened the door and got out.

"Come on, Louella, move outa there an' lemme carry Bilsy."
He lifted the hunchback in his arms. "Pore little bastud don't
weigh hardly nothin'."

Louella yawned, stretching her soft body. "Night, Grand-
pa. Thanks for the ride."

The old man waved a bony hand. " 'Twarn't nothin'. Doan'
git a chanst to celebrate like this ever' day." He yanked nervously on the gear lever and the machinery screamed in
protest.

"Put the clutch in, God damn it," Bubber yelled. "All the
way in!"

The old man nodded, but at the gate, where he shifted into
second, he ground the gears again.

"Godamighty!" Bubber stood in the darkness, his feet wide
apart, holding Bilsy in his arms. "He thinks he's still drivin'
a model T." He spat disgustedly. "You better go in first,
Louella. I didn't reckon we'd be this late."

Louella crossed the screened porch. She went through the
open door, swinging her hips, and down the dark hall that led
to the kitchen. Bubber followed, Bilsy's feet bumping noisily
along the wall. Louella opened the kitchen door and blinked
in the strong light. " 'Lo, Nora," she said apprehensively.

The woman at the sink turned around, a wet dishcloth in
her hand. Her mouth was thin with anger; her cheeks were
sucked in, making deep hollows under her cheekbones. Her
eyes were a smoky brown, with little points of fire in them.
Her hair had been red once, but now it was a dull and lifeless
copper. She wore it pulled back from her forehead with an
almost savage severity. She was about thirty-two; she looked
forty.

"Well!" she said explosively, slapping the dishrag down.
"It's about time!"

Bubber came and stood in the door, completely filling it
with himself and his grotesque burden. He looked once at his

wife, then walked across the kitchen, kicked open the door of a small bedroom—evidently an unused servant's room—put Bilsy down on the unsheeted mattress. He came out and closed the door. He put his back against it. "Hear 'bout the trial?"

Nora had not moved. "I heard about it." Her fingers twitched. "An' I heard about what went on afterwards. Drivin' through the nigger section, drunk as all get-out, hootin' an' hollerin' an' chunkin' bricks through winders. I heard about it, all right. Cissie Robertson jest had to phone me every half hour so she could enjoy tellin' me. An' me sittin' here with supper ready, an' you out there drinkin' an' makin' an everlastin' fool of yourself, as if we hadn't had enough mis'ry with your drinkin' already. An' now you bring home that piece of drunken white trash to clutter up my house, an' you stand there an' ask me if I heard anything!"

"Godamighty," Bubber said. "We do a little celebratin', an' you act like it was the end of the world."

"Celebratin'!" Nora's voice rose shrilly. "Celebratin'!" She came and stood in front of him, her thin face distorted. "You, with a breath that'd stink up a polecat an' . . . ." She stopped and stared at him. *Where'd you git that lipstick?*"

Bubber rubbed a hand guiltily across his mouth. "Lipstick? Oh, that came from Louella. That's right. It was from Louella." He laughed uneasily. "Reckon she was just showin' everybody how glad she was her uncle wasn't goin' to jail. That was it, wasn't it, Louella?"

Louella leaned against the table, her face sullen. Nora looked her up and down. When her husband's sister died, she had agreed to take Louella into her home. Lately she had begun to hate her adopted niece; she was not sure why. She said, "You better git to bed, Louella."

Louella was not afraid of many things, but she was afraid of Nora. She went.

[43]

Bubber yawned. "Maybe that's what we orta do—stop this yammerin' an' go to bed."

Nora glared at him. "I'll go to bed when I'm good an' ready! An' when I do, I don't want you messin' around me, Bubber Aycock, with your big dirty hands an' your stinkin' corn-likker breath. You can go sleep with your smelly little hunchback. Go on!" She walked over and kicked open the door where Bilsy lay, bluish face turned upward, snoring faintly. "Go on, sleep with your crooked little half-wit! You care more about him'n you do about me anyway."

Bubber narrowed his eyes. "You lay off'n Bilsy, now, you hear? He can't help bein' what he is. Now you lay off'n him, or by God you'll find yourself back in Atlanta in that ten-cent store, that's where you'll be, sellin' pink pants to niggers. . . ." His voice rose to a jeering taunt. "An' that's where you belong. Yeah, that's where you belong! Whyn't you go on back there? You're no damn good to me. Go on back, an' maybe that mealy-mouthed preacher you got up there'll come around an' pray over you twice a day!"

"You leave him outa this!" screamed Nora. "He's a man of God, an' you're not even fitten to mention his name. So help me, if it weren't for him I'd a left you long ago! *He's* the one who believes there's some good in everybody! *He's* the one who says the marriage vows gotta be kept, no matter what! An' you stand there an' blow your stinkin' breath an' try to talk him down!"

Bubber moved suddenly. He crossed the kitchen, brushing past Nora, not looking at her. "You'll open your ugly mouth once too often," he said. He went out. The back door slammed.

Nora stood still for a moment. Then she picked up the dishrag and went and sat in the straight chair by the table. Her fingers plucked at the coarse mesh of the cloth. Once she would have wept, but not any more. Her head trembled a little, but there were no tears.

[44]

BUBBER went to the shed that served as garage, backed out his mud-stained sedan, gunned the engine until it stopped coughing, then drove back along the silent road, past Neal's house, where the windows were dark, over the groaning bridge, up the other side. Occasionally his heavy lips moved as he talked to himself. "Sleep with a hunchback, hey? I'll show her who I'll sleep with, by God!"

An image of Geneva came up in his mind, and his thoughts ran hot and fast, the way they always did when he thought about her. He remembered the first time he had seen her, two years ago when she first came to work in Minelli's store. She had stood there in the gloom, her black hair piled on top of her head, not kinky but soft, her thighs pressed against the counter so that her flat belly bulged a little when she leaned forward. She was always leaning forward, wrapping a package, or tying one, so that you could see the white part in her hair and the golden valley between her breasts. Bubber moistened his lips. A yellow skin, sure, but almost white. Plenty white enough.

He'd had plenty of girls, but he'd never touched a yellow one until he met Geneva. Even now some obscure part of him considered it faintly degrading; he hoped his friends would never know. Mrs. Minelli, the old witch who ran the store—she probably knew, or suspected. And the niggers knew—they always knew. But nobody else. He'd been too careful, ever since the day he had stopped his car outside the store and called to Geneva, who was sweeping the steps. "Git in, girl," he'd said, holding the back door open, "I got some aigs at home I want you to bring back to the store."

There had been no eggs, and Geneva had known it. He

had seen the mockery in her eyes as she put the broom against the wall and climbed into the car. He had watched her face in the mirror, smiling faintly. It had not changed even when he turned off the road and sent the car lurching through the sand and pine needles on an old lumber road.

She had obeyed him when he stopped the car and told her to get out—it was near midday, hot and still. She had walked ahead of him down the little road. Of her own accord she had turned off at a place where the pine saplings formed a low green wall, and when she turned around he saw that she had unbuttoned the front of her dress. She flexed her knees and lay down on the amber pine needles, locking her hands behind her head, her underarms the color of old ivory. She was always like that, cool and deliberate at first. But more than once she had left the marks of her teeth on his neck or shoulders, left them so plain that he had had to be careful for days that Nora did not see them.

They had a place, now, where they met—usually at night, always by prearrangement. Geneva's old grandmother, Elvira, sometimes carried messages between them. Their meetings were short and violent. They never discussed anything; sometimes they hardly spoke to each other. Bubber always paid her; it was insurance against losing her. He supposed there were plenty of black men in her life; he did not like to think about it. When he did, he wanted to kill the slut, to pour gasoline over that gilded body and set fire to it, so that if he could not have it all to himself, nobody else could have it. And there were other times when he wished she were white, so that he could get rid of Nora and set himself up openly with Geneva. Although Nora would never divorce him. That was the funny thing about Nora, he reflected grimly: cold as a lizard in bed, but jealous as all hell. Maybe it was the religion in her. Take the way she had looked at Louella tonight, enough poison in that one look to kill a person....

At Minelli's store he turned right and drove along the Atlanta highway for half a mile. Every hundred yards or so, Negro cabins flanked the road, gray in the faint moonlight. A few had electricity. In the rest, the mellow light of oil lamps stained the night.

When he came to the cabin where Geneva and Elvira lived, Bubber slowed down. He peered through the windshield. The cabin was dark and silent. He looked at his watch and swore softly to himself. Then he turned the car and drove back to the store.

The lights were still on. Bubber parked the car. He took a pack of cigarettes from his shirt pocket and tossed them on the seat. Then he got out, went up to the screen door, pushed it open, and walked in.

On his right, half hidden behind a glass case full of penny candies, a massive white woman with gray hair was shelling peas. She glanced up, black eyes alive and gleaming in her still face, then went on with her work.

"Howdy, Miz Minelli."

"Hello."

Bubber slapped the pocket of his shirt. "Plumb outa cigarettes. Lemme have couple packs, will ya?"

"What kind?"

"You should know. Been sellin' 'em to me long enough."

The woman got up, unsmiling, and pushed the cigarettes across the counter. She took the money and unlocked a wooden drawer to make change.

Bubber leaned his weight on his hands, and the worn boards creaked. "Geneva around?" He tried to make it sound casual.

Mrs. Minelli's eyes remained as black and impenetrable as the eyes of a turtle. "Aimin' to celebrate a little?"

Bubber drummed his thick fingers. He knew his attempt at deception with the cigarettes had failed and he hated Mrs.

Minelli. "Just had somethin' I was fixin' to ask her." He jerked his head toward the rear of the store. "She back there?"

Mrs. Minelli shook her head. "Didn't come to work today."

"Not at all?"

"Not at all."

"She sick, you reckon?"

Mrs. Minelli lifted her shoulders in an old-world gesture. "These yellow ones, they are even lazier than the black ones." She opened a pod with a dirty thumbnail and let the peas rattle into the pan. She said, from under sardonic eyelids, "Her grandmother is back there. Would she do?"

Stinkin' ole bitch, Bubber thought furiously. He clenched his jaw muscles till they ached. "Maybe she could tell me what I want to know," he said finally.

He turned and went into the back of the store, his shadow marching ahead of him, black and enormous. He went past the shelves of canned goods, around the rusty iron stove, past the tins of kerosene until he came to the narrow alcove where the dry goods were kept, bolts of cotton cloth stacked almost to the ceiling. Here another light bulb dangled nakedly. Under it sat an ancient Negress the color of saddle leather, smoking a corncob pipe and sewing. She jumped up when she saw him and put the pipe in her pocket, live coals and all. "Howdy, Mr. Bubber; howdy, howdy!"

Bubber loomed over her. "Where's Geneva?"

The wrinkled face assumed an expression of concern. "Why, Geneva, she right po'ly today, couldn' hardly git out de baid, so I tol' her, I say to her . . ."

"Never mind what *you* told her! *I* told her I'd likely be lookin' for her, an' now she ain't here. Why ain't she?"

"I jes' done tole you, Mr. Bubber, she got a mis'ry in . . ."

"Damn your black hide, old woman," Bubber roared, "you're lyin' an' you know it! Godamighty, how is it lyin' to white folks comes so easy to you niggers?"

[48]

The sad monkey eyes looked at him with sly derision. "Maybe 'cause we's had to do so much practicin', Mr. Bubber," the old voice said.

XV

IN HARLEM, later that night, Nathan Hamilton came home. He moved easily through the heat-sodden streets, past the reeling ash cans, under fire escapes clotted with sweltering humanity, through the pools of radiance cast by the street lights on the black asphalt. Once a girl spoke to him, a single questioning obscenity from the shadows. He paid no attention. He had worked late at the trade school where he was an instructor. He was tired.

He came at last to the apartment building where he lived. It was clean and well kept, with a self-service elevator. There was nothing squalid about it, although it rubbed elbows with dreadful squalor. He rode up to the fourth floor, where he had a one-room apartment. The telegram was stuck into the crack of the door.

He picked it up slowly and held it for a moment in his hands. They were slender hands, and strong, with putty-colored palms and a few tool nicks in the close-grained skin. Without opening the envelope, he unlocked the door and went in. He pressed the light switch, moved over and placed the telegram on the mantel. Stepping back, he lit a cigarette. He inhaled deeply, letting the smoke trickle from his nostrils. He pulled down his tie and loosened his collar, keeping his eyes on the telegram.

The mirror above the mantel gave back his familiar image: brown skin, firm mouth with rather thin lips, small delicate ears set flat against his head. His hair was short; it fitted his skull like a cap of black caracul. A balanced face, but nothing distinctive, nothing memorable. Name: Nathan Hamilton, no middle initial. Age: twenty-five. Sex: male. Height: five feet ten. Weight: one hundred sixty-two. Race: Negro. Religion: none. Criminal record: none. Marital status: widower. Occupation: teacher. Specialty: automobile engines. That was all.

He picked up the telegram, glancing once around the apartment. It was neat, precise—a methodical man's room. Across the street a restaurant sign pulsed rhythmically, throwing spurts of greenish brilliance. Abruptly he moved to the door, switched off the overhead light, went over to the window sill. He opened the telegram, sitting there in the semidarkness, hunched against the intermittent flashes of light.

After a while, he read it.

CHAPTER 2

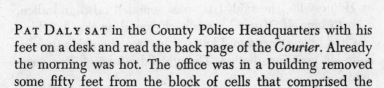

PAT DALY SAT in the County Police Headquarters with his
feet on a desk and read the back page of the *Courier*. Already
the morning was hot. The office was in a building removed
some fifty feet from the block of cells that comprised the
County Jail, but the same sour miasma of sweat and disinfect-
ant, stale food and urine, pervaded both buildings. Daly was
used to it.

He got up, crossed the room, tapped on the door of his
superior's office, and opened it a crack. "You busy, Chief?"

Matson, the County Police Chief, glanced up from his desk
with hard, colorless eyes. He was a steely-looking character,
stringy and tough. He had not been in office long.

"*Courier* don't say nothin' about them shenanigans in
Nigger Town last night." Daly's fat face looked grieved. "How
come they always give them city cops a break? If it'd been
us, now, they'd a said we were failin' in our duty to keep law
an' order."

Matson grunted. "Anything happens after sundown, that
paper can't be bothered with it." He turned his head and spat

accurately into an enamel cuspidor. "How much damage they do, anyway?"

Daly shrugged. "Not too bad. Broke a few winders. Busted into Huggins' dry-cleanin' place, an' messed up a lot of clothes. Chased a few niggers but didn't rightly hurt none of 'em. They was in a pretty good humor, I reckon."

A policeman stuck his head through the door. "Feller to see you, Chief. Reporter, he says; talks like he's from up Nawth."

Matson rasped a hand across his chin and looked at Daly. "Better see 'im, hey?"

Daly shrugged again. "Either way, you lose."

"Send 'im in," Matson said.

Melady came in with his aggressive rolling gait. He identified himself and came straight to the point. "I'm doing a story on Hainesville," he said. His voice sounded crisp and alien, even to himself. "I need some background on that lynching you had here a year ago. I know it happened outside the city limits, in your jurisdiction. Thought I'd ask you a few questions."

Matson had taken a match from behind his ear and was chewing it. "I wasn't Police Chief then," he said slowly. "Maybe you'd learn more readin' some back numbers of the papers. They told everything—and then some."

"I'll check the papers when I get around to it," Melady said. "You learn more from people than you do from newspaper morgues." His bright terrier eyes fixed themselves on Daly. "You on the force at the time of the lynching?"

"Yeah," said Daly. "I was here."

"What happened?"

Daly hitched uncomfortably at his pistol belt and glanced at Matson. "Feller was drivin' four niggers back to his farm one afternoon. Mob stopped him down by Morgan's Creek, killed all four of 'em. That's what happened."

"The 'feller' couldn't recognize any of the killers?"

"That's what he said."

"What was the 'feller's' name?"

Daly looked again at Matson, then back to Melady. "Aycock. Pa Aycock."

"Father of these two Aycocks who were acquitted yesterday?"

"That's right."

Matson took the match out of his mouth and spat again into the cuspidor. "All this is old stuff, mister. What you gettin' at?"

Melady grinned maliciously. "The truth, I hope."

"The case is closed," Matson told him. "Why not let it stay that way?"

"As a police officer, I should think you'd want to see the case solved."

"I would," Matson said. "I would."

"You don't act much like it."

"Maybe," Matson said, "maybe it's because I don't like nosy reporters. Especially when they come from up North."

"I don't like dumb cops, either," Melady said. "No matter where they come from. But sometimes I have to deal with them."

Matson got up with a slow stretching motion. "Open the door, Daly!"

Melady looked amused. "Sure," he said. "Go on. Throw me out. I'm on my way to the mayor's office anyway. He'd love to hear about it. So would my magazine."

Matson put his hands down on the desk. He leaned forward; his face looked tight and dangerous. "I'm very sorry that we can't supply you with any more information."

"That's all right," Melady told him. "I'll get it elsewhere." He waved a jaunty hand and went out.

"The little bastard," Matson said evenly. "I'd like to meet him when I'm out of uniform sometime."

Daly rubbed the back of his fat neck, a gleam of reluctant

[53]

admiration in his eyes. "He's got guts, for such a little runt."

Matson spat. "Don't take much guts to tease a dog when you know he can't bite."

Daly made a remark he had made countless times in his long and reasonably successful career. "Reckon you're right, Chief," he said.

ii

AT NOON the sun stood so straight up in the sky that there were no shadows. At the crossroads, Minelli's store crouched behind its barricade of tin signs, muffled in heat and silence. Outside the screen door, a ginger-colored cat lay limply on the top step. An occasional car whined past.

Bubber climbed out of his dusty sedan and went into the store. He had timed his arrival to coincide with Mrs. Minelli's siesta. Each day shortly after noon she retired to some private region of the store, leaving everything except the cash drawer in charge of Geneva.

Bubber noted with satisfaction that Mrs. Minelli's chair was empty. There were no other customers. Geneva stood behind a counter, leaning back against the shelves. When she saw who it was she stretched her arms sideways in a gesture that pulled her dress tight across her breasts. She lowered her chin a little; her dark eyes looked interested and scared.

"Soap," Bubber said. He always asked for some minor item; it was part of the camouflage he maintained.

Geneva turned and reached for the soap. Bubber came up to the counter so that when she turned back his face was close to hers.

"Elvira tell you what I said?"

Geneva nodded. She leaned forward and began to wrap the soap. She was smiling a little.

[54]

"You be there," Bubber said hoarsely. "Nine o'clock."

She tied the package and bit the string. Her teeth were small and even and very white. Bubber knew how sharp they were. He was sweating. He put his hands on the counter and made himself keep them there. "Where were you yesterday?"

Geneva looked at him insolently. "Sick."

"Don't lie to me," Bubber said in a furious whisper. "You weren't sick. You were with somebody an' you were just too damn hawg-lazy to crawl outa bed. Well, give your black boy friend a message from me. You tell him to remember what happened to Buckeye Miller! You tell him that, you hear!"

Geneva looked at him steadily. She said nothing. Near the front of the store there was the faint sound of a door opening. Bubber straightened quickly. "Nine o'clock," he said. He turned and walked away, his weight making the floor creak. The door that led to Mrs. Minelli's room was open. The black turtle eyes regarded him sardonically.

"Get what you wanted?" said Mrs. Minelli.

"Naw," said Bubber harshly. Anger made him forget his caution. "But I'm gonna git it. It's gonna be delivered, see? An' it better be good!"

He jerked open the screen door. The ginger cat lay across his path. He drove his foot at it, but it fled under the store, untouched.

"Stinkin' ole bitch!" Bubber muttered. He opened the door of his car and wrenched the wheel around. The engine caught; the car moved away.

iii

"Hell, yes," the barber said reminiscently, "business was wonderful. Reckon I did more business in the first ten days after the lynchin' than I usually do in a month."

He tied the cloth around Melady's neck and tilted back the chair. He was a small rabbit-faced man with soft hairless hands. He chewed gum, and one eyelid dipped resolutely in time to the champing jaws.

"Yes, sir," he said. "Just about this time last year. Reporters was thick as flies. Cameramen too." He began to whisk up the lather in a china mug. "You a reporter?"

"Me?" said Melady. "I'd just as soon be dead."

"Well, anyway, they was here in droves. People didn't mind 'em at first. But they got sick of 'em." He drew the brush along Melady's chin. "Some of 'em wrote some mighty mean things about this town." He shook his head. "Mighty mean."

"What was at the bottom of it?" Melady asked. "What got the whole thing started?"

The razor slapped slickly against the strop. The rabbit face loomed nearer, eyelid pulsing malevolently. The razor touched Melady's skin; he closed his eyes.

"It all started from nothin'," the barber said. "Know what I mean?"

Melady grunted sympathetically through the lather.

"Farmer out here a ways had a field hand named Buckeye Miller. A big, mean nigger. This farmer—his name was Dillinger—heard Buckeye quarrelin' an' fightin' with his wife. He went to separate 'em, an' first thing you know, Buckeye stuck a knife in him."

"Kill him?"

"Naw. Sent him to the hospital, though." He pronounced it "horspital."

"Why was Buckeye beating up his wife?"

The razor whittled gingerly at Melady's upper lip. "Well, *some* said it was 'cause she was too friendly with Dillinger, know what I mean? An' *others* said it was 'cause Buckeye was foolin' around with some yaller gal an' his wife didn't like it.

[56]

Anyway, Dillinger went to the hospital an' Buckeye landed in jail."

Melady opened one eye. "What became of Buckeye's wife?"

"The wife? Oh, she went to stay with her brother. He worked down the road a ways for an old farmer named Aycock. They kept pesterin' the old man to get Buckeye out on bail. He did, an' on the way home this mob stopped him down by Morgan's Creek an' killed all four niggers."

"Four?"

"Yeah. Buckeye's wife had a sister who worked here in town, an' she was ridin' back with 'em. Good-lookin' gal, for a nigger. Reckon the mob thought so too, 'cause they . . ." The rabbit face leaned close and whispered something. Melady's hands clenched, then relaxed.

"You say somethin'?" asked the barber politely.

"I said, I hope she was dead by that time."

"Well, they was all good an' dead when they got through with 'em."

Silence for a while. The fan droned. The razor purred.

"If Buckeye was the one they wanted," Melady said at last, "why did they kill the others?"

"Aycock said it was because Buckeye's wife recognized the leader of the mob, an' called his name."

"But Aycock couldn't remember the name, of course."

"Reckon he thought it was better to disremember it."

The noise of the razor ceased; the hot towel appeared.

"Where was Dillinger all this time?" Melady asked.

"Him? Oh, he was still in the hospital. *He* wasn't in the mob." The towel descended wetly. "Reckon they didn't hardly need him. They took eighty-ninety slugs out of them coons. Feller lived down the road a piece heard the shootin'. Said it sounded like a canebrake burnin'. Bay rum?"

Melady shook his head.

"But like I said, business was mighty good, what with the reporters an' the cops an' the F.B.I. They *say*"—the confidential whisper again—"the F.B.I. is still on the case. Got men scattered around here still, waitin' for a break. Know what I mean?"

Melady sat up and stroked his chin. It was a good close shave. "Think they'll get one?"

"Naw," said the barber. "Not hardly. Anybody was gonna talk, they'd've talked by now."

"How many people you suppose could name one or more members of the mob if they felt like it?"

The barber gave a quick, surprising bark of laughter. "Quite a few could. An' lots more think they could. But nobody will. Everybody'd know who talked, see? Because everybody's watchin' everybody else, wonderin' how much the other feller knows, or whether the stranger who moved in next door is really— Say!" For the first time there was a silence in which the jaws did not champ and the eyelid remained ominously still. "Where'd you say you was from?"

Melady climbed down from the chair and pulled up his tie. He put on his coat and held out a bill. He looked at the rabbit face hovering anxiously before him. "I didn't say," he told him. "Keep the change."

iv

THE place where the brick had gone through the plate-glass window was covered by a piece of cardboard. There were still a few slivers of glass on the street, glinting in the sun. Yancey kicked one into the gutter. He glanced around. Then he pushed open the door with the splintered lettering: "Dry Cleaning, Pressing and Dyeing," and went in.

Huggins and his wife and the girl who helped them were

[58]

still cleaning up the place. Huggins was a portly, middle-aged Negro, very dark, with a mustache of frosted silver. His wife was fat and shapeless. When she saw Yancey her face went all to pieces and she began to cry. She fled behind the partition. The colored girl went with her.

Yancey looked around, his eyes appraising and angry. "Sorry to hear about this, William."

Huggins dug into the pile of clothes in front of him and held up a stained garment. "Ink. Took the inkwell right off the desk an' th'owed it. Look." He pushed his fingers through a rent in a dress. "Knife done that. How come they do this to me, Yancey? I ain't done nothin' to them. I pay my taxes. I give to the Red Cross an' all those white folks' charities. How come they do this to me?"

Yancey brushed some fragments of shattered mirror off a straight chair and sat down. "You make money. You dress well. You drive a new car." He shrugged wearily. "What's the use of askin' why, William? You got off light, I reckon."

Huggins shook his head. "I heard about it an' come right down here. I fought to build this business; I'd of fought to keep it. But they was gone. Nobody here but a city policeman, standin' guard. So there wouldn't be no lootin', he said! Where was that cop when they busted the winder and kicked in the do', that's what I'd like to know! Where was he then?"

"Prob'ly standin' across the street, watchin' 'em."

"Yeah, but suppose this had been a white man's sto'?" Huggins said with sudden ferocity.

Yancey shrugged again. "How much damage, William? That's what I came to find out. Can you handle it yourself? If you can't, there's an organization I know of has a fund for this sort of thing."

Huggins wiped his mustache slowly. A certain dignity came into his face. "I can handle it, I reckon. You better save that fund for people who have real bad trouble."

Yancey got up from the chair. "You'll make out all right, William," he said. "Better go see about that woman of yours. Tell her it ain't no use cryin' over spilt ink." He hesitated at the door and drew the corners of his mouth down wryly. "Tell her it might have been blood."

V

FROM behind his cluttered desk at the Apex Tire and Rubber Company, John Haddon, lately buck sergeant in the 36th Division, looked out at the world with brooding eyes. He had been a fine athlete as a boy; his body had brought him a certain fame, and he had respected it a great deal. He had been a tough, aggressive infantryman, sure that no bullet would touch him. The land mine on the north bank of the Rapido River had taken off his right foot just above the ankle. The stump had healed well; his limp was hardly noticeable. The real scar was in his mind.

He stayed behind his desk as much as he could. A man behind a desk was expected to be only half a man. When he came out from behind it, he did not talk much, and he found that he grew angry easily. He was terrified of making advances to a woman and being rebuffed because of his wound. It had happened, once. That was why, so far, he had not attempted to touch Helen Cantrell. But she was photographed in his mind, and in his mind he had touched her often. He was thinking of her when the convertible slid up beside the gas pumps. Through the glass front of his office he saw Shep beckoning to him.

He got up slowly and went out, feeling the reluctance tug at him. There were times when he resented Shep, resented the fact that he had been an officer, resented his money, his assurance, his position in the town. A position, Haddon felt, acquired by the accident of birth, nothing more. He said, making it sound friendly enough, "Hello, Shep."

Shep ran one hand through his stiff hair. "Boat's acting up, John. I had a lot of trouble with it this afternoon. Think you could run out and take a look at it tomorrow?"

"I guess so." Haddon felt a sudden twinge of envy. "Need it to take out a girl?"

Shep laughed. "I might. It helps sometimes. Any time you want to try it yourself, just let me know." He leaned back, his eyes amused, as if he knew what was in Haddon's mind. "That Helen really fills a bathing suit, doesn't she?"

Haddon said, "She's not the one you had in mind, is she?"

"Helen?" Shep shook his head. He tapped his forehead. "Nothing up here. She'd bore me stiff."

"Her sister doesn't bore you?"

"No," Shep said. "She doesn't."

Haddon leaned his forearms on the car and wondered what he could say that would be annoying. "She looks cold, to me."

"Cold? No. Inexperienced, maybe. Not cold."

"Have you . . . ?"

"No."

"Then how can you tell . . ."

"By her mouth," Shep said, not letting him finish. "Ever notice how she shoves that lower lip at you? I like that."

Haddon felt the familiar resentment churn inside of him. Confidence, arrogance—these had been his weapons, once. He said abruptly, "You won't get anywhere with her."

Shep's eyes crinkled at the corners. "Think you'll do any better with the fair Helen?"

Haddon looked at the ground. "I don't make any bets on myself any more."

"God's sake, John!" Shep sounded exasperated. "The war's over! How long you going to keep on playing this sensitive-veteran role? What the hell, you don't need two feet to make love. You don't even need one foot!" He bent down and started the engine. "Get wise to yourself, man!" He flipped a hand. "Be seeing you." The car moved away.

Haddon stood looking after it, eyes narrowed against the slanting sunlight. Then he wheeled and limped into the semi-darkness of the garage. A pair of colored mechanics were at work in one of the pits, greasing a truck. Haddon halted beside it. "Junius!" His voice was harsh. "Thought I told you to get the tires changed on that Buick. What the hell's it still standing there for?"

The Negro wiped the sleeve of his coverall across his forehead. "We got plenty of time, Mr. John. Man ain't comin' for it till after seven."

"Suppose you do what you're told," Haddon said, "and quit answering back!"

He went into the office. The door slammed. The other mechanic looked at Junius, tight-lipped. "Mean-talkin' son of a bitch!"

"Aw," said Junius easily. "Mr. John's all right. He cain't he'p it. He's got a mis'ry in his mind, tha's all."

vi

"Lotta people in this town felt bad about that damn lynchin'," the taxi driver said. He craned his neck so that he could watch Melady in the mirror. His eyes, behind their dark glasses, were red-rimmed and weary. "Like me, Mack. I ain't got nothin' against the niggers. They gotta live. I know it ain't a man's fault if his skin is black. I felt right sick when I heard about that killin', and a lotta other folks did too."

He stopped for a traffic light and leaned forward on the

wheel. "But shucks, when all those newspaper fellers wrote what they did, and everybody started blamin' Hainesville, and all them Yankee radio commentators started soundin' off—well, you know how human nature is. People get sore. Nobody likes to be blamed for something they didn't do. And the respectable people here in Hainesville didn't have nothin' to do with that lynchin'."

"No?" said Melady.

"No," said the driver. "You know who I think done it? Some of them convict guards, from over in Clayton County. They're a mean, tough lotta bastards, and most of 'em hate niggers. Hell, they *must* hate 'em if they make a livin' outa settin' all day long in the hot sun with a shotgun on their knees watchin' 'em sweat! And you know somethin' else? That Dillinger—that feller who got cut—he'd been a convict guard himself. Don't you reckon some of his pals decided they'd have themselves a little nigger-killin' just to settle accounts for their old buddy?"

"I wouldn't know," Melady said. "Don't you think the Aycock brothers were in on it?"

"Oh, they probably was. I ain't sayin' so, mind you. Don't quote me! But I bet those convict guards organized it."

"I don't see how they could have moved so fast," Melady objected. "Aycock didn't tell anybody he was taking Buckeye out on bail, did he?"

"Shucks," said the driver. "They knew Buckeye was in jail. They might have fixed it up with somebody at the jail to let 'em know if anybody bailed Buckeye out. One phone call would a done it. But hell, I don't know. I'm just guessin'." He slowed down. "We just about covered the town now, Mack. Anything else you want to see?"

"I don't think so," Melady told him. He massaged his face with his hands. "I've seen enough for one day. Just run me back to the hotel."

"OH, AUNT GULEY," Unity said miserably, "it was awful. I made Lester let me go down there this morning when I first heard about it. Those poor people had worked so hard to build up that little business. It was a shambles: ink, broken glass, smashed mirrors—you never saw such a mess. I felt ashamed of being white!"

They were on the porch. The green roller shades were down; the sun thrust horizontal fingers through the cracks, making a kind of filtered suboceanic light. Unity was sitting in the swing. Behind her, Aunt Guley moved slowly along the window boxes, watering plants. She was a tall, angular woman in her early sixties with large melancholy eyes and hair which, astonishingly, showed no sign of age. It was as brown and glossy as a chestnut.

"I wrote a story about it," Unity went on, "but Lester blue-penciled most of it. Said it was too strong."

"Probably was," said Aunt Guley.

"It was the truth!"

"That's just what I mean," said Aunt Guley. "The truth is too strong for most people."

She put down her watering can and sat down beside Unity. Aunt Guley had never married. She had maintained spinster quarters of her own in Savannah, but when the Cantrells moved to Hainesville she had announced her intention of going with them. Nobody had objected, so here she was. She had a tendency to hide from people behind an air of gentle distraction that could be very misleading. But she did not hide from Unity.

"You're just like your father," she said now. "Always trying to make things better than the good Lord intended them to be. You'll find a lot of grief that way."

"I suppose so," Unity said. "But I feel so helpless. And I get so mad. When I get mad, I feel sick. I've been feeling sick for a year, now."

"Mad about what?" Helen had come out on the porch, full of the vitality she always displayed once the working day was over.

"Mad about what they did to Huggins' place," Unity said. "Or don't you even know about that?"

"I heard about it," Helen said. "And I think it's a shame. But honestly, Unity, you get too excited about these things. Isn't it silly to get so worked up over things you can't help—or control? I think it is."

"It's the penalty of having a conscience, child," Aunt Guley told her.

Helen tossed her hair. "I've got to run down to the grocery store for Mother. Supper's almost ready."

Unity watched her sister go down the path. "No use blaming Helen," she said. "Her attitude's the standard one. Deplore it—and do nothing. I'm not much better, really. I don't do anything, either. I don't know *what* to do." She was silent for a while. "I did try to work on Shep a little bit. He's got the—the strength. And the position. He could do something, if he wanted to."

Aunt Guley picked up a fan made of palmetto. "You're in love with him, aren't you?"

Unity said nothing. She would have resented the question from anyone else. Not from Aunt Guley.

The fan moved languidly. "Have you asked yourself why? Or don't people bother to do that any more?"

"You can't always analyze those things, can you?" Unity leaned back in the swing. "He annoys me sometimes. He's so overbearing; so—so contemptuous of people weaker than him-

[65]

self. And yet, I admire that, in a way. When you're full of un-certainties yourself, it's a relief to be with someone who's so positive, so sure." She pressed her thumbnail down on the arm of the swing. Hard. "Maybe I like to be dominated. I don't know."

"I knew a man like that once," Aunt Guley said mildly. "I always wondered what enormous weakness he was concealing under all that display of strength."

"I don't think Shep is covering up any weakness," Unity said. "He's just—well, he's just what he is, that's all. I'd like to change him a little, make him see . . ." She stopped suddenly, and laughed. "Speak of the devil!"

Shep had driven up and parked at the curb. He got out and opened the gate. Aunt Guley stood up. "I'll go and give your mother a little help."

"Don't go," Unity said. But Aunt Guley was gone.

Shep came up the steps two at a time. "Just driving by," he said easily. "Thought I'd ask you to go riding with me tomor-row after work. Doing anything?"

"I'll be working," Unity said. "Wednesdays I have to stay late down there."

"How about Thursday, then?" Shep sat down beside her.

"That would be all right, I think."

Shep looked at her closely. "What's the matter? Something on your mind?"

"I was just talking to Aunt Guley about the vandalism down at Huggins' dry-cleaning place. I guess that's still on my mind."

Shep offered Unity a cigarette. When she refused, he lit one for himself. He stretched out his long legs and contemplated the toes of his shoes. "Aren't you getting a little too involved in all this? Personally, I mean?"

"I've been involved in it personally from the beginning."

"From the beginning?"

"You know Hattie, our colored cook?"

"Hattie? Yes."

"She has a son, Nathan. Nathan Hamilton."

Shep blew a thin stream of smoke. "The one who used to work at John Haddon's garage?"

Unity nodded. "You knew him, then?"

"Sure. He was about the best mechanic in town. Came out and fixed the speedboat a couple of times. Had a good war record, too, didn't he?"

"I don't know about that. All I know is that when the lynching happened, he'd been married only a month. And his wife was one of the ones they killed."

Shep whistled faintly. "Pretty rough."

"It was horrible. And in a way, it was my fault."

"*Your* fault?"

"Yes. I sent Nathan away. Or rather, he was away because of us. We needed some things from Savannah—Daddy's will, for one thing; it was just after he died—and I sent Nathan down there. If he'd been here, his wife wouldn't have tried to spend the night with her sister. She wouldn't have been in that car, and . . ." Unity's voice trailed off.

"Damn bad luck," Shep said at length. "Still, I think you're silly to blame yourself."

"Oh, I don't blame myself, exactly," Unity told him. "But I was the one who had to tell Nathan what had happened. I won't forget that in a hurry."

"What became of him?"

Shep frowned.

"He went to New York. Hattie has a sister up there, and he went to live with her. He didn't want to stay here. I don't blame him."

"I don't either," Shep said. "But I do blame you for clinging to the thing this way. What's done is done, for God's sake! You can't change it. The things you're talking about are like John Brown's body—they're moldering in the grave. We're alive."

He put his hand on hers; it was the first time he had touched her. "But they're dead."

She moved her hand away. She wanted to be touched by Shep, but not now, not while she was discussing this subject. "They're not dead," she said sharply. "The tensions are still right here in Hainesville, the secrecy, the whisperings, the wonderings about who knows what. Look at that trial yesterday! Look at what happened last night! How can you say it's dead?"

"All right," he said. "What do you want me to do? Buy Huggins a new window?"

"You might start by doing that. But fifty dollars in an envelope pushed under a door isn't going to do any good. You've got to take a stand, Shep, and let people know it. The only thing that'll do any good is public opinion. Somebody's got to lead it." She stood up. "I'd better go in now. Sorry I've talked so much."

"That's all right." He went with her to the door.

"Think about what I said, will you, Shep?"

"I told you before, I'll go to considerable lengths to please you."

She shook her head. "I don't want it that way. I want you to do it because you think it's right."

His gray eyes were amused. "When you need help, it's better not to question the motives of the people who help you. You might give some thought to that."

He touched her hand again and went down the steps into the red eye of the setting sun.

viii

IN HARLEM, the same ruddy glare coppered impartially the evil-smelling brownstones, the refuse in the gutters, the sagging clotheslines, the peddlers' carts, the scrawny cats, the gritty windshields on the gritty cars. . . .

Nathan Hamilton took the elevator to the fourth floor and let himself into his apartment. The shades were down. It was neat and quiet. Every morning, after he left for work, his aunt came up from her apartment on the floor below and cleaned the room thoroughly. It was one of many services rendered by his Aunt Cele.

He crossed over to the mantelpiece. The telegram lay where he had left it. He had forgotten to destroy it and had worried about it all day. But his Aunt Cele had not found it. He put it in his pocket.

He took off his coat, reached under the bed, and pulled out a suitcase. Opening a bureau drawer, he began to pack. From under his shirts he took a Luger pistol wrapped in a flannel rag. He had bought it from an infantryman in Italy, complete with two clips of ammunition. He had never fired it. He weighed it in his hand; the checkered grip felt cold and lethal and uncompromising. He put it in the suitcase.

When the packing was finished, he took off his shoes and lay down on the bed. There was still the problem of his Aunt Cele. He could lie to her, or he could tell the truth, but he could not go away without seeing her.

She was expecting him for supper. He watched the clock. A few minutes before seven he got up and put on his coat and shoes. He walked down to the floor below, let himself in with the key he had. His suitcase he put in the coat closet, out of sight. Then he went into the living room.

"That you, boy?" His aunt came to the kitchen door, an apron over her dress, a floury spoon in her hand. She was his mother's sister, but she did not look like Hattie. She was a giantess, with steel-colored hair and black eyes sunk behind high cheekbones. It was a strong face, creased with sternness and good humor. "Lord," she said, "it's too hot to breathe,

[69]

let alone cook!" With the income she had from her two beauty parlors, Aunt Cele could have had a dozen cooks had she wanted them. She didn't want them. She preferred to do things for Nathan herself.

"Sit down, boy," she said. "Supper's about ready." After thirty years of Harlem, the South was still in her voice.

The table was laid by the window. Aunt Cele did not approve of eating in the kitchen. It was something she had escaped from, a badge of inferiority she no longer had to wear. She brought soup in a covered tureen and sat down opposite Nathan. She looked at him sharply, some finely tuned mechanism inside her picking up vibrations that disturbed her. "Things all right at the school?"

Nathan unfolded his paper napkin carefully. There was no use lying to Aunt Cele. He decided to get it over with. "I'm going down to Hainesville for a while." He held his plate out resolutely, bracing himself for the explosion.

Aunt Cele's mouth grew thinner. "I knowed it!" Whenever she was upset, the carefully built edifice of her grammar collapsed. "I knowed it!"

Nathan held the plate steady. "How did you know, Aunt Cele?"

She did not touch the ladle. Her voice grew shrill. "How did I know? I know everything you thinkin', boy! I seen you a-broodin' an' a-studyin' these last few days! But I got this to say to you right now, Nathan." She pushed back her chair, her eyes bright with anger and fear. "You is wrong, do you hear me? Wrong! You can't do no good down there. What's past is past, and what's dead is dead. That ain't no place for you to go!"

He said, "I've got to go, Aunt Cele."

"To do what?"

He did not try to answer her. He put his empty plate down

[70]

gently. She reached across the table and put her brown, veined hand on his wrist. "Don't think I ain't got no feelin', boy. An' don't think I don't understand. Because I do. I know how it hurts, in your heart an' in your mind. But whatever you do, it won't bring Lydia back. Or the others. They're dead an' buried almost a year, now, an' I reckon they're at peace. Leave 'em that way, boy. You ain't got no call to go."

He took out the telegram from Yancey and pushed it across the table. She read it, holding it far away from her eyes.

"Yancey!" she said. "That Yancey! How come he's sendin' telegrams to you?"

"I asked him to."

She shook her head angrily. "Did *he* give you this fool idea of goin' back down there?"

"No, it's my own idea."

She got up and moved her chair close to his and looked earnestly into his face. "Boy, maybe I'm bein' selfish. Maybe this las' year I done growed too fond of you, Nathan. Maybe I did. But even if I'd never seen you before, I'd say the same thing. Don't go. You can stay up here an' amount to somethin'. You been here a year, an' you *do* amount to somethin'. Now you're fixin' to throw it all away. For what? Answer me that! For what?"

He did not answer her.

She looked at the telegram. "Acquitted! Course they was acquitted. That's the way things are down there. One man ain't no good against that system, Nathan. It's been that way for hundreds of years. Nothin' you can do is goin' to change it. The white folks is on top—an' they's goin' to stay there."

He had not wanted to argue, but now he felt himself driven to it. "That's just it! Why do you think they murdered Lydia and the others? Because they knew they could get away with it, that's why! Because they knew nothing would happen! And

[71]

when people see 'em walking around down there, free, unpunished, untouched by the law or anything else, then they figure they can do it too."

His aunt tried to speak, but he kept on, crumpling the paper napkin in his hand. "You're wrong when you say it's over and done with. It's not! They had those three men in court yesterday. They let 'em go. You think that doesn't matter? I say it's an invitation to all the others to go out and kill more of us! Why not? It's legal!"

He stopped, breathing hard. His aunt watched him, her proud and noble old face full of anxiety and a certain bitter contempt. "Trouble with you, Nathan," she said slowly, "your skin is black like mine. Your skin is black, but you think white!"

He shook his head. "Somebody's got to teach 'em different. Somebody's got to show 'em that it *can* happen to them. Somebody's got to break the pattern. Up to now, I couldn't do anything because I didn't know who did it. But now I know—I know three of 'em, anyway."

The woman sat very still, as if considering how best to deal with a stubborn child. "You're all upset, boy," she said gently. "Why don't you get a good night's sleep an' think about it in the mornin'?"

He took an envelope out of his pocket and showed it to her. "I got my tickets at noontime. The train leaves tonight at nine-fifteen."

Aunt Cele got up and went into the kitchen. She turned off some gas jets and came back. Her face was set like stone.

"Nathan Hamilton," she said, "now you listen to me. I never said this before, an' I ain't never goin' to say it again. But I'm a rich woman. Yes, I am. I got money, an' I got a business, an' it's all left to you. I made my will that way, not two months ago. All to you, every last cent. But not if you go back to that place. No, sir. I'm warnin' you, Nathan. I mean it."

He shook his head. "I'm sorry, Aunt Cele. I've got to go."

[72]

She threw her hands out wildly. "They'll kill you sure as they killed Lydia an' the others!" Then suddenly she grew calm. She turned her back on him. "If you leave this house tonight, go for good. Don't come back. I don't want no blood in my house."

He made a tired gesture with his hand. "There you are," he said. "That's what they all say. Let blood be spilled anywhere else. Don't spill it on me." He stood up. "I'm sorry I told you, Aunt Cele. You're the only one who knows. Remember that. You're the only one who knows."

She kept her face turned away from him. "Go on," she said. "Don't talk to me. Go on. Go."

He went out and got his suitcase. He listened for a moment, but there was no sound from the living room. He let himself out and closed the door.

In the street he started walking toward the subway, the suit-case bumping against his knee, heavy and final. He had two hours before traintime, but that did not bother him. It was cooler, now. The stars were beginning to show through.

ix

BUBBER sat motionless in the doorway of the toolhouse, wait-ing for Geneva. Above him the wind sighed in the pine trees. Ahead of him, silver in the moonlight, the great cone of saw-dust towered against the sky. Down in the bottomlands by the river the insects piped their shrill chorus. Bubber smoked quietly, holding down his impatience. Geneva was late.

The place was an abandoned sawmill about a mile from Minelli's store, somewhat less from Geneva's cabin. A faint dirt road, almost invisible now, led from the highway to the sawdust mound. The whole country was dotted with these pyramids, by-products of sawmills which operated a timber concession for a while, then moved on leaving a few weather-beaten sheds and these useless monolithic cones of tawny, coarse-grained stuff. Now that most of the pine went to the paper mills, the sawdust piles were no longer rising with such regularity. But the old ones would last for a long time.

This particular mill had been abandoned only two years before. The sheds still stood, and one toolhouse was as weatherproof as it had ever been. Bubber had bought a mattress and a couple of blankets to leave in it. So far they had not been stolen.

He looked at his watch; Geneva was fifteen minutes late. He gritted his teeth and swore under his breath. Maybe the bitch wasn't coming at all. Maybe she had found someone she liked better. Maybe she was through.

Bubber ground out his cigarette with a savage gesture. By God, if she thought she could get away with anything like that she'd find out she was wrong. She had tried it once before, messin' around with Buckeye Miller so that everybody knew about it. Even Buckeye's wife! Well, Buckeye was dead now, and if everybody thought he was dead because he had cut a white man, so much the better. That was reason enough to kill any nigger, but that was not *the* reason Buckeye was dead. He was dead because he messed around with Geneva. Bubber clenched his great fists. He had to have her, that was all, and if anybody, white or black, tried to take her away from him, they'd get what Buckeye Miller had got—one way or another.

The wind stirred the pine trees in a vast sigh.

It's like a fever, Bubber thought; a God-damn fever in your blood. Nobody knows what it's like until they've had it. It's a burnin' in your innards. Only one way to cool it, an' that don't last long. No, sir, don't last long! He chuckled suddenly to himself.

If it weren't for Nora, he thought, he would bring Geneva

[74]

into his house as cook or hired girl and be done with all this horsin' around in the woods, waitin' in the dark, wonderin' when Geneva would come or if she'd come. If he had her in the house, what's more, he could keep his eye on her and see that no black bastard came nosin' around. . . .

He stood up suddenly and went into the toolhouse. He picked up the mattress in one hand, spilling the blankets on the floor. He came out and flung it on the ground. It fell double, uncoiling itself slowly, like a living thing. Bubber stared at it. That was better. He liked to see what he was doing. The half-moon would give light enough.

A twig cracked across the clearing. Bubber grew tense and still, like an animal listening. His eyes probed the shadows. Then suddenly the tension went out of him and he leaned back against the toolhouse, his body relaxed and expectant. Geneva came toward him across the clearing, picking her way delicately through the long grass, her face blank and savage in the moonlight.

CHAPTER 3

Unity opened her eyes. She always woke a few minutes ahead of time; she liked to ease herself into a new day. Half awake, half asleep, drowned in a sort of delicious languor, she waited for the burr of the alarm clock.

Sometimes, even in August, the early mornings in Hainesville had a sparkling freshness, an almost upland crispness. Today had it. The sunlight lay along the floor, cool and golden. Somewhere a mockingbird sang. Unity heard the tuneless whistle of the newsboy on his bike, then the solid thump of the *Courier* landing on the front porch. She smiled drowsily; it was such an American sound.

Hearing the *Courier* reminded her of her request for a raise. Probably won't get it, she thought gloomily. She remembered Lester's sly suggestion that she use her influence with Shep to increase the paper's revenue. Damned if I will, she said to herself, what do they expect me to do—sell my lily-white body for an extra half page of advertising?

She turned the idea over in her mind, surprised at the guilty sense of urgency it gave her. What's the matter with you? she asked herself sharply, suddenly wide-awake. You've known other men before, liked some of them quite a lot. You've never felt like this.

Maybe it's glands, she thought wryly, or all this hot weather, or getting so worked up about the trial. Maybe it's being without Daddy's restraining influence—no symbol of authority any more. Maybe it's a subconscious fear of growing old, or not getting married, or dying a foolish virgin, or something.

Whatever it is, it's real enough, she thought grimly. Like sharp, pleasurable little knives. . . .

Shep. An image of him came up unbidden in her mind, the gray slanting eyes, the heavy eyebrows, the straight mouth. What are you going to do, she asked herself suddenly, when he gets tired of just sitting around and talking? He's getting restless already; he shows it. He won't settle for a good-night kiss in the porch swing; he's not that kind. Are you going to give him a maidenly "no" and risk losing him? You're twenty-three, my girl! What are you going to say? Have you got your script prepared?

The alarm clock rattled. She reached over and turned it off. Helen did not stir. Unity got up and went to the window, stretching her arms above her head, breathing deep. The air was cool and challenging against her flesh. Turning back, she pulled off her nightgown, wadded it, and threw it at Helen's head.

"Wake up, lazybones!"

Helen groaned and opened one eye. Unity bent and touched her toes. Her body felt springy and alive.

"Unity!" Helen sat up. "Get away from that window! The neighbors will see you!"

"Lucky neighbors," said Unity, but she ducked into the bathroom.

Fifteen minutes later she came into the kitchen and brushed her lips against her mother's cheek. Mrs. Cantrell always rose

[77]

early. She liked to prepare breakfast herself; she would not let Hattie help her.

She was a small woman, gray-haired. Her face had dignity and strength without hardness. Unity wondered, sometimes, whether her mother had ever known really turbulent emotions. If she had, they were fully disciplined now. Her calmness was the most striking thing about her.

This urgency, this yearning that had troubled her lately—where did it come from? Unity asked herself. Surely not from this placid woman moving tranquilly around the kitchen. From her father, that gentle and saintly soul? Hardly! Where, then?

What would parents think, she wondered, if they could look into the minds of their children and see the slow unbidden thoughts and desires coiling there? Would they be startled? Understanding? Dismayed? She watched her mother's calm face. How could she confide in anyone so remote, so withdrawn from the hot actualities of living?

"Sit down, child," her mother said. "Your eggs are getting cold."

ii

BY TEN o'clock the freshness was gone from the morning. In the law offices of Mayhew & Kane, Melady sat down, tensing himself against the inertia that seeped out of the walls and eddied around him.

"I understand," he said, "that you were assigned by the Governor to make a special investigation of the lynching you had here last year. Is that right?"

Horace Kane toyed with the watch chain strung across his paunch. His face was bland and affable. When he opened his mouth to speak, his lips made a faint smacking sound, as if he enjoyed the taste of his own words. "That's right."

"Mind if I ask you a few questions?"

Again the preliminary kissing sound. "For publication?"

"Possibly."

Kane nodded slowly, but the good humor went out of his eyes.

Melady took out a small notebook and held it in his hand. "In the first place, why did the Governor choose you?"

The fat shoulders lifted almost imperceptibly. "I've been a lawyer here for thirty years. I imagine the Governor thought I was qualified to make the investigation."

"Did you turn over the results to the grand jury?"

"Naturally."

"But they still lacked enough evidence to bring an indictment?"

Kane pursed his mouth and pinched it with thumb and forefinger. He let go and opened it with the tiny kissing sound. "Yes."

Melady looked down at his notes. "Apparently the mob used a rope to tie the hands of the colored men. Was an effort made to trace it?"

Kane shook his head. "It was ordinary one-inch rope. Might've been lying around in somebody's car for years."

"Didn't the F.B.I. analyze it for dust, or other clues?"

"Reckon they did," drawled Kane, "but they couldn't go around checking the back of every car in Haines County, now, could they?"

Melady's mouth tightened. "Any ballistics check on the bullets taken from the bodies, or from the surrounding trees?"

"Oh, sure." Kane tapped his blunt fingers. "But they were mostly shotgun slugs. You can't trace them to any particular weapon. We did drag up some empty shells from the bottom of the creek. But we never found guns to match 'em."

[79]

"Did you look very hard?"

Kane half closed his eyes. "The F.B.I. had over a dozen men on the case, Mr. ——"

"Melady."

"Mr. Melady. They had orders from the White House to break the case. I think we can assume they weren't playing tiddlywinks all the time."

Melady stood up and closed his notebook. "Know anybody who might give me more information—anyone who had some special knowledge or insight into the case?"

Kane made his mouth into a snout again and pinched it thoughtfully. "There's a colored undertaker, has a place over on Primrose Street. Name of Yancey Brown. He probably knows as much as anybody—if you can get him to talk."

"Undertaker?"

"That's right." Kane hoisted his bulk out of the chair and moved to the window. His coat was wet where the chair had touched it. "No way for you to know it, my dear sir, but the undertaker in a smallish Southern town is just about the most important person there is, on that side of the color line. More important than the preacher, even. He has a telephone, as a rule—that makes him a kind of message center. And he's on pretty intimate terms with his own people. Anything goes on, he knows about it. In fact"—he turned and looked at Melady— "comes the black revolution, down here, the small-town undertakers will be the commissars."

Melady stared back at him. "You're joking."

"No," said Horace Kane. "I'm not."

Melady said softly, "Is that why your law firm agreed to handle the defense for the Aycock brothers in the trial day before yesterday?"

Kane smiled with everything but his eyes. "Our services are for sale to anyone who can pay for them, Mr. Melady."

"I see." Melady moved toward the door. "I was thinking,"

[80]

he said slowly. "The Governor was in a pretty tough spot over that lynching, wasn't he? The heat was on from Washington to solve it. But with an election coming up, a solution might have been embarrassing. Especially in the rural counties. Am I right?"

Kane said nothing.

"Seems to me if I'd been the Governor," Melady went on, "I'd have appointed an investigator who sounded good on paper, but who could be relied on not to investigate too hard. Wouldn't you have played it that way, Mr. Kane?"

Kane opened his mouth so sharply that there was no time for the kissing sound. "I resent that insinuation! The Governor of this state is an honorable man!"

"Okay," Melady said carelessly. "I notice he got re-elected, though." He opened the door and looked back. "Thanks for the tip about Yancey Brown." He went out, closing the door gently behind him.

iii

EVEN now, a year after it had happened, Pa Aycock disliked crossing Morgan's Creek, especially if he was alone. He was alone this morning, headed for town on a routine errand. It was a right pretty morning, he thought—cooler than most. It would be hot later, when the sun got high. But it was nice while it lasted.

He drove past Neal's farm, the cotton stretching away on either side of the road in green mathematical rows. Good thing field hands weren't so scarce this year. The old man spat through the window over his left elbow. Last year, now, there'd been hell to pay trying to get the crop in.

The thought touched a sore spot in his mind, and his wrinkled face grew sour and aggrieved. "They didn't have no call to kill *all* them niggers," he said loudly, as if he were arguing with another person, not just talking to himself. "That Buckeye, now, he was a mean nigger, sho' 'nuff. Maybe *he* got what was comin' to him; I ain't sayin' he didn't. But the others hadn't done nothin'—nothin' at all, except maybe pester me a little to git Buckeye outa jail."

The car came to the top of the ridge. He ground his gears harshly and started to creep down the steep incline toward the creek. Even on such a shining morning as this the water looked muddy and sullen, hemmed in by the reddish cypress. The front wheels clanked on the strips of iron. The sound brought it all back to Pa Aycock with piercing clarity.

It was Bubber's fault, he thought angrily. All Bubber's fault. If he hadn't stopped to see Bubber that day, none of it would have happened. But he *had* stopped. He nodded sagely to himself, as if confirming some new discovery. "Right there," he said, "was where I made my big mistake. Yes, sir, my big mistake."

It had been a day like any other, to start with. The morning was sticky and hot. Buckeye Miller was in the Haines County Jail. Buckeye's wife was staying with her brother, a tenant farmer on Pa Aycock's place. Good farmer, too. Every day they came and begged him to get Buckeye out of jail "befo' the white folks gits mad an' does somethin' to him."

The white folks got mad, all right. As it turned out, Buckeye would have been better off in jail. But his wife and his brother-in-law didn't think so. "They sure pestered me," Pa Aycock said self-righteously. "They pestered me until they pestered themselves right into hell!" He laughed, then abruptly grew sober. Maybe they didn't *all* go to hell. Buckeye, now, he might've gone there. A bad nigger—talked too big, cut a white man, wasn't even faithful to his wife—slept with that yellow slut Geneva whenever he could. Leastwise, that was

[82]

what they said afterwards. But hell, what else could you expect with niggers? Not much better'n animals, most of 'em. Pa Aycock gave a cackle of sudden mirth. Couldn't blame Buckeye for tomcattin' around with that Geneva, now; maybe in his younger days he'd have gone sniffin' around her himself. . . .

Still, he thought, sternly recalling himself to the ethics of the matter, they had no call to kill all of 'em. Field hands were too damn scarce. He'd needed an extra hand himself, those burning August days. That was why he had let himself be persuaded to go bail for Buckeye.

The car had crossed the bridge, now. It inched past the place where it had been stopped that afternoon a year ago. Quiet, deserted, now. Peaceful, almost. But that day . . . Jesus, the old man thought, how them nigger wimmin had screamed! He could hear 'em still.

About two o'clock that afternoon he had left his farm. He'd had Buckeye's wife and her brother with him in the back seat of this selfsame car. They had driven past Bubber's house to see if Nora or Louella wanted a ride to town. Bubber had been in the yard, tinkering with a tractor under the blazing eye of the sun. He had come over to the car, his meaty face red and sweating, his shirt clinging to his bull shoulders. "Nora and Louella done gone to town," he said. "Be back in an hour or so. Why you goin'?"

When told why, Bubber had spat disgustedly on the ground. He said, staring directly at Buckeye's wife, "Whyn't you let that black son of a bitch rot in jail? He cut a white man, didn't he?"

"Hell, Bubber"—Pa Aycock could hear his own voice, half blustering, half apologetic—"I need hands to git my cotton in. That Buckeye's mean, but he can work. I done phoned the Sheriff's office; they said I could have him for five hundred dollars. I'll git my money back when he comes up for trial."

Bubber's eyes were hard as glass. "We don't want no mean knife-totin' nigger runnin' around here loose."

Damn you, Bubber, Pa Aycock had thought; always buttin' in! Aloud he said, "He won't tote no knife on my place; I'll see to that."

The car had lurched away, leaving the sweating giant standing there, glowering after them.

In town, in the fetid atmosphere that enveloped the jail and the Sheriff's office, he had put up the bond, had arranged to collect Buckeye on the way home. Then he had spent a couple of hours in town, buying a few things, talking to friends. Buckeye's wife and her brother disappeared to attend to their own affairs. They were to meet him at the jail not later than five o'clock.

Two hours. Not much time for somebody to plan an ambush and assemble an armed mob. But the mob was assembled, armed, ready and waiting just the same.

He had returned to the jail a few minutes before five. Buckeye was released, hulking, sullen, indifferent alike to his wife's joy and the prospect of at least temporary freedom. They had started back in the sultry, breathless afternoon. Buckeye's wife had her sister with her. Comin' out for a visit, she said.

"Them wimmin would be alive right now," Pa Aycock said, again addressing the empty air. "They'd be runnin' around this minute, sassy as jay-birds, if they'd had the sense God gave a mule. But no, that fool wife of Buckeye's couldn't keep her mouth shut. Had to go to screamin' at Bubber an' callin' him by name. . . ."

That was the part he could remember most vividly, the thin ear-piercing screams, the chattering that sounded like a fear-crazed monkey: "Doan' kill him, Mr. Bubber! Please, 'fore Gawd, doan' kill him!"

Bubber had hesitated, the shotgun dangling loosely in his big hand. Then he had jerked his head at Neal and three of the others. "You four," he'd said. "Bring 'em along." Just like that.

Funny, Pa Aycock thought, the women fought worse than the men. Of course, they had the men tied, by that time, with an old towrope taken from somebody's car. But neither Buckeye nor Jason, his brother-in-law, had tried to resist. They had seemed paralyzed. What had Jason said? "I ain't done nothin', boss." And held out his roped hands in a queer, pleading gesture.

Whitey Lawrence had hit him over the head with the barrel of his pistol. "Shut your black mouth, nigger!" Whitey's voice was shrill and strained, as if he were the one being lynched. They were pretty drunk, all of them. The bottles were out of sight, but the smell was strong on their breaths and their eyes showed it, red and narrowed and a little crazy.

The blood ran down Jason's face, slow and surprisingly thick, like strawberry jam. "Come on," Bubber had said. "Hurry up. We ain't got all day." That was when Buckeye's wife had called his name.

They opened the car door again and got the women. They fought like fiends, but the white men dragged them, one man on each arm, toward the little clump of pines. They struggled and shrieked, flopping like scarecrows, their feet kicking up pine needles and dust. The white men lost patience and beat them around the head with their fists, but they would not go quietly. Their clothes were shredded. Their arms were wrenched almost out of their sockets; they ceased to function like arms and became boneless ropes. The men with the guns stood waiting. At the end, Buckeye's wife seemed to go completely mad. When they threw her against her husband, she fell at his feet, her teeth snapping blindly, a whitish foam on her lips. The other woman turned her face against a pine tree and prayed.

Bubber counted, "One, two, three!" The ragged volley

crashed out. From where he sat behind his steering wheel, Pa Aycock saw splinters fly, high up on one of the pine trees. Somebody had lost his nerve and was shooting high. Nobody could have missed at that distance except on purpose.

Both Negro men died instantly. They sagged forward, the ropes that bound them to the trees still holding them up. The women had stopped screaming, but they still writhed. Bubber fired his second barrel point-blank into Buckeye's wife. The charge made her body bounce once, then it was still. He walked away, not looking back, while the others finished the second woman. Finished her and then some.

Things they did to her, Pa Aycock reflected, made it just as well she *was* dead.

He had sat in his car through it all—not scared for himself, although one of the Nelson twins stood on the bridge all the time and held a gun on him. Not scared, just angry because nobody had consulted him, and because field hands were hard to get, and they were killing too many. He caught Bubber's eye once, but Bubber just looked at him stonily as if he'd never seen him before, and Neal refused to look at him at all.

Whitey Lawrence came up, though, breathing hard and swaggering a little, now that it was all over. He stuck his head in the car window, so close that Pa Aycock could see the coarse yellow stubble on his chin and smell the sour liquor-breath. "You recognize anybody you see here, old man?" A stupid question. . . .

They let him go, then. He didn't cross the bridge. He backed his car into the little side road where part of the mob had been hiding, and turned back toward Minelli's store. In his mirror he could see the cars and some of the men crossing the bridge. Slowly, like figures in a dream.

Well, they'd come looking for a nigger to kill, and by God they'd killed four. He hoped they were satisfied.

He parked outside of Minelli's and went in. The pay telephone was fastened to the wall. There was no booth. He put a nickel in the slot and asked for the Sheriff's office. When a voice answered, he said, "That you, Carfax?" Carfax was deputy sheriff. "This is Aycock. I'm out here at Minelli's store. They jes' done gone an' killed my niggers." He hesitated. "You better come on out here, or send somebody. What's that? Yeah, all four of 'em."

He remembered how Geneva, that yellow slut, had looked at him in the fading light.

The F.B.I., the local police, the State Police—none of them had been able to shake his story for the very good reason that it was true. He only told one lie—when he said he had recognized no member of the mob. He had recognized them all.

But that was a lie everyone knew he had to tell, so it didn't matter much.

All Bubber's fault, he thought again, driving fast along the red dirt road, the steering wheel vibrating under his gnarled hands. Bubber had planned the whole thing, called the mob, picked the spot for the ambush. . . .

Why? That was the question he had never quite succeeded in answering.

Just because Buckeye had stabbed a white man in a drunken quarrel? Not likely—Bubber didn't care enough about Dillinger to go to all that trouble on his account.

Then *why?*

Because Bubber liked the sight of blood, and thought the opportunity too good to miss? Hardly. Bubber was mean, but he had other ways of satisfying his meanness.

Did he have some special reason for wanting to get rid of Buckeye? Was there a personal grudge? Not that anyone knew of. Did Buckeye have anything that Bubber wanted? Well, he had a wife, but so did Bubber. He had a poor tenant farm; Bubber had a rich one of his own. He had a little money; Bubber had much more.

Well, then?

The Pontiac came to the crossroads and stopped. A figure was standing in the doorway of Minelli's store. Even at that distance the silhouette had a tigerish grace about it, a symmetry that certainly did not belong to Mrs. Minelli.

Geneva.

Pa Aycock ground his gears and drove out onto the highway. He swung left, toward town. He had not found any reason why Bubber should have desired Buckeye's death. He decided that thinking about it was a waste of time. Damn niggers, he thought, whatever they got, they had it comin' to 'em.

On his right, a line of cabins fronted the road. A chicken from one of these started to cross the concrete, changed its mind, and stood stupidly still. By holding his course, Pa Aycock could have missed it. He moved his hands slightly. There was a thud under the left front wheel. Pa Aycock looked in the mirror. The chicken lay huddled in the road; a few feathers floated grayly in the sunlit air.

"That'll teach 'em to keep their damn chickens off the road," he said aloud.

He felt obscurely relieved and began to whistle as he drove on into Hainesville.

iv

At three o'clock that afternoon the phone in Melady's hotel room rang. He turned away from his typewriter and picked it up. "Yes?"

"Colored feller down here named Brown. Says you wanted to see him."

Melady drew the back of a hand across his forehead. It

came away wet. "Oh, yes. Send him up, will you?" He hung up, went into the bathroom, and splashed water into his face. Even the water was warm. He went back into the bedroom, took out his wallet, and extracted a ten-dollar bill. He folded it twice and put it in his pocket. Then he opened the door and looked out into the hall. A slight Negro with gold-rimmed glasses was coming down the corridor.

Melady signaled to him. "Yancey Brown?"

Yancey nodded.

"Good." Melady held open the door. "Nice of you to come."

"That's all right," Yancey said.

"Sit down, won't you? Cigarette?"

Yancey eyed him warily. "No thanks." But he sat down.

Melady paced up and down with his rocking-horse gait. He ran a hand irritably through his tight steel-wool hair. "I don't blame you for being suspicious," he said. "If I were you, I wouldn't trust any white man. But what I told you on the phone is true. I *am* a writer for a big magazine. I *don't* have any ax to grind down here. I'm a reporter, that's all—a feature writer, if you know what that is."

He glanced at Yancey with his quick brown eyes. Yancey said nothing.

"I came down to cover that trial day before yesterday," Melady went on. "The trial didn't interest me as much as Hainesville itself. I figured that if I spent a few days looking around here, I could write a story about a town that committed murder and got away with it. Or rather, I thought I'd be able to prove that it didn't really get away with it—that it was paying for it, every day, in countless little ways." He stopped suddenly. "Do you know what I mean?"

Yancey nodded. "I know what you mean."

"Well, it's not so easy," Melady went on. "It's harder than I thought. The thing's not dead, by any means, but it's gone underground. And nobody wants it dug up. Nobody whose skin is white, anyway." He wheeled around. "But *your* skin isn't white. And they tell me you're a smart fellow. How'd you like to help me crack this case wide open? I could make it worth your while."

Yancey said, "Who gave you my name?"

Melady told him.

Yancey nodded slowly. "Suppose I tell you something you can print. Suppose I just give you my point of view. Don't you know it'll be read down here? Don't you know lawyer Kane'll see to it that people know you talked to me? Why do you think he gave you my name? Because he'd like an excuse to run me out of this town, that's why. What can I say to you that won't do more harm than good?"

Melady sat down on the bed. "But you know who was in that mob, don't you?"

Yancey looked at his hands. "I know people who think they know."

"Afraid to talk?"

"Afraid? Yes. But it's more'n just bein' afraid. It's knowin' that even if you do talk, it won't do no good. Look at what happened at the trial."

"I looked at it." Melady pulled out the ten-dollar bill, scowled at it, then shoved it back. "All right; you win. I don't like to pry information out of a man and then use it to hurt him. But I wish you'd tell me one thing. Not for publication; just for my own information. What are you doing about all this, Brown? What are you *doing*—you and people like you? Don't tell me you're just sitting with folded hands waiting for things to get better."

Yancey smiled thinly. "No, our hands aren't exactly folded. But we have to move slow. Seems like every time we take a step forward it kicks up a storm that pushes us two steps back. We have to inch along, tryin' to look like we're standin' still." He stared out of the window. "But we keep movin', I reckon."

"What do you consider the main issue?" Melady asked. "Segregation, I suppose."

"You people," Yancey said, "you people from up North! You mean well, but sometimes I think you're so busy bein' liberal and broad-minded you never take time to figure things out. Segregation? Hell, that's a side issue! Sure, I'd like to see a movie when and where I want to see it, or eat in a decent restaurant if I'm hungry. But that's not important, not really. Give us the vote, and justice in the courts, and we'll sit in the back of streetcars till doomsday."

Melady said, "I thought you were beginning to be able to vote."

"We are," Yancey told him. "And some of the whites are gettin' scared. They've got legislation on the fire right now that would require each voter to explain any passage in the Constitution if called on to do so. Well, who do you think would be called on? We would, of course." He shifted impatiently in his chair. "If they pass that one, we're back where we started ten years ago."

"What'll you do then?"

Yancey shrugged. "Start all over again, I suppose. What else can we do? Of course, we have our hotheads, like any other minority. And the Communists aren't asleep. Some of our big colored organizations . . . Well, let's not get into that." He stood up. "I'd better be goin' now. Sorry I couldn't help you more."

Melady held out his hand. "I'm sorry I can't help you."

"Maybe you can," Yancey said. "Just write about things as they are here. Don't exaggerate; just tell the truth. Maybe you'll change some people's attitude a little. That'll help."

"I wish," said Melady, "that I could buy you a dinner. Right here in this stuffy hotel."

Yancey opened the door and smiled. "Thanks," he said. "My wife's a much better cook." The door closed behind him.

WHEN it was fully dark, Nathan Hamilton drove into Hainesville and parked on Primrose Street a block away from the funeral parlor. He had bought the car in Atlanta—a 1939 Dodge, battered but still serviceable. He pulled down his hat, walked past the show window, and rang the bell. While he waited, he stared at the tenantless coffin. When the door opened he said quietly, "Hello, Yancey."

Yancey stood there, his shirt a white blur in the darkness. A newspaper dangled from his hand. Then he stepped back. "Come inside, Nathan."

They stood together in the dim parlor with its folding chairs and sad, artificial flowers. Nathan said, "You expecting me?"

"Sort of." Yancey opened a door that led to the basement. A sharp smell of chemicals came up out of the dark. "Let's talk down here, shall we?" He started down. "Alma's upstairs."

"How is she?"

"Alma? She's fine."

They went down into the embalming room. Yancey pulled down the shades and turned on the glaring lights. He leaned against one of the mortuary slabs. His face looked tired; the overhead light made deep shadows under his eyes. "Why'd you come, Nathan?"

"You know," Nathan said.

"I wish you hadn't."

"I had to come. I've got a job to do."

Yancey turned his head away angrily. "Why couldn't you do it on your own, then? Why come and tell me?"

"I need a place to operate from, Yancey. I can't hide in the woods."

Yancey took off his glasses and began to polish them with the end of his tie. "You want to stay here, is that it?"

"Just a few days. Just long enough to do this job."

"I've got to talk you out of this crazy notion, Nathan."

"You can't. Aunt Cele tried. She couldn't. Nobody can stop me, Yancey. No use trying."

"I know a way to stop you."

"How? By going to the police? I haven't done anything— yet."

"No, not the police. But if I told the organization about this, they'd stop you."

Nathan lit a cigarette. "Think so?"

"I know so."

"Why?"

"Because they don't believe in violence. They think it just breeds more violence."

"They couldn't stop me."

"Yes, they could. All I've got to do is pick up that phone and call Atlanta. They'd have a car here in two hours."

"A car? What good would that do?"

"They'd take you out of Hainesville. By force, if necessary."

"My own people would do that?"

"Yes."

"Well," Nathan said, "you'd better phone them."

Yancey did not move.

"Go on," Nathan said. "Phone them."

"I'd rather talk you out of it myself."

"I told you, you can't. I know exactly what I'm going to do. The Aycocks first. Then Shoup."

"You're no killer, Nathan."

Nathan said, "Every man's a killer, if you give him a reason." He ground out his cigarette. "Can I stay here?"

Yancey turned his head and ran his hand along the edge of the slab. "No."

[93]

"I thought you were my friend, Yancey."

"I am. But you try anything like this, there'll be trouble. Bad trouble. I don't want my house burned down, or my wife and baby hurt."

"I had a wife," Nathan said. He straightened up suddenly. "I know you, Yancey. I've known you all my life; you can't fool me. You want 'em dead just as much as I do. Your mind tells you one thing, but your heart tells you another, doesn't it? That's why you won't use that phone. Part of you agrees with me, and that part is stronger than you are. Sure, it's a risk. Sure, they may burn your house down. But maybe they won't. Maybe they'll be afraid to! Have you thought of that? Fear isn't a one-way street." He took a handful of Yancey's shirt front in his fist and rocked him slowly back and forth. "Suppose somebody's nerve cracks. Suppose Shoup gets scared when he sees what's happening and tells all he knows. Suppose . . ."

"Suppose they kill you first," Yancey said.

Slowly Nathan relaxed his grip. "Well," he said, "I've nothing to lose."

"Maybe you haven't," Yancey said. There were drops of sweat on his forehead. "But the rest of us have."

"All right," Nathan said. "All right. Forget it."

"You're welcome to stay here," Yancey told him, "if you'll just promise . . ."

"No," Nathan said. "No promises. I know a place I can go where I won't have to make any promises."

"Where? To your mother?"

"Never mind where." Nathan walked over to the door that led into the alley. He slid back the bolt that held it. "Just pretend I never came. Just make believe you never saw me. That'll make it easy for you, Yancey. You'll have all the satisfaction and none of the risk."

Yancey said, "I'm sorry, Nathan."

When the door had closed, he went over and bolted it. He stood still a moment, head bent as if he were listening. Then he turned out the lights and climbed the stairs.

On the second floor, in a chintz-covered armchair by the window, Alma was sewing. She looked up as Yancey came in. "Who was it?"

Her husband sat down and blotted his forehead with his sleeve. "Nathan."

Alma stopped sewing. "You sent him away?"

Yancey said, "I had to."

Alma said nothing.

Yancey looked at her angrily. "I tell you, I had to!"

"Because of me and the baby?"

"Yes."

Alma glanced down at the sewing in her lap. She raised it to her mouth and bit a thread off close to the cloth. "If he comes back again," she said, "let him stay—you hear?"

vi

HELEN lay on the bed and stared across at her sister. "Hurry up, Unity. It's almost midnight."

"All done," Unity said. She folded the note she had written and tucked it into an envelope. She was wearing an old bathrobe and slippers. She had been washing her hair; a towel was wrapped turban-wise around her head.

"Who's the lucky man?" Helen asked.

Her sister smiled. "An elderly gentleman who doesn't even know I exist. Judge Miles Winter. He presided over that Aycock trial. I've written him a fan letter."

"Good Lord!" Helen's violet eyes expressed wonder, then boredom. "I thought it was someone important."

"He is," Unity said. "I've invited him to Sunday dinner."

"Sunday dinner! Do you think he'll come?"

"He might."

"I won't be here, thank goodness. I've asked John to go on a picnic."

"Well, then, we'll just have to struggle along without you." Unity came over and sat on the edge of Helen's bed. "Have a good time tonight?"

Helen hugged her knees. "I suppose so. I never knew anyone quite like John. He's so quiet, so—so *tense*. He likes me; I know that. But he hasn't even tried to kiss me."

"That must make him practically unique," Unity said dryly.

Helen lay back on the bed. "He's all wound up about that artificial foot of his. Won't swim, won't dance, won't even talk about it. I'd like to make him see how unimportant it really is." She corrected herself with sudden fervor. "I'm *going* to make him see it."

"Well, good luck to you." Unity stood up. "Want a glass of milk? I'm going down to get some."

"No thanks." Helen yawned. "Hurry up, Unity, do."

Unity went out into the dim hall and down the stairs. She groped her way through the dining room, pushed open the door that led to the kitchen, and stopped. Her heart gave a violent lurch. The door that led into the yard was open; she could see the moonlight, pallid on the porch. In the doorway was a figure, facing her.

Unity's hand shot out and found the wall switch. Light blazed through the kitchen.

"Why, Hattie!" Unity leaned against the wall. "Heavens, woman, you scared the wits out of me. I thought you were a burglar!"

Hattie stood there, looking even more frightened than Unity felt. She was wearing an old raincoat over her nightdress. In her hand was a plate piled with food.

"If you're going to raid the icebox," Unity said crossly, "why don't you turn on the light instead of creeping in here like a ghost?"

Hattie backed through the open door. "Didn' want to 'sturb nobody. Jes' got to feelin' lil bit hongry, tha's all."

"Well, that's all right," Unity said. "But turn on the light hereafter, will you?"

"Yes'm," said Hattie. She disappeared.

Unity went to the door and watched her vanish into the garage. A suspicion formed in her mind, hovered for a moment, then dissolved. She got her milk and went back upstairs. "You don't suppose Hattie has a boy friend, do you?"

"Hattie?" Helen looked shocked. "She's much too old. Why, she must be all of fifty!"

Unity turned out the light. "Wait'll you're fifty, and someone says that about you!"

Helen yawned again in the darkness. A little breeze swayed the light curtains. Unity kicked off her covers. Perhaps tomorrow would be cooler. Tomorrow she was riding with Shep. Tomorrow, she thought sleepily. Tomorrow . . .

CHAPTER 4

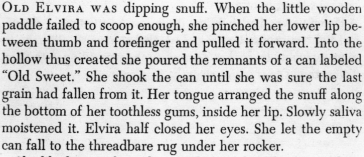

OLD ELVIRA WAS dipping snuff. When the little wooden paddle failed to scoop enough, she pinched her lower lip between thumb and forefinger and pulled it forward. Into the hollow thus created she poured the remnants of a can labeled "Old Sweet." She shook the can until she was sure the last grain had fallen from it. Her tongue arranged the snuff along the bottom of her toothless gums, inside her lip. Slowly saliva moistened it. Elvira half closed her eyes. She let the empty can fall to the threadbare rug under her rocker.

She liked to sit thus, alone in the weathered cabin with its stale, familiar smells: hair oil and lilac-scented face powder, kerosene and bedbugs, wet wash and burnt fat. Geneva had gone to work. Sullenly, after a quarrel brought on by Elvira's request for money to buy more snuff.

The old woman scowled at the recollection. She had fixed Geneva's breakfast, hadn't she? She mended her clothes and carried her messages, didn't she? Soon she would get up from her rocker and make Geneva's bed. All she wanted, in return for these and other services, was enough money to buy food and an occasional can of Old Sweet. And what did she get? Contempt and abuse. No respect no more, Elvira thought, shaking her head. No respect for nobody.

When *she* was a child, now ... The memories came flooding back to her. "Older you gits," she mumbled to herself, "better you remembers, seems like. . . ."

She had been born in a cabin much like this one. Two rooms, thin walls plastered with newspapers to keep out winter drafts, windows with swinging shutters—no glass. A pump in the front yard, an outhouse in back. She could see her mother kneeling in front of the brick fireplace in the early morning, a stick of lightwood in her hand. She could remember the sudden flare of light as the resin-soaked kindling caught, the way her mother's face looked, momentarily washed clean of fatigue by sleep. She could remember how cold the floor felt on winter mornings when she crawled out of the bed she shared with her two sisters, the way the corn bread looked, burnt black and brown on the outside, how the coarse grains tasted, crunched between her teeth.

She could hear her older sister laugh, a thin child in a faded dress, with spiky pigtails and legs like sugar-cane stalks. She could see her, rolling on the floor with the baby pig they had tamed, jumping up quickly when their mother spoke.

Respect, thought old Elvira, shifting her snuff. They taught us respect. . . .

A shadow fell across the floor and she jumped, startled out of her reverie. "Howdy," she said automatically. "Howdy!" The man came in and stood in front of her chair, looking down at her. She peered up into his face, her eyes blinking worriedly, a flicker of recognition lighting her fragmented memories. "Ain't you Hattie Hamilton's boy?"

Nathan pulled up a straight chair and sat down beside her. He opened his hand. Folded against his palm was a five-dollar bill. He held it up. "Auntie, you never saw me in all your life. Anybody asks you, you never saw me at all."

He dropped the money into her lap. The wrinkled fingers closed over it; an ironic gleam lighted the old eyes. "Naw suh! Sho'ly hasn't. Ain't never seen you at all."

"There's another one of those for you," Nathan said, "if you'll help me."

Elvira's eyelids drooped. "Whut I'se got to do?"

Nathan stood up. He took a kerosene lamp from the table, crossed over to the window facing the Atlanta road, and balanced it on the sill. "All you have to do is light this lamp at a certain time." He came back and sat down beside her. "And answer a few questions about Geneva."

Elvira drew back a little. "You ain't fixin' to hurt my Geneva?"

"No," said Nathan. "Nobody's going to hurt Geneva."

The old fingers smoothed the five-dollar bill, patted it, folded it. "Awright," Elvira murmured. "Ax me. I'se listenin'."

ii

MELADY climbed the musty stairs that led from the street to the *Courier's* editorial offices. He hesitated at the top, looking around distastefully at the littered tables, the overflowing scrap baskets, the copy paper stuck haphazardly on spikes. These damn Southerners, he thought; they'd rather be sloppy than neat. No excuse for working in a mess like this. To the office-boy-receptionist he said, "Tell your city editor that Mr. Melady would like to see him."

Pip stared at this abrupt salutation, then got up, shambled over to Lester's office, knocked once, and went in.

Melady waited, rocking back and forth impatiently on his toes. A girl came through the room, cool in a lavender dress.

[100]

Melady recognized her. It was the girl he had watched at the trial. She gave him a faint smile and sat down behind an antiquated typewriter. She bent forward, her profile sharp and clear in the cluttered room. Melady watched her with his bright, inquisitive gaze.

Pip came back and nodded toward Lester's office. "In there," he said laconically.

Melady went in. The editor indicated a chair, but did not bother to rise. His eyes were red-rimmed and bloodshot. Melady remembered the stooped shoulders and the silver hair; this man had also been at the trial. In the press box.

Lester leaned back and surveyed the newcomer with a certain malevolence. He had overdone it again the night before; his head throbbed and his tongue felt sandy and too big for his mouth. Melady glanced once at Hester, sitting quietly at her desk against the wall. Her long legs were tucked gracefully under her chair; she held her head so that the birthmark was not visible. Melady sat down and proceeded to identify himself.

Lester knuckled his nose and sniffed. "Might as well tell you," he said sourly, "this town has had about all the publicity it wants. If you think everybody's going to fall flat on their faces at the mention of your magazine, you've got another think coming."

Melady eyed Lester for a moment, made his estimate of the man, and acted accordingly. "My magazine doesn't expect favors. It pays for what it gets." He took out his wallet and extracted a pair of fifty-dollar bills. He laid them on the editor's desk. "I want to take a look at your files. I have some questions I want answered. I may need some stenographic help. I might even borrow one of your reporters as a guide." He nodded at the money. "Will that cover it?"

"Well, now," Lester said in an altered voice. "I don't know if that's necessary."

Melady smiled a little. "First of all, can you lend me some-one who knows their way around your morgue?"

"Why, yes," Lester said. "I think so." He got up, came around the desk, and opened the door. "Unity! Look here a minute, will you?"

Unity came in and was introduced to Melady. "Help him all you can," Lester said graciously. "Dig up whatever he wants."

"I'll try." She glanced at Melady. "Want to start digging now?"

"If you're free." Melady turned back to Lester. "I'll let you know if I need anything else."

"By all means," the editor said. He watched the door close and picked up the two fifty-dollar bills. "Interesting fellow," he said to Hester's rigid profile.

"Very."

Lester sniffed thoughtfully. "About this—ah—retainer he of-fered us. Better not to say anything about that—eh?"

"Us?"

"Well, naturally, you'll be in on it if he has to have any typing done. Let's say—" He hesitated, choosing a figure, then discarding it because it seemed too big. "Shall we say twenty per cent?"

Hester's fingers twitched as she fitted them onto her key-board. "You overwhelm me," she said.

Down the corridor, in the room with the big wooden tables and dangling green-shaded bulbs, Unity pulled out the folder marked "Lynching—Hainesville" and handed it to Melady. "Most of the clips we have are in here."

Melady put the folder down on the table. "I'll look at it in a minute." He fished in his pocket. "Cigarette?"

"No, thanks."

"I saw you at the trial," Melady told her. "What did you think of it?"

Unity closed the file slowly. "I don't think my reaction was typical."

"No?" Melady looked interested. "What was it?"

She shook her head. "I can't give it to you in capsule form. I'm sorry. It's just not that simple."

Melady lit his cigarette and dropped the match on the floor. "Why not have lunch with me? You can do the talking. I'll listen."

Unity hesitated. "All right," she said finally. "I've been trying to find somebody who will listen. You're the first volunteer."

"Come back in an hour," Melady told her. "By then it'll be time to eat." He looked down at the folder. "If this stuff doesn't ruin my appetite."

iii

NATHAN moved slowly down the incline that led to Morgan's Creek. His shoes were covered with red dust; his shirt, wet with perspiration, clung to his back. He had left his car in a side road a mile away. He did not want to leave tire tracks in this area.

When he came to the bridge he stopped, shifting the brown paper parcel he carried from one hand to the other. It was very quiet. Insects hummed in the long grass; above the strips of metal on the bridge the heat waves shimmered fiercely. There was no wind. The cypresses and the dwarf pines were still.

He turned right and moved along the faint path that parallelled the creek. Twenty paces brought him to a clump of pines somewhat taller than the rest. The trunks of these trees were as thick as a man's thigh. He stared at the rough wood; there were scars in it. He put out his hand and touched one of the holes. It was very small; the bark was growing back over it now.

This was the place.

His ears picked up the sound of a car's engine, coming from the far side of the creek. He stood very still, listening. When he heard the metal strips clank, he stepped back into the undergrowth. A green Ford came off the bridge, shifted gears, and flashed out of sight. The driver was the only occupant. The glimpse Nathan had was too short for positive identification. It might have been Neal Aycock.

Nathan came out of his hiding place, still carrying the brown paper parcel. He went back to the bridge and crossed it, walking carefully, watching the sluggish water flow beneath him. He went up the steep slope on the other side. The climb made his heart pound; his breathing was rough and labored. Sweat poured down his face, but his hands felt cold.

At the top of the hill, the farmhouse came into view. Nathan began to walk more quickly. Once he looked back; his feet left no marks in the baked clay.

When he came opposite the gate in the wire fence, he halted. The farmhouse seemed lifeless, deserted. Nathan opened the gate. He took the parcel he had been carrying from under his left arm. It was a brown paper bag. He thrust his right hand into it.

As he walked forward a pair of small mongrel dogs burst from under the farmhouse, yapping fiercely. Nathan stood still. The dogs stopped ten feet away. They snarled, showing their teeth, but did not try to bite. After a while Nathan moved forward again. He went up on the porch, ignoring the dogs. He knocked twice with his left hand. His fist made a hollow, empty sound. There was no response. Behind him the yard was dimmed suddenly as a cloud moved across the sun. The dogs ceased their barking. Silence settled down, leaden, oppressive. Somewhere, out of sight, a rooster crowed feebly.

Nathan moved off the porch quickly, as if contact with the farmhouse was unbearable. The dogs followed him in hostile silence to the gate. He closed it and went back down the road toward the creek. When he came to the bridge, he crossed to the other side and sat down on the low stringpiece that took the place of a railing. Slowly his heart ceased its heavy pounding.

The sky had a yellowish tinge, now; the air was sticky, humid. In the south, thunderheads were piling up. Nathan looked at his watch. It was after three o'clock. He put the paper bag carefully on the weathered wood beside him. He had waited a year; a few hours more could make no difference. Neal Aycock had gone to town. Sooner or later, he would have to come back.

iv

ELVIRA walked slowly through the pulsing sunshine, head bent, eyes on the ground. All day she had been torn between desire for certain things that her money would buy, and reluctance to walk the half mile of sun-baked highway that lay between her cabin and Minelli's store. The two five-dollar bills were pinned inside her dress. They gave her marvelous visions. She saw herself choosing items with regal carelessness from the shelves, handing the money to Mrs. Minelli, then waiting—unheard-of novelty—for change. She thought of snuff, and her mouth watered.

She shuffled into the store at last. Mrs. Minelli sat behind the counter, impassive, toadlike. Elvira took a soft drink out of the washtub full of tepid water, opened it, drank it slowly. Mrs. Minelli watched her.

At last Elvira spoke: "Whey Geneva?"

"Sent her to town," Mrs. Minelli said. "Needed some things."

Elvira brightened. She had had unpleasant thoughts of being forced to share her wealth with her grandchild. She began to move briskly around the store, peering at the colored labels on the shelves. When her arms were full, she came and stood triumphantly in front of the counter.

Mrs. Minelli said, "You got money to pay for all that?"

Elvira unpinned a five-dollar bill and handed it over. She watched the heavy face in front of her with secret glee.

Mrs. Minelli looked at her suspiciously. "Where'd you get this—steal it?"

Elvira scowled. "No, ma'am."

"Then where'd you get it?"

"Man give it to me."

"What for?"

Elvira shook her head.

"What for?"

Elvira felt herself goaded beyond endurance. "For answerin' questions, tha's what for! Man ax me questions. I tell him the answers an' he give me fi' dolla's! Tha's the truth!"

"Questions about what?"

Elvira looked over her shoulder, then remembered her granddaughter had gone to town. " 'Bout sump'n, tha's all."

"About what?"

"Neh' min'," Elvira said. " 'Bout sump'n, tha's all." She was not going to tell Mrs. Minelli the rest of it. She had said too much already. She clutched the groceries she had bought, the candy, the tins of snuff. "Lemme have my change, please, ma'am," she said grandly.

Mrs. Minelli opened the wooden drawer and made change.

NEAL AYCOCK came out of the Farmers' Mutual Exchange and looked at the sky. The rain had slackened until it was a thin steel curtain, barely visible. Some colored children were playing in the new puddles in the street, their laughter shrill in the freshened air. Across the wet roofs of Hainesville, thunder growled at the heels of the retreating storm.

Neal went back inside, collected his packages, came out, and put them in the green Ford. The car was clean, except for raindrops, but he took a cloth and wiped it off carefully. When he was satisfied with it, he got in and drove rapidly out the Atlanta road.

At Minelli's store he turned right. The red clay was slippery. When he came to the incline leading down to the creek, he shifted gears. The car crept down cautiously, like an animal uncertain of its footing. The light was fading; along the creek the pines and cypresses were black against the greenish sky. The night chorus of insects had begun.

The car's wheels bumped onto the bridge and rolled slowly forward. Neal swore suddenly and slammed on the brakes as a figure stood up directly in his path. He reached down and switched on his headlights. The figure moved forward into the cone of light: a Negro, soaking wet, carrying something in his hands. The car stopped. Neal leaned out of the window. "Move, you damn fool, unless you want to swim!"

Nathan moved quickly to his left. He opened the door and slid in beside Aycock. He closed the door awkwardly with his left hand, holding the covered Luger in his right. He slid the paper bag from the automatic. "Back up, Aycock."

Aycock's pale eyes looked at the Luger, then at Nathan's face. "You drunk, nigger? Or just crazy?"

Nathan raised the muzzle an inch so that it pointed between Aycock's eyes. "Back up. I want to talk to you."

Slowly the Ford moved backward until the wheels were on the wet clay. Nathan gestured with his head. "Pull over there. Turn out your lights."

Aycock moistened his lips with his tongue. "You better give me that gun, nigger, before somebody gits hurt."

Nathan leaned back against the seat. He was shivering. This man killed Lydia, he thought, and waited for the lightning flash of anger, but it did not come. He just felt cold. He said, "Remember what happened here a year ago, Aycock?"

"I remember four dead niggers," the white man said. "You must be aimin' to join 'em." One of his hands left the wheel and strayed to the door handle at his side.

"Keep your hands on the wheel," Nathan told him. "And your eyes in front of you." An acrid smell came to his nostrils. He had smelled it before, in the war. It took him a moment to recognize it. It was Aycock, sweating. It was the smell of fear.

"You can't win, nigger," Aycock was saying. "Even if you git me, my friends'll git you. They won't shoot you, neither. Oh, no, it won't be nothin' pleasant like that. You want to know what they'll do? I'll tell you. They'll stand you on this here bridge. They'll tie your hands an' put a noose over yore head, an' set the bridge afire. Then you can either burn or jump an' stretch yore neck." He swallowed convulsively. "Better hand me that there gun!"

Nathan felt a sickening distaste rising in him. He thrust the slim muzzle forward. The pistol leaped in his hand; the noise it made was appalling. Aycock's head jerked once. His eyes had a look of surprise and disbelief. Then all expression went out of them.

Nathan did not look at him. He took out a handkerchief and rubbed the pistol carefully. He put it in Neal's limp

fingers. It slipped out. He let it lie on the seat. He opened the
door of the car. His ears were ringing; his nostrils were full
of the clean smell of cordite. He stepped out. Gradually, along
the banks of the creek, the startled insects were resuming their
piping chorus.

vi

AT SHEP TOWNSEND's cabin, the two horses tethered to the
porch railing stood damp and dejected, with drooping heads.
Inside, on the couch that faced the fire, Unity moved her head
suddenly, ending the long kiss. She pushed at the strong, demanding hands. "No, Shep!" she said. "No! Please don't."

He held her a moment longer, watching her through half-
closed eyes as if he considered her protest a sham, a token resistance, a conventional move in an old and universal game,
nothing more.

She stopped struggling. "I mean it. Please."

He slid his hand slowly out of the gap he had made in her
clothing. His eyes were angry. "One thing I can't stand, it's a
woman who's a tease."

She got up and stood by the fire, buttoning her shirt. She
was wearing faded blue jeans and scuffed jodhpurs. She had
a yellow ribbon around her hair.

Shep clenched his fist. "I ought to rip that damned shirt
right off you." He lit a cigarette; the match shook a little in
his fingers. "You deserve it."

She had taken a comb from her pocket and was running it
through her hair with short nervous strokes. She put the yellow hair-ribbon on the mantelpiece. Still she said nothing.

"Only reason that I don't," Shep went on savagely, "is that
you'd love it. You'd love every second of it. And your con-

[109]

science wouldn't bother you, because you could blame it all on me. Well, I'm not giving you that satisfaction. Not this afternoon, thank you."

She put the comb in her pocket and stared into the fire.

His voice changed suddenly. "Unity, come back here, please."

She shook her head. "I can't, Shep."

"Why not? You're no child, for heaven's sake. We're not exactly strangers. I called you a tease a minute ago, but you're not. You're perfectly capable of giving yourself to a man if you like him, and the circumstances are right. Or don't you even know that much about yourself?"

"I came in here to get out of the rain, not to . . ."

He said dryly, "You didn't exactly object to a few preliminaries."

"I know."

"Don't you know enough about elementary biology to realize that it's silly to start this sort of thing and not finish it?"

"Yes."

"Then come back here." He held out his hand.

"No."

He got up suddenly. "I haven't got much patience with fuzzy-mindedness, Unity. Suppose you give me the reason for this maidenly coyness of yours. If it makes sense, I'll try to respect it. If it doesn't, let's let this beautiful friendship lapse."

She found it easy to turn her anger with herself against him. "You're a spoiled young animal, that's one reason! Maybe you'd better take your ultimatum somewhere else."

They stared at each other. Then Shep laughed. "Maybe I'm rushing things a bit," he said. "But there's something about you— Well, I'm sorry."

She took a deep breath. "So am I."

They sat down on the couch again, close but not touching.

"You're right," Unity told him. "Part of me doesn't want to say no. Believe me, it doesn't. But—well, for one thing, my father was a preacher, you know. We didn't talk much about sex around the house, but there were a lot of unspoken taboos. You can't brush them aside."

"Most people do, sooner or later." He leaned back and looked at her. "Matter of fact, I've always envied those people their confusion of sex with sin. Whatever else it does, it makes sex twice as stimulating when they finally get around to it." He pushed off one of his riding boots and held out his foot to the fire. "Is that your only reason?"

"There may be one other. I'm not sure. It wouldn't make much sense to you."

"I'd rather know it than not know it. If I know it, perhaps I can do something about it."

"All right, then. It has to do with Hainesville. You not only live in Hainesville, you know. You *are* Hainesville."

"You flatter me."

"In my mind," she said slowly, "it's not very flattering."

"Look," he said, "I know Hainesville isn't as historical as that charming old coastal city you came from. We haven't got hand-wrought balconies and churches copied from models in London. We weren't captured by Sherman in the Civil War and we weren't even here when the Revolution was fought. But Hainesville is a damn good town; there's nothing wrong with Hainesville."

"I doubt if the country as a whole would agree with you," she said.

He had been pulling on his boot. He stopped and stared at her. "Are you referring to the lynching?"

"Yes."

He put the boot down on the floor. His face grew red. "Damn it all, Unity, are you saying you won't let me make love to you because a bunch of ignorant cracker farmers got drunk and shot four field hands? I think you're out of your mind!"

"I didn't say that."

"You're practically saying it."

She shook her head wearily. "Let's skip it, Shep. I knew you wouldn't understand."

He stood up suddenly. A muscle jumped in his cheek. He looked so angry that for a moment she thought he was going to strike her. Then he controlled himself. "You're right," he said calmly. "I'm spoiled. People seldom say no to me about anything. When they do I don't like it, and I get mad." He stamped his heel into his boot. "There. Is that apology enough?"

She smiled at him, feeling relief wash through her. "More than I deserve." He was not going to leave her. She had not lost him.

He was watching her closely. "Think your resistance will be as high tomorrow?"

"I don't know."

"Then maybe I'd better see you tomorrow."

"Maybe you had." She laughed, full of her sudden happiness.

"Same time?" Shep asked.

"Sure." She stood up. "We'd better be getting back now, though."

They went out onto the porch. One of the horses nickered quietly. She waited while he locked the door and put the key in its hiding place under the eaves. A purple twilight held the cabin and its guardian pines. At the foot of the bluff, the river glimmered. Moored in midstream, the speedboat nosed to and fro against the current like a restless hound.

Unity said, "Do you leave the boat anchored out there all night?"

"Sometimes," he told her. "Haddon was working on the engine today. Guess he left it out."

They mounted and rode slowly down the dirt road, the horses' hoofs quiet on the pine needles. Shep shifted in his saddle. "John seeing much of your sister?"

"They go out together occasionally."

"Well, I hope she doesn't give him the treatment you gave me this afternoon." He touched the horse with his heels. "Come on, let's canter back. It's cool enough now."

vii

PIP pedaled furiously through the dusk-filled streets, his porcupine head bent low over his handle bars. His bicycle lamp had a loose connection; it kept going out. He slapped at it ferociously, skirting black pools of rainwater. This was the residential section of Hainesville. On either side of the street, houses sat back primly behind their lawns. The air had a smell of wet grass.

In front of the Cantrells' house he braked to a stop and began trotting up the path. The bicycle, abandoned, seemed to hesitate for a moment, then fell over into the street directly in the path of the convertible nosing in to the curb. Shep stopped the car with a jerk.

"Why, it's Pip!" Unity said. "It's our office boy. Something must be wrong down at the *Courier*. Call him, will you, Shep?"

Shep whistled through his teeth. "Hey, you! Who're you looking for?"

The boy came back to the car. His hair stood on end; he was sweating. "M-m-m-Miss Cantrell," he panted. "Got a message for her from M-Mr. Crowe down t' th' paper. Oh. There you are!" He looked at Unity reproachfully, as if he suspected her of hiding from him. "N-n-no wonder your phone don't answer!"

Unity said, "Let's have the message, Pip."

"Oh. Yeah. The message!" His face brightened. "Mr. Crowe wants you to come down to the office right away, if you kin. Big news story's done broke, and he's gone down to cover it, and Miss Fagan's home with her summer cold, and there ain't nobody there but me." He backed away and righted his bicycle. "And I want to get down to Morgan's Creek quick as I kin to see what's goin' on."

He threw one leg over the saddle and slapped at his head-lamp, which winked, then glowed feebly.

"Wait a minute," Shep said. "What big news story? What's all the excitement?"

"Neal Aycock," Pip called, pushing himself out into the middle of the street and balancing precariously. "Shot himself through the head down by Morgan's Creek. Right where they had the lynchin' a year ago. Same place eggsackly." He started down the street, then thought of something and swooped back. "Remorse, we figger it must be! Remorse!" He turned again and pedaled away. Halfway down the block he turned and yelled the word again. "Remorse!" His voice cracked on the last syllable and echoed eerily in the quiet street.

Unity looked at Shep. "I told you it wasn't dead!"

Shep said calmly, "Guess I'll run down and take a look for myself. I'll drop you at the *Courier* first—all right?"

Unity looked at the silent house. "Everyone must be out. I'd better leave a note— No, I'll phone later from the office."

Shep let in the clutch; the car moved away. He came to a red light, looked casually both ways, then drove through it.

"Shep," Unity asked hesitantly, "do you think this man Aycock really shot himself?"

Shep shrugged. "Those countrymen aren't exactly the sensitive, brooding type."

[114]

"Then you don't believe it could be what Pip said?"

"Remorse? Hardly."

They drove the remaining blocks in silence. Shep pulled the car over to the curb and stopped. Above them the editorial lights of the *Courier* blazed brightly.

She got out, shut the door, and looked at him through the open window. "You're going down there now?"

He nodded. "Thought I'd take a look."

She seemed suddenly upset. Her hands clutched the window sill and her voice shook a little. "And if it isn't suicide?"

"Well," said Shep, "if he didn't kill himself, then sure as hell somebody killed him." He put his hand behind her head suddenly, pulled her face to him, and kissed her on the mouth. He released her and let the car begin to move. "Be seeing you," he said.

viii

IN THE darkness near Morgan's Creek Pat Daly wheeled his motorcycle so that it blocked the road at the top of the incline. The red mud was slick and treacherous. He slipped once to his knees and swore.

Down near the bridge, car headlights made a pool of radiance and across it dark figures moved to and fro. Another car came toward him and Daly flagged it down. He walked forward, flashlight in hand, his khaki shirt moth-colored in the darkness. He peered at the driver.

"Oh, hello, Mr. Townsend." His voice sounded as if he had injected civility into it at the last moment. "We're stoppin' all cars, now. Don't want sightseers messin' up the tracks—if there are any tracks."

"What's it all about, Pat?"

The policeman hunched his thick shoulders. "Got a call

about an hour ago sayin' there was a dead man in a car down here by the creek. Turned out to be Neal Aycock. That's about all, so far."

"Who found him?"

"Couple of youngsters who'd been fishin' downstream a ways. They were comin' across the bridge just about dark and found him."

"Dead long?"

"Doc Fosburgh said not."

"Body still here?"

"No, ambulance came and got it. Car's still there, though. Matson don't want it moved or touched until mornin'."

Shep offered Daly a cigarette. "Suicide?"

"Thanks. Well, it looks kinda like it. Gun was on the front seat, right beside the body."

"What sort of gun?"

"One of them foreign jobs—German, I think."

"A Luger? That's funny."

Daly shrugged again. "I've seen a few around. Some of the boys brought 'em home from overseas."

"Any fingerprints?"

"Don't know yet."

"Mind if I take a look?"

Daly hesitated. "I'm not supposed to let anybody go down there. But shucks, any tracks there might have been are trampled flat by now. Just don't touch Aycock's car, or Matson'll murder me."

"Thanks, Pat." Shep eased the big car down the slope, feeling the tires slip on the rain-soaked clay. At the bottom, he turned off the engine and got out, leaving the lights on. A green Ford sedan was pulled over to the side of the road, almost in the ditch. Two or three other cars were grouped at a respectful distance from it. Shep saw Lester Crowe's white head bent over a notebook in which he was writing something—an interview, evidently, with one of the discoverers of the body, since the answers were being given in a high-pitched treble. Another policeman stood looking on, his badge glinting in the headlights.

Shep walked over to the Ford and peered in. He could not see much. The car smelt of stale tobacco and dogs and sweat, that was all. A hand touched his arm and a gruff voice said, "Stand back, please. Chief's orders." It was the other policeman, grudgingly respectful.

Shep turned away. Lester Crowe came up to him, snapping a rubber band around his notebook. "Didn't expect to see you down here, Shep. Who told you about it?"

"Your office boy, I believe," Shep said. "I took Unity back to the paper."

Lester sniffed and put the notebook away. "That's good. It never fails. Big story waits until just after everyone's gone home, or got sick, or something. Then—bam! It lands on you."

Shep said, "The other Aycock been told about his brother's death?"

"He was down here a few minutes ago, with his father. Bubber looked mad and his father looked scared. Thought I'd drop in and have a little talk with 'em before I go back to the office and write the story."

Shep glanced around. "I'll follow you," he said. "I can get back to the highway on the other side. It's longer, but easier than turning around in this muck."

He went back to his convertible, swung in behind Lester's taillight, and crept across the bridge. Ahead of him the coupé danced as it hit the wet dirt. Lester gunned his engine; the car shot up the slick, oily surface. Halfway up the slope it slowed and stopped. Then, wheels churning, it slid sideways into the deep drainage ditch. The engine coughed and died. From inside came Lester's voice, hoarse with rage, "Oh, *Jesus Christ!*"

[117]

Shep got out, climbed the muddy slope, and helped Lester extricate himself. They stood in the road and stared at the mired vehicle.

Shep said, "You're in there until morning, my friend. Even then it'll take a tractor."

Lester clutched his white hair. "Why does everything happen to me? This morning my secretary doesn't come in; she has a cold. Shipment of newsprint is due; doesn't arrive. Tarleton calls up and says he doesn't like the tone of yesterday's editorial. Aycock waits until seven P.M. to shoot himself. Now this. By God, if I had a fifth of bourbon I'd crawl right back in the car and drink it all and let the whole damn thing go to hell!"

Shep laughed. "Come on," he said. "I'll drive you to the Aycocks', and then down to your office. How'll that do?"

"It'll help, believe me," Lester said gratefully.

The Aycock farmhouse blazed with light. When they knocked, a lean figure came to the door, walking with a slow deliberate step that was almost a prowl. It was Matson.

"We've been down by the creek," Lester told him. "Thought we'd stop and have a word with Bubber and the old man, if they're here."

"Yeah," said Matson, "they're here." He preceded them along the narrow passage. "These people don't know nothin'," he said over his shoulder. "Bubber's wife, she's gone to Atlanta to see her folks for a coupla days. Left this afternoon and took that girl, Louella, with her." He pushed open the door and stood aside. Lester and Shep went in.

The Aycocks, father and son, were seated at opposite ends of the kitchen table. Bubber had his sleeves rolled up, his hairy forearms resting on the table. He had a glass in his hand. His face was red and forbidding. Bilsy Shoup sat on the drainboard by the sink, his knees drawn up to his protruding chest, his big-eared head sunk between his shoulders like a gargoyle's. Another man in blue overalls with a heavy gold watch chain looped through one of the straps stood watchfully in a corner. He was young—about thirty—with sallow skin and lank black hair.

Matson said, "These fellers want to talk to you, Bubber. One of 'em's from the paper."

Bubber scowled and said nothing. Pa Aycock spoke up in his sandpapery voice. "Neal didn't have no call to kill hisself. No sir! He had a good farm an' money in the bank. . . ."

Bubber's heavy voice drowned him out suddenly. "Some nigger done it!" He pushed the glass away. He turned his head and stared at Matson. "Like I tol' you! Some nigger done it!"

The man in the blue overalls nodded. "That's right," he said gently. "I'm satisfied some nigger done it."

Matson spat accurately into the sink. "Maybe so." He narrowed his eyes and squinted at the ceiling. "Maybe so. But I don't believe there's a nigger in Haines County'd walk up and kill a white man in that particular place. No sir. Not on the banks of Morgan's Creek."

Bubber nodded his head. "Some nigger done it."

Shep had been leaning against the door, watching first one face and then another. Now he said, "Who'll be next?"

They all stared at him.

"Jesus!" said Bilsy Shoup loudly.

Bubber closed his big fists slowly. "Let 'em come on around. Jest let 'em come on around. Nothin' I'd like better."

The man in the overalls cleared his throat apologetically. "Neal, now, he had some right funny ways. Maybe he made some suggestions to somebody and somebody didn't like 'em."

Pa Aycock shook his head violently. "Neal never made no suggestions to nobody," he declared. "He lived real quiet like, him and them dogs of his'n."

Bubber looked up at the editor malevolently. "Some damn

nigger done it," he said. "That's all you need to know. Put that in your paper. Some damn nigger done it. Now, git out of here. Go on; git!"

Lester stood still for a moment, evidently searching for a reply. He found none that suited him, and went out. Shep followed him into the dark hall. He closed the door, but not before he heard Bilsy Shoup's querulous whine, "Jesus, Bubber, you think some black bastard's gunnin' for all of us?" and the heavy rumble of Bubber's voice as he began to reply.

Matson came out on the porch behind them and watched them go down the steps toward the car.

"Say, Chief," Lester called.

"Yeah?"

"Who was that other man in there, the one in the overalls?"

"Feller named Dillinger, cousin of the Aycocks."

"Isn't he the one who . . ."

"Yeah, he's the one."

"Thanks. Take it easy."

Shep backed the convertible, then straightened it out. "Dillinger had something to do with the lynching, didn't he?"

Lester gave a tired sniff. "Whole thing started when he got himself stabbed."

"That's right," Shep said. "I remember now."

They drove through the muddy back roads until they reached the highway.

"If we see a taxi," Lester said, "let me take it. You've chauffeured me around enough for one night."

"I'll drop you at the *Courier*," Shep said. "It's no trouble."

"I've got to go out to Hester's place," the editor told him. "Got to pick up some stuff she's been typing at home today. No use your going way out there."

"Hester? Hester Fagan?"

"That's right—my secretary. You know her. Worked for your father, didn't she?"

"Yes, she did."

"Damn shame about that birthmark," Lester said after a while. "Without it she'd be a good-looking woman." He pointed suddenly. "There's a cab, Shep."

Shep did not slow down. "I'll drop you at the office, then go get your papers for you. I've nothing to do."

"But . . ."

"Don't argue," Shep said. "I want to do it."

ix

ALONE in the *Courier* office, Unity waited for Lester to come back. One or two routine calls had come in; nothing important. She had pulled another chair close to her own, had propped her feet on it. She hated cockroaches.

She felt tired and depressed. The afternoon with Shep had been too full of tension. She shook her head. Her own behavior had dismayed her. She had thought herself more emancipated, more—she chose the word deliberately—adult.

It was a pity, she thought, that she had lacked the courage to give Shep the real reason for her refusal of him. It was so simple. Something in her, stronger than herself, had felt that it was wrong, that was all. Morally wrong. Next time the restraint might not be there—she did not know. This time . . .

She knew perfectly where these principles of hers—prejudices, Shep would call them—had come from. She could see her father, slouched in his old leather chair, the stubby pipe, the long, good-humored face above the clerical collar, the thick gray hair falling in a kind of forelock. She could hear his voice, too. . . .

"The universe is fundamentally ethical, Unity. Never forget that. Don't take my word for it; just look around you, at the people you know. They're all the proof you need that experiments in selfishness don't pay. It's so obvious, I don't see why it isn't apparent to everybody!"

A dreamer, in a way, an idealist. He had never given up his belief that it was possible, somehow, to unify the different Protestant sects. Hence his first daughter's name: Unity. A hopeless, quixotic task. Still, that was why he had moved to Hainesville, really: to sow his ideas in a smaller field. A gentle soul, without the ruthlessness that a great reformer needs.

When had those impromptu lessons in ethics begun? It was hard to say; certainly early enough to make a deep impression. Unity could remember demanding, with the petulant logic of childhood, "If God wants me to be good, why doesn't He make me good? He can do anything, can't He? Why doesn't He do that?"

And the patient answer, "Because if He *made* you good, that wouldn't be real goodness. What credit would it be to you? Don't you see, nobody can *make* you good—not even God. The goodness has to come from you—or it's no good at all."

Then, later, when they had a cottage at the ocean, the long walks on the beach in the summer evenings, the sand damp and firm and crusted with millions of shells, the jetty black and glistening where the river coiled into the sea, the splendor in the west as the sun went down, and the restless, unfolding curiosity of adolescence . . .

"Why is the world so beautiful, Daddy?"

"I suppose because its Creator loved beauty."

"But why"—groping, troubled by some vague sense of contradiction—"how can it be so full of ugly things? You know, spiders and snakes and things."

The crinkle at the corner of the eyes, the jet of pipe smoke, sweet-sour, comfortingly familiar. "Some snakes are very beautiful. So are some spiders. At least, their webs are."

"But they *bite* people!"

"Only in self-defense as a rule."

[122]

The sense of frustration, the determination, somehow, to make a point. "But there *are* ugly things."

"Usually man-made ones."

And once, when she was about fifteen, after a transgression that she now knew to be common enough, universal probably, but which then seemed unforgivable, the blackest depths of sin, she had been shattered, inconsolable. Her father, hearing her muffled weeping, had come to her in the middle of the night. He had sat on the edge of the bed in the dark, saying nothing at all, just holding her hand, until she sobbed out her terrified conviction that she was utterly lost, beyond all compassion or hope of redemption.

"Oh, I don't know," her father said. "Whatever it is, it can't be that bad. If you're sorry enough, which evidently you are, you'll be forgiven."

"But how do you *know* I will?" She could remember it all so well, the sad hush-hush sound of the waves on the beach, the dampness of the pillow under her cheek, the warmth of her father's hand, her terrible need for reassurance.

"The sun will rise tomorrow morning, won't it?"

"Yes."

"Well, when it does, you'll have a new day in which not to do the thing you did. That's all forgiveness is, really: new opportunities for doing better." He disengaged his hand and touched her hot cheek. "Go to sleep, now, child."

The education of Unity Cantrell . . .

She heard the familiar footfall on the stairs. Lester was back.

X

HESTER FAGAN lived alone in a housing development on the western edge of town. Somebody, in grandiose mood, had named it Fairmont Manor. It consisted of small, two-story brick buildings, each divided into half a dozen apartments. Enough shrubbery had grown up to conceal some of the raw ugliness of the place, and it had certain advantages: rents were low, bus service was good, and there was a wry sort of neighborliness to be had among the tenants, mostly white-collar workers with too many children. Hester had despised it when she first moved there after her mother's death. She still didn't like it, but she had grown used to it. People no longer stared at her; that was something.

She took a certain pride in her two-and-a-half-room apartment. One of the few compensations for solitude, she often thought, was the absence of responsibility for others, the chance to concentrate earning power on the gratification of personal whims and tastes. The apartment showed it. The walls, carpet, and slip covers made pleasant combinations of gray, maroon, and chartreuse. Her mother's books and her own almost filled one wall. In one corner was a big cabinet radio-phonograph. To own it, she had paid a dollar a week for two years. In the opposite corner she had her desk and typewriter. There were small matching prints along the walls, set in indented frames of white plywood. Compared to the drab and chaotic living rooms in other Fairmont Manor apartments, full of broken toys and the smell of wet laundry, this room was an oasis of serenity and charm. It was also, by the same comparison, sterile and lonely.

Expecting Lester, she had straightened cushions and emptied ashtrays, but she had not bothered to dress. Her cold was better, but it was still real enough. She had exchanged her old blue wrapper for a newer dressing gown, black with white piping. She had tied a white scarf around her throat and brushed her hair and put on some lipstick. That was plenty, she thought, for His Sniffiness. She took the pile of typescript from the desk and was fitting it into an envelope when the buzzer sounded. She went to the door and opened it.

"Hello, Hester," Shep said. And after a while, impatiently, "Can't I come in?"

She held the door wider. "Certainly. You startled me for a minute, that's all. I was expecting someone else."

"I know. Your worthy boss." He came into the room and stood looking down at her. The part in her hair was very white. He could smell the musky scent she always wore. It still excited him; he wondered if she could feel his excitement. He said, lazily, "He's an awful bore, Hester. Doesn't he get on your nerves?"

She turned her back abruptly. Her heart had been hammering ever since she opened the door, and this annoyed her. "Lester's all right," she said. "He knows his job."

Shep laughed. "He doesn't know how to drive on muddy roads, though." And he told her what had happened.

Hester picked up the envelope. She bent her head to lick the gummed flap, and for a moment all Shep could see was the left side of her face, clear and undamaged against the black of the dressing gown. The excitement stirred in him again. "Hester?"

"Yes?"

"How are things with you? I don't hear much about you any more."

"No reason why you should." She held out the envelope. "I get occasional reports on you, though."

She meant Unity, of course. He did not want to discuss that. The two women were in completely different categories in his mind. He wanted to keep them there. He took the envelope and balanced it in his hand. "Had supper?"

"I'll probably fix myself something here. I'm not hungry."

"I am. Why don't you eat with me? We can drop this by your office first."

She looked at him steadily. "Eat with you where?"

"There's plenty of canned stuff at the cabin."

She sat down on the arm of the chartreuse sofa and lit a cigarette. "You were the one who called it off, Shep. Why do you want to start again?" She blew out the match with a thin contemptuous stream of smoke. "Won't your new girl friend come across?"

He felt a stab of anger, then a grudging admiration. Same old Hester, shrewd and bitter. "Seeing you has a lot to do with it," he told her. That was true enough. He had been undecided until he saw her.

She made a little negative gesture with her hand. "What's the use, Shep? There's no future in it." She stared at the glowing tip of her cigarette. "Is there?"

Shep looked around the quiet room. He swung one of his long arms in an inclusive arc. "Is there any future in this?"

"At least I know where I stand with this."

"You always knew where you stood with me."

"That's right. And once bitten . . ."

"That's a silly proverb. I always thought it should read, 'Once bitten, twice bitten.' That's what usually happens, anyway."

Hester pressed her lips together. "Not to me."

"All right. You've got a mind of your own. Make your own decisions. But does that mean you won't eat supper with me?"

Well, here it is, she thought. Here it is again. You can refuse now, and make it stick. But don't kid yourself; it's your last chance to say no.

He doesn't love you, she told herself with scorn and contempt. He never did. He likes your body, and maybe he even likes your face, because some men get a kick out of things like that. And he'll take anything you want to give him, because that's the kind of man he is, and nothing you do or say will move him. Not an inch, forward or back.

What the hell, she said to herself, you've been through it once. Was it worth it? Were the times in the cabin and the two trips to Atlanta worth all the rest of it? The misery and the heartbreak, the loneliness and the jealousy and the curdled hopes, the change of job and the rest of it? Was it worth it? Is it something to begin again? Of course it isn't, you fool, you utter fool. And yet . . .

There really isn't any future, she thought confusedly. It's always today, no matter what you do. And look at my todays, just look at 'em! She felt a sudden loathing so violent and profound that she knew it must show in her face—loathing for herself, for her life, for this room, for Shep Townsend, for Hainesville. What had she done to deserve all this? Someday, someday . . . She did not complete the thought. She said to Shep, keeping her eyes lowered so that he would not see the hatred in them, "Sit down and wait for me, will you? I won't be long."

She dressed quickly, looking at herself sardonically in the mirror, despising the electric needles of excitement that kept pricking along her spine. She picked up her pocketbook and threw a final glance at her image.

"So long, sucker," she said.

xi

UNITY stepped off the bus and watched it move away like some gigantic glowworm through the tunnel of the trees. She began walking quickly toward home. Faintly, far behind her, she heard the courthouse clock striking the hour. Ten o'clock. Not late, really, but the weariness she had felt at the office was now an aching fatigue. Probably lack of food, she thought. She had eaten nothing since her lunch with Melady—and then she had done more talking than eating.

If Hattie's light was on, she decided, she would ask her to fix some soup and sandwiches. She was too tired to make the effort herself. She was not conscious of hunger; she was past that stage. But she knew she should eat something.

She wanted to talk to Hattie anyway. Her Sunday dinner for Judge Winter was expanding. She had invited Melady, who had accepted, and Lester, who said he would consult his wife. She might as well ask Shep, she thought. It would be a mixed group, but an interesting one. She began placing the people mentally at the table, smiling at the thought of Melady next to her Aunt Guley. He was an odd little man; aggressive and yet somehow detached, as if life were a beetle on a pin that he held up for his own examination. Perhaps that made him a good reporter. He seemed honest, anyway. And he had been a sympathetic listener.

That was more than could be said for Shep, she thought dryly.

She opened the gate and went up the familiar brick path. She swung around the house without going in and came to the garage. The light was on in Hattie's room. Unity thought of calling her, then decided against it. Aunt Guley usually went to bed early; she did not want to disturb her.

She went through the open garage doors and slowly up the pitch-dark stairs. In Hattie's room a radio was playing softly—a Christmas present from Unity and her sister. The door was pushed to, but not firmly closed; a thread of light showed, faintly illuminating the landing. Unity groped for the knob, found it, pushed the door open an inch or so.

"Hattie?"

There was no reply. She opened the door wider. Hattie's old bureau was in her line of vision, the mirror reflecting the brass bedstead on the opposite side of the room. Unity drew in her breath sharply. A man was sitting on Hattie's bed. His back was to the door, but his head was raised alertly, as if he were listening. He reached out suddenly, snapped the radio off. He turned around. In the mirror, his eye met Unity's.

[128]

"Nathan!" Her voice was high and breathless, as if something had knocked the wind out of her. He got up from the bed, came over and held the door wide.

"Hello, Miss Unity." His face was set and curiously controlled. He did not look like the Nathan she had known.

Unity walked forward three paces. She saw Hattie rise from a chair near the window, her face frightened and miserable. Nathan closed the door.

Unity waited until she thought her voice would be steady. "What are you doing here, Nathan? I thought you were in New York."

"I was," Nathan said. "I came back."

"Why?" She knew why, she had known why from the moment she saw him, but she asked the question anyway.

Nathan said, "I had a job to do."

Unity went over and put her hands on the brass bedstead. The metal was cool and firm under her fingers. Her fatigue was gone, suddenly; she felt strong and clear-headed. "The Aycocks, you mean?"

"Yes," Nathan said. "The Aycocks."

Unity swung around and faced him. "Murder," she said clearly.

Nathan shook his head. "Not murder. Execution."

Hattie began to weep with choking gasps and soft mewing sounds. "You stop him, Miss Unity," she said brokenly. "I tried. I can't do nothin' with him. You stop him."

Unity looked at the man in front of her. Nathan stared back. His eyes did not waver.

"Well, Miss Unity?" he said.

CHAPTER 5

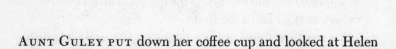

AUNT GULEY PUT down her coffee cup and looked at Helen with her wide, tranquil eyes. "What's wrong with Unity?" she asked.

"Unity?" Helen looked blank. "Why, nothing's wrong with Unity."

"Yes," Aunt Guley said, "there is."

They were sitting at the table in the dining room, the windows wide open to the freshness of the morning. Mrs. Cantrell was in the kitchen. Unity had gone to work. Helen should have gone, too, but she was late, as usual.

Aunt Guley nodded toward Unity's plate. "Didn't eat any breakfast, for one thing."

"Maybe she's in love," Helen said. She finished her toast and stretched her arms over her head. "In love," she repeated dreamily.

"Maybe she is," Aunt Guley conceded. "But it's not that."

Helen got up and looked at herself in the mirror over the sideboard. "What else could it be?"

"I don't know," Aunt Guley said. "I was asking you."

MELADY sat on the bed in his hotel room with the phone held between one hunched shoulder and his chin. He had a cigarette in one hand and a pencil in the other. With the pencil he was making angry doodles on the back of the telephone book. His face was unshaven and exasperated. Talking long-distance with Cunningham always irritated him. He had been talking for ten minutes.

"I tell you," he said, "my being here is a real break. We ought to exploit the hell out of it—that's why I want a photographer. This whole town has been living for a year in a state of dynamic tension. All it needed was a push to upset the whole applecart. Whoever shot Neal Aycock gave it that push. Things are going to happen. I don't know what things, but I can feel 'em coming. I spent an hour prowling around this morning. Hell, nobody's talking about anything else!"

"I don't see why you can't get a local photographer," Cunningham said. "There must be somebody in Atlanta. . . ."

"Nuts to that," Melady snapped. "I don't want some temperamental local yokel. I want one of our own people, so I can make 'em do what I want. You know photographers; none of 'em have any brains. How about Matthews—can I have him?"

"He's on the Coast," Cunningham said. "I'll send you Simpson."

"Oh, my God!" said Melady. "Not Simpson. Anybody but Simpson."

"She's in Asheville," Cunningham said. "On a polio story. I'll phone her and pull her off it."

"I don't want a woman," Melady objected. "This isn't that kind of a job."

"Stop being such a prima donna," Cunningham said coldly.

"Simpson's as good as they come, technically, and you know it."

"I know," said Melady, "but . . ."

"No buts," Cunningham said. "You asked for a photographer. All right, you've got one. She'll get there tomorrow. You can keep her for twenty-four hours; that should be enough. Have her fly back with the film. Tell her not to try to get it processed there. We'll be running it close as it is. When will I get some copy?"

"I'll have to rewrite, now," Melady said. "I can get some stenographic help from the local newspaper office, though. Suppose I air-mail three or four thousand words tomorrow night, how'll that be?"

"Better put it on the wire," Cunningham told him. "We'll have to rewrite at this end."

"My copy? Don't be silly."

"Listen," Cunningham said, "you're good enough to get away with that kind of talk, but you're not as good as you think you are."

"Are you?" said Melady. He grinned suddenly. "Keep cool, Sidney dear. It's going to be another stinker down here. Tell Simpson to wear her sun helmet—the long-legged bitch."

"I'm busy," Cunningham said in his dry, humorless voice. "Suppose you hang up and get to work?"

"Okay," said Melady. "Good-by, Sidney dear." He reached over and cut the connection. He waited a moment, then flashed the operator. He felt energetic and good. Being on the spot was a terrific break, and when the breaks started coming on a story they usually kept coming right to the end.

"Hello, honey-chile," he said when the operator answered. "Think you-all could get me the *Courier* editorial office?"

"You know," said the operator, "down here we can always spot Yankees by the way they use 'you-all' in the singular. Sure, I'll get you the *Courier*."

"Oh," said Melady. He blinked. "Thanks, you-all."

IN A car parked outside a faded-yellow house in Atlanta, Louella squirmed impatiently. Sun glared through the windshield, heating the straw seat-covers until they were painful to touch. Louella sat with her dress halfway up her thick thighs. She had opened both doors for coolness. Her lipstick was smeared and her brassy hair was damp with sweat. Nora had been inside the house for an hour.

Louella thought of her aunt with fear and loathing. Above all things, she hated waiting. Today her impatience was like a fever. She was afraid that unless they hurried, her uncle would be buried before they got back to Hainesville. Louella had never seen a dead person; she was determined not to miss the opportunity.

Nora had assured her that the funeral would not take place until the next day, but Louella was not convinced. She had read somewhere that in hot weather it was necessary to bury corpses quickly. Furthermore, she did not trust Nora. She had noticed that adults had no scruples about lying to children when convenient, especially when it was "for their own good." Nora might easily have decided that it was for Louella's good not to go to the funeral—hence this delay in Atlanta. Louella writhed on the hot seat.

To divert herself, she wondered how large a hole the bullet had made, how much blood there had been. If she could just get home in time, she would see for herself. She glanced resentfully at the sun-bleached yellow house. Why didn't Nora come?

Inside the house, in the front parlor with the limp lace curtains, Nora closed her gloved fingers over her pocketbook and stood up. "Thank you, Reverend. I reckon it's the will of God.

That's what I figgered you'd say, anyway, the minute I heard about it." She sighed. "Like you said in the sermon, their iniquities shall find them out. Only repentance shall save them." She held out her hand, her face quiet and almost handsome in its solemnity. When she wore her best clothes, an echo of her lost looks came back to her.

The Reverend Theodore Martinson was a gaunt young man, rather pale, with earnest, worried eyes behind very clear, rimless glasses. His voice was deep and controlled, except when he let it go during his sermons in startling bursts of fervor. Women remembered the quality of the voice long after they had forgotten the words the Reverend Martinson had spoken.

He was a well-meaning soul who was sometimes perplexed by the magnetism he exerted over his female parishioners. He had prayed earnestly for guidance, and had been rewarded by a conviction that the Lord would hardly tolerate in one of His own ministers qualities which might be damaging to the Lord's own work. This tendency to see the will of God at work in everything was apparent throughout the Reverend Martinson's philosophy. He preached it constantly in his virile, resonant voice. It was hardly an optimistic view of life, but many people dissatisfied with their lot found solace in it.

He had known Nora Aycock for two years—ever since the night she had spoken to him at the church door after one of his sermons. She was visiting her parents in Atlanta, she told him. She added that she had a problem about which she would like to consult him.

The problem, naturally, concerned her own happiness, or rather her lack of it. It had not taken the Reverend Martinson long to discern where the trouble lay. Her husband sounded like a drunken brute at best, and something unspeakable at his worst. Still, the woman loved him, or seemed to, and the young preacher made an honest effort to lighten her burden. He talked of the opportunities for character-building presented by great troubles; he said the Lord for some reason known only to Himself seemed determined to assign to some people the heaviest loads they could possibly bear. He even implied that somehow this must be a mark of favor, since such people were so often blameless.

As he talked, Nora always sat quietly, her hands in her lap, her smoldering brown eyes fixed on the minister's face with an intensity that made him more uncomfortable than he cared to admit. He liked helping people; he felt that it was his duty and his mission, but he sensed something potentially explosive about Nora. He wondered, sometimes, if his gentle words about the sanctity of marriage and the spiritual value of self-sacrifice might be keeping the lid jammed down on a seething caldron of resentment which one day might explode in his face. Or in somebody's face.

On this particular occasion, Nora had talked only of her brother-in-law's death. She had heard about it when she returned from church service the night before—the message had been telephoned from Hainesville—and she had instantly connected it with the sermon she had just heard. She hoped the Reverend Martinson would verify the connection. What he said seemed to satisfy her.

She came out into the sun-washed street feeling peaceful and refreshed. She saw Louella sprawled in the car, and a white-hot needle of anger stabbed her. "Louella! You git them skirts of your'n down where they belong!"

Lately, the thought that Louella was turning into a woman had infuriated Nora. She did not admit it to herself, but that was the reason she had brought her niece to Atlanta on this trip instead of letting her stay at home as usual. She did not want to leave her with Bubber.

She slid behind the wheel, glancing tight-lipped at Louella's mutinous face. She raced the engine of the old sedan. "You want to grow up to be a tramp?"

Louella tossed her brassy hair. "I wouldn't mind!"

She said it partly to annoy Nora. And partly because it was true.

iv

"DOVE season opens Sunday," Bilsy Shoup said, a look of anticipation on his pinched face. "Bubber, you fixin' to go?"

The three men were sprawled on the porch of the farmhouse. The great oak tree cast a dense shade, but still it was hot. Somewhere a locust whirred. In the dust under the porch the chickens held their wings away from their sides.

"Ain't missed openin' day in twenty years," Bubber said. "Ain't gonna miss this one."

"It's right hot for doves," Dillinger said.

"They'll be a few around."

A sad-faced hound wandered up on the porch and flopped down beside Bilsy. The hunchback scratched it gently behind the drooping ears. "Ain't this here one of Neal's dogs? Where at's the others?"

Bubber said, "Pa took Nellie over to his place."

Dillinger plucked a splinter from the porch railing. "Who took that big mean one Neal had—what was his name—Rex?"

"He's dead," Bubber said. "Snake-bit. Moccasin hit him, down in the swamp. Leastways, that's what Neal told me."

Dillinger picked his teeth thoughtfully with the splinter. "An' now Neal's dead too. Funny, ain't it?"

Bubber raised his head. "What's so funny about it?"

"Yeah!" Bilsy echoed him fiercely. "What's so funny?"

"Nothin'," said Dillinger hastily. "Nothin'."

Bubber stared at the floor. "Maybe you're right," he said slowly. "Maybe it *is* funny. *I* was the one who done the beatin' in the icehouse. Neal, he just stood lookin' on. Bilsy was there; he'll tell you the same thing. Neal never laid a finger on that nigger. I was the one who roughed him up. Hell, I admitted it right there in the courtroom." He pronounced it "coatroom." "So if somebody was fixin' to pay us back for *that,* why'd they pick on Neal? I was the one they shoulda shot."

Dillinger stroked his chin. "Maybe Neal was easier to git at. Most people knowed he drove into town an' back ever' day near sundown."

Bilsy Shoup looked up fearfully from the stick he was whittling. "Bubber, you reckon somebody's fixin' to git us too?"

Bubber pushed him with affectionate roughness. Whenever he spoke to Bilsy his expression changed subtly and his voice softened. "You stop your frettin', half-pint. Ain't nobody goin' to hurt you long as I'm around."

"Maybe not," Dillinger said. He thumbed his gold watch chain, his eyes fixed on some remote object on the skyline. "Jes' the same, I'm beginnin' to be glad I missed that there lynchin' bee. Yes sir, I'm plumb satisfied I was in that hospital." He shook his head. "Some fellers I know ain't sleepin' so good since they heard about Neal. No sir. Ain't sleepin' so good at all." He pushed back his lank black hair and eyed Bilsy speculatively.

The hunchback looked appealingly at his protector. "He's wrong, ain't he, Bubber?"

"Aw, shut up," Bubber said to Dillinger. "If you can't talk sense, go on home." He got up and squinted at the sun. Nora and Louella should be back from Atlanta before long. He wondered if he had time to go down to Minelli's and see Geneva. He decided he hadn't. He wet his lips regretfully. "God damn," he murmured to himself. "God damn."

IN THE office of the Apex Tire and Rubber Company, the phone rang. Haddon answered it, recognizing at once the slow confident voice.

"John, this is Shep—Shep Townsend. Is the boat okay? Thought I might use it this afternoon."

"It's okay," Haddon said. "Wasn't much wrong with it. I put in new plugs and reset the points. It's all right now."

"Thanks, boy," Shep said, and hung up.

Haddon put the instrument back in its cradle. Through the glass wall of his office he saw Pat Daly talking to one of his assistants. A moment later the policeman came in. He looked hot and harassed.

"Howdy, John." Daly sat down on the edge of the desk. "Jes' checkin' up on sump'n. Did the city cops ask you to keep an eye out for transient cars or strangers? Ask you to report anything suspicious?"

Haddon shook his head.

Daly sighed. "I figgered they wouldn't. Lazy bastards."

"What you after?" Haddon said. "Man who shot Aycock?"

"We ain't sure yet that he didn't shoot himself."

"Why check up on transient cars and strangers, then?"

"Well," Daly began uncomfortably, "we . . ."

"You guys better start using your brains," Haddon said coldly. "That is, if you have any. Whoever shot Aycock isn't driving around in the open. Why waste my time with silly questions? Why don't you go to somebody who might know some answers?"

"An' jest who," Daly asked sarcastically, "might that be?"

"Why don't you go talk to Yancey Brown? If the killer has a black skin, Yancey'll know about it. But no—that wouldn't occur to you. It's too simple. You cops have got to think of something really stupid, like checking transient cars and suspicious-looking strangers!"

Daly got up and hitched uneasily at his pistol belt. He decided to change the subject. He nodded at the wall calendar that hung behind Haddon's desk. "Nice," he said admiringly. "I could do with some of that."

Haddon did not answer him.

"Well," Daly said, "be seein' you, John." He went out.

Haddon swung around in his swivel chair so that he could see the calendar. It was typical filling-station art, a leggy nude wearing a sombrero and cowboy boots, nothing else. He stared at it for a moment, then got up stiffly and took it down. He limped over to the men's washroom, opened the door, and hung the calendar on a nail, out of sight.

He closed the door. A customer was coming toward the office across the sun-baked concrete. Haddon moved quickly behind his desk and sat down. He pulled up his chair so that the lower half of his body was completely hidden. At once the tension went out of him. He waited for the customer, his brown face calm and handsome, his hands relaxed on the desk in front of him.

vi

IN THE dark-paneled room on the third floor of the courthouse, Judge Winter brushed idly at a fly and heard the springs of the old couch squeak. "You know, Saunders," he said, "I find I can think much better with my feet above my head. What d'you suppose accounts for that? Increased flow of blood to the brain?"

These questions called for no answer, and got none. The fly buzzed and was still.

"Yes, sir," the Judge resumed, "this Aycock business is very interesting. Remember I asked you whether the injured party might be justified in taking some sort of action outside the law? Well, apparently I had something there."

"Looks like it, sir," murmured Saunders dutifully. He was beginning to be less afraid of the Judge. He had discovered that His Honor, like many able souls, was highly susceptible to flattery and not too concerned with distinguishing it from sincere admiration. Now, obviously, the old boy wanted to have his ego stroked by a discussion of the apparent fulfillment of his prophecy. A prophecy, actually, that he had never made. Well, thought Saunders, with an irreverence that would have terrified him a week earlier, let's throw him a fish. Aloud he said, "Do you think a local Negro could have done it?"

The Judge half closed his eyes. "I'm not sure a Negro did it at all. The killing was planned, obviously; it wasn't any spur-of-the-moment job. The killer selected that particular site for two reasons. One"—the Judge held up a bony finger—"it was an easy place for a man on foot to stop a car. All he had to do was appear in front of it on the bridge. And two: he wanted it to look like a crime of retribution—what better way to divert suspicion from yourself, if your skin was white?"

"Interesting theory," Saunders conceded. "But where's your motive?"

The Judge looked like a man who has constructed an elaborate sand castle to please a child only to see it kicked down. "Motive?" he snapped. "There could have been a dozen different motives!"

"Of course there could," Saunders agreed hastily, despising himself.

The Judge was silent for a while. "Funny how people reacted to my remarks to the jury the day they acquitted those fellows. I had two verbal commendations, one disapproving letter—signed; two threatening notes—anonymous, of course.

And this." He fumbled in his pocket and produced an envelope. "Invitation from a young lady to take Sunday lunch with her family. Very genteel way of showing her enthusiasm, I must say. However, I made inquiries and found that she is a young lady of superior qualities—mental and physical. So I'm damn well going. . . ."

He opened his eyes and saw that his young law clerk was not really listening. "You approve, of course, of innocent young girls being pursued by lecherous old men?"

"Yes, sir," said Saunders, and saw that he had been trapped. "I mean, no, sir," he added feebly.

There were times when he heartily wished himself back in law school.

vii

IN THE Headquarters of the Haines County Police, Pat Daly opened the door of his superior's office. "Benny's here, Chief."

Matson raised his cold, colorless eyes from the report he had been reading. "Bring him in."

Daly turned around and beckoned. At once a bundle of old clothes that had been huddled on a bench in the outer office arose and pranced—Daly could think of no more descriptive term—into Matson's office. It stopped in front of the desk. Two eyes as bright and friendly as a Cairn terrier's gleamed from under tangled eyebrows. An arm flapped in greeting, a rusty voice said, "Howdy, Chief!"

Matson looked at the apparition in front of him. In spite of the temperature, the little man wore two overcoats, one on top of the other, with the collars turned up. A knitted stocking cap was pulled down over his ears. His seamed and hairy face might have been borrowed from an ancient monkey. He stood there patiently, mouth stretched in a broken-toothed grin, the sleeves of the outer overcoat covering all of his hands except the tips of his fingers. On his feet, mismated shoes turned sharply outward, giving him a penguin stance. This was Benny. If he had another name, no one knew it. He was just Benny.

Matson opened the top drawer of his desk, took out the Luger that had killed Neal Aycock, and pushed it across the blotter. He leaned back and began to chew a match. Benny's dirty paws crept out of his sleeves. He picked up the pistol, stroked it lovingly, carried it to the window. His head came down and he sniffed at it. His fingers explored it, slipped out the clip, ejected the shell in the chamber, and clicked the hammer all in one smooth and lightning motion. He put the loose shell back in the clip, slid the magazine home, and sighed. He turned back to the desk and shook his head.

Matson stopped chewing his match. "Never seen it before?"

"Nope."

"You sure?"

"Yup."

"Seen any other Lugers around here?"

"Yup. A few."

"Well, how can you tell one from another?"

Benny smiled tolerantly. "I kin tell."

"That's right, Chief," Daly said. "He can tell."

Benny had unbuttoned his outer coat, revealing a row of canvas pockets stitched to the inner lining. From one of these he now produced an object wrapped in dirty flannel. He came close to Matson, who wrinkled his nostrils distastefully.

"Look, Chief." Benny flipped back the cloth, revealing an enormous blue-steel revolver. "Webley, four-five-five! Got it in a trade over in Clayton County. Sell it to you cheap!"

Matson looked disgusted. "Where in hell would I get ammunition for a cannon like that? Go on; get out of here. No, wait a minute." He took a piece of paper from the desk drawer.

[142]

"Write your name and address on this; we might want to see you again."

Benny stared sadly at the floor. Behind him Daly caught his superior's eye and shook his head. Matson crumpled the paper. "All right," he said. "Go on. Beat it!"

The overcoats trailed out dejectedly .The door closed. Matson looked at Daly. "That was a waste of time. He's so dumb he can't even write his name."

Daly shrugged. "He's been tradin' guns around these parts for fifty years. I bet he knows ninety per cent of the pistols in this county by sight. Anyway, you said to try everything."

Matson turned his head and spat into the crusted cuspidor. "You're damn right I did. And you know why. If we don't come up with a solution pretty damn quick it'll be just too bad. God damn it"—he threw the Luger back into the drawer and slammed it shut—"why do all the dirty crimes have to happen in our territory? If somebody had to shoot Aycock, why couldn't they shoot him inside the city limits?" He spat again. "You ask the city police to check on strangers and transients?"

"Yeah, but they ain't doin' much about it. They like to watch us squirm." Daly scratched his head. The Chief's question had reminded him of something. "Thought I might go over and talk to Yancey Brown. He knows just about everything that happens in this town where niggers are involved."

Matson looked skeptical. "Suppose he does. What makes you think he'll tell you?"

"I dunno. Me and Yancey get on pretty good."

"Well, go see him, then, for God's sake. Make him see that we got to move fast. Tell him if we don't find a suspect soon, some innocent people are gonna get hurt. His own people. Tell him that."

"Okay," Daly said. He went out and closed the door behind him. Through a window he could see Benny climbing into his ancient truck. The little man was teetering uncertainly, like

[143]

an overstuffed scarecrow. Daly glanced at the patrolman on duty at the switchboard. "That Benny," he said. "So loaded down with guns he can't even get into his own truck!" He picked up his cap. "I'll be back. Goin' over to have a little talk with Yancey Brown."

He went into the courtyard that separated Headquarters from the jail, swung his leg over his Harley-Davidson, kicked the starting pedal twice. From the barred windows above his head a few faces looked down, morose and indifferent. He gunned the engine, let in the clutch, and rolled through the archway into the street.

In front of Yancey's funeral home he stopped, walked up the steps past the coffin window, and rang the bell. There was no answer. He waited, then rang again.

Across the street, on the tiny porch that clung to the front of a sagging house, an old colored man peered anxiously at the motorcycle and the broad back of the policeman. Finally he got up and hobbled out into the blast of sunlight. " 'Scuse me, Cap'n—ain' nobody home. Yancey done gone to Atlanta today. Took his wife an' baby een de car. Won't hardly be back 'fo' dark, I reckon."

Daly came down the steps, a resigned expression on his face. "You tell him Lieutenant Daly was lookin' for him, you hear?"

The old man bobbed his head nervously. "Sho' will, Cap'n. Sho'ly will tell him."

He stood there in the street, a bent, worried figure. The motorcycle roared away.

viii

IN THE Palace Drugstore the ceiling fan revolved with a drowsy humming sound. Pop Hallíday swished the wet rag across the marble top of the soda fountain and leaned forward confidentially. "If you ask *me*, it was a white man killed Neal Aycock. Somebody figgered Neal was goin' to shoot his mouth off about the lynchin', an' so . . ." He put his forefinger to his glistening forehead and made a popping sound with his tongue.

Dr. Frank Fosburgh stirred his coke with a straw and looked at Pop with tolerant contempt. Fosburgh was a short, compact man with untidy clothes, a competent general practitioner who had inherited enough money to stifle a certain early brilliance. He had a wry, sardonic humor with which he liked to baffle and confuse his patients. It was his way of constantly reminding himself that he was superior to them. Still, he was a good doctor.

"Which member of the mob are you accusing, Pop? Might as well be specific, while you're solving the case."

Pop blinked his moist eyes, and for a moment his pink face looked solemn and scared, like the face of a child who has opened a closet and mistaken an overcoat for a ghost. He ducked his head furtively. "Ain't sayin'." He sidled down the counter, polishing as he went, pleased with the answer he had given. It sounded mysterious and important, as if naming the killer was something he would do at the proper place and at the proper time. Well, he told himself righteously, he knew a lot more than most people. Feller runs a drugstore, he gets to hear a lot of things. Yes, sir, a lot of things.

He became aware that the stool in front of him was occupied. He jerked up his head. "Yes, ma'am?" He blinked again. "Oh, hello, Hester. What'll you have?"

Hester Fagan tugged at her hat brim. "Coke with ammonia, Pop."

"Ammonia? Sure. Hardly get any calls for ammonia cokes any more. What's the matter? Nerves jumpy?"

"That's right," Hester murmured. She had not heard the

question, or rather, she had not absorbed it. Some fraction of her mind made automatic response; the rest of it went on wrestling with its problem.

In the corner the phone booth stood, black and empty as an up-ended coffin. It drew her like a magnet. It had been drawing her all day. She could not phone Shep from her office —not with Lester snuffling over his papers behind her. But she could phone from outside. At lunch she had resisted the temptation; besides, she knew Shep would be out of the office himself. But the afternoon had been torture. She had sat at her desk pretending to work, her traitor mind reconstructing the evening, every drink, every word, every easy inevitable move. She shivered. She had never known Shep to be so . . .

She looked at the clock over the prescription counter. Half past four. If she were going to phone, she had better hurry. Shep might leave his office; he might go home.

What had he said that would give her real hope? Nothing. She caught a glimpse of herself in the mirror behind the counter and winced. Who was she to think about love with a face like that? She clenched her hands until the nails bit into her palms. The coke with ammonia was placed before her. She picked it up, spilling a little. Five yards away Dr. Fosburgh watched her with sudden professional interest. She did not see him; she drank half her drink and put it down.

Don't phone him, you fool, she said to herself. If he wants to see you again, he'll call you. If he doesn't, nothing can make him. Go back to the office like a good little girl. Work hard. Accept reality. Sublimate everything.

She said, "Give me a couple of nickels for a dime, will you, Pop?"

What are you going to say, she jeered at herself as she walked into the stifling darkness and pulled the shuddering door shut behind her. "Thanks for a lovely evening, Mr. Townsend, and when can I expect you to marry me?" She put the

[146]

nickel in the slot and dialed the number she knew by heart. She would think of something to say when she spoke to him.

"Townsend Lumber Company." There it was: the bright, empty, idiotic voice. The first hurdle.

Hester put her free hand in her pocket to stop its shaking. "Is Mr. Townsend there?"

"Who's calling, please?"

Ah yes, they always asked that; she should have remembered. "This is Hester Fagan."

"Why, *Hester*!" The bright mechanical voice was suddenly full of honey and mockery. "Fancy hearing from *you* again." That would be Lois, the blond one. The switchboard bitch, they used to call her, and later a simplified version: switch-bitch. "Just a moment, please."

Now the second hurdle. Shep had a new secretary: the voice was crisp and unfamiliar. "I'm sorry, Miss Fagan, he just left. Can I take a message?"

"No," Hester said, sick with some nameless emotion, relief, regret, she did not know which. She tried to hold herself back and could not. "Do you happen to know where he went?" Humbly. Oh, it was awful, this begging for crumbs.

"Why, I think he's going home. And then, I know, he has an engagement for dinner. . . ."

Hester bit her lip. Hang up, you little fool, she warned herself, hang up. You're going to get hurt; you're asking for it; you're begging for it. "That's just it," she heard her voice saying. "I'm a little mixed up. I don't know whether my engagement with Mr. Townsend is for tonight or . . ." Oh, you imbecile, you hopeless driveling idiot, do you think any woman will believe that? Don't you know she'll check with Shep in the morning? Then he'll know. . . .

"Well," said the voice doubtfully, "I don't *think* so, Miss Fagan." And now the thin edge of malice, the feline satisfaction. "I heard him talking to Miss Cantrell, and, well . . ."

"*Miss Cantrell?* Oh, I see. Thank you very much." The click of the receiver, the light going out as she pushed the door half open, then the numbness and the red flashes of anger beginning to burn in the breathless dark. How could he do this to her after last night, how could he? That Unity, that smug idealist, that ineffectual liberal, that preacher's daughter, that colorless *child!*

Abruptly her rage leveled itself at Shep. He thought he could have them *both*, did he? He thought he could take whichever was most convenient, whichever pleased him most at the time. Or had her flash of intuition in her apartment been right—that he had invited her to the cabin only because of his lack of success with Unity? A wave of humiliation welled up inside her. She felt as if she were going to be sick. She pushed the creaking door of the booth wide, but still she could not breathe: her throat was full of the brassy taste of despair.

She had to do something. She could not just stand there. She had to smash the glass in the door, or scream, or go back to the counter and hurl the remnants of the ammonia coke in Pop Halliday's horrible hairless face. She had to do something, however futile, however childish. Something that would hurt somebody, as she was being hurt.

She would call Unity, she decided, call her on the phone and say to her, "You're having dinner with Shep Townsend, aren't you? Well, give him a message for me, please. Tell him I know now why he wanted to sleep with me last night. It was because he couldn't sleep with you. And tell him another thing. Tell him that's the last time I'll oblige him. Tell him that over your coffee, will you, Unity dear?"

She still had a nickel clenched in her hand, hot and slippery. All she had to do was drop it in the box and dial the *Courier's* number. Unity would still be there. Good little Unity never left work early. She would have to pick up the telephone; she would have to listen while Hester said those things to her. If there was relief in merely thinking them, what would saying them do? She tried to imagine the effect on Unity. One thing she was sure of: Shep Townsend's dinner engagement would be canceled.

And Shep would know why eventually, and Shep would hate her—Hester—and the gleaming grain of hope would be gone—gone for good, this time.

I can't do it like that, she thought. I can't tell her. All I can do is see that she finds out. For herself. Gradually. If she still wants him then, there's not much I can do about it. But maybe she won't. She's a prude, at heart. She'll think she can never trust him. And by God, she'll be right.

She dropped the nickel in the box and dialed the number. She could not go back to the office today. She could not sit there and watch Unity go off to meet Shep. But there was one thing she could do; one small brick she could move into position in the edifice she intended to build. "Let me speak to Pip," she said.

When he answered, she identified herself. "I'm not coming back today, Pip. Tell Mr. Crowe my cold's bothering me, will you? And, Pip, is Miss Cantrell still there?"

"She's here," Pip said, "but she's t-talkin' to Mr. Crowe."

"Well, listen. In the top right-hand drawer of my desk there's an envelope, sealed, with no address. Give it to her before she leaves, will you? Tell her I meant to give it to her this morning, and forgot."

"S-sure," Pip said. "I'll tell her."

She came out of the booth, pulled her hat brim down, and walked toward the door.

"Hey, Hester," Pop Halliday cried, "you ain't finished your coke!"

She did not hear him. She was wondering how it was possible to love a person you loathed and despised. It's yourself

[149]

you love, really, she thought with sudden bitter insight. That's why it hurts so much. . . .

Dr. Fosburgh watched her go. "Something must be bothering Hester," he said. "Didn't even see me." His vanity was piqued a little. She had seen him clearly enough a year ago, when she needed him. Funny, he thought, how much a doctor in a small town knew about what went on in people's lives. He lit a cigarette. Someday, perhaps, he would write a book; doctors, he had read somewhere, were naturally good observers and writers. He had a brief, pleasurable daydream in which his book became a best-seller, acclaimed by critics, praised by other doctors. He fumbled briefly for a title, found none that pleased him, and gave it up. There was no hurry about it, anyway, he thought with sudden irony. Unless he wanted to be sued for libel, he'd have to wait until all his patients were dead.

ix

LESTER CROWE leaned back in his chair and stared at Unity. What in hell's the matter with these women, he thought. Hester goes around all day grimmer than death, and now here's this one looking pale and nervous as a witch. What's eating *her*? Brooding about that raise she asked for? Lester felt a faint twinge in the place his conscience once had been. Well, damn it, he thought, I'll take it up with Tarleton soon as I get a chance. What with this Aycock business, there just hasn't been time, that's all.

Aloud he said, "One more thing. That Yankee character—what's his name, Melrose, or something—he called up this morning. Asked if he could borrow you tomorrow afternoon. Wants to go out and cover Aycock's funeral, of all things. With a photographer. I said you'd take him—okay?"

Unity nodded.

"He wants Hester to help him with some typing in the morning." Lester sniffed. "Seems to think he owns the *Courier* or something. But I told her she could go," he added magnanimously. "Might make a few extra dollars. By the way, I'm taking up the matter of that raise for you next time I see Tarleton."

Unity said, without enthusiasm, "Thanks, Lester."

Lester stood up. "What's the matter with you today? Female complaint, or something?"

"No," Unity said. "I'm all right."

"You don't act like it," Lester told her. "You better go on home a little early. Maybe the heat's getting you down or something. Go on; go home. It's almost quitting time anyway."

"All right," Unity said.

In the outer office, she pulled the dusty cover over her typewriter. She had tried all day to bury herself in her work, to ignore, to forget. She had failed. The knowledge that was in her lay in the pit of her stomach, heavy and cold and immovable. She turned out the light over her chair. She stood there motionless, seeing Nathan's set face, hearing her own voice, frantic and futile.

She had stayed in the garage for half an hour, trying to make him see beyond his fixed objective, trying to make him understand what would happen if they caught him, what it might mean—not just to himself, but to his mother, to every colored person in Hainesville.

Useless.

"Nothing will happen if they don't catch me, Miss Unity," he'd said. "And they won't catch me, unless you tell 'em where I am."

She had begged; she had pleaded; she had warned him that if he persisted there would be an explosion. Whether they caught him or not. "You don't know this town any more," she had said desperately. "It's changed in a year. It's guilty; it knows it's guilty. That's why it's dangerous!"

She told him about Huggins. She told him about the broken glass in Primrose Street. Nothing she said moved him; nothing shook or altered his purpose.

She picked up her pocketbook and moved away from her desk. You've got to do something, she said to herself. You can't just drift. You *can't* . . .

Pip stopped her at the head of the stairs, an envelope in his hand. "M-m-miss Fagan, she asked me to give you this. S-said she forgot to give it to you herself."

Unity took it. "Thanks, Pip."

She came out into the flat yellow sunlight and started to walk to the bus stop. A vacant taxi slowed hopefully. She could not afford it, but she stepped inside and gave the driver the address. She looked at her watch. Shep was supposed to pick her up in an hour. I can't face it, she thought. I can't go out with him. Not unless I tell him . . .

The streets moved past her, familiar, placid. The envelope Pip had given her was still in her hand. She tore off one end and looked inside. It contained a piece of yellow ribbon; nothing else.

Unity let it slide out onto her palm. She stared at it, puzzled. It was the ribbon she sometimes wore around her hair when she went riding. She had worn it yesterday afternoon, and left it on the mantelpiece at the cabin. She remembered, now. But how had Hester . . .

"Here y'are, Miss," the driver said.

She put the ribbon in her purse, took out money, paid the driver. She started up the path, still groping for an explanation. Perhaps Shep had left it at the office, and Hester had forgotten to give it to her.

The garage came into view. She gave it an almost frightened glance, quickened her pace, and ran up the steps.

The business about the ribbon was not important. She would ask Shep about it later—if she remembered.

Her Aunt Guley was watering the ferns in the hall. She gave Unity an anxious look. "Everything all right, dear?"

"Yes, thanks," Unity said in a tight, unnatural voice. She ran up the stairs to her room and closed the door.

x

THE law offices of Archibald Pope in Atlanta were in a shabby building but there was nothing shabby about the furnishings; they were somber and expensive. Yancey was not kept waiting. Pope was expecting him.

The lawyer was a tall, thin Negro, carefully dressed, with a dreamy, preoccupied expression that hid what was said to be one of the best legal brains in the South. He shook hands with Yancey; they had known each other a long time.

"Sorry to make you come all the way up here," Pope said, offering a leather box of cigarettes, "but New York is worried. Thought I might as well talk to you before I made any report." His glance flickered to the telephone. "I don't care much for talking on that party line of yours."

Yancey lit a cigarette and nodded without speaking.

"What really happened, Yancey? Who killed Aycock? Was it one of our people?"

Yancey took off his glasses and polished them. "Yes," he said finally, "it was."

"You'd better tell me about it."

Yancey told him.

Pope got up and walked to the window. He stood there, tall and stooped, like an angular crane. "It's easy enough to follow Hamilton's thinking," he said at last. "He figures that if he puts enough pressure on the town, somebody will crack; somebody will get panicky and talk, and maybe the whole case will break wide open. There's a certain logic in that. But . . ."

"But?"

"But if he gets caught—as he will if he keeps on—he'll do us terrible harm. Any justification he may have will be forgotten. He'll be lynched himself, for a homicidal maniac, and every person with a black skin will suffer."

Yancey said slowly, "It's almost worth it!"

Pope came back to his desk and sat down. "That's childish, Yancey. These Aycocks, they deserve to die, I grant you. But we can't jeopardize the whole movement just for the satisfaction that may come from an act of personal vengeance." He leaned back and closed his eyes. "I know what you're thinking: that it's easy for me to sit here in a comfortable office and lecture you, that I don't understand the humiliations you undergo every day. You think I've forgotten the anger and the frustration and the bitterness. Well, I haven't. I lived in a small town once, and things were worse then than they are now. Much worse. We're not doing too badly, Yancey. You may not see it from where you sit, but the tide is coming in. Slow—slow. But it's coming. We've got more friends than you realize. Lots of white people, right here in the South, are helping us. . . ."

Yancey said nothing. The office was quiet except for a sleepy horn or two in the street. On the mantel, a clock ticked.

Pope made a tent of his fingers. He stared at the wall over Yancey's head. "Trouble is, people try to keep hurrying the tide. New York is the worst offender. Hurry, hurry. Magnify incidents. Put chips on shoulders. Step on toes. Demand complete justice, complete equality. Not later. Now. Action— that's the word they always use. They have to have action. They can't seem to realize that action always brings reaction."

He sighed. "You can't knock a wall down with your head or your hands, Yancey. You've got to dig under it—undermine it slowly, until it falls down. The wall we're trying to overthrow is weakening. But what happens when somebody like Hamilton comes and starts thundering on it with his bare fists! Why, the people behind the wall wake up, and they come out and strengthen it, of course. Tragic." He shook his head. "Tragic. Sometimes I don't blame the whites for thinking we're racially inferior. Emotionalism, Yancey, that's our trouble. We feel too much. People who feel, can't think."

Yancey said, "People who can't feel, aren't people."

Pope smiled. "We've gotten a bit off the subject, haven't we?"

"What do you want me to do?"

"Do you know where to find Hamilton?"

"I think so."

Pope picked up a paper cutter, tapped it on the blotter. "Go and talk to him. Tell him I want to see him. Here."

"Suppose he won't come?"

"In that case, it may be necessary to bring him."

"I see."

Pope stood up. "Get him in here as soon as you can. If he agrees to come, fine. If not, you'd better phone me."

"All right."

"Need any money?"

"Not right now. The undertaking business is pretty steady."

"Just an old Southern planter, eh?" Pope smiled at the threadbare joke, then grew serious. "You're doing a fine job for us, Yancey. No one does it better."

Yancey stood up. "I do what I can."

"Going back now?"

"I brought Alma and the baby in to buy a few things. When I leave here I'll meet 'em and go on back."

"Try to see Hamilton soon, will you? We can't afford to

have him caught. And sometimes the police are smarter than you think."

Yancey nodded. At the door he turned back. "Tell me something."

"What?"

"If you knew the only way to stop Hamilton was to tell the cops about him, would you do it?"

Pope hesitated. "That situation could hardly arise. We can always stop him ourselves, if it comes to that."

"Answer the question," Yancey said.

"No, I would not turn him over to the police."

"Why not? You said he's a terrible threat to everything we're working for."

Pope smiled. "I wouldn't do it because I'm a Negro—and because in the last analysis my heart rules my head. Does that satisfy you?"

"Yes."

"Why did you ask?"

"Only because sometimes I wonder what sort of men I'm working for." He opened the door. "I'll try to see him tonight or early tomorrow."

"Good," Pope said. "The sooner the better."

xi

IN THE huge department store that covered two blocks—the halves connected by subways under and ramps over the street—Yancey's wife and small son had almost finished shopping. Alma was wearing her city clothes; she looked respectable and neat. Albert was very clean, very dark, and very solemn. His great liquid eyes looked out upon the world with a pleading expression as if begging for favorable notice or—failing that—then no notice at all.

White people passing through the narrow corridor smiled at the colored mother and her little boy. The saleswoman who was trying to find shoes to fit Albert was patient and kind. Alma had almost forgotten the anxiety and tension that had come into the store with her. She seldom came to Atlanta. When she did, the crowds and traffic confused her.

Another child—white—was also being fitted, and somewhere this happy mortal had acquired a large red balloon. Albert's eyes came to rest upon the balloon and remained fixed there, filled with unutterable longing.

The mother of the white child caught the glance. She hesitated, then stooped down and whispered in her little boy's ear. He frowned and shook his head. She whispered again—some effective bribe, evidently, for he shuffled forward, balloon in hand, and thrust it in front of Albert's fascinated nose. "Here!" he said ungraciously.

Albert reached out a small brown paw and grasped the string. He looked doubtfully at his mother.

"It's all right," the white woman said encouragingly. "He can have it."

"Oh," said Yancey's wife. "That's very kind of you!"

The two women looked into each other's eyes and a flash of understanding passed between them, so intense, so unracial, that they were both embarrassed.

"It's surely kind of you," murmured Alma in her low chiming voice. "We thank you."

"Not at all," said the other awkwardly, and moved away.

Albert's face was beatific. "I got me a balloon!" he said. The rapture in him struggled to find expression. "A *red* one!"

His mother felt his happiness as if it had been her own. "My, my!" she said admiringly. "Ain't that fine, now, ain't that fine?" The saleswoman came with the shoes and the change. "Thank you, ma'am. Come on, Albert. Time for us to meet Daddy."

[157]

Yancey was waiting for them on the corner outside the door. He smiled at the sight of the balloon, raised his eyebrows when he heard how Albert had acquired it. He took the packages from his wife. "I left the car over on Henry Street, honey. We can walk to it, if we take it slow."

So they took it slow, walking sedately along the hot, crowded streets, out of the main shopping district, into the squalid borderland between the areas recognized as black and white. Albert trotted ahead, his balloon floating bravely. At each corner, Alma called him back and took him by the hand. Yancey watched them over the armload of bundles; he was proud of his small family.

Two blocks from the car, in front of a pawnshop where some idlers stood, an eyelid drooped to command attention, a pale hand with yellow-stained fingers plucked a cigarette stub from a neighbor's lips, held it a moment, then flipped it in a short accurate arc against the red balloon. Deliberate. Unmistakable.

The scene as Yancey sees it is very sharp and clear in the slanting sunlight. It will always be in the present tense; it will never go away into the past. There is the sharp slap of the explosion as the balloon vanishes, Albert's baby features contorted with fright and grief, Alma's hand clapped suddenly to her mouth, the foxlike faces of the loungers, elaborately unaware. Inside there is the sickening shock of anger colliding with the conditioned reflex of caution. And suddenly he hears his own voice, shaking, furious: "You had no call to do that!"

Then the unbelieving silence, thinly pierced by Albert's wailing. The slow gathering together of the group in front of the door, the imperceptible hunching of shoulders, the reply, soft, almost coaxing: "Nigger, you tryin' to tell me I busted that balloon a-purpose? You just fixin' to call me a liar, is that it?"

Now he knows he must do something quickly. He feels his

wife shrinking against his arm. He hears his son's choked crying. Abruptly he stoops and picks up Albert with his free arm, knowing that a child is protection—they will not hit him with a child in his arms. And in hideous camouflage he says, as if Albert were an adult who could understand the fantastic joke, "Never mind, Albert; everybody's balloon gets busted sooner or later; yours just got busted sooner, that's all."

He wrenches his mouth into a ghastly smile to show that he has accepted this outrage as a boyish prank, a harmless joke, nothing more, and he moves on, his face working a little, out of range, out of danger.

They let him go; they do not call him back, as they might have done had he not confused them. He comes to his car and they all climb in. Albert is still sobbing; he will not be comforted. "Hush, child, hush," his mother says. And she says, "We'll get you another one, baby, a big red one, big as the sky, big as the whole world, all for you."

Yancey begins to shake all over and he finds he cannot stop. "God damn them all," he says to his wife. His throat is dry and tight; tears run down his face, but he does not care. "God damn their stinking souls to hell!"

Yancey's wife is drying the baby's face. "Not all," she says. "One of 'em gave us the balloon. Remember?"

xii

UNITY lay on the bed in her room, staring at the ceiling. She had not changed; she was still in her office clothes. There was a knock and Hattie came in. They had not seen each other since the night before.

"Mr. Shep's done come for you," Hattie said.

Unity sat up slowly and swung her legs to the floor. She

[159]

pushed at her hair; her eyes looked hot and feverish. "Hattie, I've been thinking about it all day. What are we going to do?"

Hattie bent down and picked up a stray stocking of Helen's. "Nothin', Miss Unity. Nothin's all we kin do."

"He's got to go back," Unity said. "Back where he came from."

"He'll go." Hattie raised her chin and straightened her thin shoulders. "He'll go when he's done what he came to do." There was a curiously resonant note in her husky voice. Pride, thought Unity suddenly; she's proud of him! She stood up and stared into Hattie's tawny eyes. "You tell him he's got to go!" Her hand gripped the bedpost. "You tell him that if he doesn't go I'll have to call in the police!"

Hattie's glance did not waver. "I'll tell him what you said, Miss Unity. But he ain't goin' to go. Not till his job is done. An' you ain't goin' to tell no police."

"No?"

"No. You ain't goin' to turn my Nathan over to no police."

"Don't be too sure, Hattie."

"No, ma'am," Hattie said calmly. "You ain't goin' to do it. You're tryin' to scare me, that's all." She turned back to the door. She lowered her head and her voice was again a servant's voice. "Mr. Shep's waitin'," she said, and went out.

Unity sat down at her dressing table. She picked up a hairbrush, then put it down with a distracted gesture. She got up, went out into the hall and down the stairs. Shep had taken the chair by the radio and was idly turning the dials. She remembered the darkened street outside the *Courier* office, the pressure of his hand behind her head, the roughness of his mouth. Less than twenty-four hours ago. Fantastic. She said to him, "Shep, would you mind terribly if I don't go out with you tonight? I—I didn't sleep much last night, and today I've felt generally . . ."

He said, cutting her off in the abrupt way he had, "You

know damn well I'll mind." He came over and stood close to her. "The boat's all ready. I thought we'd go downriver somewhere and cook a steak. There's an island just below the railroad bridge where . . ."

"Please, Shep." She put her hand briefly on his arm. "Let's have a drink here and . . ."

"I believe you're afraid to go. Is that it?"

She shook her head. "No, I *want* to go really, but I'd be such poor company that— Well, let's not quarrel about it. Go out and wait in the porch swing. I'll bring the drinks."

"All right," he said sulkily. He went out, letting the door slam, but when she followed a few minutes later he looked at her quizzically. "I don't know why I put up with you, Unity. Really, I don't. You're always crossing me up, one way or another."

She smiled a little. "Maybe subconsciously you like it."

"I don't think so. I like it better when I get my own way."

"Think you'll get it?"

"I usually do." He raised his glass. "Let's drink to it, anyway."

They touched glasses and drank.

"Since you're driving me out into the night," Shep said, "you might at least tell me when I'll see you again. Tomorrow afternoon? You don't work Saturdays, do you?"

"Tomorrow I'm covering a funeral," Unity said, and told him about Melady's request.

Shep frowned. "I don't like that much. People are bound to resent these Yankee snoopers, and if you're associated with 'em, they'll resent you too. I suppose Lester never thought of that." He kicked the floor moodily. "What's this fellow like, anyway?"

"He's coming to midday dinner on Sunday," Unity said. "You can meet him then. I was going to ask you and a few others." And she told him her plans.

"Sounds fine," Shep said. "I'll be shooting in the morning; dove season opens Sunday. But we'll be through before noon. I insist on sitting beside you, that's all. With Aunt Guley on my other side. Next to you, she's my favorite girl."

"Is she? I didn't think she was your type."

"Aunt Guley? Of course she is. That air of helplessness doesn't fool me. I never knew anyone more ferociously aware of what goes on. For example"—he glanced at her sideways—"she knows how you feel about me."

"Does she?" Unity murmured. "I doubt it."

"Why?"

"Because I'm not sure that I know myself. There are things about you . . ."

"That you'd like to change, eh?"

"Yes." She was amazed, sometimes, at the way he could penetrate her thoughts. "Yes, I would."

"Perhaps," he said shrewdly, "that's one of the main attractions. I appeal to the reformer in you."

"I'm not a reformer."

"Oh, yes, you are. Look at your attitude about the lynching, your preoccupation with the trial. Didn't you say you'd asked Judge Winter to come on Sunday? What prompted that but the reformer in you?"

She did not answer him; the point was unanswerable. She said, finally, "Did you go down to Morgan's Creek last night?"

"Yes. And over to the other Aycock's place afterwards, acting as chauffeur for your estimable boss. He got stuck in the mud—did he tell you?"

"No. Lester doesn't mention incidents unless he's the hero." She hesitated. "Do you think it was suicide, Shep?"

He shook his head. "I'm inclined to agree with Bubber Aycock."

"What did he think?"

"He kept saying, 'Some nigger done it.' I think he's right."

[162]

Unity put her drink down slowly. "Suppose he *is* right. Do you think, given the circumstances, there's any—any justification for that sort of—of crime?"

"Well," Shep said placidly, "I suppose you could argue that Aycock had it coming to him."

Unity's hands twisted nervously in her lap. "Then if you knew who the killer was—if you knew where he could be found, would you go to the police?"

"The police? I suppose so. That's what they're for, isn't it?"

"But there might be another . . ."

"Lynching?"

"Yes!"

"Well," said Shep, "they'll have to catch him, first."

xiii

LATER, when it was dark enough, Yancey Brown drove his car from Primrose Street to the house where the Cantrells lived. He parked in the shadows, walked quietly up the path and around the house to the garage. He climbed the narrow stairs, lighting his way with the small flashlight he had. He knocked; there was no answer. He tried the door; it was locked.

He came back down the stairs, crossed over to the house, and moved up quietly to one of the kitchen windows. Hattie was washing dishes. She was alone. Yancey went up on the porch and called her softly by name.

Hattie gave a violent start, then controlled herself. She came to the door, a dish clutched against the front of her apron. "Who's there?"

Yancey bent close to the screen door so that she could see his face. "It's me, Hattie. Where's Nathan?"

Hattie came out on the porch. Strong moonlight, pouring through the trellis, made a mottled leaf pattern on her face. "Nathan?" she whispered. "He's in New York."

Yancey put his hand on her shoulder. She was trembling, a tremor so light and quick that it was like a vibration. "Listen, Hattie, you don't have to lie to me. I know that Nathan's here. He came to me before he came to you. I have something important to tell him. Where is he?"

"I don't know!" The whites of Hattie's eyes shone wildly. "I ain't seen him all day."

"He'll be back, won't he?"

"Yes, but he'll be gone again befo' daylight."

"Gone where?"

"He don' tell me. He jes' goes." Hattie looked fearfully over her shoulder. "The police—they don' know he's here, do they, Yancey?"

"Not yet."

"You want me to tell him to come by your place?"

"No," said Yancey quickly. "No, I'll come back here. Early tomorrow. Very early. You tell him to wait for me. Tell him it's important, you hear?"

"I'll tell him," Hattie said. "He may not pay me no min' But I'll tell him."

CHAPTER 6

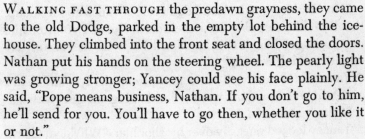

WALKING FAST THROUGH the predawn grayness, they came
to the old Dodge, parked in the empty lot behind the icehouse. They climbed into the front seat and closed the doors.
Nathan put his hands on the steering wheel. The pearly light
was growing stronger; Yancey could see his face plainly. He
said, "Pope means business, Nathan. If you don't go to him,
he'll send for you. You'll have to go then, whether you like it
or not."

"How soon?"

"Depends on what I tell him when I phone him today. I'll
have to call him this mornin'."

Nathan turned his head and looked at the man beside him.
"I don't understand you, Yancey. Why you telling me all this?
Are you for me or against me?"

Yancey rubbed his mouth with the back of his hand. "I was
against you. But something happened in Atlanta yesterday.
Never mind what. You tell me how much time you need. I'll
help you get it."

"What about Pope?"

"I'll tell him that I saw you and talked you out of it. That you've gone, that you've left Hainesville, that it's all over."

"Will he believe you?"

"I've never lied to him before."

"Sooner or later he'll know."

"I'll say you double-crossed me and didn't go. Or that you went and came back, that's all."

They were silent for a while. The air began to be full of the soft sleepy chirping of small birds. Ahead of them, the cross on a church steeple caught the first rays of the sun. Above it, the sky was a pure bottomless blue. Yancey found that he resented the coming of daylight. It made him feel naked, exposed. He said again, "How much time you need, Nathan?"

"I don't know exactly. Shouldn't be much longer."

"Who's next—Shoup?"

"No. He'll have to be last. I don't care so much about Shoup; that'll be like stepping on a cockroach. But if I go after him now, and get him, the other one'll be twice as careful. He might even leave town."

Yancey said slowly, "I know more about the lynchin' than I ever told you. You don't want to let that big one get away."

"I don't aim to."

Yancey looked uneasily over his shoulder. "Why'd you leave the gun there?"

"I thought that if I could make 'em think it was suicide for a day or two, I'd have more time to work out this other plan."

"You got a plan?"

"I've set a trap. Just got to wait until he walks into it, that's all. Won't be long, now. He likes the bait."

"Bait?"

"Geneva. Geneva Holland."

Yancey spat through the window.

"I figured it out on the way down here," Nathan said. "On the train. I thought that business would still be going on. It is.

I had a little talk with Elvira. She told me where they meet. I spent all day there yesterday. Sooner or later . . ."

"Suppose they meet at night?"

"I'll be there. Elvira's going to let me know. We fixed up a signal. I'll see it when I come out of the woods after dark. Then I'll go back and wait, that's all."

"You goin' back there today?"

"I'm going there now. It's a good place to wait. Nobody comes there."

"What do you do with your car?"

"Hide it in the woods."

"Nobody's recognized you, have they? Nobody's seen you but Hattie and Elvira?"

Nathan said slowly, "Unity Cantrell knows I'm here."

Yancey's face looked suddenly tired. "Oh, my God!"

"She won't talk," Nathan said.

"Why not? She's white. If she knows you're . . ."

Nathan shook his head. "She won't talk."

Yancey said angrily, "Anybody trusts a white person in a case like this must be crazy."

A truck rumbled up and parked outside the icehouse. A white man got out, yawning, and began to unlock the heavy doors.

"I'd better get moving," Nathan said. He leaned forward and turned on the ignition. "Want me to drop you by your place? It's still early enough to be safe, I reckon."

Yancey shook his head. "Cops were around askin' for me yesterday. I don't know yet what they wanted. I'd better walk." He opened the door and slid out. "How're you fixed for food, Nathan? Want Alma to make you some sandwiches? You gotta eat somethin', sittin' out there all day."

"I don't get hungry," Nathan said.

UNITY came into the church slowly and sat down in one of the rear pews. At once a stale sad odor of dust and sanctity rose up around her, the sterile aroma she had associated with religion since childhood.

On Saturdays—there being no Sunday edition of the *Courier*—she did not have to work. She sat quietly, hands folded in her lap. She did not try to pray. More than once in the past year, when a problem had seemed too big for her, she had come here and sat thus, wondering how her father would have handled it. She felt closest to him here.

A shaft of sunlight fell across the empty pulpit, gilding the dust motes in the dry air. It was easy to visualize her father standing there, hands on the pulpit railing, his earnest face full of gentleness and compassion.

What would he have advised her to do? How would he have met the situation? Help me, she said desperately inside herself, help me.

There was no real solution to the problem, no way out. If she told the police about Nathan, they would seize him, sweat a confession out of him. Or say that they had. A mob could do the rest. If it did, the whole town might explode. Race riot. The words had an incredibly ugly sound. All the other words were latent in them. Murder. Blood. Death.

She had to shield him, she told herself; she had to protect him. Not for his own sake. Not because he had found a kind of sanctuary under her roof. But because the lives and welfare of so many others depended on it.

And yet, if she let him stay . . . She beat her fist silently against the cushioned seat. She could *not* let him stay, knowing what she knew. It made her an accomplice in a design appalling in its brutality, in its negative savagery. A design by no means finished. A design that had barely begun.

She had to get him out of Hainesville. *She had to.*

How many generations, she wondered suddenly, was Nathan from the jungle? Five or six, at the most. Could that explain . . . She bit her lip; it was idiotic to think like that. That was what Shep would probably say, if he knew.

Shep. If only he could be made to listen, to understand.

She bent her head, staring at the tile floor where each little hexagonal fitted with such crafty exactitude into the endless pattern of the whole. Each in its place, inevitable, purposeful. . . .

Shep would never listen, she knew that. Or, if he did, he would have only one solution. Action, drastic and final.

She began to review the other possibilities. Lester? He was a coward at heart; he would not help her. Melady? There was something solid, something dependable about that little man. But she hardly knew him. Besides, he was a reporter; the temptation to exploit his knowledge might be too great. Her mother, Aunt Guley, Helen—what could they do? Nothing. Confiding in them would only be a cruelty, selfishly calculated to relieve the pressure on herself.

She raised her head and stared at the texts painted on the wooden gallery that ran along the sides of the church, the gallery where, on certain occasions like weddings or funerals, the colored people were allowed to sit. The colored people. . . .

She stood up quickly. She had her answer. Or, if not an answer, at least a hint, a suggestion, a lead to follow. "Thank you," she said under her breath. "Thank you."

She went out into the brilliant, smiling day.

iii

AT THE rear of the filling station across from Minelli's store, the four men stood close together in the narrow shade. Dillinger had his hat pushed back from his lank hair. His thumb was hooked through his watch chain. He talked slowly, watching the three faces in front of him.

"Ain't no doubt about it," he concluded. "Matson says somebody put that there gun in Neal's hand after he was shot. Fingerprint man came down from Atlanta. That's what he said, too. Bubber's right. Some nigger done it. I'm satisfied some nigger done it."

The taller of the Nelson twins spat on the ground and smeared the red dust with his shoe. "We oughta show 'em," he said. "Right after the funeral. We burn down two, three nigger cabins, they won't shoot no more white men in a hurry."

Whitey Lawrence rubbed the yellow stubble on his chin. "Mebbe it'd work out that way, mebbe not."

Dillinger scratched his shoulders against the sun-warped planking with a slow circular motion of his back. He was enjoying himself. "You mean, somebody might take a notion to shoot *more* white men, that it, Whitey?"

The other Nelson twin drawled, "You gittin' yeller, Whitey? Mebbe we orta change your nickname, hey?"

"Naw," protested Whitey in a high-pitched whine. "You know damn well I ain't yeller. Still, I think we oughta let Matson catch him a suspect an' then . . ."

"Burn 'em out!" said the first twin. "Fire's the thing. They don't like that. You burn a few cabins, an' them niggers'll see to it themselves that whoever done that killin' don't do no more. Burn 'em."

"Dynamite's good, too," Dillinger said. "I know some fellers over to Clayton County, convict guards. They been workin' on that new road through the hills. Bet they'd have a stick or two they could spare."

Whitey said, "You start somethin' like that, first thing you know they'll send so'jers an' put this place under martial law."

Dillinger turned on him with sudden ferocity. "*You* kin talk. *You* ain't never had no black bastud stick a knife in *you*. Well, I have!" He jerked open the neck of his shirt, showing the long bluish scar across his upper chest. "You see that? Buckeye Miller done that. But he ain't goin' to cut no more white men. 'Cause he's dead. An' every nigger in this county knows why he's dead! An *they* gonna think twice before they cut a white man. Yes, sir! Don't you fergit it!"

"I ain't fergittin' nothin'!" Whitey moved away from the group and climbed into a half-ton truck that stood by the pump. "I'll see y'all at the funeral. Gotta git on into town now."

He started the engine. The truck moved away. Dillinger and the Nelson twins watched it with their light, steady eyes.

"You reckon that son of a bitch gittin' yeller?"

"*Gittin'* yeller?" Dillinger spat. "He's been yeller all the time."

iv

WILLIAM HUGGINS stood behind the counter in his dry-cleaning establishment. It had reopened for business that morning. The shattered mirrors were replaced, the inkstains were gone from the walls. Everything was as it had been before, except that the plate-glass window was still broken, and possibly Huggins' smile was not quite so evident. However, he smiled now. "Good mornin', Miss Cantrell."

He liked this slender white girl. When she had interviewed him for the newspaper story her sympathy and indignation had been genuine. The story, as it finally appeared, had minimized the damage. But Huggins had an idea that it was not her fault.

Unity put her elbows on the counter. "I've one or two dresses at home to be cleaned, William, if you'll send for them. We'll try to use you for that sort of thing from now on."

William made a note of it. "Thank you, ma'am."

Unity lowered her head and stared at the varnished counter. "William . . ."

"Yes, Miss Cantrell?"

"I have a problem. It concerns a . . . a colored friend of mine. I can't discuss it with my own people, not even my own family." She hesitated; five seconds passed.

William stroked his frosted-silver mustache. "Reckon we all get problems like that, Miss Cantrell. Sooner or later."

"If you had a friend who . . . who was in trouble, and there wasn't much you could do to help him, where would you go, William? Among your own people, I mean. Who's the strongest, the most influential person? Who'd be the one most likely to help? The one you could trust most?"

"In Hainesville?"

"Yes, in Hainesville."

Huggins took the pencil and wrote a name. He pushed it across the counter. "Do you know him?"

Unity shook her head. "I've heard of him, though."

"If anybody can help you," Huggins said, "he can."

"Can I trust him?"

"I wouldn't tell you about him if you couldn't."

The door opened and a customer came in. Huggins straightened up quickly. "You want him to come and see you?"

"I'd rather go and find him. That would be quicker."

Huggins bent and scribbled the Primrose Street address. He held out the slip of paper. Unity took it. "Thank you, William."

[172]

She knew where Primrose Street was. Too far to walk, really, but she did not want to wait for a bus. She wanted to see this Yancey Brown. She wanted to get it over with.

She chose the shady side of Blanchard Street, and set out, curbing her impatience. She had all morning; she did not have to meet Melady until midafternoon. She went past the Palace Drugstore and crossed the courthouse square. Under the dusty trees the grass was burnt to a lifeless brown. Later there might be a thunderstorm; already an oppressive sultriness was in the air.

She passed the pawnshops that marked in some subtle but definitive way the boundary between the white and colored sections. Near the eastern edge of the town she turned right into Primrose Street.

Primrose itself was paved. It bisected shorter dirt streets, uniformly drab. In front of the gray-faced houses, squatting in the dust, chocolate children played with spools and broken-headed dolls. They watched Unity pass with wide, untroubled eyes.

She came to the funeral parlor, stared for a moment at the coffin in the window, then climbed the steps and rang the bell. A slight Negro with gold-rimmed glasses opened it. He looked at her, aloof and somehow hostile.

"Are you Yancey Brown?"

"Yes."

"Could I speak to you about something?" She added, "William Huggins sent me."

Yancey opened the door wider. "Come in, please."

She went in, glancing curiously around her at the paper flowers, the rows of chairs, the wooden altar covered with black cloth. Yancey pulled one of the chairs away from its fellows. He took out a handkerchief and dusted it. Unity sat down. "Thank you," she murmured.

Yancey said nothing. He folded his arms, watching her.

Unity said, in a nervous rush of words, "My name is Unity Cantrell. I've come to ask your help. Before I can tell you about my . . . my problem, I must ask you to give your word that what I say to you will be held in strictest confidence. No matter whether you help me or not. I must be absolutely sure . . ."

Yancey said, "I already know about your problem, Miss Cantrell."

She stared at him in the twilight of the shuttered room. "You *know*?"

"Yes, I've seen Nathan."

Something in his voice, something cold and abrupt, dismayed her. The sense of relief that someone shared this knowledge of hers, that she was not alone with it, vanished almost before it began. This man did not trust her; there could never be any true alliance with him. They might have the same knowledge, the same motives, the same impulse to action, but they could never act together. The ancient barrier of their skins was between them.

She said, confusedly, "But if you know . . ."

Yancey pulled up a chair and sat down. He leaned forward, so that his thin face was not far from Unity's. "Go home, Miss Cantrell. Try to forget all this. It doesn't concern you. Go home."

She had a queer awareness that for the first time in her life a Negro was speaking to her as an equal, without the faint implied disparity so familiar, so habitual that she had always taken it for granted. She said sharply, "It does concern me. If Nathan is caught . . ."

"It's his risk, isn't it?" Yancey demanded softly. "And mine, maybe. Not yours."

Unity stood up, anger working in her. She had been trying to help; she had been excluded. She said harshly, "Huggins sent me to the wrong place. I'm sorry!"

[174]

Yancey moved over to the window. He peered through the slats in the green shutters. "My father was a veterinarian, a self-made one. Sometimes, when he didn't know what to do for a sick animal, he'd say, 'Leave him be; if you don't know what to do, don't do nothin'.'" He turned around. "That's pretty good advice, Miss Cantrell. I'd take it, if I were you." He walked over and opened the door, letting in a blinding block of sunshine. "Thanks for comin' down here," he said more gently. "Not many people would take the trouble. Go home, now, and try to ease your mind a bit. I'll do everything I can for Nathan. I promise you."

Unity hesitated. "Make him go, that's all. Make him see that he's got to go. Now, before it's too late."

Yancey looked at her gravely. "I'll do what I can," he said.

She walked down Primrose Street slowly. Ahead of her, thunderheads were building up in the glaring sky. The air was heavy, lifeless. She felt drained, exhausted. She felt, obscurely, that she had failed.

v

HESTER FAGAN walked east on Blanchard Street toward the Eagle Hotel. As she walked, she kept her head turned to the right, as if engrossed in the contents of the shop windows. The mannerism was entirely unconscious. She was not thinking of her scarred face. She was thinking of Shep.

Yesterday, abandoning what was left of her pride, she had telephoned him again. Again she had progressed as far as the secretary. And again she had been stopped by the cool voice, full of professional regret: "I'm sorry, Miss Fagan; he's in a meeting right now." That was all. No suggestion that she call later; no indication that Shep might call her.

In a meeting. At the lumber company, she knew, visitors came and went in the front office, but nothing happened that could be classified as a meeting. There *were* no meetings; the word itself had a hollow, unconvincing sound.

It meant, of course, that he had left instructions with the secretary not to be disturbed. In her imagination, she could hear his voice, calm and faintly bored, "Oh, by the way, if that Miss Fagan calls, I'm not available. Understand?" Walking slowly, in the thick white sunshine, she dug her nails into the palms of her hands until the pain balanced the misery in her mind.

She stopped, suddenly, in front of a hardware store. Inside, at the ammunition counter, a tall figure was buying shotgun shells. Shep? The figure turned slightly. It was not Shep. The silhouette was similar, that was all.

Dove season opens tomorrow, she thought; Shep will be there. He had taken her with him once. She could remember his profile under the battered cap, the fine wrinkles at the corners of his eyes, the touch of his hand as he cautioned her to keep still. She could remember the easy fluid movements of his body as the gun came up to his shoulder, the way the walnut stock compressed his cheek, the bark of the explosion, and the way the tension went out of his face afterwards. She could smell the warm, earthy smell of him and hear his voice, half exasperated, half amused: "Don't shut one eye, Hester. Keep 'em both open. You'll never hit anything squinting like that!"

She never did hit anything, but she didn't care. She had been with him.

She went out of the sunlight into the dim lobby. She went up to the clerk. "I'm to do some secretarial work for Mr. Melady."

"Oh, yes," the clerk said, staring. "He's expecting you. Room 208. Go right up, please."

[176]

When Melady opened the door, she faced him resolutely, head up. If he was startled by her appearance, he didn't show it. "Hello," he said. "Come on in." He indicated the desk and portable typewriter. "There's our workbench. Sorry the room's so small and stuffy, but I guess we'll survive."

Hester took off her hat and tossed it on the bed. She sat down at the typewriter, then got up and moved the chair to the right so that the scarred side of her face was against the wall. She tapped the space bar a couple of times and looked at Melady.

"I'll dictate a new lead," he said. "Then it'll be mostly copying. One carbon, please."

They worked steadily for two hours. He was fast, but she kept up with him easily. The pile of manuscript grew. At one o'clock Melady leaned back and lit a cigarette. "That'll do for now," he said. "I can finish up the loose ends after lunch." He nodded at the manuscript. "What do you think of it?"

"The article?"

"Yes."

"It makes lively reading," Hester said slowly. "And the facts are accurate enough. But I think the general impression it creates is misleading."

"Misleading? How?"

"Well, you're probably not even aware of it. But you've made all the white people villains and the black people saints. In reality, it's not that way at all."

Melady drew hard on his cigarette. "No?"

"No. There are good colored people and bad ones, and the proportion of bad ones is pretty high. Certainly as high as it is among the whites."

Melady said dryly, "My investigations make that rather hard to believe."

"You believe what you want to believe, don't you?" Hester

said. "I know I do." She leaned back in her chair. "You talk about your investigations. How can you possibly expect to absorb it all in four or five days? How can you hope to understand it unless you live down here for a while? You think our antipathy for the Negroes is based on prejudice, pure and simple. Well, it isn't pure and it certainly isn't simple. It's based on a lot of things, some of 'em perfectly valid."

"Such as?" murmured Melady.

"You want a specific example? All right, it's not hard to find one. I remember once, when my mother was alive, we had a colored cook. Very faithful; very kind. She had a daughter, nineteen or twenty, who got pneumonia. We took her in and nursed her through it—and I mean nursed her! We also paid all the doctor's bills. When she was strong enough, she walked off—with profuse thanks, of course. But also with a pair of my mother's earrings. We got 'em back later, when she tried to pawn 'em. That's the sort of thing they do down here. Senseless, stupid, dishonest. And they do it all the time. Go look at the police court records, if you don't believe me."

"If you educated them better . . ." Melady began.

"That's right," Hester said sardonically. "Twist it so that it's all our fault. You have a queer compulsion to do that, don't you? And I think I know why. You're a writer. You like dramatic situations, with good solid villains and noble heroes. Everything black or white. You don't like to face the fact that it's mostly gray. If you did, you'd weaken the essential elements of your drama, wouldn't you? You'd have nothing to beat the drums about, nowhere to lead your crusade!" She smiled a little. "You might even lose your bread and butter."

Melady looked nettled. "When you're writing about a town like Hainesville, you don't have to invent villains."

"I agree. But for every town that's had a lynching in this state, there are a hundred that haven't. Why don't you write about them? Because they're not melodramatic enough, that's why. They won't build you any circulation."

"That's not fair," Melady said sharply. "You might as well ask us not to report the criminal activities of a burglar because the other members of his family aren't burglars. How do you expect to correct an evil if you don't expose it?"

"What makes you so sure that exposing it will correct it?" Hester demanded. "How do you know it won't just perpetuate it? That's the question you really ought to ask yourself."

Melady felt that the conversation was beginning to press against convictions he could not afford to have shaken. He said, "Well, it's an interesting point of view. Maybe I'll quote you."

"Go ahead," Hester told him. "It'll weaken your article, though."

Melady grinned suddenly. "You're a smart girl. Too smart for this place. How about a drink? I think we've earned one."

"I wouldn't mind," Hester said. She watched Melady rummage in his bag, produce a bottle, and go into the bathroom. I like him, she thought; he doesn't crowd you. He listens to your point of view. I could talk to him; I could tell him about Shep, even. He'd understand; he knows what it is to be on the fringes of things. He's been there himself. . . .

Melady came back with the glasses. He gave her one and raised his own. "I mean it," he said. "You're not only a good typist—you've got brains. Any time you want a job in New York, just holler."

Hester took a swallow of her drink; it was very strong. "You'd better be careful. I might take you up on that some-day."

"Don't you like Hainesville?"

"Not very much."

"Lonely?"

"Yes."

Melady put down his drink and massaged his face with both hands. "New York can be lonely too." He hesitated. "Mind if I say something personal? Two things, really."

"Go ahead."

"You're a very handsome woman; you should always remember that."

She was genuinely startled; to conceal it she gave a forced, jolting laugh. "Depends on where you sit, doesn't it?"

"That's the other thing I wanted to say—although it's none of my business. That birthmark—it can probably be fixed."

She raised one hand to her face in a hesitant gesture. "*Fixed?*"

"There's a man in New York—a doctor I know of—who treats facial birthmarks with X-rays, or radium, or something. Some friends of mine had a little girl as badly marked as you. Worse, I think. It took quite a while, but the mark is almost gone, now. Some tiny scars are left, but they're to be removed by surgery. The child's going to be perfectly all right."

"Oh," said Hester, "I'm glad."

"He might be able to do the same for you."

"Me? Oh, no. I couldn't afford it, for one thing. Anyway," she looked down at her drink, "it's too late, now."

"Too late for what?"

"Just too late, that's all. I'm thirty-three."

"What of it? I'm thirty-seven, and I don't consider that too late for anything."

"You're less defeated than I am." She finished her drink in a long gulp. "Thanks for telling me, anyway. I'm glad about that little girl."

"Look," Melady said, "if you had a New York job you'd probably make enough money to take treatments. I'd be . . ."

There was a rap on the door. Melady opened it. "Well," he said, "look who's here!"

A lean woman in slacks came quickly into the room. Her

[180]

hair, cut short, made an untidy but not unattractive frame for her face. She had a green scarf around her throat, the color vivid against her sunburned skin. A camera in a leather case was slung over her shoulder. "Hi, Shorty," she said in a husky voice. She saw Hester and stopped. "Am I interrupting something?"

"You are," said Melady. "But never mind." He waved a hand at Hester. "Miss Fagan, Maggie Simpson, one of our staff photographers, said to be very good."

Simpson barely nodded to Hester. "God, what a dump! Do they speak English? How long do I have to stay here? Not overnight, I hope. I couldn't bear it."

Melady shrugged. "Soon as you get enough pictures to make a decent spread you can drive back to Atlanta and catch a plane. That's what Cunningham said." He turned to Hester. "Thanks for the help. If your boss doesn't pay you for it, let me know."

"He will," Hester said a bit grimly. She picked up her hat and went out.

Simpson sat down on the bed. "Where'd you pick up that blighted American beauty?"

Melady was putting on his coat. "From the local newspaper. She's a crack typist. And smart, believe it or not. As for her looks, I imagine you prefer the fluffy ingénue type anyway, don't you?"

Simpson looked at him levelly. "You're a bastard, Joe."

"I know," he said. "Well, come on; I suppose I've got to buy you lunch."

vi

IN THE elevator, Hester leaned against the wall, feeling the alcohol burn slowly inside her. She had not had a drink since the night with Shep. You shouldn't drink at all, my girl, she told herself. It makes you do things you always regret. Also, it makes you sorry for yourself.

She tugged her hat brim down and went out of the elevator. God, she thought, if that man in New York—that doctor—could really do something, I'd throw this hat away, I'd burn it!

She crossed the lobby and went out into the street. The afternoon lay ahead of her, blank and empty. What had Melady said? "I'm thirty-seven, and I don't consider that too late for anything." Maybe that was the trouble; maybe she let herself be defeated too easily. She wanted to see Shep; she had a right to see Shep. Well, then, why not go and see him? Now, on Saturday, when he'd be home. Now!

She raised her hand and a taxi slid forward from the rank in front of the hotel. She gave the address and sat back, knotting her fists, watching the driver's curious glances in the mirror. You'll regret this, a small, smug voice said somewhere inside her. She did not try to answer it.

The Townsend house crouched in its well-tended grounds behind a tall iron fence. Shep's convertible was parked in front. Hester hesitated, her courage almost failing her. Then she went quickly up the long walk, up the white marble steps. She rang the bell and waited, her heart beating too quickly. She gave a violent start when Sam, the fat black butler, opened the door.

"Hello, Sam." Her voice sounded as if she had been running. "Mr. Shep at home?"

"Who's that, Sam?" It was Mrs. Townsend, Shep's mother, following her own well-bred voice to the door. "Why, Hester, how nice to see you after all this time."

"Is Shep here?" Hester hadn't wanted to see Mrs. Townsend; she was in no mood for brittle pleasantries.

"Why, no-o-o-o," Shep's mother said hesitantly. "I think he went out, didn't he, Sam?" She did not wait for Sam to reply. "I'm sure he'll be disappointed. Is there any message?"

You know, don't you, thought Hester. You know, and you're afraid for your precious son, and you're lying your head off right now to protect him. Because you don't think I'm good enough; you never thought I was good enough. So now you say he's out when he's not. All right. *All right.*

"No, thank you, Mrs. Townsend," she said clearly. "No message."

She turned and walked back down the marble steps. When she had almost reached the street, she heard the front door shut with a click that sounded triumphant and final.

vii

IN THE stiff front parlor of the Aycocks' farmhouse, strangely morguelike with its unscarred linoleum and seldom-used furniture, the mourners were departing. They had escorted the Aycocks back from the cemetery, had drunk tea and eaten some of Nora's small cakes in an atmosphere of dreary and self-conscious formality. They were glad to be leaving. The Aycocks were glad to see them go.

When the door closed on the last of them, Louella shot a furtive glance at Nora to make sure she was unobserved, then swept the last two cakes from the plate into her mouth. She munched dreamily, tired and content. She had had a moment alone with the corpse, before the funeral, and had satisfied her curiosity about the bullet hole. The undertaker had concealed some unpleasant realities from the world at large, but not from Louella.

Bubber stood up and stretched. He took his coat off, loosened his tie, pulled his red suspenders away from his sticky shirt, and let them snap with a wet slapping sound. "How 'bout a real drink, Pa?"

A roll of thunder muttered faintly. "Fixin' to rain," Pa Aycock said. "Glad it held off till now. Me, now, I doan' like puttin' nobody in a watery grave."

"It said 'Weatherproof' on the casket," Louella offered helpfully.

"Louella, you hush!" Nora began moving around the room, collecting plates and teacups with sharp clicking sounds. "Seems like nobody has respect for the dead any more." She glanced at her husband. "Or for the livin', if it comes to that."

"Stop your fussin'," Bubber said irritably. "I declare, you get worse every day." He beckoned to his father. "Come on, old man. Let's go into the kitchen an' git us a drink."

Pa Aycock got up from an unyielding sofa. He was dressed in a shiny serge suit and a stiff collar that was too big for his stringy neck. He looked smaller than he did in overalls and, if possible, grayer.

" 'Pears to me," he said in his papery voice, "you two would try to stop fightin', jest for tonight, anyway. Outa respect for Neal."

Louella found a half-eaten cake on an abandoned saucer and stuffed it in her mouth. "If they didn't fight," she mumbled, "they wouldn't have nothin' to do."

"Haw!" said Bubber explosively. He had started to leave and now he looked back over his shoulder. "That's the truth, believe me!"

A knock sounded on the front door.

Nora opened her thin mouth. "See who that is, Louella."

Louella disappeared and came back in a moment, excitement on her face. "Reporters," she announced. "One from the *Courier* an' two from a New York magazine!" She repeated her last words as if she did not believe them herself. "New York magazine!"

Nora put down the china she was carrying. "What they want?"

"Talk to Bubber; talk to all of us. Ask questions. Take pictures. You know what? The photographer is a woman! She's got a little bitty camera hung around her neck, an' she's already takin' pictures of the house an' the yard. An' you know what?" Louella watched Nora to gauge the effect of this additional bit of information. "She's wearin' pants! Brown checked pants!"

"Well," Bubber said, "we're all dressed up fit to kill. Might as well let her take our pictures, I reckon. Lady photographer in pants!" He shook his head wonderingly and slapped his father on the back. "What you know about that, old man? Ever git your picture took by a lady wearin' brown checked pants?"

"Louella!" Nora brushed her hair back with an angry gesture. "You tell that woman to git off'n our place. You tell her we just had a buryin' here, an' we don't want no reporters pokin' their noses into our lives. You tell 'em to git, you hear!"

Bubber looked at his wife derisively. "Ain't the reporters you object to—it's the pants. I know you!"

"You stand there," Nora began, "with your brother not cold in his grave, an' . . ."

Pa Aycock broke in uneasily. "She's right, Bubber. Nora's right. Any other time we could talk to 'em, but not right now. 'Tain't fitten, somehow. 'Tain't a question of pants or no pants. It's a question of—" He groped for a word. " 'Tain't fitten," he ended helplessly.

Bubber glared at him. "Old men an' naggin' women—I'm sick to death of both of 'em!" He jerked open the door that led into the hall. "Stay here, then. Stay here an' mope about a dead man who wasn't no account even when he was alive. I'm gonna have me a drink!" He went out and slammed the door. They heard his heavy footsteps retreat along the corridor to the kitchen.

"Louella," Nora said, "go tell 'em to git off'n our place."

Her niece hesitated. The prospect of being rude to the New Yorkers was pleasant, but the vision she had conceived of her own picture appearing in a magazine was pleasanter still.

"Louella!"

Louella went, dragging her feet. She opened the screen door about six inches. Melady and Unity were standing near the steps. Simpson was sitting on the porch railing fumbling with her light meter. A greenish pallor was spreading over the sky.

"Y'all might as well go," Louella told them. "We jest had a buryin' here; my aunt don't want no reporters hangin' 'round."

"We understand how she feels," Melady said. "But after all, we've come a long way, and—well, it might do her good to talk to us, don't you think? Get her mind off her troubles, maybe. . . ."

He looked around as Unity nudged him. She shook her head slightly. There was no use trying to cajole these people, once they had made up their minds.

Simpson spoke up impatiently. "Come on out, bright eyes. I've got the camera all set, just for you." She loosened the green scarf at her throat and swung her tailored legs. Louella stared at her, fascinated. "Come on. It won't hurt. Do something interesting, though. Bite the pretty gentlemen there in front of you, or kick him, or kiss him. Or fall down and have a fit. Don't just stand there with crumbs all over your face."

Involuntarily Louella wiped her mouth with the back of her hand, a childish gesture that smeared her lipstick. She stepped out onto the porch. Simpson raised her Leica indolently and snapped her. "This is no good," she complained to Melady. "They probably don't even dress like this on days when there's no funeral."

A door banged inside the house, there were quick steps in the passage, and Nora appeared. "Louella! I told you to git rid of these people!" She came out into the greenish light, her face set and bitter. She snatched at Louella's wrist. "Git back inside, you hear me?"

"Ah," Simpson murmured. "Action!"

She raised her Leica again; the tiny click of the lens sounded. She lowered it, twisting the knob that renewed the film. Louella stood unmoving, and suddenly Nora struck her across the face with the back of her hand. "You heard me! Git!"

Simpson half raised the camera. "Damn," she said mildly. "Don't suppose you'd do that again, would you?"

Louella stumbled through the door; she began to wail, a ludicrous, muffled sound that retreated down the passage toward the kitchen. Nora turned to Simpson. "You too! Git off'n this place. Take them fancy pants of your'n somewhere else." She began to walk across the porch, her body bent forward at the waist, her eyes hard and glittering. Simpson raised her camera and snapped it in Nora's face.

"Look out!" Unity cried suddenly.

"You git!" Nora said venomously. Her hand came around in a sweeping arc. Simpson saw the blow coming and ducked so that she caught it on the back of her neck instead of full in the face. She swung her legs over the railing and dropped into the flower bed. Nora leaned over the railing, her face crimson. "Git off'n this place," she screamed. "Git!"

Simpson was on one knee and Unity saw, to her astonishment, that she was still taking pictures, her face calm and amused, her hands moving with quick, certain gestures.

The screen door flew open and Bubber appeared on the porch. He held a glass in one hand, and stopped so suddenly that the liquid slopped over. "Nora!" His voice boomed out, rough with fury.

His wife straightened up with a sudden queer dignity. "All

right!" she said. She was breathing heavily and her fingers twitched. "All right!" She walked past Bubber and into the house. In the silence Simpson's camera continued to click. She was taking pictures of Bubber, now.

Melady gave an embarrassed cough. "Mr. Aycock?"

Bubber looked at him curiously. "Yeah?"

"I'm sorry if we upset your wife." He hesitated. Simpson had risen to her feet and was brushing herself off. Unity had moved down to help her.

"Aw, that Nora," Bubber said disgustedly. "She gits excited." The first drops of rain spattered into the dusty yard. He kept watching Simpson as if she were some rare and interesting animal.

Melady said, "Suppose I come back and see you when things are a little quieter around here."

"Sure," Bubber said absently. "Any time." He drank from the glass in his hand. A puff of wind stirred the dusty oak leaves over their heads with a dry whispering sound. The rain stopped, as if too exhausted to continue.

Melady walked down the steps. "Come on," he said in a low voice. "There's a limit to everything. Let's get out of here."

The three of them climbed into the front seat. Melady swung the car in a circle and headed for the gate. In the mirror Unity could see Bubber still standing on the porch, watching them.

Simpson touched the back of her neck tenderly. "Charming people! Remind me to ask Cunningham for a bonus, will you?"

Melady grunted. "Occupational hazard, that's all."

Unity said nothing. She kept thinking of Bubber Aycock standing on the porch, the amber liquid from the glass slopping over his huge hand, the sandy hairs bristling at the neck of his shirt. Nobody can kill him, she thought dully; he's too big, he's too powerful, he's too alive.

Simpson was staring out at the red clay banks that flanked

the road; they looked almost purple in the livid light. "The Deep South," she said. "My God, when they wanted to secede, why didn't we let 'em?"

Melady said nothing. Unity found herself too dispirited to reply.

Simpson felt the back of her neck again. "God, what a dump!" she said.

viii

MELADY turned the car into the Cantrells' street. They had dropped Simpson at the Eagle, anxious to collect her things and be gone. The thunderstorm had by-passed the town; the streets were dry; the lawns had a parched look in the slanting light.

Melady slowed down. "Well, we didn't get much, but it wasn't your fault. I may try it again tomorrow or the next day, now that I know the way." He shook his head wearily. "I can describe those people, all right; I can make the reader see 'em. But I'd never really understand 'em, not if I studied 'em for fifty years."

"It's a shame," Unity said, "that you have to base your opinion of the South on something like that. There's another side, you know. A side with decency and good manners and courage and—and grace. That's the South I knew, once. I wish you could know it too."

Melady was not listening. He killed the engine and leaned back. "I'm even beginning to doubt the value of what I'm doing," he said. "That's never happened to me before. I'm beginning to wonder if writing about it won't just harden the crust of prejudice and violence. I don't know. I just don't know."

Unity did not answer him. She was staring at the convertible parked in front of the house. Shep was here. She opened the door and stepped out. "Come in for a minute, won't you? There's someone here I'd like you to meet."

Melady sighed. "I ought to get back and kiss my little helper good-by. Well, all right. Just for a second, though."

As they came up the path, Shep's long figure uncoiled itself from the porch swing. Unity made the introductions and watched the two men measure each other coolly. Shep said, "How'd you make out?"

She told him, and he nodded. "Lucky it wasn't worse." He looked at Melady. "Some people feel that reporters are sort of like buzzards, you know. All right at a distance. But unpleasant when they get close to you."

Melady said, "People who don't like buzzards shouldn't leave corpses in their front yard."

Shep grinned suddenly, as if he liked the temper of the reply. "What exactly are you after down here?"

Melady shrugged. "Local color, I guess."

"I could put you in touch with plenty of that," Shep told him. He hesitated. "What are you doing at five o'clock tomorrow morning?"

"Sleeping, I hope."

"Ever shoot a dove?"

"No."

"Like to try it?"

"Sure," said Melady slowly. "I'll try anything once."

"I'll pick you up at four-thirty," Shep told him. "Where are you staying—the Eagle?"

Melady nodded. "I have no equipment—do I need any?"

"Just buy some blue jeans and a pair of cheap shoes. I'll find a gun for you."

"All right," Melady said. "Nice of you to take the trouble."

"It's no trouble, for a friend of Unity's."

[190]

"Four-thirty, then," Melady said. "I'll be in the lobby. I hope the local color is bright and gay at that hour."

"It's your risk," Shep told him. "I think you'll like it."

They watched the little man go down the path and drive away.

"That was generous of you," Unity said to Shep. "What made you do it?"

Shep flung himself back into the swing. "Well, I figured he's been saturating himself with racial stuff, the way they all do. Thought I'd show him that occasionally we shoot something besides field hands." He pulled Unity down beside him. "What d'you think made him accept? He doesn't like me."

"Doesn't he? How do you know?"

"I can tell. Why did he accept?"

"Probably wants to study you. That's his business."

"I suppose so," Shep said. "He looks like the analytical type." He stared at her. "Something's still bothering you, isn't it?"

"Yes," Unity said. "I'm afraid so."

"Want to tell me about it?"

"I wish I could, Shep. I can't."

"Why not?"

She knotted her fist. "I can't, that's all. I can't."

Shep narrowed his eyes a little. "Suit yourself." He stood up. "See you tomorrow, I guess." He went down the steps, down the path. He did not look back.

ix

BILSY SHOUP dropped the oily rag and peered lovingly through the barrel of his automatic shotgun. "Remember las' time you an' me sat aroun' cleanin' guns, Bubber?"

They were sitting on the steps of the Aycock farmhouse.

Dusk eddied in the yard. Nighthawks made passes in the air around the big oak tree, chasing insects.

"Ain't likely to fergit it," Bubber said. He had finished cleaning his own gun; it lay across his knees. Now and then he drew back the recoil spring with his thumb—most men would have had to use the heel of their hand—and let it slam forward. His little eyes watched the nighthawks circling. "Louella," he called, "bring me them shells on my dresser, you hear?"

"How come we went to the icehouse that night anyway?" Bilsy asked, fitting stock and barrel together. "I disremember."

"It was Neal's notion. We had to get them guns cleaned; he figgered it was a nice quiet place, that was all."

"You see that nigger watchin' us?"

"Naw, can't say as I did." Bubber turned his head and roared: "Louella—you hear me?" The girl came out on the porch, dropped a box of shotgun shells beside him, and flounced away. He fitted two into the magazine and pumped one into the chamber. "Course, we were all a little likkered up by that time. *You* made a lot of noise, I remember that."

Shoup's long melancholy face looked aggrieved. "I didn't talk no more'n anybody else. *I* seen that there nigger watchin' us clean them guns. But I never figgered he'd tell no grand jury about it."

Bubber grunted. He half raised his gun, then let it fall again. "He wouldn't have, neither, if he'd had good sense."

"Why you reckon he talked?"

"Oh, some of them uppity Northern niggers got a holt of him, told him they'd pertect him if he talked."

Shoup gave his high-pitched laugh. "He needed pertection, all right, the afternoon we went back there. You shore poured it on him." He shook his head admiringly. "You shore did."

"He had it comin'." Bubber raised his gun suddenly and

fired twice. The gun spat streaks of orange flame into the dark; the explosions seemed to lift the roof. One nighthawk fell like a stone just beyond the tree; another veered crazily, dropped a feather or two, and fluttered away.

"Right nice shootin', Bubber," the hunchback said. " 'Specially in this light."

Bubber disassembled his gun and picked up the ramrod. The oily rag pushed a wisp of smoke out of the barrel.

"You reckon we goin' to do any good tomorrer?" Bilsy asked. "Been mighty warm for doves. I don't see why they got the season set up thisaway, nohow."

"We'll git some. Everybody in Haines County with a dove-field'll be shootin' 'em. That'll keep 'em movin'."

"What time you want me here?"

"Any time before light." He laid the pieces of his gun carefully on the porch. "You ready for me to take you home?"

"Might as well go before Nora gits back," Shoup said. He sighed. "What's she got against me, anyway, Bubber? I never done nothin' to her."

Bubber walked out into the yard, the hunchback at his heels. He bent down and picked up the dead nighthawk. "Want this bull-bat? Eats good as chicken. No?" He tossed the bird across the fence, into the road. "Nora? Hell!" He wiped his mouth reflectively with the back of his hand. "Ever since she started gittin' religion she's been sour on everybody. It ain't jest you. Oh, maybe she hates you a little bit extry because I like havin' you around. She's the most jealous damn piece of . . ." He stopped, frowning, opened the car door, and slid behind the wheel.

Bilsy got in on the other side. "Whyn't you give her somethin' to be jealous for?" He looked at Bubber slyly. "Or do you?"

"If I did," Bubber told him, "I wouldn't go around makin' a fuss about it."

"I heard of a feller had a jealous wife over to Carrolton. Well, seems like she found out he was playin' around, and one night after he was asleep, she took a razor, an' . . ."

"Yeah," Bubber said. "I heard about that too. Never did believe it, though." He switched on the lights. They passed Neal's farmhouse, white and empty in the darkness. "Feller would a bled to death, for one thing. Never heard that he did, did you?"

"Naw," said Bilsy. "Never heard nothin' like that."

They came to the creek; the katydids were in full chorus. The tires boomed hollowly on the metal strips of the bridge.

"Damn," Bilsy said nervously. "If some nigger *did* kill Neal because of—well, you know—he'd sure as hell like to catch the pair of us now, wouldn't he?"

"I wish he'd try," Bubber said. "I just wish he'd try. But he won't. They're jest as yeller inside as they're black outside."

The car lurched unmolested up the opposite bank. "I heard a rumor," Bilsy said, "jest a rumor, mind you, that you kinder liked 'em when they was yeller outside."

Bubber drove steadily, his face impassive. "Who told you that?"

"Well, now," Bilsy said. "I don't rightly know. They was a bunch of us somewhere, an' somebody jes' happened to say . . ."

Bubber turned and looked at him. "Somebody, who?"

"I swear, Bubber, I didn't pay him no mind, an' I don't hardly recall . . ."

The car stopped with a shuddering jerk. Bubber's hand fastened on the overalls covering Shoup's protruding chest and lifted him bodily off the seat. The meaty face, twisted with rage, quivered an inch from the hunchback's sallow features. "You tell that somebody if I find out his name, he's gonna git killed! Not jest beat up, like that nigger in the icehouse. Killed! And I don't care whether he's black, white, sound, or crippled, you hear?" He flung Shoup back into the seat so hard that he bounced. He lifted his hand as if to strike him. Shoup cowered away from him, terrified. "Don't, Bubber!" he cried. "I was jest funnin'—honest I was. Jest funnin,' that's all!"

Bubber started the car again and drove for ten minutes in silence. They came to the farmhouse where Shoup lived. Bubber flung open the door and stared at him balefully. "Someday you're gonna talk yourself into good trouble. Now git!"

Bilsy hopped out like a spider and scuttled across the road. "See you tomorrer, Bubber?" There was an apology in the whining voice.

"What the hell," Bubber muttered. "You don't know no better, I reckon." He swung the car in a tight circle. "All right. See you then."

He drove back along the dusty road, his thoughts churning sullenly. So they knew about Geneva, did they—or thought they did? Well, let 'em talk. It'd take more'n a bunch of rumors to make him give up Geneva. He hadn't planned to see her this week end, what with Neal's burial an' all. But now . . .

"I'll show 'em," he muttered. "I'll show 'em . . ."

When he came to the turnoff for Morgan's Creek he kept straight on, following the wide dirt road until ahead of him he saw Minelli's store. As he stopped in front of it, the door opened and Elvira came out into the lavender dusk. Bubber relaxed, watching her. This meant he would not have to face Mrs. Minelli's knowing eye.

He waited until Elvira had walked fifty yards down the road, then drove up alongside her. Their conversation was short.

"All right," Bubber said finally. "You tell her, now. Tomorrer night; nine o'clock. I'll be expectin' her."

"I'll tell her, Mr. Bubber," the old woman said. She watched the car drive away. Wouldn' give me a ride no-how! she

[195]

thought spitefully. Well, tomorrow night she would light her lamp. There would be a certain satisfaction in that.

X

NEAR midnight, Unity threw back the crumpled sheet, reached for her dressing gown, and stood up. The room was quiet except for Helen's steady breathing. The night was very still. On the wall behind the bed, leaf shadows cast by the street light made a pattern.

She fumbled for her slippers and put them on. She had had enough of this. She could stand it no longer.

She went down the stairs, trying to make no noise. She went through the kitchen, out onto the back porch. The moon was bright. Somewhere a cat yowled sadly. Unity pulled the dressing gown tighter around her. The air was warm, but she was shivering. She hesitated, listening to the muffled thudding of her heart. The lights were out in Hattie's room.

She made herself go down the steps and walk over to the garage. She went up to Hattie's door quickly, not giving herself time to change her mind. She knocked. "Hattie!" She knew the old woman would recognize her voice. "Let me in. I've got to talk to Nathan!"

For a moment there was silence; then she saw a thread of light appear under the door. She waited. The lock turned; the door opened. It was not Hattie. It was Nathan. He had taken off his shirt and shoes. His undershirt looked very white against his skin. If he had been sleeping, his face did not show it. "What is it, Miss Unity?"

"I've got to talk to you, Nathan. Please let me in."

He stepped back and opened the door wide. Unity went in. Hattie was sitting up in bed, the sheet pulled up around her chin. She looked very small, very fragile, like a chocolate doll.

A quilt and a pillow lay near the door. Unity swung around and faced Nathan. She was no longer shivering. She said, calmly, "Nathan, you can't stay here any longer. You've got to leave. Tomorrow."

Nathan said nothing. He picked up his shirt slowly, and slipped it on. Hattie said, in a tense whisper, "You ain't goin' to no police!"

"Yes," said Unity slowly, "I am." She had thought it all out, lying sleepless on her bed. She had rehearsed it in her mind until she knew it by heart. Now she said it. "I can't go on being a party to all this. It means I'm as guilty as you are. I haven't any choice. I'm going to tell them, in the morning."

Nathan was buttoning his shirt; his face was impassive. "They can't prove I've done anything."

Unity said, "Do you want to risk it?"

Hattie came across the floor, her head tilted back, her jaw thrust out. She stopped in front of Unity. "You ain't gonna tell nobody nothin'."

Unity looked down at her. "Yes, Hattie, I am."

Nathan was watching her. "What if I agree to go, Miss Unity?"

"I'll forget I ever saw you."

Hattie said fiercely, "You better fergit it anyway! You better . . ."

"Hush!" Nathan said to his mother. He turned away from them and sat down in the rocking chair by the window. He took cigarettes out of his pocket and lit one. Outside, the cat cried again, a low anguished sound. Nathan crushed out the cigarette. He said suddenly, "All right, I'll go. I got one of 'em. That's enough. I'll go."

Unity let her breath out slowly. "Do you mean that?"

"Yes."

"Do you promise . . ."

"Yes."

"Nathan!" Hattie whispered. "You said . . ."

Nathan stood up. "I'll go tomorrow." He opened the door. "You can stop worrying," he said to Unity. "Better go back and get your sleep."

"If you don't go," Unity said, "if you break your promise . . ."

Nathan took her elbow gently and led her to the door. "I don't break promises, Miss Unity."

He watched her disappear down the narrow stairs. He closed the door and locked it. He went to the window, waited until he saw Unity open the kitchen door and go inside. He turned back into the room. Hattie was sitting on the edge of the bed. She had taken a bottle from somewhere and was pouring herself a drink. Her hands shook. The neck of the bottle chattered along the rim of the glass. "You think she'd do that, Nathan? You think she'd go to the police?"

Nathan came across the room and took the bottle away from her. He switched off the light. "No. She was bluffing. Trying to scare me off, that's all."

"Then you ain't . . ."

"No." She heard him lie down on the quilt that was his bed. "She asks you tomorrow, you tell her I'm gone. But I won't be gone."

Hattie finished her drink in one gulp and put the glass on the floor. She lay down slowly. The springs creaked. "Then how come you promise her like that?"

Nathan did not answer her. Hattie lay still, listening to his breathing. "Nathan?"

"Yes?"

"How come you promise her?"

Nathan moved impatiently in the darkness. "To give her some peace, that's why. She's a good girl. I didn't come down here to worry her."

In a clock tower, not far away, a rusty-throated bell was striking twelve.

[198]

CHAPTER 7

DRIVING THROUGH THE predawn darkness, they had not talked much; the car's radio had filled the silence. The headlights followed the dirt road through the pines until the windows of the cabin gleamed ahead of them. Shep stopped the car. "We'll pick up the guns here. Want to come in?"

Melady followed him up on the porch. The moon was down. Overhead stars glittered coldly. From the river a silver mist was rising.

Shep threw the beam of a flashlight under the eaves, found the key, unlocked the door. "Don't know if I've got one that'll fit you. My arms are pretty long. Still, it doesn't matter too much."

Melady watched him go to the gunrack and select two, a double-barreled and an automatic. He handed the latter to Melady. "Here you are. Sixteen gauge, modified. Ammunition's in the car." He swept the beam of the flashlight like a sword. "Sorry it's not daylight; I'd like to show you the place. We'd better move on, though. They'll be waiting for us."

"Far from here?" Melady asked. The heavy shoes he had

bought felt clumsy on his feet; the new blue jeans were tight and uncomfortable.

Shep locked the door and put the key away. "Couple of miles. We can make it in five minutes."

They made it in four. Half a dozen cars were there ahead of them, the occupants standing around a fire built in the angle formed by the crossroads. There was a streak of pale yellow now along the eastern sky. The fire snapped, throwing orange sparks.

Melady climbed out stiffly. Shep was already fumbling in the trunk of the car. He handed over a musette bag. "Here's your ammunition."

"What size shot d'you use?"

"Oh, seven and a half. Eights are all right. Doesn't take much to stop a dove. People think it does, but that's because they usually shoot six feet behind 'em and just knock out a feather or two with the edge of the pattern. If you've never shot doves before, you'd better give 'em what you consider a normal lead, then double it."

"Are they that fast?"

"The easy wingbeat fools you—makes you think they're going slower than they are." Shep closed the trunk and straightened up. "Come on." He moved toward the fire. The circle parted to let them in; a murmur of recognition met Shep. "Hello, boys," he said. "Brought a friend of mine along." He indicated Melady. "Visitor, down from New York."

The murmur was repeated, with less enthusiasm. Melady felt the pale eyes measure him briefly, then fall away. He looked at the lean, hard-bitten faces under the peaked shooting caps, the faded khaki shirts, the dusty boots, the long gun-barrels gleaming in the firelight. Stonewall's foot cavalry, he thought; by God, they haven't changed since Chancellorsville.

From the half-open window of a sedan parked near the fire

a melancholy pointer poked a nose full of entreaty. The fire-light shone greenly in its eyes. Its owner fondled the soft ears, arguing gently with a little hawk-faced man who stood beside him. Their voices were slow and easy in the damp air. Like an endless yawn, Melady thought.

"Takes ten weeks to make a puppy, Jawn, Ah'm a-tellin' yuh."

"Sixty-three days."

"Ten weeks, man!" Slow, high-pitched, good-humored. The word "ten" was two syllables—tay-en.

"Somebody tell this hyuh bullheaded ol' fool it only takes a bitch nine weeks to have a litter!"

"Jawn's right, Luke." Even the word "right" slurred to the point where it became ra-a-a-ht.

"Aw, shuh!"

The argument died. The sky lightened slowly. Somewhere a rooster crowed, a thin sound, lonely, challenging. The pointer shook its head, ears flapping loudly. Shep shifted his feet. "Everybody here, John?"

"Near 'bout enough," said the little hawk-faced man. He was, Melady decided, the farmer who owned the field. "Reckon we might's well git started." He glanced around the circle of faces. "Shep, you an' yore frien' take th' far end—one in each corner. We'll sorta spread out enough to keep 'em movin'."

"Thanks," Shep said, and Melady knew that they had been given the best stations. He followed Shep out of the circle of firelight. As he did, two small figures detached themselves from the shadows behind the parked cars and glided along in their wake. Melady glanced back at them curiously.

"Pick-up boys," Shep told him. "They always know when a dove-shoot is on. Damn useful, too. A dead dove's mighty hard to see sometimes; feathers blend with the ground. But these pickaninnies will hunt till they find 'em."

"Do you pay them?"

"I usually give 'em a quarter. But they'd be happy with a bird or two to take home. Or half a dozen shotgun shells for their old man to hunt rabbits with."

They entered the vast field, walking between rows of dead cornstalks taller than a man's upraised arm. The soil was dry and soft. Melady's shoes sank into it; once or twice he stumbled. Shep walked easily, almost without noise. The gray light was filtering through rapidly now. Without warning a monstrous shape lurched up out of the ground not ten feet away and went crashing through the cornstalks, grunting and snuffling. Melady clutched his gun convulsively. "My God! What was that?"

"Hog," Shep said laconically. He kept on walking. "John's probably got some peanuts in here. Hogs root 'em up, and that attracts the doves." He plodded on for another thirty yards. "Ugly customers, some of those hogs. They won't attack you, but they'll eat a dove in one bite if they get it before you do. They'll eat anything, and they've got mean teeth. I knew a farmer once, had a heart attack in a field like this. When they found him, hogs had eaten most of his face."

Melady grunted. "Charming little story."

"File it under local color," Shep said, and laughed.

They went on and on; the field seemed endless. Melady heard a whistle of wings and saw some blurred shapes knifing through the tops of the cornstalks. "Those doves?"

"Yes. They fly low in this light. Better not shoot until they get higher. You might pepper somebody on the other side of the field." Somewhere behind them, as if in contradiction, a gun banged hollowly and a moment later pellets rattled on the cornstalks around them. Shep swore gently. "Always one in every crowd."

They came to the end of the field where the pines were massed, dark green, solid. "This'll do for your stand," Shep said. "Keep your eyes open when you hear anybody whistle or yell 'Mark!' These birds are right on top of you, sometimes, before you know it. I'll be over in the other corner in case you want anything."

He moved away, his khaki clothing blending instantly with the tawny field. One of the colored boys followed him. The other came up to Melady shyly. He was about nine years old, dressed in a patched cotton shirt and ragged trousers. He was carrying an empty wooden box and this he now up-ended in a furrow for the white man to sit on. Melady said, loading his gun, "What's your name, boy?"

"Leroy."

"Well, Leroy, I've never shot doves before. You'd better tell me what to do."

"Yassuh," said Leroy earnestly, but that was all. He was no conversationalist.

A low whistle came from the corner where Shep had taken his stand. Melady turned and saw three birds driving straight for him through the luminous air. They looked and flew like small pigeons; their long, curved wings drove them in effortless flight. Forty yards away they changed course and strung out momentarily in line. Melady swung on the lead bird and pressed the trigger. The gun kicked solidly; to his astonishment he saw the last bird waver and fall. Leroy went off through the cornstalks as if released by a spring. Melady watched him, feeling both elated and foolish. Farther up the field another gun bellowed twice and a second bird dropped. The third soared up and away.

Leroy came back proudly with his quarry. The bird was quite dead. It lay in Melady's hand, warm and light, the slate-colored feathers on its back not even disarranged, the graceful white-barred wings folded around the ruddy breast like a shroud. A bluish film covered the eyes. A single drop of blood, ruby-colored, clung to the delicately curved beak.

Melady stared at it, tasting the faint bitter regret that had always lessened his pleasure in hunting. When birds were killed outright, like this, it was not so bad. But when they were crippled—

In the next two hours his conscience did not torment him unduly because he shot only three more birds. He had plenty of chances; the ground around his box was littered with empty shells. He just could not hit them. They flew past him with maddening regularity, usually to fall victim to an old farmer two hundred yards away who rose up against the skyline, fired his single-barrel with deadly effect, then subsided like a gnome into the gray earth.

At eight-thirty Shep came back, picking his way along the edge of the field, gun held slantwise across his shoulders. "Had enough?"

"I think so," Melady said. "I'm disgracing myself, anyway."

"Just a matter of practice, that's all."

A single dove wheeled into the field and was cut down by the old farmer.

"Doesn't he ever miss?"

"Shotgun shells cost so much he can't afford to miss."

"Tell me something," Melady said. "Why do you get such a kick out of this sort of thing?"

Shep looked surprised. "Hunting? I don't know, exactly. It takes a certain amount of skill, I suppose. You've got an ounce or so of shot traveling three or four hundred feet a second. You've got an unpredictable target moving forty, maybe fifty miles an hour. Takes a certain craftsmanship to make 'em meet. Exercising any skill is fun, isn't it?"

"Do you get as much fun out of shooting clay pigeons?"

"No, I wouldn't say so."

"Perhaps what you really like is killing something."

Shep shrugged. "Maybe so. Man's a hunting animal, isn't he?"

Melady kicked at a clod of earth. "If that's your basic philosophy down here, no wonder that girl—that Unity—no wonder she's miserable in Hainesville!"

Leroy made an apologetic sound and pointed. A pair of doves came lancing through the pines; the sun was in their eyes; they did not see the men with the guns waiting below.

"You take 'em," Shep said sharply.

The birds whistled overhead. Melady did not raise his gun. "We've got enough. Let 'em go."

Shep threw him a disgusted glance. The birds were well beyond them, out of normal range, but the long double-barreled slammed once. The rear bird spun into the ground.

"Watch him," Shep said. "I just winged him."

Both colored boys sprinted away, feet kicking up puffs of dust. Shep broke his gun and blew the smoke out of the barrel. "What were you saying? That you didn't think Unity belonged in Hainesville, or something?"

Melady was annoyed. He had wanted the doves to have their chance to live. "That's not exactly what I said, but it's close enough."

"What's wrong with Hainesville?"

The colored boys came panting back. Shep's boy had won the race; he handed the bird to Shep. It was uninjured, apparently, except for a broken wing. It lay in Shep's big hand, head raised alertly, eyes bright and questioning. Shep was watching Melady, waiting for an answer.

"For God's sake," Melady burst out, "put the thing out of its misery!"

Shep looked down at the dove. He shifted his gun to the crook of his arm, held the bird's body with one hand, pulled its head gently forward with the other. He raised it to his mouth. His teeth closed on the neck with a quick pressure—not enough to break the skin, but Melady heard the vertebrae snap with a sickening crunch. The bird quivered and was still. Shep spat out a gray feather that had clung to his lips. He saw Melady's face and shrugged again. "That's the quickest way. The most painless."

Melady reached forward and took the bird from him. It was dead, he knew, but he could feel life vibrating in it, a strong humming, like a dynamo. He was furious. "You asked me what was wrong with Hainesville." He held up the bird so that the head lolled sideways on the broken neck. "That's what's wrong with it!"

Shep stared at him contemptuously. "Come on," he said. "Let's go."

ii

UNITY looked anxiously around the table at the faces of her guests. There was a sudden tension in the dining room. It was Melady's fault. He had steered the conversation to this point. Deliberately, Unity felt.

The day had started well. Hattie had assured her that Nathan was gone. She had ducked into the garage to satisfy herself, had found no sign of him. She had spent the rest of the morning helping Hattie prepare the dinner, feeling as if an intolerable weight had been lifted from her. All through the long meal she had been happier than she had been in days.

"After a dinner as fine as this one," said Judge Winter soothingly, "we really shouldn't quarrel."

"I'm not quarreling," snapped Mrs. Crowe. "I just don't intend to sit here and listen to insults." She glared at her husband. "Why don't *you* say something?"

Lester sniffed gently and stirred his demitasse. "You don't seem to need any support, my dear."

Melady ran one hand through his wiry hair. "All I said was

that if a Negro did kill Neal Aycock, I could hardly blame him. I don't see anything insulting about that."

Mrs. Crowe stared around the table. She was a full-busted woman with a nasal voice and, apparently, firm opinions. "I must say, I'm beginning to think I'm the only one in this room who really represents what the people of the South feel about this race question. I grew up in a county where the blacks outnumbered the whites. I've known 'em all my life. Some are better than others, but the general run of 'em are shiftless, lazy, and dirty. Especially dirty. Look at any of their cabins! They'd rather be dirty than clean. Half the time you can smell 'em. Faugh!"

Aunt Guley widened her mild eyes. "Perhaps we don't smell so nice to them, either."

Everyone laughed except Mrs. Crowe.

"Living in dirt is a sign of poverty and ignorance everywhere," Unity said. "The Negroes have no monopoly on that. If we'd educate them decently, they'd begin to live decently."

"If we educated them decently," Lester said gloomily, "they'd begin to expect a lot of things they couldn't have. The South isn't rich. Its soil is worn out. There's a limit to the wealth it can produce. It won't support a much higher standard of living for those people."

"In that case," Melady suggested, "they might move out of the South into areas of more opportunity."

"That would be fine!" Mrs. Crowe said emphatically.

"Their schools are a lot better than they were," Mrs. Cantrell said to Melady. "Even so, to make them the equal of the whites would cost millions. Don't you think it's a little unfair to ask the white people of the South to shoulder that cost? After all, the amount the colored people pay in taxes is infinitesimal."

"Well, the rest of the country will never do it," Mrs. Crowe stated. "All they contribute is criticism."

Judge Winter smoothed his tawny hair. "Some of the criticism is justified, my dear lady. I don't think we can pretend the Negro can count on equality under the law as it is administered in the South today."

"What's more," Melady said, "when these lynchings and other outrages occur, it plays right into the hands of the Communists."

"You have your mass murders in the North," Shep drawled. "You just don't call them lynchings, that's all."

"*And* race riots! *And* discrimination!" echoed Mrs. Crowe with satisfaction.

"The Communists will never lack for things to criticize," Judge Winter said gently to Melady. "When they do, they'll invent some."

Melady furrowed his forehead. "It all seems to boil down to whether or not you think a Negro is racially inferior—or even mentally very different from a white person. If he is, then perhaps inferior treatment of him is justified. That's the way most Southerners seem to reason, anyway."

"That's no justification for ill-treatment," Unity said sharply. "If it were, you'd be justified in maltreating anyone, white or black, who could be proved your mental inferior."

"But they *are* inferior," Mrs. Crowe cried. "My heavens, two hundred years ago their ancestors were running around in the jungle with rings in their noses!"

"What were *your* ancestors doing two thousand years ago?" Melady asked her pleasantly. "Probably running around in bearskins, or tattooing themselves blue."

Mrs. Crowe looked at him stonily. "Where you come from, you don't have the problem. Consequently you know nothing about it. But you love to exploit it. You love to come down here looking for the worst; that's the truth of the matter! Why don't you write about the good side? Why don't you report that the first hospital ever built exclusively for Negroes was financed, equipped, and organized by the white people of Savannah! Write a story about that!"

"If you didn't have Jim Crow," Melady reminded her, "you wouldn't have to build them separate hospitals."

Mrs. Crowe flushed. "You mean to tell me you'd like to be in the same ward with a colored patient?"

"I wouldn't mind."

"Well, I would!" Mrs. Crowe's bosom trembled with the vehemence of her emotions. "And so would ninety-nine per cent of the people in the South." She looked angrily from under her heavy eyelids. "It's easy enough for you people from the North to say we should like the Negroes and try to uplift them. Well, we *don't* like them, and we're going to keep them in their place. That's not a theory; that's a fact! Whether we *should* like 'em or not is beside the point. We don't!" She paused for breath, then plunged on. "Furthermore, while you're talking about rights, seems to me the right of a human being to dislike something is a pretty fundamental right in itself. If I don't want a Communist teaching my children at school, that's a prejudice, isn't it? But who says I'm not entitled to it?"

"You're entitled to that prejudice," Melady began, "because a Communist teacher threatens your way of life. . . ."

"Well, people who advocate opening our hospitals and restaurants and theaters to niggers"—she caught herself—"Negroes, *are* threatening my way of life!"

"In most parts of the country that sort of thing is permitted without causing any undue . . ."

"I don't *care* what happens in any other part of the country," Mrs. Crowe cried. "Let 'em have chimpanzees in their theaters if they want! Or let 'em have laws keeping chimpanzees out. That's their business. We won't interfere with it!"

"What you're really defending," Melady told her, "is the right of a minority to persecute a smaller minority. Isn't that it?"

Mrs. Crowe was not daunted. "It's not our fault we're a minority," she said scornfully. "We're only a minority by force of arms, don't forget that. We tried to get out of your precious Union. You people defeated us and held us against our will. But that doesn't mean we have to pretend to like it. We don't! We're a separate country, in our own minds, and don't you forget it!"

There was an awkward silence. Mrs. Cantrell glanced helplessly at Unity. These are your guests, the glance said. Do something!

Unity said hesitantly, "Judge Winter, how would you go about solving the problem? What would you suggest if by some miracle your recommendations could be adopted?"

The Judge dropped his handsome head on his chest and considered the question. Everybody waited. At last he looked up. "Trying to balance the ethics of the situation with the realities involved certainly isn't easy. Still, here are some things I'd recommend. First"—the yellow eyes flicked briefly toward Melady —"and this will not please *you*—I'd advocate the retention of segregation until it breaks down of its own accord in fifty or a hundred or two hundred years. Any legislation that tries to end it now will fail just as Prohibition failed, because it won't have the support of the people. In fact, like most unenforceable laws, it will only aggravate the situation.

"Secondly, I'd make stronger efforts to give the Negroes equality of education, with the Federal Government bearing the expense. There's no reason, as Mrs. Cantrell said, why the South should carry the whole load. And the load would be heavy.

"Third"—he was ticking off the points on his fingers—"I'd see to it that they got justice under the law, using Federal guarantees if necessary. In some cases, we'd have to by-pass the jury system." He smiled thinly. "There would be considerable uproar about *that*.

[210]

"Fourth, I'd safeguard the Negroes' right to vote—a right theoretically guaranteed to them by the Constitution, of course, but constantly under attack in some places. . . ."

"Wouldn't you run into difficulties over segregation?" Melady asked. "Suppose the Negroes elected a colored man to represent them in the legislature. Where would he sit?"

"It would be very difficult," the Judge admitted. "He would have to sit in a special section and vote from there."

"Wouldn't that be absurd?"

"Human nature is often absurd," said the Judge. "But I think the colored people would rather have a representative voting from behind a railing than not have one voting at all."

Lester said slowly, "Would you favor laws guaranteeing the Negro freedom from discrimination in getting jobs—and advancement in jobs?"

"No, I wouldn't," the Judge replied. "That's something that seems to me to interfere with the rights of the employer. It's unenforceable anyway. And why not leave something to the enterprise and ingenuity of the colored people themselves?"

Mrs. Crowe gave a derisive snort. The Judge looked at her coldly, then went on.

"Finally," he said, "I'd use all available media—schools, churches, newspapers, radio stations, women's clubs, everything—to stress the advisability of these changes from the purely selfish standpoint of the white people's self-interest. The South will always be at a disadvantage until the Negro is pulled out of the mire. A lot of thinking people are beginning to realize that. The trend is unmistakable."

Mrs. Crowe looked disgusted. "People always seem to think a trend must be right just because it's a trend. Aren't there ever any wrong trends? How about the trend toward a depression, or the trend toward another war?"

"Madam," said Judge Winter, making her an ironic little bow, "you are almost unanswerable."

Lester mumbled something that sounded like "Always has been."

Shep said, in his lazy drawl, "What do *you* think, Miss Cantrell? You haven't said a word."

Aunt Guley pursed her lips thoughtfully. "We could always assimilate them, couldn't we? That's what the Chinese do."

"*What?*" cried Mrs. Crowe.

Aunt Guley looked helpless. "Well, of course, everybody'd be a little darker than they are now. But most of the young people spend hours sitting in the sun anyway, trying to get darker, and . . ."

"Guley!" Mrs. Cantrell rapped on the table. "Stop teasing everybody!"

"Well," said Aunt Guley wistfully, "they *asked* me."

Mrs. Cantrell pushed back her chair. "Shall we go into the other room and let Hattie clear away these coffee things?"

Lester glanced regretfully at his watch. "I'd better get back to the office. My secretary will scold me." He sighed. "After thirty years in this game, I still can't get used to working on Sunday." He bowed in the courtly way he had. "So if you'll excuse us, Mrs. Cantrell . . ."

Unity said, "I'll be down in a little while, Lester."

The editor patted her hand. "Don't bother. Take the afternoon off."

They stood on the porch, watching the Crowes move down the path. "I'd better go too," Melady said. "I have some rewriting to do. My editor in New York is a frustrated writer himself. So nothing anybody ever writes is quite the way he wants it."

"That must be trying," Judge Winter said. "I'll walk along with you, if I may." He turned to Unity. "Thank you, my dear. I'm sorry to have missed your sister. If she's half as charming as you, I'm doubly sorry. Mrs. Cantrell, Miss Cantrell, my thanks to you and my compliments to your admirable cook."

He retrieved his hat and stick from the rack in the hall. "Now, sir," he said to Melady, "if you are ready . . ."

They walked slowly along the shaded streets, the Judge's cane making small tapping sounds. There was little traffic. From hidden lawns came the whir of mowers. Somewhere a piano tinkled, brittle and somnolent.

"You started that discussion deliberately, didn't you?" the Judge asked after a while. "Not very good manners, young man."

"I suppose not," Melady admitted. "Still, a writer can't always afford to have manners."

"You'd probably write better," the Judge observed, "if you did."

They walked on in silence through the drowsy sunshine.

"That Crowe woman," Melady said at length. "Listening to her makes me think that what you've got down here is a white problem, not a Negro problem. Is her attitude typical?"

"She's typical of an uncomfortably large majority, I'm afraid."

"But they're so inconsistent. She hates the colored people, and yet I'm sure she wouldn't hesitate to entrust her child to one—assuming she had a child—to be fed and bathed and cared for by one of these untouchables."

"That's right."

They stopped and waited for a street light to change.

"I think I know what it is," Melady said finally. "They've got a guilt complex about the Negroes. They knew slavery was morally wrong—and they'd probably have freed the slaves themselves in another decade or so. But they weren't allowed to salve their conscience that way. The Yankees came down and freed the slaves forcibly. That left these people with a guilt feeling they never could get rid of. The Negroes make 'em feel guilty, subconsciously, and they hate 'em for it."

The Judge smiled. "A pretty theory, my dear sir. But it

[213]

doesn't fit the case. One of the things that should be obvious to a clear-eyed observer like yourself is that the lower you get in the social scale—I'm talking about the whites, now—the more violent is the antipathy for the Negro. If your hypothesis were correct, Southerners of the upper classes, whose ancestors owned the slaves, would be the most prejudiced of all."

Melady decided to abandon a subject which offered such endless possibilities for confusion and entanglement. He said as much.

The Judge gave his stick a twirl that was almost jaunty. "Well, now," he purred, "if you've learned that much, perhaps your stay down here hasn't been entirely wasted."

iii

"How on earth," said John Haddon, "did you know about a place like this?"

He was leaning on his elbow, chewing a spear of grass. He had his shirt open at the neck, his sleeves rolled up above his sinewy forearms. In the intense sunlight, his hair was blue-black; his profile was as brown and somber as an Indian's. Beside him, Helen knelt on the blanket they had spread for their picnic. She was collecting paper plates and other debris. Her dress had a low, square-cut neckline. Haddon watched her as she leaned forward.

In front of them the ground dipped quietly into the river. It was a backwater rather than the main stream; no current ruffled the surface. Cypress grew straight and tall out of the dark water, each reddish trunk meeting its reflection precisely at the base in a queerly inverted Gothic effect. A few strands of gray moss dripped from the branches. This was low country, fifteen miles downstream from Hainesville. They had left their

[214]

car half a mile away, on the main road. It was very quiet; when a jay-bird flew down in a flash of blue and screeched at them, the sound was a desecration.

Helen laughed. "Sounds silly," she said, "but my boss in the bookstore is a bird lover. She talked me into getting up early one morning—it was a Sunday, too—to come down here and watch birds with her through field glasses. I was pretty bored, but I thought I saw picnic possibilities. Was I right?"

"You were right."

"Wasn't too much of a walk for you, was it?"

Haddon frowned. "No." Any reference to his lameness always brought a sullen reaction. Usually Helen avoided the issue, but not today.

"John," she said hesitantly.

"Yes?"

"Why do you let that artificial foot bother you so much? It doesn't bother anyone else."

He gave a short mirthless laugh. "Nobody else has to live with it."

"Oh, I know it must be—must be *difficult*, but you let it interfere too much. I mean, well—" She hesitated, choosing her words carefully. "It *can't* be as bad as you think! After all, lots of people go through life with worse disfigurements than that. Look at Hester Fagan, for instance. Now there's real tragedy! But your foot—that's a war wound, an honorable sacrifice you made. I don't . . ."

"Let's not talk about it, shall we?"

Helen lifted her chin obstinately. "I *want* to talk about it. I want to make you see that it makes no difference to me as a—as a woman! I wouldn't be upset by the sight of it, honestly I wouldn't. I know it disturbs you to talk about it, but maybe if we *do* talk about it some of this twisted attitude of yours will disappear. It *is* twisted, John; it's not normal. It's . . ."

"Listen," he said savagely. "I used to run a hundred yards in

[215]

ten and one-fifth seconds. I could high-jump six feet. Now look at me! Strapped into a steel-and-leather contraption with a nice soft nest for that shrunken thing they call a stump, and a thumbtack to hold my sock up! You say the sight of it wouldn't upset you. Well, if the sight of it makes me want to vomit, what wouldn't it do to you? What wouldn't it do to any woman?" He stopped, breathing hard. He rubbed the back of his hand across his forehead and looked at the smear of perspiration. "You think I'm not normal. Well, you're right! I'm not a man; I'm a stump, with a man attached. And I don't want your pity or anybody else's, see?"

"Wait here a minute, will you?" Helen took a small canvas bag that lay with the picnic basket, and moved down the path, out of sight. She was gone perhaps three minutes. The swamp was utterly quiet. A fish jumped between two cypresses. Haddon lay motionless, watching the spreading ripples. His chest rose and fell under his damp shirt. His fingers plucked nervously at the tough brown grass.

An object flew over his shoulder and dropped on the ground in front of him. He stared at it, then turned his head quickly. Helen was standing behind him. She was wearing the black bathing suit that fitted like a second skin. Her cap was in her hand; the sun made a golden nimbus of her hair. Haddon sat up. "What do you think you're doing?"

"We're going swimming," Helen said calmly. "You and I." She nodded toward the swimming trunks that had fallen in front of Haddon. "I bought those for you. Out of my hard-earned wages. Hope they fit."

Haddon stared at her. He swallowed once. "You know I don't swim."

Helen dropped to her knees beside him. She had planned this moment with the greatest care. "I know you do. Why do you think I brought my swim-suit, and one for you? So that we *could* swim, out here where nobody can see us. Where you don't have to worry about what people think. Go on." She picked up the trunks and dropped them in his lap. "Hop behind the bushes and change. Quick, now! No arguments!"

He made no move. He sat there rigidly, half turned toward her. She bent closer; her hair swung across his face. She picked up his hand, laughing a little to herself, and tried to open his clenched fingers so that she could put the red trunks in them.

"Helen!" he said warningly.

She misunderstood. "Don't try to argue with me," she said, "you silly, stubborn man. Do as I say; it won't hurt you." She dropped his hand and began to unbutton his shirt. "Here, I'll help you." She looked at him from under her long lashes, pleased with her own daring. Her fingers worked swiftly, touching his skin occasionally. Her breath was warm in his face; the tip of her tongue was clenched in her teeth as she concentrated on her work. "There!" she said as the last button was unfastened. She tugged the shirt back from his hard brown chest. "You can do the rest."

Still he did not move. She leaned forward, her breasts straining under the black satin as she tried to peel the shirt from his shoulders. He made a sound deep in his throat. His arms closed around her.

"John!" she said, still laughing as she was pulled down beside him. She heard the tearing sound as he ripped at her shoulder straps. She saw his face and felt the violence of his hands. "*John!*" She was quick and young and strong. She brought up her knee hard, twice. She heard him gasp and felt his hands relax. She rolled away from him, the stiff grass scratching her skin. She came up on her knees ten feet away from him, her hands holding the torn straps of her swim-suit, her eyes full of pity and terror.

He stared at her, his lips trembling. "That's right! Run away! Run from me! I can't catch you. Hop behind the bushes, you said. Hop! Hop! That's all I can do. Like a toad. Hop!"

The blue jay flew into a sweet-gum tree and perched there, head on one side, examining them curiously.

Helen put her hands on the ground. Slowly she crawled back to the blanket. Haddon did not touch her. He was shivering. She took his right foot in her hands and unlaced the shoe. She drew the shoe off, forgetting that she did not have to. She pushed his trouser leg up to his knee and fumbled with the straps she found there. The artificial limb came away in her hands. There was a flannel jacket covering the stump. She pulled it off. She held the maimed leg in both hands for a moment, looking at it. Haddon watched her, braced against his arms. His face was very pale.

Helen looked up at him. "You see? There's nothing to be afraid of." She drew her hands in suddenly. "There," she said. "There. There."

iv

"You really have no excuse now," Shep said. He clasped his hands behind his head and leaned back in the swing, watching Unity with his eyes half closed. "You have the afternoon off. It's going to be a nice evening; moon's almost full. The speed-boat's still ready, and the island in the river is still there. I haven't got a steak, this time, but there's plenty of corned beef hash in the cabin. I want to go. How about you?"

Unity did not reply immediately. She was looking out over the peaceful garden. "Speaking of the cabin," she said at last, "there's something I've been meaning to ask you. How did Hester get the hair-ribbon I left out there Thursday afternoon?"

"Hester?"

"Yes. She had my yellow hair-ribbon. I left it on the mantelpiece out there. At least, I thought I did."

Shep stood up and shoved his hands into his trouser pockets. He looked angry. "Why don't you ask Hester?"

"I haven't seen her since Friday. I meant to ask you sooner, but I forgot."

"Maybe you left it in the office, and she found it there."

"I don't think so. I never wear it to the office."

Shep moved his shoulders impatiently. "Hester likes to be mysterious about things; it makes her feel important." He reached down, took Unity's hand, and pulled her to her feet. "The moon will rise about seven," he said. "Do you want to watch it with me, or don't you?"

Unity did not look at him. "Yes. Yes, I do."

"Let's go, then. Let's not waste any more time."

"Shall I bring my swim-suit?"

His eyes crinkled. "If you think you'll need it."

"I'll go and tell Mother I won't be here for supper." She pulled her hand free slowly. "Wait for me, Shep."

"Hurry up," he said. "I've waited long enough."

When she disappeared, he lit a cigarette, flipping the match over the porch railing. Damn that Hester, he thought; she's going to make trouble if she can. I should have known better. Well . . . He blew a stream of smoke in twin jets from his nostrils.

Unity came back. She had changed into slacks; her canvas beach-bag dangled from her hand. "I've got one errand first, Shep. Aunt Guley's used up the last of her hay-fever pills. Mother phoned Pop Halliday and he's refilling the prescription. Do you mind if we pick it up before we go to the cabin?"

Shep threw his cigarette away and took the beach-bag from her. "I don't mind anything," he said, "now."

V

LESTER came into his office and hung up his yellowed panama. "Lord, I thought that dinner would never end! Anything stirring?"

"Oh, sure," Hester said. Her voice sounded thick and sardonic. "The mayor has been assassinated, the courthouse has burned down, Pat Daly has confessed to murdering Neal Aycock. Otherwise it's just a quiet Sunday afternoon."

Lester stared at her. "What in hell's got into you?"

"What do you think?" She pointed. The bottle of bourbon stood in the middle of her blotter. "Same thing that gets into you." She saw Lester's face change. "Oh, don't worry. I'll buy you a new one. But you know"—she swung around and leaned forward, her slender hands on her knees—"it gets damn gloomy around here on a Sunday. Lonely, too, when everybody else is at a party. So I thought, well, *I'll* have a drink, cheer myself up. So I had two drinks. Maybe three." She swung back, facing the wall. "What the hell, Lester, I'm not really drunk. I'll be all right in a few minutes."

The editor walked over, picked up the bottle, and looked at it critically. He put it down again. "Well, can't say I blame you, really." He looked at the undamaged side of her face, feeling something that was close to pity. "But look, Hester; I told Unity she could take the afternoon off. That means we're shorthanded. I'm going to need you."

Hester nodded solemnly. "Fine. Like to be needed."

"Tell you what you do. Walk down to the drugstore—the Palace stays open on Sunday. Drink a couple of cups of black coffee and eat something. Then come on back here and . . ."

"Don't want any coffee."

"God damn it!" Lester brought his fist down on the desk so

[220]

hard that the bottle rocked. "You do what I tell you! Most any-body else would fire you for this. I'm trying to *help* you, you crazy female! Go on! Go!"

Hester got up, took her hat from its peg by the washstand, pulled it down, and crossed over to the door. She hesitated. "Thanks, Lester. I'm sorry."

The editor grunted and picked up the telephone. "Get going," he said without looking at her. "And hurry back."

She went down the narrow stairs, bracing herself against the dizziness that pushed at her. You *are* a fool, she said to herself. Drinking on the job! My God, you must be out of your mind! Because *she* gave a dinner party and *he* was there and *you* weren't. So you steal a bottle out of the boss's desk and slug yourself with it. Fine, Hester, fine!

She bit her tongue sharply. Funny, how it came in waves. She did not drink much, as a rule. When she did, she could always make herself sober momentarily, by an effort of will. At least, she could make herself think she was sober.

What are they doing now, she asked herself. What are their after-dinner plans? Afternoon off for Unity? How nice, how convenient! How thoughtful of dear old Lester! How useful for Shep!

She went around the corner, walking fast in the still, hot afternoon, and stopped. The familiar convertible was parked outside the drugstore; Shep was sitting at the wheel. Alone.

Hester felt her throat tighten. She walked forward, suppressing an impulse to turn around and go the other way. This was what she wanted, wasn't it? A chance to talk to Shep.

He caught sight of her when she was perhaps ten yards away and nodded. "Hello, Hester."

He looks strange, she thought—tense and worried. She came up to the side of the car. She put her hands on the window sill, then drew back. She did not want him to smell the bourbon on her breath. "Shep?"

[221]

"Yes?"

"I tried to get you by phone. Twice. And once I even went to your house."

"I know," he said with controlled impatience. "Mother told me. I'm sorry I missed you."

"When can I see you, Shep?" That's right, the mocking voice cried inside of her. Stand right here in the street and beg. "I've got to see you, Shep," she said desperately. "I can't go on like this."

"Like what? Look, Hester, I'll give you a ring one of these days, but right now I'm busy. Would you mind . . ."

"Busy?" The word had a jarring sound in the quiet street. "You don't look very busy to me! You're not in a meeting, by any chance, are you?"

"In a what? Oh." His eyebrows came down angrily. "Listen, Hester, I'm trying to be patient with you." His eyes flicked past her to the entrance of the drugstore. "I'm waiting here for someone who's getting a prescription filled. We're supposed to take it back to the house quickly. Now will you please . . ."

"Someone!" She pounced on the word. "As if I couldn't guess who! Your sweet little dewy-eyed social reformer. Your innocent conquest-to-be! Does she know about us? Have you told her how . . ."

Shep slammed his hand down on the wheel. "Shut up, Hester! I know you're trying to cause trouble between Unity and me. Well, you can just relax because I *am* going to tell her about us—in my own way and in my own good time. And if you don't keep your . . ." He cut the threat short. Unity had come out of the drugstore.

"All right, Shep," she said. "I've got it." She seemed to recognize Hester for the first time and paused uncertainly. "Oh, hello, Hester."

Hester held onto the car door, swaying a little. "There's something I want to say to you, Unity."

"Hester!" Shep's voice was flat and cold.

Unity made a little gesture with the package she was carrying. "Won't it keep till morning, Hester? We . . ."

"It's kept long enough," Hester said harshly. "It's time you knew a few things—for your own good. Do you remember that hair-ribbon I returned to you? You left it at the cabin, didn't you? Do you know how I got it?"

Unity glanced at Shep. He was staring straight ahead, his hands gripping the wheel. "Why, no, I don't. Does it matter?"

"Does it matter?" Hester repeated, mocking her. "Does it matter if *he* took me to the cabin two hours after you left it there? Does it matter that he took me there to sleep with him—and I did?" She felt a savage exultation, watching Unity's face. She knew she had caused all the damage that was necessary, but she could not stop. She plunged on, the words tumbling out in a scalding flood. "Does it matter to you that I was his mistress for three years? That once he made me pregnant? That Dr. Fosburgh took care of it and *he* paid the bills? Oh, it was strictly a cash transaction! Fosburgh never knew who the man was. Nobody ever knew, till now! Does it matter?" She thrust her head forward like a striking snake. She screamed it again. *"Does it matter?"*

Unity had taken a step backward. She looked once at Shep, as if waiting for his denial. When none came, she said, very calmly, "Thank you for telling me this, Hester." She wet her lips with her tongue. She said to Shep, "I think I can get myself home." She turned quickly and ran back into the drugstore.

Shep looked at Hester. "Thank you," he said. "Thank you so much. Now I won't have to tell her anything." The engine of the car caught with a subdued roar. "Keep away from me from now on, you ugly bitch. I hope to God I never see or hear of you again!" The gears clashed. The car shot forward.

Inside the drugstore Unity leaned against the soda fountain

feeling nausea churn within her. Pop Halliday came forward, his hairless face floating toward her like a worried moon. "What's the matter, Unity? Don't you feel so good?"

She shook her head, unable to speak.

He puttered a moment behind the screen and came out with a glass. "Drink this."

She pushed it away. "I'll be sick."

"Come on," he said, coaxing her. "Make you feel better."

More to rid herself of him than anything else, she swallowed the bitter liquid. For one ghastly moment she thought it would come back up, but it didn't. She sat down weakly on one of the stools, resting her damp forehead in her hand. It's not real, she thought. It's all a nightmare.

"Better now?" Pop Halliday inquired brightly.

"Oh, yes," she lied. "Much better. Just let me sit here, will you?"

"You sit there just as long as you want," Pop said sympathetically. Another customer came in, and he pattered away.

Unity waited five minutes. Then she took a nickel out of her pocketbook, went into the phone booth, and dialed the number of the taxi rank in the courthouse square. "Send a cab to the Palace Drugstore, please." She hung up and leaned against the wall of the booth. She felt as if she had been beaten.

vi

"COME IN," said Melady impatiently. He had the carbon of his article spread out on the bed, marking sections for revision. Cunningham had echoed Hester's criticism. Too one-sided; too biased; too much of a tract. Nobody, it seemed to Melady, gave a damn about the truth any more. Everything had to balance. Everything had to be trimmed and evened up, so that nobody would be offended. God damn the public any-way, Melady thought; stupid, cruel, blind, and all-powerful. "Come in, I said!"

Hester came into the room. She closed the door behind her and leaned against it. Melady stood up. "Hullo," he said, sur-prised. His voice sharpened. "What's the matter?"

She brushed past him. She went blindly forward and sat on the edge of the bed, holding herself very erect. "It's nothing," she said, speaking low and fast. "I shouldn't have come here, I know. It was just that I—that I had nowhere else to go. I didn't stop to think. I just had an idea that you might ..."

Her teeth came down on her underlip. How can he under-stand, she thought drearily, when I haven't told him any-thing? He must think I'm drunk, or crazy, or both. Well, maybe I am. I don't care if I am. I don't care about anything, any more.

Melady went back to the bed slowly. He pushed the papers aside and sat down. He did not touch her. "Want to tell me about it, Hester?"

She took a deep shuddering breath; her face crumpled. She rocked forward, covering it with her hands. She rolled side-ways, away from him, and slid from the bed to the floor. There was nothing pretty or controlled about her weeping. Ugly, choking sounds came from her, as if she were strangling. The tears ran wetly through her fingers. She pressed her face against the bedspread. With her clenched fist she began to beat a slow agonized rhythm on the dusty carpet.

Melady watched her, sitting very still. At last he got up, went to the window, and pulled down the shade. He walked back to the bed and stood over her in the twilight he had created. From his wallet he took some bills and folded them. He stooped down and put them in her hand, closing her fin-gers around them. "That'll get you to New York," he said. "Consider it a loan—strictly business." He tossed two keys,

[225]

linked together, onto the floor beside her. "These will let you into my apartment up there." He went over to the desk and typed a few words, the sound staccato in the quiet room. He ripped the paper out of the carriage. "Here's the address. Nobody's there. Make yourself at home until I get back there two or three days from now. Then we'll find you a job and a place to live. We'll also look up that doctor."

Hester made an inarticulate sound of protest.

"Don't argue," Melady said. "If you don't get away from this place now, you'll never go. You'll be trapped here, for good." He picked up his coat. "I'm going downstairs and send a couple of telegrams. Be out of here when I get back, will you? Tears make me nervous. I'll see you in New York."

He went out and closed the door. Hester sat up slowly. She looked at the money, the keys, the typed slip of paper. Her dress was twisted above her knees. She straightened it. She got up, finally, and looked at herself in the mirror. Melady's comb was lying on the bureau. She picked it up and began to rearrange her disheveled hair. She felt empty, hollowed out, released from all emotion. Her job? Leave it. Her apartment? Close it.

She put the comb down. She remembered how she had looked at herself in the mirror the night she went to the cabin with Shep. That was finished now. Everything was finished. "Well," she said silently to her reflection, "what are you waiting for?"

vii

HELEN ran up the path through the slanting shadows and into the house. She stood in the hall for a moment, undecided, hugging her secret to her, but eager to share some of it. The living room was empty. The house was very quiet. Sunday was Hattie's night off. On Sunday evenings, her mother and Aunt Guley went to the Parish House for supper. Unity was probably out with Shep.

Helen frowned, deprived of an audience. Then she climbed the stairs, walked down the hall, and tried to open the door of the room she shared with Unity.

It was locked.

Helen rattled the knob. "Unity! Are you there?"

"Yes," said Unity's voice.

"What's the matter? Are you sick, or something? Let me in!" She rattled the knob again. "I've got some wonderful news!"

"Just a minute." Unity's footsteps came to the door. The key turned. The door opened. The sisters confronted each other, Helen's face eager and animated, Unity's expressionless.

"Why're you locked in?" Helen demanded. "Are you afraid, or something?" The importance of her own news overcame her. "Unity, guess what? We had the most wonderful afternoon. He—he asked me to marry him. I said I would!"

Unity wrinkled her forehead as if she found it difficult to grasp Helen's meaning. "John Haddon? Marry him?"

"Yes. Oh, Unity, it's so *wonderful*—you don't know—I mean—" Helen stopped and stared at her sister. "Aren't you glad? I mean, aren't you even *excited* a little? I thought . . ."

"Of course, dear." Unity put her arm around Helen's shoulder. "I'm happy, if you are." She turned back into the room and sat down on her bed. Her hands twisted slowly in her lap.

Helen followed her. "Unity, what's the matter with you? Don't you feel well? What's happened? Where's Shep?"

"Shep?" Unity repeated sharply. "He's gone!" She got up and moved to the window, staring out into the fading light. "Tell me about you and John."

Helen said, "What's wrong, Unity? Do you want me to make you some tea, or something . . . ?"

"No." Unity swung around. She went back over to the bed and sat down again. "I'm all right. Nothing's happened. Tell me about John."

"Are you sure you want to hear about it?" Helen looked doubtful and distressed.

"Of course I do," Unity said. She gripped the bedspread and made her hands still. "Tell me all about it."

viii

LOUELLA came into the kitchen where Nora was drying the last of the dishes. She kicked at the worn place in the linoleum. "He says he ain't gonna take us to the show. Says for us to go ahead an' go by ourselves."

Nora swabbed the sink with her roughened hands. "What's he got to do that's so almighty important?"

Louella shrugged petulantly. "How should I know? All I know is you said we'd go see this movie when it came to town. Less'n we go right now, we ain't gonna see it."

Nora flung the dish towel across the drying rack. "All right, we'll go. Anything to git out'n this place for a while."

When they went out on the porch a few minutes later Bubber was sitting in a rocking chair with his feet on the railing. The moonlight silvered his dusty shoes and half of his bulky body. His face was in shadow; the glowing cigarette in his lips moved as he spoke.

"Have fun now, y'all."

Nora said, "How come you ain't comin' with us? What made you change your mind so sudden like?"

"Aw, them mushy movies ain't no fitten way for a man to spend his time." Bubber stretched, raising his great arms above his head. "I might take the truck an' run over an' see Bilsy. Or again I might jes' go to bed."

"Come *on*," Louella whined, tugging at Nora's sleeve. "We'll miss the first part of the show."

Bubber watched them walk across the moon-whitened yard, get into the sedan, and drive away. For five minutes he sat there, smoking, listening to the small night sounds magnified by the stillness. Then he stood up, threw his cigarette away, went into the kitchen, and got the flashlight that hung on a nail over the sink. He glanced at the wall clock. Ten minutes to nine. "Gonna be late," he mumbled. Well, Geneva had kept him waiting more than once; wouldn't hurt her to spend a few minutes alone in the dark.

He went through the kitchen door to the shed and backed out the truck. He drove swiftly down the road to Morgan's Creek, over the bridge, up the ridge on the far side. Where the dirt road met the paved highway he slowed momentarily. There was a light in Minelli's store; Sundays made no difference to Mrs. Minelli. He turned right. At Elvira's cabin he slowed again; a kerosene lamp burned steadily in one of the windows. He chuckled and drove on.

A quarter of a mile beyond Elvira's cabin he swung the truck into the narrow track and drove until he was sure it was no longer visible from the highway. He killed the engine, switched off the lights, got out, and listened. Wind droned softly in the pines; there was no other sound. Bubber tapped his hip pocket to make sure the pint of corn whisky he had brought with him was in place. It was. He decided to have an anticipatory drink. He uncorked the bottle with his teeth, took a long swallow, and coughed. Strong stuff. He reached into the truck for the flashlight, then decided he would not need it. The moonlight was bright enough.

He began to walk along the sandy road, feeling the hot impatience rising in him. Four days—no, five, by God, since he'd been with Geneva. Too long. But it would be all the better for waiting. He lengthened his stride, walking faster. An owl hooted dolefully somewhere in the shadows. A rabbit ran out in front of him, then ducked back into the long grass.

The road curved suddenly and he could see the great mound of sawdust, gleaming like a pyramid of lead. He crossed the moonlit clearing. The door to the toolhouse was half open. Geneva was inside, then. The impatience was hot in him now, pulsing, unbearable. He pushed the door wide and entered. Moonlight followed him, making a pallid rectangle on the floor, filling the small room with a luminous half-light. He could see the mattress lying where they had left it, the blankets folded and undisturbed. That was where Geneva should have been, waiting for him. He could not see her. And yet, the cabin was not empty. Some faint human smell, some tiny sound, told him that he was not alone. His body tensed suddenly. A shadow moved among the shadows.

"Geneva! What you doin'?"

The shadow drifted close to him. A paralyzing blow struck him just below his breastbone. He felt no pain, but something grated horribly against one of his ribs. The breath went out of him with a whistling grunt; then the blow came again, lower down, this time, and he felt a hot burning in his side.

He clutched at the hand that held the knife. His fingers closed on a man's forearm. Hard. Wiry. He wrenched with all his strength, felt the bone break like a green stick, heard his assailant's agonized gasp. He brought up his other hand, clutching for the unseen throat. His fingers found it but there was no strength in his grip. He felt his knees begin to buckle and the sudden salt taste of blood in the back of his throat. Through the confusion in his mind the thought came clearly that some black admirer of Geneva's had ambushed him— probably with her knowledge and consent. He tried to bellow his pain and rage but he made only a guttural choking sound.

The shadow swayed away from him, crouching, bent. It fled through the open door. . . .

He was down on all fours, close to the mattress. Blood poured from his mouth, pattering darkly on the floor. He coughed horribly, fighting for air. His elbows gave and he fell forward heavily on his face. Then the wind blew the door gently shut and the toolhouse was full of darkness and all was quiet except for the choking sounds he made and the far-off wailing of a locomotive whistle somewhere in the night.

Minutes passed. Eight. Ten.

Geneva came slowly across the clearing, humming to herself. She knew she was late, but the knowledge did not bother her. She was wondering how much money Bubber would give her this time, and how she would spend it—that was all.

She pushed open the door of the toolhouse and saw Bubber lying on the mattress, his face turned toward the door. For a moment she thought he was asleep, then she heard the slow strangled breathing and the bubbling sounds. She took three quick steps forward and squatted beside him. "What's wrong?" She shook his shoulder. "You sick?"

Bubber opened his eyes. "Doctor," he whispered. "Get him. Run."

Geneva did not move. She put out one slim finger and touched the dark stain on the floor. She held up her finger and sniffed at it like an animal. "Somebody done cut you!"

"Yeah," Bubber panted. "An' less'n you git me—git me a doctor—I'm gonna tell 'em"—he wheezed horribly—"you done it!" He coughed, a strangling sound. Geneva felt a spray of blood cover her like a fine mist. She threw up her hand to ward it off and backed out of the toolhouse. Outside, the night was bright and peaceful.

Her first impulse was to run back to her grandmother's cabin, hide herself in bed, pretend she had never left it. But Bubber's threat had terrified her. If the white folks thought *she* had done it . . . She began to run. She fled across the clearing, along the sandy road. Her hair whipped back from her face; her eyeballs gleamed white and panicky. It was almost a mile to Minelli's store and the telephone. It would take her all of ten minutes, running fast, but she would do it. Not for pity, not for love. She had a stronger motive. Fear.

ix

AT TEN TWENTY-ONE, just as Lester had decided that the Monday edition could be locked up, the phone jangled. He picked it up, glowering at Hester's empty desk. Ordinarily, she would have handled the call. "Yes?"

"That you, Lester?" It was Pat Daly's voice, tense with a subdued excitement.

"Of course it's me. Who else would be around here this time of night?"

"Well, if it ain't too late, there's one hell of a story down here for you—and a hell of a headache for us."

Lester jabbed the point of his pencil irritably into the blotter. "What is it this time?"

"They got Bubber Aycock!"

"*Got* him? You mean he's dead?"

"Near about. Hospital don't think he'll live. We found him less'n an hour ago, bled 'most to death in an old sawmill two, three miles from his farm."

Lester swore under his breath. He pulled a pad of yellow copy paper toward him. "Who did it? You holding anybody?"

"We got one suspect. Leastways, I reckon she's a suspect. Nigger gal named Geneva Holland—bad actor from way back."

"*Black?*"

"Well, mostly yeller."

Lester scribbled furiously. "Why you holding her?"

"She turned in the alarm. Said she was out for a walk and found Bubber there, stabbed. 'Cordin' to her, he asked her to run for a doctor. Time we got there he was unconscious. He's a tough bastard, all right. Anybody else'd be dead."

"You couldn't learn anything from him, then?"

"He came to in the ambulance and talked to Matson a little bit. Said it was a man who jumped him and that he broke his arm for him. Maybe he did, at that. The knife was on the floor."

"Then the woman *didn't* do it?"

"Hell, Lester, I don't know. She could have been mixed up in it. She had his blood on her clothes, an' she led us right to him."

The editor sniffed. "Lord, what a mess!"

Daly laughed. "You said it. Matson's fit to be tied. You should see him—orderin' roadblocks, phonin' Atlanta for more men, oh, he's raisin' hell! Didn't want me to call you, but I told him it'd have to come out sometime."

"That's right." Lester reflected that the *Courier*'s annual Christmas present to Daly was money well spent. "You suppose Aycock's been meeting this nigger wench for moonlight strolls pretty regular?"

"He's been meetin' somebody. They had a cozy little setup out there—mattress, blankets, all the comforts of home. I'm satisfied it was this yeller gal. She worked at a store a mile or so away. Minelli's place. You know it, don't you? Moonlight strolls!" Daly gave a throaty chuckle. "I wouldn't mind a short stroll with a piece of that myself!"

Lester threw an upward glance at the clock. "Could I see her if I came down there?"

"I doubt it; Matson's in the cell with her now, givin' her the business. But you could see her tomorrow, I reckon."

"What about Aycock's family? They know about it yet?"

"Hell, we can't *find* 'em," Daly said plaintively. "Farmhouse is empty. Matson's got a motorcycle man waitin' out there now."

"Don't think his wife could have done it, do you?"

Daly snorted. "You don't fix a setup like that to entertain your wife!"

"No, but if your wife finds out about it, she's likely to drop in and entertain you."

"Gawd!" Daly sounded startled. "That's right." Then disbelief crept into his voice. "Naw, that couldn't be. White woman wouldn't use a knife like that, in the first place. Anyway, I've known Nora for years. She's a pretty good citizen."

"It's the good ones that surprise you." Lester looked at the clock again. "Hell, Pat, I'm not going to try to cover the whole damn story tonight. I'm shorthanded again—secretary got drunk and walked out on me. No, by God, it's too late, and too damn complicated. No use implying Aycock had a black mistress, for instance, until it's proved. Not fair to his family, for one thing. I'm just going to say he was stabbed, and that you're holding a suspect. How's that?"

"That'll please Matson. Makes it sound like we've got the case half solved."

"I was also thinking of writing a short editorial saying you'd *better* solve it."

"God's sake, Lester," Daly protested, "give us a chance. Damn thing only happened an hour ago. Matson's touchy enough now. You start writin' editorials and he'll be like a bear with a sore head!"

"That's your problem," Lester said unfeelingly. He stared at the notes he had made. "You're positive this man is Bubber Aycock, aren't you?"

"Hell, yes," Daly said. "I helped carry him into the hospital, didn't I? If you don't believe me, go down there and see for yourself—if he's off the table yet, which I doubt. Look, I've talked too long already. See you tomorrow."

"All right, Pat." Lester hung up moodily. Damn that Hester, he thought; if she hadn't vanished . . . He looked again at the clock. "What the hell!" he said aloud. Blaming Hester was just an excuse. He had plenty of time, really. A younger, more energetic man would rush down to the jail, would cover the hospital, would interview the victim's family, would get a detailed story off to the wire services. . . .

So what? Lester asked himself sourly. I'm not a fireball cub reporter bucking for a Pulitzer Prize. I'm a second-rate country editor who always takes the line of least resistance. Why change now?

He twisted a sheet of copy paper into his typewriter. He decided to write the editorial first. He ran one hand through his white mane, lit a cigarette, placed it on the edge of the desk, and began to type:

Last night's bloodthirsty attack on a white man within a week of the apparent murder of his brother should be a matter of serious concern to every law-abiding citizen of Hainesville. The police must work night and day until the criminal or criminals are apprehended. And every citizen must aid the police. In a sense, we are all policemen. Let every one of us examine his memory and keep his eyes open for possible clues. The blackest crimes are often solved by observant civilians. . . .

He stopped and drew hard on his cigarette, reading what he had written. It sounded all right. Matson could hardly object. When everybody was made responsible, no individual could be singled out for blame. Lester smiled and bent over the machine. When he finished, he would reward himself with a drink. Just one. The clatter of the typewriter began again.

Y ANCEY opened the door and felt a little chill wind of pre-
monition blow between his shoulder blades. "What is it,
Hattie?"

Nathan's mother came in out of the dark and leaned against
the wall. She had been running; her breath hissed through her
flat, upturned nose; her chest heaved convulsively. She had
an old scarf thrown over her head; one hand held it under her
chin. Her eyes were in shadow.

Yancey closed the door. "What is it? Something wrong with
Nathan?"

Hattie nodded, fighting for breath.

Yancey jumped to the worst possible conclusion. "They got
him!"

"No." Hattie moved over on her spindly legs and sat down
on one of the folding chairs. "But he's hurt."

"Hurt?"

Hattie touched her right wrist with her left hand. "Arm.
Done broke his arm. Broke it right in half. Jes' hangin' by the
skin."

"Where is he?"

"Home. My place. He's hurtin' real bad, Yancey. We got
to do somethin'."

"How'd it happen?" Yancey asked slowly. He thought he
knew.

Hattie shook her head. Her breathing was more normal,
now. "He ain' tol' me nothin'. Jes' come home, come home like
that lil while ago. Had his arm buttoned up inside his shirt.
Like this. When I went to take it out, he got sick. All over the
floor. He's hurtin' bad, Yancey. We got to do somethin'."

A peculiar knock sounded on the door. Three raps, then

two, then one. Hattie shrank back and pulled the scarf around her face.

"It's all right," Yancey said. He opened the door. A colored boy in his middle teens stood there. He spoke to Yancey in a low voice. The undertaker listened, head bent. "All right," he said at length. "Go on back. Tell Morrison to see what else he can find out."

He closed the door and turned back into the room. He took one of the dusty paper flowers out of its vase and began to shred it slowly, letting the pieces fall to the floor. After a while Hattie got up and touched him on the shoulder. "Yancey! He's hurtin' *real* bad!"

Yancey shivered slightly. "Yeah. I know. Well, we can't fool with a doctor, but I can set a bone, I reckon. You wait here."

He went upstairs. Hattie heard a murmur of voices, then Yancey came back. Alma was with him. She was wearing an overcoat over her nightdress. Her feet were bare. She went up to Hattie, looking at her with dark, compassionate eyes. "Don't fret yourself too much. Ask the Lord to help you. He will."

Hattie covered her face with her hands.

"Come on!" Yancey said savagely. "None of that, now!" He was ashamed of himself, even though he knew it was the tension in him finding release. "We got no time for cryin' and such!"

Alma opened the door for them. "You remember what I told you," she said to her husband. "If he wants to come back here, you let him."

Yancey muttered, "Keep the door locked till I get back." He followed Hattie down the steps into the dark. "Don't hurry, now," he warned her. "You'll just make people look at us. Walk slow."

Hattie put her hand on his arm, as if touching him gave her

strength and confidence. "They won't git him, will they, Yancey? The police won't find him, will they?"

Yancey turned into the lane where he kept his car. "Don't fret, Hattie." It was Alma's phrase; he could think of no better one to offer.

The streets were quiet, almost empty. They parked near the house. No one noticed them. They came to the garage, quiet under the bright moon, and climbed the narrow stairs. Hattie opened the door with her key. "I done brought him, Nathan. Here's Yancey."

Nathan was sitting on the bed. He had a pillow in his lap, resting his right forearm on it. The arm looked out of line, unnatural. Midway between wrist and elbow a purple discoloration and swelling marked the break. The room was hot and full of the sour smell of vomit. Nathan's shirt was plastered against his body; his forehead and upper lip were rimmed with sweat. He let his head fall back against the brass bedstead. "Hello, Yancey."

Yancey went over to the bed. He bent and touched the swollen arm. "Can you move it?"

"Only with my other hand."

"How'd you drive yourself here? With one hand?"

"I had to."

"Hurt much?"

"Not so bad, now. It burns some."

Yancey turned to Hattie. "Get me some strips of cloth. Long ones. Tear up a sheet, if you have one." He peered under the bed. "I can use one of those slats for splints, I reckon."

Nathan ran his tongue across his lips. "I didn't exactly count on this, Yancey. He was stronger than I thought. Even with a knife in him."

Yancey said, "You didn't finish the job."

"You mean Shoup? Well, he . . ."

"No, not Shoup. Aycock. He's not dead."

[238]

Nathan sat up slowly. "How do you know?"

"I got word from Sam Morrison. He's night porter down at the jail. Geneva found Bubber right after you left him, and called the police. He's in the hospital; she's locked up."

Nathan clenched his left fist. "He's got to be dead!"

"Well, he isn't. Could he have recognized you?"

"No. It was too dark."

"Does he know he broke your arm?"

"If he's alive, he does. If he can remember anything."

"Well," said Yancey, "if he's told the cops that, it's just too bad. They're settin' up roadblocks all around the town. That's what Morrison said. All they've got to do is look for somebody with a broken arm. If you could hide *that*"— he pointed at the arm—"I'd take a chance and run you up to Atlanta tonight. But you can't hide it."

"No," Nathan said, "I can't hide it." He drew his left sleeve across his forehead and winced. "Maybe if you tie it up I can walk down to the freight yards and get in a boxcar. They'll watch the passenger trains, but they won't watch the freights. I could—"

Yancey shook his head. "You're in no shape to ride a freight, Nathan. That takes two arms, and a lot of luck. You got one arm, and looks like your luck is tryin' to run out. You better stay here, right here, till you get over the shock of this thing and the town quiets down." He looked around the room. "You been safe here so far; you'll be safe a while longer. I'll talk to Pope again; maybe he'll figure out something." He closed his lips in a thin line, then opened them again. "There's gonna be hell to pay, anyway, one way or another."

Nathan said wearily, "Maybe I just better give up, Yancey. Just go down to the jail and give myself up."

"No!" Hattie looked up from the sheet she was tearing. "No!"

Yancey shook his head. "We'll get you out of here somehow,

Nathan. We got to, that's all." He held out his hand. "You got those bandages ready, Hattie?"

Hattie gave them to him. Yancey reached down, lifted a corner of the bed, and pulled out one of the thin slats. He flexed it in his hands, then broke it over his knee into halves, then quarters. He chose two pieces about the same length and put them on the bed. He took a clean handkerchief out of his pocket. He handed it to Nathan. "Better put that between your teeth and bite on it. This'll hurt."

CHAPTER 8

Unity sat by the window, a dressing gown around her shoulders. In the bathroom, Helen splashed happily. The sun was warm on Unity's face. She pressed her fingers against her aching eyeballs. I won't go to work, she thought; I can't face it, that's all.

It was not the prospect of work that dismayed her; it was the thought of seeing Hester.

Come on, she said to herself. Show some guts. Pull yourself together. So what if he did sleep with the woman, what if she was his mistress; what if she was stupid enough to have an abortion? That's ancient history, now. Who do you think he is, anyway? Sir Galahad?

She got up, crossed over to the bedside table, picked up her compact, and went back to the window. She flipped open the lid. Her face stared back at her, slightly distorted by a flaw in the glass.

Make up your mind, she told herself fiercely. Are you a prude or aren't you? If you are, you'd better get him out of your system. Now. Before you get hurt even worse. And if you're not a prude, if you want him on any terms, you'd better stop moping. You'd better swallow your pride. No, not swallow it. Wrap it around you, layer on layer, until not even the thought of Hester can get through it.

Hester. In the cabin. On the same couch. Oh, it was the *timing* that she could not forget, could not rationalize. Two hours after she had left him. Maybe less. How could he have done it, how *could* he? She put her burning face in her hands. The metal of the compact was cool against her cheek.

All right, said the icy voice inside of her, the untouched voice, you might as well face that too. Why did he do it? Because you . . . What had he said? *One thing I can't stand, it's a woman who's a tease. . . .*

Abruptly she shifted her anger from Shep and from herself. Hester. That troublemaker. That scar-faced *bitch*! What right had she to *say* those things, even if they had happened? Damn her! *Damn her!*

Unity stood up. She hurled the compact across the room. It struck a picture on the opposite wall, smashed the glass, and spun to the floor. It lay there, face down, bits of broken mirror around it, its halves spread open like some kind of stricken butterfly.

Helen appeared at the door of the bathroom. "Unity!" Her face was stupid with amazement. "What on earth . . ."

Unity said, "It's nothing." She walked over to her bed and got into it. Her hands were shaking. She put them under the sheet. "I'm not going to work. I don't feel like it, that's all. Call Lester for me, will you, and tell him. Tell him I won't be down today."

Helen sat down on the side of the bed. "Unity, what is it? Is it Shep? Maybe if you . . ."

"It's nothing," Unity said again. She made herself try to smile. "I'm all right. But I'm not going to work today."

Helen looked worried; frightened, almost. "You stay there. I'll bring you a tray."

"I'm not hungry."

"Just orange juice and coffee," Helen said soothingly. "You'd better eat something."

She went out. Unity closed her eyes. The blast of anger had cleared her head, somehow, had made her feel better. I've got all day, now, she told herself. I'll work it out. By tonight I'll know what to do.

In twenty minutes Helen came back with the tray. She put it down beside the bed. "Feeling better now?" She did not wait for an answer. "I'm late; I'll have to run. Aunt Guley said she'd phone Lester for you." She stooped and kissed her sister's cheek. "All right?"

Unity nodded.

"Oh," said Helen, "I almost forgot." She had the *Courier* tucked under her arm. "Somebody stuck a knife in that other Aycock man. Story's on the back page." She laughed. "I knew you were interested in all that business, so I brought it up. Thought it might take your mind off your troubles."

She tossed the paper on the bed. The door closed behind her.

ii

"Oh, the police are trying to sit on it, naturally." Melady dangled the base of the telephone over the side of the bed so that the kinked wire uncoiled slowly. "They wouldn't let me see the colored girl when I went down to the jail this morning. Hospital's out of bounds for reporters, too. Aycock's still alive, I guess—if he was dead, they'd hardly be able to suppress *that*. And I heard a rumor that he'd told the cops . . . What?"

He listened to Cunningham's dry whisper coming from eight hundred miles away.

"Hell, yes, the town'll be crawling with 'em before the day's over. But for once we're on the inside of a national story, Sidney dear. A big one. Nobody outside of Hainesville got very excited about Neal Aycock's death. But now they will. This pot's going to boil, believe me. In fact, you've got a situation here that could get very ugly. Very ugly, very fast. I wouldn't be surprised to see some troops moved in before the week's over. If . . ."

"I wish to God you'd kept Simpson," Cunningham said querulously. "We'll have to have a follow-up story next week and we'll need some more pictures. As for this edition, the timing couldn't be worse. Well, we'll have to recast, that's all. We seldom get a chance to handle spot news almost as fast as the newspapers. We can't afford to muff it. What's your program?"

"Thought this morning I'd see what I could pick up in the town. Then this afternoon go out and interview Aycock's wife, if she's available, maybe check on the place where this colored girl worked. I also have a notion this Negro undertaker would be worth seeing again. . . ."

"All right," Cunningham said. "I'll give you a final deadline of midnight. Phone it. I'll stay here until I hear from you."

"Okay," said Melady, "only this time don't give me any of this rewrite business. I'm the one who's looking at the thing. You're not. Try to remember that, will you, Sidney dear?"

"There won't be time for any rewrite," Cunningham said stiffly. "Does that make you happy?"

"Deliriously," said Melady, and hung up. He rubbed his chin reflectively. I'm going to get myself fired, someday, he thought, acting like that. What makes me so damned suicidal where Cunningham is concerned? Speak up, Dr. Freud; I can't quite hear you. He grinned to himself and flashed the operator. "Get me the *Courier*, honey-chile."

"Okay," sighed the operator resignedly, "you-all."

"Good morning," Melady said when Lester finally answered. "Did your secretary turn up missing today? If she did, it's partly my fault. Thought I'd better call up and apologize."

"My God." Lester sounded exasperated. "I'm glad to get some explanation. Found a note here this morning saying she was going away indefinitely. Hell of a thing, at a time like this! What got into her, anyway?"

"I don't know. Something was driving her crazy, that was obvious." And he told the editor what had happened.

"I must be jinxed, that's all." Lester, clearly, was interested in Hester's problems only in so far as they affected him. "I got another girl, but she's not worth a tinker's damn. Scared of her own shadow. She's out bawling in the bathroom now because I snapped at her." Melady heard him sniff sadly. "You trying to keep up with this Aycock business?"

"I read your editorial," Melady told him. "Everyone must keep their eyes open for the killer—isn't that what you said? Well, that's what I'm doing. Haven't blinked once since I read your inspiring words."

"I know it stank," Lester said. "You don't have to rub it in. Hell, there wasn't time to do any better. You ought to try putting out a paper sometime all by yourself, even a lousy six-page job like this. Sometimes I wonder why I do it."

"Why not let that Cantrell girl help you more? She's no fool."

"All women are fools." Lester sounded disgusted. "She didn't show up this morning, either. Her aunt said she has a headache or some damn thing." He sighed. "If you stumble across anything interesting, for God's sake let me know, will you? I'm too shorthanded to do much leg-work."

"If I corner the killer I'll call you up."

"I'm serious," Lester said sourly.

"So am I," Melady told him. "So am I."

iii

BILSY SHOUP came into police headquarters and walked straight up to Daly's desk. His hat was pushed back; his forehead was shiny with sweat. He leaned forward so that his thin face with its sunken cheeks was only inches away from Daly's broad red one. He was breathing fast. "Pat, I gotta have some pertection. You gotta give me pertection."

Daly recoiled a bit from the fetid breath. "Give you what?"

"They got Neal, di'n' they?" The hunchback's high-pitched voice rose higher. "They got Bubber, di'n' they? I'm next, Pat." He thumped himself on his protruding chest. "Me. Bilsy. I'm next. I'm *next*!"

Daly shifted his weight and the chair creaked. "Aw, c'mon, Bilsy. You're gettin' all het up over nothin'. Why'd anybody want to bother with you?"

"I was there! I was there in the icehouse, wasn' I? Neal was there, an' they got him. Bubber was there, an' now . . ." Under the wide hat Bilsy's sallow face worked convulsively. "Is he dead, Pat? Is ol' Bubber dead?"

"Naw!" The policeman shook his head. "Not yet." He looked at the clock. "Wasn't dead an hour ago, anyway." He pushed at some papers irritably. "Go on home, Bilsy. Ain't nobody gonna bother with a runt like you. We got plenty else to worry about." He jerked a nail-bitten thumb. "Matson's in there now with a feller from Atlanta, arguin' about how many highway patrolmen they gonna give us till this thing's cleaned up. You go on home an' stay there. Ain't nobody fixin' to bother with you."

Bilsy's Adam's apple bobbed. His face grew red. "You wastin' all these men on road blocks, you can afford to send one out to my place!" He knotted his fingers into a claw and pounded with it on Daly's desk. "I know what them murderin' niggers are after! They want me to talk! They want me to tell what I know, see? If I do, then they'll leave me alone. If I don't, they're comin' after me." He stood back and shouted, a ridiculous and terrifying figure. "Well, you gimme that pertection, or I'm gonna tell! I'm gonna name names, too! I'm goin' up to Atlanta and I'm gonna talk, you hear?"

Daly stood up quickly. "You wait here. An' stop your fool hollerin'. You wait here."

He went into Matson's office and closed the door. Bilsy subsided on the long wooden bench that occupied one wall. He twisted his hat brim nervously. Slowly the flush died out of his face, leaving it pinched and yellow, like a parchment-covered skull. The policeman at the telephone switchboard eyed him contemptuously.

In five minutes Daly came back. He stood over Bilsy for a moment without speaking. "All right," he said at length. "Go on home. We'll put a man out there for a couple of nights. Matson okayed it."

Bilsy pulled at his long nose, his eyes suspicious. "When's he comin'? I want him there afore sundown, you hear?"

"Go on home," Daly said impatiently. "He'll be there."

He stood watching the twisted figure sidle out through the door and disappear down the hall. "He's gonna be scared stiff, the rest of his life!"

The policeman at the switchboard spoke from under his headphones. "Wouldn't be no great loss, would it? If they did get him, I mean."

Daly wiped his mouth slowly. "I wouldn't shed no tears."

iv

"No," Yancey said in a low, hurried voice, "I'm not at home. It's a pay telephone, not a party line. Even so, I wouldn't mention names, if I were you." He hesitated, looking over his shoulder. Nobody was near the booth. "You know what happened, don't you?"

"I can read the papers." Pope's voice sounded angry. "I thought you told me . . ."

"I did," Yancey said. "I told you wrong. Don't ask me why. I'll try to explain when I see you. The question is, what we better do now."

"Get him out of there! Get him out of there!"

"I can't," Yancey said. "He's hurt."

"Hurt?"

"Broken arm."

"Well, he can walk, can't he? Walk him to a car and drive him out of there."

"I can't do that either," Yancey said. "They know he's got a broken arm. They're watchin' for him. Every road."

Pope sucked his breath through his teeth with a hissing sound. Finally he said, "Is he out of sight? Now, I mean?"

"Yes."

"Your place?"

"No. Another place."

"We've got to get him out of there, Yancey. I can see what's coming. If Aycock dies you've got a fine chance of a full-scale race riot. You'll have trouble even if he doesn't die. Then what happens? They send the National Guard, this time. They may declare martial law. They do that, they search the whole town. It's been done before. And if they find him, it's just too bad."

"What you want me to do? Take him out through the woods? That'll be no picnic, especially after dark."

"No," Pope said slowly. "We can do better than that. You've got a hearse, haven't you?"

"A hearse?" Yancey's voice rose sharply. "Yes, I got an old one."

"Will it run as far as Atlanta?"

"Yes. But I told you, they've set up roadblocks. We . . ."

"They'll be looking for a live man, not a dead one. You've got coffins, haven't you?"

"Yes, but . . ."

"You can make him look like a corpse, can't you? If you've got a real corpse, put both coffins in the hearse. They won't even look at 'em."

Yancey felt the sweat trickling down between his shoulder blades. "We'd be takin' an awful chance. I think it would be better to sit tight and wait. . . ."

"You can't wait, you fool! Don't you know there are white men—politicians, some of 'em—who've just been waiting for a situation like this? Don't you think they're going to exploit it? Of course they are! We've got to move, and move fast!"

"You can talk!" Yancey said with sudden sarcasm. "You don't have to drive that hearse. You don't have to run that roadblock. All you have to do is give the orders. I got a wife and child down here. They need me alive, not dead in a ditch. I'm not gonna do it, see?"

Silence for ten seconds, broken only by the humming of the wire. Then Pope said gently, "Suppose somebody stole your hearse, Yancey. Suppose they took it without your knowledge. Suppose you left it in front of your place tonight and it just vanished?"

"Who do you think would drive it?"

"I can buy that sort of courage, Yancey."

"Send a man down here, you mean?"

"Yes."

"Why don't you get your own hearse and everything, then?"

"By God, Yancey!" Pope's voice cracked out in sudden fury. "It's your fault we're in this mess! If you hadn't lied to me, we'd have had him out of there before now, and you know it! Now stop being a miserable little coward, and do what I say! Our man will get to your place after dark. You'll arrange the rest of it, or you'll regret it the rest of your life! Is that clear?"

Yancey muttered, "It's clear enough. What time will he come?"

"I don't know yet," Pope said more quietly. "I have to find him, first. Sometime before midnight, anyway. Stop being frightened, will you? It'll work. We've pulled off jobs that involved much more risk. Go and tell your friend that he's leaving tonight. Make your own arrangements at that end. All we can supply is the driver. Go on. Get started." His voice softened suddenly. "I know it's tough, Yancey. But once he's out of there, you'll feel much better. We'll all feel better."

"All right," Yancey said. He pressed one hand flat against his belly. He felt sick. "I'll go tell him."

v

SHORTLY after twelve Lester looked up at the apprehensive back of his new secretary. "Get me Pat Daly down at County Police Headquarters, will you?" He waited, drumming his fingers on the desk. "That you, Pat? Lester. Anything new?"

"Not much," the policeman said. "We got those roadblocks set up. Anybody with a busted arm tries to get out, we'll get him. That's about all."

"You better get him," Lester said heavily. "Town's pretty tense. You heard about the meeting tonight?"

"Yeah." Daly sounded uneasy. "Nine o'clock, courthouse square, ain't it? City cops are gonna keep an eye on it, but shucks—they won't do nothin' if trouble starts." He hesitated. "Who called it, anyway, Lester? You know?"

"I don't know for sure. You might ask old Horace Kane. *He'd* know, I bet." The editor sniffed. "Matson get anything more out of that yeller gal?"

"Not yet."

"Well, if she says anything, let me know, will you? Call me if anything breaks."

"I'll try, Lester."

The editor put the phone back in its cradle. "Going out for a while." He stood up and took his panama from the rack. "Be back after lunch."

In the shimmering street he stood still for a moment, almost as if he were listening. He liked to say, sometimes, that a good newspaperman could smell trouble before it happened. Perhaps it was true. Anybody who'd worked in Hainesville as long as he had was bound to have an affinity for its moods. Moods and tenses, Lester thought wryly. It was the tension that interested him now.

He walked slowly along Blanchard Street, turning his sharp ferret face from side to side. Spotting tangible evidence wasn't easy; there was almost none. A few more countrymen gathered in little knots on street corners—perhaps. A few less colored people on the streets—maybe. A certain wariness in certain faces—or was it all imaginary? The town was too still, that was it—too quiet for high noon on Monday. Even the traffic sounded muted.

He turned into the Palace Drugstore and sat down at the soda fountain. The marble felt cool under his hands; the ceiling fan droned softly. "Fix me some iced coffee, will you, Pop?"

The drugstore, he knew, was a nerve center. Any pressures

within the town found outlet, sooner or later, here. "Thanks, Pop." Lester stirred the coffee distastefully; he did not really want it. "What's new? Everything seems kinda quiet."

Pop Halliday's hairless face tried to look portentous. "Too quiet." He slid the sugar bowl along the counter. "Too quiet." He leaned closer to Lester. "Hear 'bout the meetin'?"

"I heard about it. You going?"

"Sure," Pop said. "Sure, I'm goin'. Dunno what'll happen, but whatever it is, I don't want to miss it. Betcha half the town is there."

"Yeah," said Lester. "Probably." He drank half his coffee, paid for it, and went out. It was not quite his usual lunch-time, but he decided to go to the Stone House anyway. It was one of the town's older residential houses, converted into a restaurant. Most businessmen ate lunch there.

He went up to the room reserved for men and stood in the doorway looking around. The room was half full; he recognized most of the faces. Judge Winter was sitting at a corner table with Shep Townsend. There were two empty chairs. Lester went over and pulled out one of them. This was no intrusion, it was the custom of the place.

The Judge greeted him affably. Shep moved his chair grudgingly; he said nothing. Lester stared at him, concealing his irritation. The Townsend Lumber Company was a big advertiser. And Shep was the Townsend Lumber Company. Even so, he might be civil. . . .

The waitress brought plates of okra soup and a bowl of steaming rice. There were hot biscuits, homemade. Shep ate in silence. Lester and the Judge discussed the Aycock affair.

"I still think a white man could be responsible," the Judge said. "Why not? Those Aycocks must have had plenty of enemies. Why assume the man who tried to get rid of them was necessarily black?"

[252]

Lester sniffed. "Maybe he wasn't. But that's what they'll assume at the meeting tonight."

"What meeting?" asked the Judge.

"I don't know too much about it," Lester confessed. "It's scheduled for nine o'clock, courthouse square. I'm told they plan to have a bonfire and some speeches. White-supremacy stuff, probably."

The Judge looked grave. "I don't like that. I don't like that at all."

Lester shrugged. "Not much we can do about it, is there?"

Shep pushed back his chair and stood up. "Sure." He fumbled in his pocket for change. "All you've got to do is bring in the killer, Lester. Then they won't have anything to raise hell about." He put the tip beside his place and walked away.

The two older men watched him go. "Arrogant young puppy!" Lester said with a vehemence that surprised him.

The Judge smoothed his tawny hair. "Maybe he's crossed in love."

"I hope so," Lester said malevolently. "I hope he's crossed but good!"

vi

"It's a risk," Yancey admitted. "It's a big risk. But we've got to take it, that's all."

"All right," Nathan said. He reached up with his left hand and gripped the brass upright behind his head. "Anything's better than just sitting here, thinking."

"How's the arm?"

"I didn't sleep much."

"I didn't either," Yancey said. He turned to Hattie, who stood at the foot of the bed, her eyes moving from one face to the other. "You got it straight, now? Eleven o'clock you help Nathan down to the corner. Be sure you're on time. I'll pick him up, take him to my place. By then the driver from Atlanta should be here." He turned back to the man on the bed. "You'll be out of Hainesville by midnight."

"That's good," Hattie said in a whisper. "That's real good."

Nathan was watching Yancey. His eyes were sunken and feverish. "You couldn't keep out of it after all, could you, Yancey?"

Yancey had opened the door. He glanced back, his face tight with strain. "You better try to shave yourself, Nathan. Somebody might be suspicious of a corpse with a beard."

He went out. Hattie moved up to the head of the bed and put her hand on Nathan's forehead. "You got lil fever," she said. "How 'bout takin' some rest, now?"

Nathan eased himself down until he was lying almost flat. He did not close his eyes. He stared at the ceiling.

"You hungry?" Hattie asked.

Nathan shook his head.

"I'll bring you some soup," Hattie said. "You jes' rest easy."

She went down the stairs, humming a jerky tune under her breath. Everything would be all right, now. Yancey would take care of everything.

As she entered the kitchen, she hesitated, then went through the dining room, up the stairs, and down the hall to Unity's room. She knocked once, gently.

"Come in," Unity said.

Hattie went in and closed the door. Unity had not dressed. She was sitting on the bed in her dressing gown; the *Courier* lay beside her. She looked at Hattie coldly.

Hattie tiptoed forward. "You don' have to worry no more!"

Unity said, "He lied to me, didn't he? Nathan lied to me."

"You don' have to worry no more. He . . ."

"I don't intend to worry any more." Unity's voice was hard.

[254]

"I'm through worrying about other people. I don't care what happens to Nathan. I don't . . ."

"He's goin'," Hattie said. "Nathan's goin'. Tonight. You don' have to worry no more. He's goin'."

Unity's expression changed. She said, sharply, "How's he going to get out of town? The *Courier* says the roads are guarded!"

Hattie gave a hoarse chuckle. She rolled her sherry-colored eyes in a kind of triumph. "Neh min' how; it's all fixed. He's goin.'"

"Who fixed it? Can you trust him?"

Hattie nodded slowly. "Got to trust him."

"Is it Yancey Brown?"

Hattie's eyes widened. "Who tol' you?"

"Nobody told me," Unity said slowly. "I guessed."

From downstairs came the sound of Mrs. Cantrell's voice calling for Hattie. "Comin'," the old woman grumbled. "I'se comin'!" She went out.

Unity got up and went into the bathroom. She threw some crystals into the tub and turned on the tap. She stood staring down at the foaming water. He's lucky, she said to herself. Nathan's lucky. I wish to God somebody would take me out of Hainesville.

vii

"ALL RIGHT," the highway patrolman said to Melady, "drive on." He stepped back, making a sweeping motion with his hand.

"Tell me something," Melady said. "How do you know what you're looking for? I mean, how do you know *I* don't make a hobby out of sticking knives in people? Why let *me* pass?"

[255]

The patrolman said, "We know what we're lookin' for, buddy. An' it ain't you. Drive on, now; you're blockin' the bridge."

Melady drove across the bridge. A hundred yards farther on he made a turn and headed back. He waved sardonically at the patrolman. "Forgot my toothbrush," he said as he went past.

It was the third roadblock he had checked. At each one the procedure had been identical—a glance at his face, a quick look into the rear of the car, another into the trunk. Nothing more. It supported the rumor Melady had heard earlier in the day, that Bubber had identified his assailant, that the police would be able to pick him up on sight.

He drove back into town and headed out the Atlanta road, toward the Aycock farm. It was midafternoon; the sun was halfway down the western sky. He came to the crossroads, hesitated a moment, then swung off the road and parked in front of Minelli's store. Before he tried to interview Nora, he would have a few words with Geneva's employer.

He got out and stood for a moment beside his car, his writer's eye picking up details that would be useful to him later: the peeling whitewash, the tin signs, the rusted drum of kerosene with the hand pump that stood beside the door, the sluggish flies, the brown cur stretched limply along the middle step. The sun was still hot. He took off his coat and tossed it into the back of the car. Across the highway, in front of the filling station, the little knot of farmers ceased their talk and watched him go into the store, stepping carefully over the sleeping dog, easing the screen door shut so that it made no sound.

Whitey Lawrence spat into the reddish dust. "Another one of them re-porters, I betcha. Orta run them bastuds outa town."

A bulky man in blue overalls removed a frayed match from

a mouth full of gold teeth. The hairs on his thick wrists glinted in the sun. "Good thing you don't act as fierce as you talk, Whitey." For such a big man his voice was curiously gentle. "Maybe he ain't no newspaper feller at all. Maybe he's jest a drummer."

Lawrence spat again. "He's a re-porter, all right. I kin tell. An' I don't like 'em nosin' 'round!"

Dillinger took off his hat and smoothed his flat, black hair with the palm of his hand. "You so curious, Whitey, whyn't you walk acrost the road an' see?"

"Yeah," said the taller of the Nelson twins, "go on over there an' see."

Inside the store, Melady leaned against the counter, meeting Mrs. Minelli's basilisk stare. "This the store where Geneva Holland works?"

"She did work here," Mrs. Minelli said.

"Mind if I ask you a few questions about her?"

The massive shoulders lifted slightly. Melady put a five-dollar bill on the counter. "I pay for information," he said. "When it's worth paying for."

The screen door slammed and Whitey Lawrence came in. He took a bottle out of the washtub, uncapped it, and took a long gulp of the purple liquid. He turned and began to prowl along the opposite wall, ostentatiously peering at the canned goods. Mrs. Minelli followed him with her black turtle eyes. She kept her mouth tightly closed.

"Now, then," Melady said briskly, "how long had this girl worked for you? A year? Two years?" He took out his notebook and put it on the counter. "Two years?" he repeated.

Mrs. Minelli nodded slowly.

"What sort of girl was she? Good? Bad? You have any idea she was meeting this white man out in the woods?"

Whitey Lawrence stopped moving. Mrs. Minelli said to Melady, "You waste your time, mister." She got up from her chair and came around the counter. She walked over to Lawrence and stood behind him. "You look for something, hey?"

The man turned around quickly. "Me? Naw. Jes' came in for a drink, tha's all." He leaned back against the shelves and sucked at his bottle. When he took it away from his mouth, a drop of the purple fluid trickled through the yellow stubble on his chin. He wiped it off. "Didn' know you was entertainin' a re-porter. Go right ahead. Don't mind me." He put the bottle in the rack, dropped a coin on the counter, and walked out, swaggering a little. The screen door slammed again.

Melady looked at Mrs. Minelli. "You let that sort of thing scare you?"

Mrs. Minelli said, "They're customers."

Melady closed his notebook, trying to conceal his annoyance. "Tell me one thing: you think this girl stabbed Aycock?"

Mrs. Minelli picked up the five-dollar bill and handed it to him. She moved heavily behind the counter and sat down. "I wouldn't stay around here, mister, if I was you."

Melady shrugged. "Why not? It's a free country, isn't it?"

"Not very," said Mrs. Minelli.

Melady put his notebook in his pocket and pushed open the screen door. The countrymen had crossed the road and were standing between him and his car, waiting. Their still, brown faces were blank and hostile. The big man with the gold teeth stood apart from the rest, thumbs in the straps of his overalls. Dillinger looked up at Melady slyly. "Git what you wanted?"

"No," said Melady shortly. He came down the steps. He was angry; his face showed it.

When he came near the car the blue and khaki figures moved closer together so that they made a living wall in front of him. The taller of the Nelson twins said slowly, "We don't like nosy strangers 'round here, mister."

"That's right," Whitey Lawrence said in his blustering voice. " 'Specially when they come from up Nawth."

Melady said nothing. He lowered his head a little. Watching him through the screen door, Mrs. Minelli thought of a small goat she had had once, when she was a child in Sicily. Sometimes the dogs would corner the goat and he would lower his head, just the same way.

Dillinger said, in his smooth drawl, "People don't mind their own business liable to git hurt, mister. You know that?"

Melady moved forward suddenly with his dancing terrier gait. He went straight up to Whitey Lawrence until not more than an inch separated their chests. Lawrence was half a head taller; Melady had to tilt his chin up to look him in the eyes. "Get the hell out of my way!" he said.

Lawrence recoiled half a step. Melady pushed forward, jostling him roughly. He shoved through the line and made two quick strides to his car. He had the door open and was about to step in when the smaller of the Nelson twins blocked it with his shoulder. He was the same height as Melady—if anything, an inch shorter. He pushed his hat back from his sunburned forehead; he was smiling a little. "You're a pretty good picker, for a Yankee. Yes sir, a pretty good picker. You pick the one man who'll step back for you. Now I call that right good pickin'." He stretched out one hand lazily and touched Melady's tie. "Yep. Right good picker. Picks nice ties, too." His hand closed slowly on the colored fabric. "Sho' nuff silk. My, my!" He cocked his head admiringly. "Sho' nuff!"

Melady said evenly, "Let go of that tie!"

Nelson tightened his grip. "Well, now, look who's givin' orders 'round here! How 'bout that?" He glanced at his companions in mock astonishment. As he did so, Melady struck him. It was a chopping blow, delivered awkwardly. It landed on Nelson's cheekbone, too high to do much damage, but it broke his hold on the necktie and sent him reeling back a step or two. Melady felt the shock of it in his knuckles, a sudden numbness that snaked up his arm and vanished. He heard his own breathing, shallow and quick. He was frightened; the thing had happened almost without volition. He put his back squarely against the body of the car. "All right," he said. "Six to one. That's the sort of odds you like, isn't it?"

He expected them to rush him, and he waited, his stomach tight and hollow, his feet planted solidly in the red dust, the knot of the tie hard and painful under his ear. But they did not. They stood watching the smaller Nelson twin, their faces eager and full of a curious innocence, like the faces of small boys watching a pair of dogs fight.

"Aw right, Tawm," Dillinger said with a kind of controlled glee. "Give it to him!"

Nelson took off his hat and flung it on the ground. He moved forward, crouching a little, fists cocked. A signet ring on his little finger caught the sun and winked like a tiny malevolent eye. The brown cur on the middle step raised its head alertly. In the doorway Mrs. Minelli brought her clasped hands up under her chin.

Melady moved to his left, away from the car. The sick, empty feeling moved with him, but the worst fear—the fear of being mobbed—was gone. He knew, now, that they considered Nelson their champion. If he could handle Nelson, none of the others would molest him. He kept circling, backing away, weighing his chances. He had boxed a little as a boy, nothing since. He had no illusions about his endurance. He might be good for one or two minutes, no more. If he was going to make any sort of fight of it, he would have to do it quickly. It did not occur to him to talk his way out of it—or try to. Or to run away. A queer, irrelevant thought of Cunningham flashed through his mind. Let him rewrite this one, he said to himself, and stepped forward and struck again, left and right.

The first blow landed on Nelson's mouth, driving his head back so that the second blow missed. The impact of fist on flesh made a wet, pulpy sound. Melady felt a knifelike pain across his knuckles, and knew that Nelson's teeth had cut him. He saw the surprise and anger in the brown face, the bright smear of blood on the twisted lips. He heard the indrawn hiss of excitement from the watchful circle around them, and, trying to follow up his advantage, he moved in again, throwing the same combination of blows dimly remembered from his childhood, the classic and difficult one-two.

Nelson jerked his head sharply so that Melady's left fist went over his shoulder. He caught the right fist on his left forearm and threw his own right hand inside, straight. The blow smashed into Melady's cheekbone. Behind his right eye a torrent of red fire exploded. The pain was unbelievable. He stumbled and fell to his knees, staring at his own hands braced before him in the dust. With his left eye he could see clearly the cuts along his knuckles. His right eye seemed to be spinning in a fiery darkness. One punch, he thought stupidly; impossible. He heard Dillinger's jeering voice, far away and triumphant, "Stomp him, Tawm!"

And another voice said, with maddening slowness, "Naw, they's about of a size. Leave 'em fight fair. Nothin' better'n a good fist fight, no-how."

His head cleared a little. He looked up at Nelson, standing over him, waiting. He knew that if he stood up another blow would flatten him before he could raise his hands, and so he lunged forward suddenly, driving his shoulder against Nelson's knees, wrapping his arms around his legs, drawing them together in a savage embrace so that Nelson went down hard on his back. His head hit the ground with a solid thump and bounced once. Melady rolled clear and came up onto his feet. In the doorway of the store, Mrs. Minelli made one hand into a fist and struck it into the palm of the other. *"Ay, cabrito!"* she said softly to herself.

Nelson got up slowly. He did not seem hurt. Red earth caked

his overalls. His face gleamed with sweat and a kind of animal enjoyment. He drew the back of one hand across his mouth, and the blood and dust mingled in a muddy smear. He came forward again, fists moving in tight circles. Melady stood still, waiting for him. He felt too dizzy to risk moving quickly. The right side of his face was numb; he could see the swelling coming up in a mound under his eye. The dancing fists came nearer; he watched them with a curious detachment, as if they were threatening somebody else. Not sixty seconds had elapsed since the first blow.

Nelson darted in, throwing his left fist like a javelin. It raked the side of Melady's head. He felt a burning sensation in his ear, and lashed out with both hands, but Nelson had bounded away. He moved around Melady, crouching, catlike. Melady turned slowly, always facing him. Behind Nelson, out of focus, he could see the tense figures of the other men and their blurred shadows. The only sound was the scuffle of Nelson's feet and his own labored breathing.

Nelson moved in again, fast. Melady speared him with his left hand, but his elbow folded like a hinge. Nelson's fist came up in a white blur and smashed against Melady's nose. He felt the numbing impact and heard the cartilage crack. There was not much pain, this time, but the force of the blow bent his knees and drove him back on his heels. He hung there, his hands dangling behind him, unable to straighten up, unwilling to go down. Nelson stepped back and measured him like a swordsman. The blow flashed in a short vicious arc. It almost missed its target—the point of Melady's chin. But it brushed the bone hard enough to send him flat on his back.

He lay there, feeling the blood come slowly down through his nostrils. The fear was all gone now—the terrible instinctive fear of being hurt. Now he was hurt, so there was nothing to be afraid of. No matter what happened, he couldn't be hurt much more. He rolled over and came up on his hands and knees. The blood dripped from his nose onto the ground, heavy, clotted. He shook his head and it flew like a red spray. Six feet away, the side of his car reflected the slanting light, calm and dazzling.

Nelson said, gasping, "Had enough, mister? If that'll holt you, crawl over to yore car an' git out of here. You want some more, jes' stan' up, that's all."

Melady raised his head and stared at him. The soft voice that he had heard once before spoke behind him. "Better do like he says, stranger. Crawl over there an' git on outa here. Don't stan' up no more. You done pretty good."

Melady moved one foot up until it was planted on the ground. He stayed there, his knuckles still in the dust, the lower half of his face a red mask. In the store, Mrs. Minelli pushed open the screen door, then let it close slowly again. "Stay down, *cabrito*," she muttered. "Stay down, little goat."

Melady got up. There was a little groan of admiration from the circle of faces. Nelson moved in.

viii

AFTER a flurry of activity in the morning, the telegraph office was quiet. A fly buzzed hopelessly, trapped by a spiderweb in the dusty window. The languid blond girl who accepted messages, bored to the point of desperation, was reduced to reading the *Courier*'s editorial page. She had read everything else. A messenger boy sat on the yellow wooden bench behind the railing, eyes closed, chin on chest. His daydream was approaching a fascinating climax.

The blond girl read the editorial about the stabbing of Bubber Aycock and found it more stimulating than she had expected. "*Let every one of us examine his memory and keep his eyes open for possible clues.*" She read the sentence twice. She put the paper down and obediently began to examine her memory, chewing her gum with a slow, even rhythm.

"Jimmy," she said finally.

The messenger boy opened a reluctant eye. "Huh?"

"Remember that trial about a week ago when they turned those Aycock brothers loose? What day was that, anyway?"

The messenger boy fingered a pimple thoughtfully. "Day after I got back from my vacation, I think."

"What day was that, silly?"

"Monday. Last Monday."

The girl sat quietly for a while, her jaws moving slowly. At last she got up, crossed the narrow office, opened a file, and began to thumb through the yellow papers, one by one.

The messenger boy closed his eyes gratefully and returned to his fantasy. The fly buzzed on.

ix

"' 'Pears to me," Pa Aycock said plaintively to Louella, "she'd talk to her own father-in-law. 'Tain't *my* fault Bubber got hisself stabbed."

Louella tilted herself back in the kitchen chair and looked critically at the nail polish she was applying to her left hand. "She ain't talkin' to nobody." Her tone made it clear that her aunt's withdrawal had her full approval. "Been locked up in that room ever since las' night. Come out to git the newspaper this mornin', that's all. Some newspaper people been here, along about noon. Real nice; from Atlanta. *She* wouldn't talk to 'em." Louella smiled contentedly. "I did, though."

Pa Aycock said worriedly, "You fixed her anything to eat? 'Pears like she'd git hungry by now."

Louella spread her fingers in a fan and admired them. "She gits hungry, she'll come out, I reckon."

"When she does"—Pa Aycock sounded grim—"you better git that there paint off'n them fingers of your'n."

Louella gave him a sulky stare, then started on the fingers of her other hand. She had hoarded the bottle of nail polish for weeks. Until now, fear of her aunt had prevented her from using it.

Her grandfather said with sudden ferocity, "What you need is a razor strop acrost that fat tail of your'n." He got up and went to the door. "An' if Bubber dies, an' you come to live with me, you're gonna git it, too."

Louella went on smearing her dirty nails. "It'll take a better man than you, Gran'pa."

The old man opened the door angrily and went out. He walked along the hall until he came to Nora's bedroom. He hesitated, then knocked.

There was no answer.

He knocked again. "Nora!"

Still no answer.

Inside the room Nora sat in the maple rocker. The shades were drawn. She had not been to bed. A Bible lay open in her lap, but she was not reading it. Her right hand rested on the round-topped maple table that she had bought in Atlanta, along with the rocker, the bed, and the dresser, the week before she married Bubber. Under her hand was the *Courier*, torn in half. From time to time she tapped her fingers on it. She rocked slowly, her face wooden in the gray light.

Pa Aycock rattled the door handle. "Nora! Lemme come in an' talk to you!"

Nora went on rocking. She made no reply.

DR. FRANK FOSBURGH stepped back and surveyed his handiwork. "You're lucky," he said to Melady. "Sure, your beak is busted, but the bones are pretty straight. They'll heal, all right. And you'll have quite a shiner for a week or two. But you managed to keep your mouth out of the way. That's the most expensive damage to fix, as a rule. Teeth don't grow back." He picked up Melady's left hand and ran an iodine swab across the knuckles. "Watch out for infection here. When you cut your hand on somebody's mouth, nine times out of ten it'll fester."

Melady raised his hand and flexed the fingers gingerly.

Fosburgh perched himself on the edge of the examining table. "You're not the type I usually have to patch up after a brawl. What happened?"

Melady's face felt stiff and sore. He could not breathe through his nose, and it hurt him to talk. "I lost my temper, like a damned fool. Got myself in a spot where I had to fight."

"Did you win? Or will I have another patient?" Fosburgh grinned. The gaps between his teeth were too large. They irritated Melady.

"I didn't win," he said shortly. "How much do I owe you?"

"Oh, I usually charge three bucks for an office visit," Fosburgh said carelessly. "Make it five and I'll give you some codeine to take tonight." He went over to a cabinet and shook some pills into an envelope. "Couple of these at bedtime will help you sleep." He added, conversationally, "You don't belong in Hainesville, do you? Don't recall seeing you around."

Melady held out a bill. "I think it's safe to say I don't belong in Hainesville."

Fosburgh folded the money and put it in his pocket. His

curiosity, clearly, was not going to be gratified. He sighed and opened the door that led to the waiting room. "Next?"

The big farmer with the gold teeth put aside his magazine when he saw Melady. "Fix you up?" he asked in his mild voice.

Melady nodded. He took one of the pills out of the envelope and swallowed it. They went out into the street together, Melady holding the lapels of his coat closed over the blood-stains on his shirt. They came to the car, parked half a block from the doctor's office. "Best thing for you to do now," the farmer said, "is go back to yore hotel, drink half a glass of straight whisky, eat a couple more of them little biddy pills, an' sleep till tomorrer mornin'." He opened the car door with a huge hand. "You jes' set easy, now. I'll drive you."

Melady got in. "You've done about enough, I think."

"Shucks," said the countryman. "'Tain't nothin'." He walked around the car and slid behind the wheel. "I wanted to come to town anyway."

The car bucked a little, moving away from the curb. Melady felt the jolts in his face and winced. "I haven't tried to thank you properly," he said to the farmer. "I don't even know your name."

"Simmons. Joe Simmons. Folks mostly call me Big Joe."

"Why did you bother to help me?"

"Oh, I dunno," Simmons said vaguely. "Liked yore spunk, for one thing. An' that Nelson—he's a little too handy with his fists, know what I mean? Likes to find somebody who ain't quite so handy, an' cut 'em up."

"I thought he was going to take a poke at you when you stepped between us."

"Me?" Simmons seemed amused at the idea. "Naw, he wouldn't do that, hardly." He chuckled to himself. "He ain't *that* foolish."

"Well," Melady muttered, "I'm glad to know there are a few like you around."

Simmons swung the car in to the curb near the hotel entrance. "Takes all kinds," he said gently. "You feel all right, now?"

Melady smiled a little, even though it hurt him. "I'll live."

"Better git in a hot bath, drink that likker like I tol' you, an' sleep right through till tomorrer."

"I can't do that; I've got work to do."

"Work?" Simmons was astonished. "You work at night?"

"Sometimes," Melady said. He felt dreadfully tired. He did not want to talk any more. He held out his hand. "Thanks again. That's about all there is to say. Thanks."

Simmons wrapped his fist around Melady's hand. His gold teeth gleamed suddenly. "You shore look funny with that there plaster 'crost your nose."

"I don't feel very funny," Melady said.

He took the keys of the car and went quickly into the hotel.

xi

HELEN came into the bedroom and closed the door. "That was Shep again. Second time he's phoned since I got home. I told him you still weren't available. He said he might come by about eight-thirty anyway. Doesn't discourage easily, does he?"

Unity said, "When he comes, tell him I'm out, will you?"

"Sure." Helen sat down at the dressing table. She stretched her lower lip and drew a lipstick across it carefully. "I'll tell him. But honestly, Unity—" She swung around, her violet eyes reproachful. "Isn't this lovers' quarrel sort of silly? I mean . . ."

"There's been no quarrel," Unity said quietly. "I just don't want to see him, that's all."

"But I thought you liked him," Helen protested. "And after all, he's quite a catch. I know girls who . . ."

[268]

"Listen, Helen," Unity said, "let's not discuss it, shall we? It's taken me all day to come to this decision. Don't shake me loose from it. I know he's a good catch. I know lots of other girls would like to have him. And so would I, that's the worst of it, so would I. But the little sanity I have left tells me he's not for me. Don't make me explain it. Just tell him I'm out, if he comes around."

"Sounds like you're afraid to see him," Helen said shrewdly. "If it's all over, why don't you tell him so yourself?"

"Maybe I will, later," Unity told her. She changed the subject abruptly. "Supper almost ready?"

"Just about."

"Are you seeing John tonight?"

"He had to go to Atlanta this afternoon. Said he'd drop around if he got back in time." She smiled. "I think he will. I'll sit up till midnight, anyway."

They went out into the hall and down the stairs together.

"I'll be glad when this day's over," Unity said.

xii

"You go on home," William Huggins said to his wife. "I got some work to do on the books. I'll be along later."

It was seven o'clock, closing time. The last customer had gone. Huggins' wife hesitated, her fat face creased with anxiety. "How long you gonna be? I don't want you . . ."

"Go on, woman!" Huggins' voice sounded impatient. "Go on home and fix yourself supper. I'll be here till ten o'clock. Eleven, maybe."

That would be long enough, he was thinking. If the meeting began at nine, it would take them an hour to get themselves worked up to the point where they might do something. An hour of speeches, an hour of bottles passed from hand to hand. Flat pint bottles, glinting in the light from the bonfires. From ten to eleven—that would be the time. If nothing happened then, maybe nothing would happen at all. "Go on," he said again. "And when you get home, lock the door. Lock the garage, too. Lock everything."

His wife went out, shaking her head. It was growing dark. Huggins turned on the lights. He looked around at the mirrors, at the chairs, at the racks of clothes hanging in their paper bags. Neat. Orderly.

He went slowly behind the counter and pulled out some ledgers. Might as well work on the books. He had nothing else to do. A year ago, he thought, he would have laughed if anybody had told him that this night he would be waiting, alone in his dry-cleaning place, to protect it from violence. But here he was.

He opened the cigar box that lay under the counter. He had gone home at lunchtime to get it. The pistol looked black and ugly against the golden wood. All his life he had been afraid of guns. He was still afraid of them.

He stroked his silver mustache nervously, then closed the lid of the cigar box. Let 'em come, he thought. They won't throw no more ink in my place. No sir. This time, they'll have to get me first.

xiii

"I'D LIKE to have you read what I've written, for one thing," Melady said. He held the telephone carefully away from his bruised ear. "And there's something else I want to discuss with you. Not on the phone. Can you come over for half an hour? You'll be paid for your trouble."

"I'm sorry, Mr. Melady," Yancey said. "I can't leave home tonight. I'm expecting some—some people. I have to be here when they arrive."

Melady touched his face gingerly. The swelling had gone down a little, but his whole head ached. Across his nose the plaster felt stiff and uncomfortable. "Well, I could come over there, I suppose."

"Wouldn't tomorrow do?" Yancey's voice sounded anxious, tense. "I could meet you . . ."

"No, it wouldn't do," Melady heard the irritation in his own voice and tried to smooth it out. "I've got to phone this thing to New York before midnight. And I want to take a look at this meeting they're having. What the hell, I'll come over to your place. It'll only take a minute. I'd like an excuse to get out of here anyway. Will you be there?"

"Yes," said Yancey, "but . . ."

"I'll be over, then," Melady told him abruptly. He hung up and looked at his watch. Five minutes to eight. Might as well forget about dinner, he thought. God knows I'm not hungry. Maybe a drink . . .

He went into the bathroom, got a glass, splashed some whisky into it, and drank it neat. His manuscript lay on the table beside the typewriter. In three hours he had rewritten the whole thing. It was good stuff, this time; he was certain of it. The words had come fast, with an unmistakable ring of finality. Angry, sure—and bitter. But good. Cunningham might object, on the same grounds as before. Well, let him! Melady drained the glass and kicked the scrap basket out of his path. He was here to write the truth, wasn't he? And truth was reality, wasn't it? If reality included the sound of your nosebones breaking and the salt taste of blood in your mouth, you couldn't ignore it, could you? Even Cunningham would recognize that.

Or would he?

Maybe you can't recognize it, Melady told himself angrily, maybe you just can't comprehend it until it's happened to you. And even then— That's the hell of it, he thought, the God-damned hopeless hell of it; you can't ever communicate it; you just can't. Not the way it really is. No matter how you write it, no matter what you do. It's not the same.

He snatched the manuscript from the table and rolled it into a cylinder that lay lightly in his hand. He glanced in the mirror once, then turned away. He looked like a battered gargoyle. He went out and locked the door. In the lobby he went up to the desk, ignoring the clerk's curious stare.

"Where's number seven Primrose Street?"

The clerk stared harder than ever, but he gave the necessary directions. He added, unable to contain himself, "Been in a car smashup, sir?"

"No." Melady stared back at him. "I just asked too many questions, that's all."

He turned and went out into the purple night.

xiv

SLOUCHED behind his desk, Daly looked indifferently at the slip of yellow paper. He straightened up suddenly, his face sharp with interest. "Where'd you say you got this?"

"Like I told you," the girl said. "I work in the telegraph office, see? And I remembered this colored man sending this wire the day the Aycock brothers were acquitted. Sent it full rate, too. That's why I remembered. So when they started getting themselves shot and stabbed and everything, I looked it up. This afternoon, at work." She pointed. "That's our file copy you got there. I'd have brought it over sooner, but I don't get off till eight o'clock."

"Wait here, will you?" Daly went quickly into Matson's office. The Chief was sitting with his feet on the desk scowling at the sergeant in charge of the motorcycle men, a thick-bodied, round-headed man named Bauer. "I don't care how much bitchin' there is," Matson was saying. "You've got your orders. Those roadblocks are gonna stay there till I say they can come down." He looked impatiently at Daly. "What is it?"

"Look at this, Chief." Daly held out the slip of paper. "Telegram sent to somebody in New York the day the Aycock brothers were acquitted."

Matson took the telegram and read it. His feet came down with a solid thump. "Where'd this come from?"

Daly gestured with his thumb. "Girl from the telegraph office remembered it. She looked it up an' brought it over here."

Matson handed the paper to Bauer. "Read that."

Bauer read it aloud, one word at a time. "*Aycock brothers acquitted. Nothing you can do about it. Better forget the whole thing. Yancey.*" He handed the telegram back to Matson. "Yancey Brown?"

"Go back out there," Matson said to Daly. "Describe Yancey to her and see if it checks." He read the address on the message. "Nathan Hamilton." He looked up at Bauer. "That name mean anything to you?"

Bauer scratched his bullethead. "One of them nigger wimmin got killed—her name was Hamilton, wasn't it?"

"You're damn right it was." Matson spat at the cuspidor; in his excitement he missed. "It fits. It sure as hell fits. But there's only one person can tell us for sure." Daly came back into the room. "Does it check?"

"It was Yancey, all right. Slender-built colored feller, gold-rimmed glasses."

"Come on, Bauer." Matson stood up. "Let's go pay a little visit on Mr. Brown. Right now."

"Want me to come?" Daly asked.

Matson eyed him coldly. "You're a friend of Yancey's, aren't you?"

"I know him pretty well."

Matson spat again, accurately this time. "Then maybe you better stay here. All right, Bauer. Let's go."

Daly said, "That's inside the city limits, you know."

Matson pulled his cap over his eyes. "You think I'm gonna call in them city cops on the first good lead we get? Don't be a God-damn fool, Daly."

They went out the side door that led into the courtyard. Daly stood there a moment, gnawing at his thumbnail. Then he went back to the outer office.

The blond girl was still waiting on the bench, and now another woman sat beside her. Daly stared at the newcomer, at the copper-colored hair drawn back from the thin face, at the circles of rouge on the pale cheeks. It was Nora Aycock. She sat there almost primly, holding her worn leather handbag carefully in her lap.

Daly thanked the languid blond girl and ushered her out. Then he came back to the desk. "Hello, Nora." His joviality sounded forced, even to himself. "Sorry to hear about your bad news. Hope Bubber's gonna pull through."

Nora did not answer. When she looked at him, her eyes had a stony opaqueness that made Daly uncomfortable. What in hell does she want, he wondered. Oughta be down to the hospital, or maybe home in bed. Looks sick enough to be in bed.

"We're workin' on the case, Nora," he said soothingly. He decided that she must have come to ask about that. "Just got a lead this minute might bust the whole thing wide open."

"You holdin' Geneva Holland here?" Nora's fingers plucked nervously at the handbag, but her face remained stiffly expressionless, the circles of rouge as round and as artificial as a clown's make-up.

"Sure, we got her," Daly said. "An' we're gonna keep her

[274]

until we know more about this business. We don't think *she* did it, mind you, but . . ." He closed his mouth firmly. Holy saints, he was thinking, I gotta be careful what I say. Wish she'd go on home, where she belongs.

"Could I see her for a minute?"

"See her?" Daly's voice rose. "What for?"

"I just want to—" Nora shut her eyes and kept them shut. "I want to thank her for doin' what she did. If she hadn't, Bubber would be dead right now."

"That's right," Daly agreed. "He sure would. But I wouldn't bother, if I was you, Nora. It's after visitin' hours, for one thing. I don't know whether the matron's on duty or . . ."

"I come all the way from home just for this," Nora said. "Won't take but a minute." Her eyes were still shut; she did not move.

"Oh, all right," Daly said wearily. Anything to get rid of her, he told himself. "I'll take you up for a minute. I can't open the cell without Matson's permission. But you can talk to her through the bars."

"That'll be fine." Nora nodded her head deliberately. She opened her eyes. "That's all I want to do."

"Take over," Daly said to the policeman at the switchboard. "I'll be back."

He led the way across the courtyard, a heavy sense of irony oppressing him. Fine thing, he thought: white man shacks up with a yeller gal, cheats on his wife two, three times a week, now wife comes to thank the yeller gal for savin' her husband's life. Fine thing!

They came into the fetid atmosphere of the jail. The deputy sheriff on duty recognized Daly; he put down the newspaper he had been reading. "Howdy, Pat."

"Want to see that nigger gal, Holland," Daly said. "Lemme have the key to B block, Dan. Just the outer door. We don't aim to open the cell."

He led the way up to the top floor, where the women prisoners were kept. Naked light bulbs threw a harsh brilliance on the whitewashed stairway, but behind the latticed steel doors the cell blocks were in semidarkness. "We put the cell lights out at eight o'clock," Daly said by way of explanation. "They ain't got much to do besides sleep anyway."

Nora said nothing; she followed close behind him.

He unlocked the green-painted door, stepping expertly on a cockroach that scuttled under his feet. "She's in the third cell on the left, Nora. Want me to stay here with you? If not, I'll go down and have a cigarette with Dan."

"That'll be all right," Nora said.

"Have to lock you into the block, I reckon. Give a holler when you're ready to come out."

Nora moved inside. The door clanked shut; the lock clicked. The place reeked of urine and sweat, of carbolic acid and vomit. She stood for a moment, looking at the unpainted wooden table that ran down the middle of the block with backless benches on either side. She heard Daly's footsteps retreat down the stairs. She went forward, peering through the bars into the cells on her left. The first was empty. In the second a figure lay motionless on a canvas bunk slung from the walls by steel chains. She came to the third cell. Geneva lay on the bunk, legs crossed, hands behind her head. Her eyes were wide open. They stared straight at Nora, insolent and a little curious.

Nora moved close to the bars. She bent forward tensely, elbows held tight to her sides. "Geneva Holland?"

Geneva did not move.

"Come here," Nora commanded. "I want to talk to you."

Geneva hesitated a moment. Then slowly she reached out, caught the chain over her head, pulled herself to a sitting position.

"Go ahead an' talk," she said. "I kin hear you."

[276]

Nora fumbled with her handbag. "I've brought you somethin'," she said. She was breathing hard. "Here, take it."

At the foot of the concrete stairs, Daly held out a pack of crumpled cigarettes. "Know who that was? Bubber Aycock's wife. Came to thank that nigger wench for savin' her husband's life. How 'bout that?"

The deputy sheriff struck a match on his thumbnail. He held it out. Daly bent his head, still smiling. The screaming began. The match fell to the floor. Daly straightened up, the ruddy color draining out of his face. The deputy sheriff's lips moved soundlessly. The dark cells came to life with oaths and uneasy mutterings. On the top floor the screaming went on, not diminishing, growing in intensity. It sounded like an animal being tortured.

They began to run, three steps at a time, up the glaring, whitewashed stairs.

xv

THE ancient hearse stood in front of number 7 Primrose Street, its tarnished silver funeral lamps gleaming in Melady's headlights. He cut his engine, switched off the lights, and got out. He went up the steps, past the show window. It was empty except for the wooden trestles, gaunt and ugly in their somber setting. Melady rang the bell.

Yancey opened the door immediately, as if he had been waiting just behind it. He stared at Melady's battered face; for a moment he did not recognize him.

"Well," said Melady, "can I come in?"

Yancey stepped back, let him in, then closed the door and locked it. Only the chapel lights were on, blue bulbs that made an eerie twilight. Yancey pushed forward one of the folding chairs. He did not take one for himself. He kept standing, as if he hoped the interview would be short.

Melady sat down. "I brought the script over. I'd like your opinion of it, as I said. But that was only one reason for coming. The main reason . . . Sit down, for God's sake, will you? You make me nervous, standing there like that."

Yancey obeyed.

Melady pulled his chair forward. "I'll be frank about this. Or try to be. You refused to tell me anything the other day. Maybe you'll still refuse. But I've got a new set of credentials, see?" He touched the X of plaster that Fosburgh had strapped across his nose. "This morning I was just an outsider looking in. Tonight I'm not. It makes quite a difference. Can you believe that?"

Yancey took off his glasses and rubbed the lenses with his tie. He did not answer.

"I'm saying it badly," Melady told him. "What I mean is this. Until this afternoon I was looking for news, nothing else. I wanted a good story; I was willing to settle for that." He got up and began to move restlessly around the room. "I suppose it's childish to have your attitude changed by a broken nose. All right, so I'm childish. But I have a personal interest, now, in breaking this case. I don't mean these recent attacks on the Aycocks; they're just secondary. I mean the original case—the lynching itself."

Yancey put his elbows on his knees and stared at the floor. The glasses, swinging from his fingers, glittered in the blue light.

"I don't know who made these attacks on the Aycocks," Melady went on. "Maybe you do. I sympathize with the man, whoever he is. In fact, I hope to God he gets away with it. But his method's all wrong. He's trying to fight fear with fear, meet violence with violence. That's no solution—you just start a vicious circle. Why did I get mauled this afternoon? Because

[278]

those farmers were afraid, that's why. They had to maul something. Today it happened to be me. Tomorrow it may be you. But it'll be somebody—you can bank on that."

Yancey put on his glasses and spoke for the first time. "It'll be somebody, all right."

"Look," Melady said. "You've got all the knowledge, haven't you? You know the facts, or most of 'em. You know the names—you practically admitted that the other day. What can you do with your knowledge? Nothing, apparently. But if I had it . . ."

Yancey looked up. "Yes?"

"I might be able to do quite a lot. For one thing, I'd have nothing to lose. I . . ."

Yancey made a negative gesture with his hand. "I've heard that before. It's not true. Everybody has somethin' to lose. You should have found that out this afternoon."

"This afternoon I was a damned fool," Melady told him. "That's why I got hurt. Look." He came back and sat down beside Yancey. "The magazine I represent is very rich. And immensely powerful. You have no idea how powerful. The men who control it like to think of themselves as humanitarians. They have to think of themselves that way to justify the money they've made and the power they have. And maybe they are, I don't know. All I know is that if I had the knowledge you have, it is quite possible that I could persuade them to . . ."

The knock at the door was loud, imperative. Yancey sprang up so quickly that the chair fell over. He caught it before it hit the floor. He went over and put his face close to the door. "Who is it?"

"County Police," said Bauer's heavy voice. "We want to talk to you, Brown."

Yancey's face seemed to shrink a little in the blue light. "What about?"

"About Nathan Hamilton, you sneaky son of a bitch." It was

Matson's voice, this time, cold and furious. "Open that door!"

Yancey took the key out of the lock and put it in his pocket. Bauer's fist hit the thin panel with a crash. "Open up, or we'll kick your God-damn door down!"

"Just a minute," Yancey said coolly. "My wife's got the key. I'll go get it."

He crossed over to the door that led to the basement, jerked it open. He took Melady roughly by the arm and pointed. "Down there. Quick!" And in a much louder voice, "Alma! Bring me the key to the front door."

Melady found himself descending the stairs, Yancey behind him. "What the hell!" he said angrily. "Let 'em find me here. Why should I hide?"

Yancey pressed the switch and the harsh overhead lights blazed out over the stone slabs, over the empty coffin that lay on the floor. He gripped Melady's shoulder and whirled him around. "Listen to me!" He stammered a little, trying to get the words out quicker. "Don't ask questions. Just listen. They're after Nathan Hamilton." He pulled Melady across the embalming room to the door that led to the alley. "He's the man who shot Neal Aycock, who tried to kill Bubber. The lynchers killed his wife; he's been tryin' to pay 'em back, I reckon. Right now he's hidin' in a garage behind a house belonging to some people named Cantrell. It's at . . ."

"*Unity* Cantrell?"

"That's right. She knows he's there. We . . ."

"She *knows* it?"

"Yes. Do you know where they live?"

"Yes, but . . ."

A heavy pounding sounded over their heads. Yancey looked up, his face sharp and alert, like a trapped weasel. "Somebody's got to warn him. We were fixin' to get him out of town late tonight. That's hopeless, now. Somebody's got to tell him the cops are here, understand?" He was unbolting the door. "Tell him they're comin' to get him. Half an hour, maybe less. Tell him to get out of there—hide somewhere else, or get himself out of town somehow." He saw Melady hesitate. "You said you hoped he'd get away with it. Well, he won't, unless you help."

"For Christ's sake!" Melady felt confused and helpless, as if he were being sucked into a whirlpool. "You don't have to tell 'em where he is, do you?"

"They'll make me," Yancey said flatly. He looked up again. The whole house shuddered as Bauer kicked violently at the door. "Wait till I open the front door; then let yourself out." He ran back to the stairs. The lights went out. Melady stood in the thick darkness, breathing hard. He put out his hand and touched one of the heavy bolts. He pushed and the door swung back. Overhead the battering ceased abruptly.

Melady stepped out into the alley. He walked quickly to the street. The police car stood behind the hearse, lights blazing. It was empty. Melady opened the door of his own car and slid behind the wheel. As he fitted the key into the lock he noticed that his hands were trembling. He gripped the wheel fiercely. Don't be a God-damned fool, he said to himself. It's not your mess. Stay out of it.

The engine caught. The car moved away.

Inside the house, Alma came down the stairs from the second floor. She looked at her husband standing between the two white men. From behind her came Albert's frightened wailing. She gripped the banister with her right hand. "What is it? What they want, Yancey?"

"Go back upstairs," Yancey told her. "Look after the baby. They want to talk to me, that's all."

Alma backed slowly out of sight. Matson thrust the crumpled telegram in Yancey's face. "You send this here wire?"

Yancey bent over it, holding it close to his eyes. "I can't read in this light. Let's go downstairs." He moved over and opened the door.

"Wait a minute!" Matson sounded suspicious. He motioned Bauer ahead of them. "You go first."

At the bottom Yancey touched the light switch again. He moved across the room slowly and leaned against one of the slabs. He put the telegram on the stone and smoothed it flat. His palms were sweating; they left dark marks on the coarse yellow paper. Bauer went over to the door that led into the alley, looked outside, then closed and bolted it.

"Now, then." Matson came close to Yancey and stood there, thumbs hooked into his belt, cap pulled down so that all of his face except his mouth was in shadow. "You sent that there telegram, didn't you?"

Yancey nodded slowly. "Yes."

"And Hamilton came down here, didn't he? And killed Neal Aycock! And stabbed Bubber Aycock! Well, *where is he now?*"

Yancey said, "If he came down here, I don't know it. You see what I said in the telegram. I told him there was nothin' he could do about it. I told him to forget it."

Matson's right hand shot out and fastened on Yancey's wrist. "But he didn't forget it, did he? He came down here as fast as he could. He ambushed both the Aycocks, and he would have got Shoup too, if he hadn't got hurt! He's hidin' somewhere in Hainesville right now, with a broken arm. An' you know where! Well, talk, God damn you! Where is he?"

Yancey said, "I don't know," and went to his knees as Matson twisted his arm behind him.

Matson said, panting a little, "You're lyin', you yeller bastard. I'll teach you to lie to me." He gave a violent wrench. Yancey groaned. His wrist, slippery with sweat, revolved inside Matson's hand; otherwise his elbow would have been broken.

[282]

Matson jerked him to his feet and clouted him on the side of his head with the flat of his hand. Yancey staggered, stumbled over the coffin, and fell sprawling. His glasses flew off. They hit the concrete floor and broke with a tiny tinkling sound. Matson pulled out his blackjack. He put two fingers through the loop and wrapped the rest of the rawhide around his fist. "You better talk, God damn you. This is your last chance. I'm tellin' you! You better talk fast!"

"Wait a minute," Bauer said.

Matson glared at him. "Wait for what?"

"You knock him out, you ain't gonna get no information. I know a better way."

"Better way?"

Bauer said, "I'll show you. But first I'll have to git his wife."

Yancey stared at the concrete floor. It looked fuzzy and out of focus. Less than five minutes had passed since Melady left. Maybe he could stall them for ten more.

"Well, go get her, then," Matson said impatiently.

Yancey looked up. He blinked in the strong light; his face looked naked without its glasses. "You won't have to do that. I'll talk." He reached up, caught the nearest slab with his uninjured arm, and pulled himself to his feet. Five more minutes, he thought. "Maybe I better begin at the beginnin'," he said weakly.

Matson spat into the corner. "Maybe you had."

xvi

HELEN sat by the radio, eyes closed, book open in her lap. She was not asleep. Now and then she smiled faintly to herself. Once she opened her eyes and looked at her wrist watch. Eight twenty-five.

The house was quiet except for the narcotic murmur of the

radio, turned low. Her mother and Aunt Guley had gone to a movie. Unity was in her room.

Helen drew her legs under her, nestling deeper into the chair. She was back on the riverbank with John, reliving the previous afternoon. Slowly, so as not to miss any of it. She made herself see it all again: the tawny sunlight, the reddish cypress, the black unruffled water. She made herself hear the rasping screech of the bluejay; she curled her toes, feeling the prickle of the rough grass. The doorbell rang.

She frowned, drawing her smooth brows together, obstinately keeping her eyes closed, holding on to her dream. The bell rang again, loud, insistent. It kept ringing.

Helen sat up. That Shep, she thought; can't wait for anything. Has to have what he wants exactly when he wants it.

She stood up. The doorbell was still ringing. Well, he was going to get a shock this time. Serves him right, she told herself, making a fuss like that! She went out into the hall, rehearsing what she would say, finding a certain satisfaction in the role that had been assigned to her.

She came to the screen door and stopped. A man was standing there. It was not Shep; he was much shorter than Shep. For one terrified moment she thought he was wearing a mask, and her heart gave a panicked leap. Then she saw that what she thought was a mask was a bandage of adhesive tape across his nose. He brought his face close to the screen; she saw the dark discoloration around his right eye. He said rapidly in a clipped, un-Southern voice, "You're Helen Cantrell, I suppose. My name is Melady. Joe Melady. I must see your sister. At once!"

Helen put one hand on the doorknob. Her thumb pushed at the catch that locked it. She did not like the look of this sudden visitor. He might be drunk. He might be—worse. She remembered, abruptly, all the horror stories she had read in the newspapers. She said sharply, "My sister's gone to bed. She doesn't want to be disturbed."

"She'll want to hear about this." The battered face came even closer to the door. "Tell her it's about the man in the garage."

Helen stared. "The what?"

"The man in the garage!" Melady rattled the door handle. "Hurry, you little fool! Don't stand there like an idiot; get her!"

Helen turned and fled up the stairs. She burst into the bedroom. The lights were on. Unity lay on the bed fully dressed except for shoes. Her hands were clasped behind her head. She said quietly, "Is that Shep? I thought I told you . . ."

"It's not Shep. It's some strange character named Melady, or something. Says he has to see you right away. About a man in a garage. But I wouldn't go down there, Unity. I've locked him out. I think he's danger— Wait a minute, Unity! Unity!"

Her sister brushed past her and ran into the hall without stopping to put on her shoes. Helen followed her to the head of the stairs. "Unity! Wait!"

Unity did not even look back.

xvii

LESTER's new secretary turned halfway around, her hand covering the mouthpiece of the phone. She looked a little less frightened, now that the long day was almost over. But not much. Every time he spoke to her, Lester half expected her to flush like a quail. She said, gulping a little, "Lieutenant Daly asking for you, Mr. Crowe."

Lester picked up his own instrument. "Yes?"

"Lester? Listen! This is Pat." Daly sounded as if he had been running. "You better get down here right away. Yeah, right away. All hell's broke loose; the lynchin' case is busted wide open. Nora Aycock, she did it. Wasn't my fault, Lester. Honest! How was I to know? She . . ."

"God's sake, Pat!" Lester cried. "Stop babbling! Make sense! What's happened?"

"Nora Aycock," Daly said again. "Come down here fifteen, twenty minutes ago. Wanted to see this nigger gal, Holland. So I let her talk to her, through the bars. Didn't see no harm. But Jesus, Lester, she had a can of lye in her handbag. Red Devil lye. Throwed it right through the bars into the yeller gal's face. All in her eyes. Christ, you never heard such screamin'! We got Doc Jenkins from down the street. He's over in the jail now, stickin' her with needles. Says she'll probably be blind. But that ain't all. Lester, you gotta come down here. I ain't got time to . . ."

"Go on," Lester snapped. "What else?"

"That Nora, she's crazy, I reckon. Gave me a list of names, all wrote out careful like. Thirteen names. Says they're the ones who did the lynchin'. Said she knows because they met at her place before the killin'. She saw 'em and heard 'em. Says she'll swear to it in any court. An' Lester, she made two other lists an' mailed 'em. One to the *Bulletin* in Atlanta, one to the F.B.I."

"The F.B.I.?" Lester clutched his white hair. "That does it! You recognize any of the names?"

"Recognize 'em? Hell, yes! The Nelson twins, Whitey Lawrence, young Buckhalter—holy saints, Lester, I know 'em all! You better jump in your car an' . . ."

"All right, all right! Where's Nora now?"

"In Matson's office. I got a man watchin' her. I didn't want to lock her up; not yet, anyway. Christ, Lester, you oughta see her—so calm it gives you the creeps. I don't . . ."

"Where's Matson?"

"That's another thing. We got a hot tip on the Aycock business. We think we know who done it. Matson went off to follow it up—he ain't back yet. I'm in charge down here, with all this goin' on. Look, Lester, I gotta hang up. Come on down, or send somebody. I can't talk no more now." There was a click. Daly was gone.

For perhaps half a minute Lester sat quite still. The F.B.I., he thought. All they ever needed was one good witness. They'll get an indictment now. Hell, they'll get convictions, this time. He stood up and reached for his hat. He looked once at the clock. "I may be gone quite a while. You just sit tight until you hear from me."

The rigid secretarial spine grew even more tense. "Yes, sir."

Lester paused, his hand on the door. "All the cops in creation couldn't break that case. One fool woman cracks it wide open." He sniffed sadly. "One fool woman," he repeated, as if he couldn't quite believe it. He went out.

xviii

SHEP stood on the porch of the Cantrell house. His feet were planted wide apart. His close-cropped hair shone like gunmetal in the moonlight. "It's fantastic! You're imagining things."

"Shep, I *saw* him." Helen's voice sounded shaky; she was not far from tears. "It was Nathan; I'm sure of it. I couldn't have been mistaken."

"But it's dark out here. You . . ."

"I heard his voice, I tell you! The three of them came around the corner, right there by the oleander bush, and went down the path."

"How long ago was all this?"

"Less than ten minutes. Oh, Shep, I'm frightened! I was trying to phone you when you arrived; I thought you ought to know. It's all so queer! Unity's been acting strange for—for days. Aunt Guley noticed it before I did. She said . . ."

Shep silenced her. "How long after Melady arrived did you see Nathan?"

"Four minutes. Five. Unity was out here on the porch with—with that man for about three minutes. I don't know what he said to her. Then she came back in and ran upstairs and got her shoes . . ."

"How did she look?"

"Look? I don't know, really. She looked scared and mad and determined, all at once."

"Say anything?"

"When she came down she said, 'I'll be back.' That's all. Then she went out on the porch and down the steps. I came out behind her and stood right here, where we're standing now. And in a couple of minutes I saw the three of them. . . ."

"Come on." Shep took her arm. "Let's get to the bottom of this. Hattie lives over the garage, doesn't she? Show me where."

They went down the creaking steps together, around the corner where the sickly scent of oleanders stained the night air. Ahead of them an oblong of yellow light marked Hattie's window. The shade was drawn. Helen ran up the unlighted stairs, Shep stumbling behind her. She knocked once, and tried the door. It was locked. "Hattie!"

"Ma'am?" Hattie's footsteps halted beside the door.

"Let me in. I want to ask you something."

The key turned. The door opened a crack. Hattie's face appeared. There was the sweetish smell of liquor on her breath, but she was not drunk. Not yet.

Helen tried to push the door open, but the old woman had her foot against it. "Hattie, I saw Nathan go out with Unity just now. What's he doing here? Where did they go?"

Hattie hesitated. "Ain' nobody here but me."

Helen said frantically, "Please, Hattie, tell me! I'm frightened. Where did they go? What does it all mean?"

Hattie allowed the door to swing wider. She opened her mouth to speak, then saw Shep looming behind Helen. She stepped back instantly and slammed the door. They heard the lock click.

"Hattie!" Helen beat on the wooden panel with the flat of her hand. "Let us in. We've got to talk to you! Where did they go? You've got to tell us!"

They stood there in the blackness, waiting. It was so quiet that they could hear the pounding of their hearts. At last Hattie said in a voice like a tired sigh, "Ain' nobody here but me." They heard her footsteps retreat.

Shep swore under his breath. "She's not going to talk. Let's get out of here." They backed cautiously down the stairs. At the bottom, Shep stopped. "Listen, Helen. You told me you heard Nathan say something. What was it?"

Helen moved down the last two steps and stood beside him. "I didn't really pay much attention. I was too amazed. And anyway, it didn't make sense." She thought for a moment. "He said something about a crisscross. It sounded like 'What about the key to the crisscross?' Something like that."

Shep's hand came out of the darkness and gripped her shoulder. "*Crisscross?*"

"Yes. Shep! Don't! You're hurting me."

He spun her around. "Go in the house, quick! Phone the County Police. Tell Matson or Daly or whoever answers to get out to my cabin, right away. Tell 'em to hurry."

"The *cabin*?"

"Nathan didn't say crisscross; he said Chris-Craft. There's only one speedboat around here that's a Chris-Craft. Mine. Don't you see? Nathan's going to try to dodge the roadblocks by going down the river. And that crazy sister of yours is helping him. Go on; do as I say! Hurry!"

"What about you? Where are you going?"

Shep was already out of the garage, running.

You must be crazy, Melady told himself bitterly, driving fast along the moon-whitened road; you must be out of your mind. Look at yourself; take a good long look. And don't pretend you're the cool impersonal newsman now. You're . . .

"Curve ahead," Unity said.

He glanced at her quickly, then back at the road. He let the speedometer move down to fifty. You never know, he was thinking, you just never know. Remember this the next time you think you can judge people. You had her tagged as the helpless type, didn't you? Unhappy. Uncertain. Incapable of any action. But whose idea was this? Who made the decision, all in a flash? Who's pushing it through? Not you, my friend; not you.

Unity's shoulder touched his as he clawed the speeding car around the curve. Something's happened to her, he told himself. It's not just this emergency; it's something a hell of a lot stronger than that. It's got to be. Maybe she's getting even with somebody, he decided suddenly. That's it. By God, maybe she's getting even with Hainesville.

The wheel vibrated under his fingers, a steady humming, and abruptly he remembered himself standing in the dove field with the broken-necked bird in his hand. He said, almost dryly, "I hope you're not planning to cross any bridges. They're guarded."

"We turn off before we come to any bridges." Unity's voice was positive, assured. "I'll tell you when."

Melady raised his eyes briefly to the mirror. Nathan sat huddled in a corner of the back seat, left hand steadying his bandaged right arm. His face was a blur above his white shirt.

He had not spoken since entering the car. What goes on be-hind that blur, Melady asked himself in a kind of despera-tion. How does it feel to have your wife murdered, then wait a year, then start murdering the murderers? What sort of corro-sion goes on inside of you? How much of you is left at the end?

The road straightened out again; the needle on the speedom-eter crept up to sixty. It's no use, Melady said to himself. You can't ever know what anyone else is thinking. All you can ever know is what you'd think if you were in their place. And even that's confused. How can you get inside a black man's skull when you can't even understand what goes on inside your own?

Lights from an oncoming car dazzled him. They came closer and closer, intolerably bright. They bored into his shrinking eyes; they seemed to split his skull. He dimmed his own lights, but got no response. A blast of rage, momentary but murder-ous, roared through him. He twisted the wheel; for a moment a head-on collision seemed inevitable. The other car flashed past, teetering on the shoulder of the road; they heard the frightened yell of the driver, a ragged sound, gone instantly.

Melady bent forward over the wheel. His face throbbed; the pain came in waves. That was childish, he told himself wearily; I might have killed us all; what's the matter with me?

"We turn off up ahead," Unity said calmly. "Just past that sign." She looked over her shoulder. "You all right, Nathan?"

Nathan said, "I'm all right."

The car swerved into the dirt road. Melady touched the brakes and slowed it down. He said, without looking back, "If they catch up with us, somehow, remember one thing. You held a knife at my back, or a gun, or something all the way out here. That'll be my story. I have no intention of going to jail for this."

Nathan did not answer. Unity said, "Nobody's going to jail."

The windows of the cabin glinted ahead of them. "There it is," she said. "Aim your headlights at the porch and keep them on, will you?"

Melady did so. He took his hands off the wheel. His fingers felt cramped, numb; he flexed them slowly. Around the car the night air was damp and cool. In the glare of the headlights the front of the cabin looked unreal, one-dimensional.

Unity ran up onto the porch. Melady saw her reach under the eaves and take the key from its hiding place. She fitted it into the lock and beckoned. Melady got out and joined her. She had the door open, now. She held out her hand. "Matches, please."

He gave her a paper folder of matches. She struck one and moved into the darkness, shielding the flame with her hand. He heard a step behind him; Nathan had come up on the porch. He stood leaning against one of the poles that supported the roof, his bandage white in the darkness, his face in shadow. Go on, said the years of training inside Melady. Now's your chance. Ask some questions. Get some quotes. Go on, what are you waiting for?

With his left hand Nathan took his right arm and moved it to a new position in the sling. His body sagged. He's in pain, Melady thought; leave the poor bastard alone. Then the habit-forming years prodded him again. He said, "Was it worth it? Would you do it all over again?"

Nathan raised his head a little. "I don't know."

"You killed one of 'em. Doesn't that give you any satisfaction?"

"I don't know," Nathan said again. He straightened up as light flared inside the cabin. Unity had lit the big kerosene table lamp. Nathan went inside. Melady followed him to the door. Death is no punishment, he thought; that's the irony of it. Has he found that out? God help him if he has.

Unity was lighting a second, smaller lamp; the match was

[292]

steady in her fingers. She replaced the glass chimney and carried the lamp over to the mantel, the shadows retreating ahead of her. She took some keys from a hook beside the fireplace and handed them to Nathan. For the first time she seemed hesitant; her forehead was creased with anxiety. "Can you really manage the boat with one hand?"

"I think so," Nathan said. There was no emotion in his voice. No confidence, no despair. A kind of numbness, that was all.

Melady stood in the doorway, arms folded, watching them. He had seen the cabin only once, and then by flashlight. Yet all the details—the gunrack, the bar, the silver cups on the mantel, the position of the furniture—all looked strangely familiar. He felt a queer conviction that somewhere, sometime, he had stood here in this same attitude, in this same room, listening to this same dialogue. His mind trembled on the brink of foreknowledge of what would be said next. When Unity did speak, the words seemed to fall precisely into vacancies waiting for them.

"How far downstream will you go? To the railroad bridge?"

Nathan shook his head. "I'll have a better chance if I get to a main road."

"You need anything else? Food, money, anything?"

Nathan moved around her and took a gun from the rack. It was Shep's double-barreled twelve-gauge. He put it on the table. A box of shells stood open on the shelf below. He dropped two or three into his pocket. He picked up the gun again. "I'll take this."

"Bird-shot won't help you much," Melady said sharply. The sense of preordination was leaving him. He was glad of it.

Nathan did not answer. He walked over to the door. He looked back and started to say something. Then he shook his head. He went out. They heard him cross the porch.

Melady took out a pack of cigarettes. He fumbled for his matches, then remembered he no longer had them. He walked over to the lamp on the table, thrust the tip of the cigarette over the glass chimney, and drew on it till it ignited. He inhaled deeply, standing there with his hands on the table. Unity sat down on the couch. They waited. In perhaps two minutes they heard the sound they were waiting for—the whine of a motorboat's self-starter, a moment later the dull roar as the engine caught.

Melady went out onto the porch. The boathouse was a black rectangle against the moon-path on the water. He saw the Chris-Craft emerge, backing slowly. Nathan's shirt was a pale smear in the cockpit. The engine coughed once; then water boiled white under the stern. The boat leaped forward. It heeled over as Nathan gave it full rudder. Even so it barely missed the end of the boathouse. A diamond plume of spray glittered briefly. Then the bow rose high, hurtling over the calm surface of the river. The drone of the engine faded, receding into the distance. The white track of the wake curved around the bend, out of sight.

Melady went back inside. Unity had not moved. "Well," he said to her, "he's gone." She did not answer, and her silence angered him. He said, "You don't think we'll get away with this, do you?"

She turned around slowly. "I don't see why not."

Melady threw his cigarette into the empty fireplace. He felt a strong compulsion to shake her confidence, to torment her, somehow, to hurt her. "I suppose you're feeling noble, now. Heroic. Self-sacrificing. Well, I'm not. I feel like a fool. Worse. Like a criminal. That's what we are, you know. Criminals."

Unity looked up at him. "Nobody made you do it, did they? Are you really sorry, or are you just scared?"

He went and stood at the window, his shoulders hunched a little, his fingers on the smooth unpainted sill. "Maybe I am scared," he said finally. "I took quite a beating this afternoon. Maybe that used up my supply of courage." He touched his broken nose gingerly. "What really scares me, I think, is the knowledge that I've stepped out of character. Twice in one day, without meaning to. I'm not the impulsive type. I'm the reverse. At least, I was."

Unity rubbed her hand along the back of the couch. "Nobody can stay in his hiding place forever."

"It's not a hiding place," Melady said angrily. "It's a way of life, a discipline that I . . ." He stopped. Twin lances of light were probing through the trees, coming rapidly nearer. He felt the leaden impact of fear in the pit of his stomach. It was familiar, now. He said, "We've got visitors."

Unity jumped up from the couch and ran to the window. The oncoming headlights struck obliquely across her face. She put her hand on Melady's arm, and he knew that she was frightened too. She whispered one word. "Police?"

"How would they know we're here? Nobody knows."

The lights swerved past Melady's car and stopped. "It's not the police," Unity said. He felt her grip tighten. "It's Shep."

Melady had been holding his breath. He let it out slowly. "I'll handle him," he said. The tension was going out of him. "Let me do the talking."

Shep was out of the car almost before it stopped. He ran down the bluff. They heard the boathouse door bang in the stillness. Unity went back to the couch. She sat there, rigid, facing the fireplace. Melady turned so that he could watch the door. There were quick steps on the porch. Shep came in.

He looked once at Melady, then crossed the room and stood in front of Unity. "What do you think you're doing? Are you out of your mind?"

Unity stared into the blackened fireplace. "There's been enough violence," she said in a low voice. "There's been enough death. I wanted to save a life, for a change."

Shep clenched his fists. "You want to save a life. So you help a murderer escape! You're mad. No, you're weak. You miserable, interfering little fool! What do you think'll happen at this mass meeting tonight when they find out the killer has escaped and a meddling yankee helped him? They'll stampede into the colored section of town and tear it to pieces. Violence? Death? You're asking for it! You're begging for it!"

Unity said dully, "I don't know what you're talking about."

"You will," Shep said. "You will unless somebody can undo what you've done. And there's only one way to do that. Bring him back, dead or alive. Preferably dead!" He whirled and took two long steps toward the gunrack. He stretched out a hand, then drew it back. Over his shoulder, he spoke to Melady for the first time. "Where's the twelve-gauge?"

Melady said, "He took it."

The muscles in Shep's back seemed to tighten. He jerked another gun from the rack. It was the sixteen-gauge automatic that Melady had used. He put it on the floor and knelt in front of the cupboard that formed the base of the rack. He pulled out several boxes of shells, looking at the labels quickly and discarding them.

"Shep!" Unity had turned around. "What are you doing?"

He ignored her. He stood up suddenly, opened a closet, and dragged out a wooden case of ammunition. It was unopened; the lid was still nailed down. He went to the fireplace and picked up the poker. He drove it into a crack between two of the top boards and threw his weight on it. There was a sound of rending wood; one board broke in half with a loud report. Shep reached into the hole and ripped the rest of the board away. He picked up a single box of shells and threw it on the table. The green cylinders spilled out, brass heads glinting in the lamplight. He swept up a handful in his left fist. His right hand still held the poker.

Unity got up from the couch and ran across the room. "Shep!" Her composure was gone. "Where are you going?"

He dropped the shells into his coat pocket. "You let him go. I'm going to stop him, that's all."

"Shep, you can't! He's . . ."

"What do you expect me to do?" His voice rose sharply. "Sit here with folded hands? He's got to be stopped. There isn't any choice!"

He tried to move past her, toward the gun that lay on the floor. She caught the lapels of his coat. "Shep!" He shrugged his shoulders and threw her off. He walked over and stood in front of Melady, dwarfing him. He held the poker in both hands, now, like a riding crop. His nostrils flared; his face looked ugly and dangerous. "As for you, why don't you go back where you came from? You stay around much longer, somebody's going to twist your God-damn neck. Like this."

He arched his wrists; the poker curved into a semicircle of sooty iron. He dropped it at Melady's feet. He took two steps backward and scooped up the shotgun.

"Shep!" Unity cried again.

He did not look at her. He went out of the cabin. They heard his footsteps cross the porch. The convertible's door slammed; its engine caught. The big car whirled in a tight circle, headlights sweeping luminous scythes through the dark. The taillight gleamed red for a moment; then was gone.

Melady bent down and picked up the poker. He tried to straighten it, found he couldn't. He tossed it on the table. He picked up the broken box of shells. He looked at the label: "Buckshot."

Unity said stupidly, "How did he know we were here?"

Melady put his hand to his face. "Does it matter?" His skin felt hot and feverish. "Let's get out of here. Nothing we can do now. Let's go back to town, for God's sake."

Unity had picked up the poker. She carried it back toward the fireplace. "You go. I'll stay here."

"Here?"

"Yes. I want to stay here until I know what happens."

Melady felt a stab of pity. "That's silly, Unity. We did all we could. I don't think Nathan's got a chance, myself. But worrying does no good. He . . ."

She said, "I'm not worried about Nathan."

There was silence for a moment, then Melady said, "So that's why you tried to stop him."

Unity put the poker down carefully on the bricks that formed the hearth. She did not answer him.

"Look," Melady said evenly. "I'm tired and fed up. I think I've got a fever. In any case, I've loused up this assignment, and I know it. The town has licked me, that's all. I want to get out of it, the sooner the better. I think you should get out of it too, but I'm damned if I'm going to coax you. Are you coming with me now, or aren't you?"

Unity said, "I'd rather wait here."

She heard him go to the door and hesitate. She heard him say, "Come on, Unity; don't be a damned fool." She kept her head down, kneeling there by the fireplace. After a while Melady went out. She heard the car start and drive away.

One of the bricks in the hearth was loose. She took it out; it felt clumsy and heavy in her hand. She held the poker against the other bricks and began to pound at it awkwardly, trying to straighten it. Her hair fell forward around her face like a curtain. If he doesn't come back, she told herself, it will be my fault.

She held the poker up and looked at it. It was still bent. She had made a little impression on it. Not much. Her hands were black with soot. She picked up the brick again. If he does come back, she thought, maybe he'll forgive me; maybe we'll forgive each other. She remembered what her father had said once, about the nature of forgiveness. New opportunities for doing better. Nothing more. She bent her head and began to hammer again, the sound of the blows loud and comforting in the quiet room.

At the turnoff to the cabin the police car left the highway too fast and met the convertible coming out. Headlights clashed like sword blades; brakes squealed; the two cars came together with a grinding jolt. The lighter police car bounced back; one light went out.

Shep leaned out of the window. He blasted once with his horn. "Get the hell out of my way!" A spotlight came on full in his face, and he knew it was a police car. "Matson?"

The Chief got out and went up to the convertible. He held his .38 loosely in one hand. "That blond girl at the Cantrells' house gave us your message. We were just about two jumps behind that black bastard anyhow. What happened—he git away again?"

"He took the speedboat—headed downstream. I'm going to cut him off at the railroad bridge."

Matson swore. "Think you can stop him?"

"If I can get there first. Channel's narrow; he'll have to come through the far span on the Clayton County side." Shep gunned his engine impatiently; it made a roaring sound in the quiet night.

Matson put his hand on the window frame and felt the metal vibrating. "Wait a minute; I'll go with you."

"Hurry up, then, or we'll lose him. Move that car out of my way."

Matson turned and spoke quickly to Bauer. "Get back into town; tell 'em what's happened. Tell Daly to alert the Highway Patrol; have him send any motorcycle men he's got out to the railroad bridge." He slapped Bauer's beefy shoulder with his free hand. "Hurry!"

The police car backed onto the highway. Bauer ground the

gears in a piercing whine. The car jumped away. Bauer pulled the siren and the sound wailed through the dark. "Damn fool," Matson muttered. "What good does that do?" He ran back to the convertible, opened the door, and slid in beside Shep. "After this, maybe they'll give me that two-way radio I been askin' for!"

Shep swung the big car out onto the highway and shoved the accelerator down to the floor. Matson's head snapped back, then forward. "How you figgerin' on stoppin' him?"

Shep kept his eyes on the road. "Double-O buckshot mainly. It'll do it, if I get close enough."

"Where's your gun?"

"On the back seat. He's armed too."

Matson wet his lips with the tip of his tongue. "How d'you know?"

"He took my twelve-gauge."

"Has a busted arm, hasn't he?"

"I don't know. If he can steer a boat, he can pull a trigger."

The purr of the engine rose to a growl. The road was a gray ribbon, flanked by fields of blurred silver; the trees fled past so swiftly that they seemed solid, motionless. They overtook the speeding police car and passed it as if it were standing still.

"How in hell did he git out here?" Matson demanded angrily. "Steal a car?"

Shep's expression did not change. He shook his head. If Helen had said nothing, neither would he.

"Think we'll cut him off?"

"It'll be close. We've got a half-mile run after we get to the grade crossing. Thank God for the moonlight, anyway."

They flashed past a warning sign. Shep braked sharply. The heavy car swerved onto the shoulder of the road. Sand sucked at the right front wheel, then let it go. The convertible shuddered as Shep wrenched it back onto the road. "Jesus!" Matson said.

The embankment where the tracks crossed the highway loomed in front of them. Shep drove up and over. The car bounced once and shuddered to a halt on the other side. Shep switched on the parking lights, and reached into the back seat for the gun. He jumped out of the car and fumbled in his pocket. He slid two shells into the magazine and pumped one into the chamber. The gun was plugged so that it would hold only three shells. He clicked on the safety; it made a metallic snick, surprisingly loud in the stillness. He rammed the third shell home. "Come on," he said to Matson.

He began to lope down the tracks, the moonlight glinting on the gun barrel. Matson stumbled after him, trying to adjust his stride to the crossties. "Wait, God damn it!" Shep did not answer.

They ran. Ahead of them and behind them the shining rails stretched away to infinity. On either side of the embankment cypress made a jungle wall of blackness, broken by occasional splinters of brilliance where the moon caught pools of stagnant water. On and on. One hundred yards. Two, three hundred. Quarter mile. Slowly Shep drew away from Matson. The Police Chief tried to lengthen his stride, missed a crosstie, and plunged forward. His pistol made a shining arc into the darkness. Cinders raked the palms of his hands. He swore desperately and skidded six feet down the embankment. Ahead of him Shep stopped and looked back. "Come on, man!"

Matson was sobbing with rage and exhaustion. "Can't. Lost my God-damn gun!"

"Leave it."

"Christ, no! I may need it."

"We'll miss him, you fool!" Shep went on, his footfalls quick and delicate, now on wood, now on cinder. Matson saw some-

[301]

thing gleam in the shadows and pounced on it. It was a beer can, new and glittering. He swore again and flung it from him. He straightened up as if to follow Shep, then changed his mind. Suppose the nigger killed Shep? Suppose the black bastard shot him and then came down these tracks with *two* guns? Where would *he* be, then, weaponless, helpless? Christ, it had to be here somewhere. It had to be! He fell on his knees and began scrabbling in the tall grass with his burning hands.

Far ahead of him, Shep ran loosely through the silvered dark. His breath came fast and easily, timed to his running rhythm. Fifteen minutes, he estimated, since the speedboat had left the cabin. The railroad bridge was five miles below his boathouse, he knew that. Fifteen minutes at roughly twenty knots. It would be close. It would be damn close.

He ran faster, holding his gun in one hand, using it to balance himself when he stumbled. Ahead of him he could see the river gleaming like spilled mercury and the gaunt skeleton of the bridge with the green railroad signals steady and unwinking. To his left a yellow glow in the sky marked the lights of Hainesville. He stopped suddenly, trying to listen. A wind had come up, moaning and sighing in the trees. He stood still, holding his breath. For one second he thought he could hear it, far away, the familiar high-pitched whine. He lunged forward again. His heart was hammering, but he did not feel tired.

The trees fell back suddenly; he had reached the river. He stopped again. The throbbing of an engine was clearly audible now. Upstream, by God! The speedboat was upstream! It had not passed the bridge. He could see nothing—yet. The river stretched calm and unbroken, curving peacefully into nothing. The whine grew louder. He could tell from the pitch just how fast it was coming. About eighteen knots. Probably as fast as Hamilton dared drive it in the semidarkness.

Shep glanced over his shoulder. Far down the tracks he

thought he saw Matson coming. He did not stop to make sure. He began to trot out onto the bridge, placing his feet carefully along the duckboards laid between the rails. They were greasy and half rotten. He slowed down; he could not afford to slip. On either side he could look down through the cross-ties at the sluggish water. He saw the moon-shadow of the bridge, the girders black against the gun-metal surface of the river. The bridge was longer than he had thought. It stretched in front of him like an endless tunnel, a nightmare network of steel and frustration.

Out of the corner of his eye he caught a gleam of white as the speedboat swept around the curve two hundred yards upstream. He heard the engine sing a higher song as Hamilton saw the straightaway and opened the throttle. The deep channel was near the far shore, where the river narrowed to plunge past a series of small islands. Shep sucked his breath in sharply. He was still out of range.

He began to run along the slippery planking, confident that Hamilton would be too intent on holding his course to see him. He came to a place where the duckboards ended and four feet of blackness intervened before they began again. He hesitated for a second, then jumped, landing with all his weight on his outstretched foot. His shoe drove through the rotten planking with a splintering sound. He felt an agonizing pain as the jagged fragments raked his shin and calf. He fell forward, still clutching his gun, his face colliding sharply with the left-hand rail. The stinging smell of creosote came into his nostrils. The rail itself was still warm from the heat of the sun.

He came up on his left knee and tried frantically to pull his right leg free. Upstream the whine of the speedboat rose to a snarl. He could see the bow wave plunging toward the bridge, the fan of the wake lengthening like a luminous arrow in the dark.

He dropped the gun and tore his leg out of the hole it had made, losing his shoe in the effort. He heard the cloth of his trousers rip. The skin of his leg was lacerated again; he could feel the blood start. But his ankle was uninjured. He snatched the gun and ran forward, clicking off the safety. The speedboat flashed under the bridge, too far away for certain shooting. Forty yards; half a second later, fifty.

Shep whipped the shotgun to his cheek and fired, pivoting on his heel, leading the hunched figure in the cockpit as if it had been a deer. He saw it lurch forward. The speedboat swerved. He fired again instantly, trying to pattern both the engine and the man. The boat swung crazily off course, out toward the middle of the river. It passed Shep sixty yards away, its speed undiminished.

Shep crouched down. He could see nobody at the wheel. He aimed carefully and put his last charge of buckshot into the forward end of the boat, where he knew the gasoline tanks to be. He saw splinters fly in the moonlight and the tiny splashes in the water where some of the pellets fell short. The boat hurtled across the river, rammed the bank, and heeled over. The motor coughed and snarled. The propeller beat the water into a futile foam. Then the engine died.

Shep rose from his crouching position. He clenched his left fist slowly, and struck himself on the thigh. Got him! *Got him!* He began to limp back along the bridge, reloading with sure expert fingers. He came to the gap in the planking and walked across on one of the rails. After that, he did not take his eyes off the boat. He knew what might happen when the liberated gasoline reached the hot engine. As he came to the end of the bridge, it did happen. A tongue of flame leaped twenty feet in the air. Shep watched it, eyes narrowed, gun ready. He tasted blood in his mouth; he had bitten through his lip when he fell. Until now he had not noticed it.

Matson came up to him, panting. He had found his gun.

[304]

"Jesus!" He tried to spit, but his mouth was too dry. "Jesus! You stopped him!"

Shep raised his automatic suddenly, then let it fall. "There he goes! Over the side." He bent down quickly and pulled the laces on his remaining shoe.

Matson caught his arm. "Where you goin'?"

"After him. You don't think I'm going to let him get away now, do you?"

"Christ, man! You said he had a gun!"

"Well," Shep said, "so have I."

"Yeah, but he can see you comin'."

"You can cover me from here."

"You're crazy!" Matson's voice was shrill. "He can't git away, now. We got more men comin'. Let's wait for 'em!"

Shep said, "That might be too late." He jerked off his coat. A dozen or more crossties were stacked beside the tracks. They were massive creosoted blocks, eight feet long. He put down his gun, dragged a tie from the top of the stack, lowered it to the ground, and let it slide down the embankment. It hit the wet vegetation at the bottom with a squelching thud.

Shep went down after it, his movements swift and certain. He stooped down, picked up the tie, staggering a little. He hoisted it to his shoulder. He looked up, his face twisted with the effort. He balanced the tie with one hand and reached up with the other. "Pass me my gun."

Matson handed it down, butt first. He moved along the embankment as Shep plowed through the tangle of bushes and cypress roots. "Don't be a damn fool! He'll hear you comin'. Even if he's hurt, he can still shoot!" He scrambled halfway down the embankment in his agitation.

"Stay up there," Shep commanded. "He's right behind the boat, I think. If he moves, pick him off with your pistol. I'm going to float down with the current. He won't hear me. I doubt if he can see me, either. Even if he does, he won't have much to shoot at. If I flush him out onto the tracks, you take care of him."

"You'll never do it." Matson's voice was hoarse. "Your gun'll get wet! You'll never . . ."

"I'll risk it," Shep said.

He came to the river and waded in up to his waist. The water stung his torn leg, but eased the pain of it, too. He stooped slowly, holding his gun aloft with one hand, until the crosstie floated free. He rested the gun on it and began pushing it steadily out into the stream. When the water was up to his neck, he looked back. Matson stood on the embankment, the pistol in his hand. Downstream, the tower of flame had subsided, but the forward end of the boat was burning with a steady crackling sound. The fire had jumped to the bank, but it would not spread far. The vegetation was too wet.

Shep felt his feet leave the bottom. He let them trail out behind him, resting his hands on the crosstie close to the gun. It supported him easily. He began to move his feet in a slow flutter kick. The crosstie responded sluggishly. He kept his head low, feeling the current nudge him. He would drift almost on top of the speedboat, and then . . .

Behind the screen of bushes, ten yards downstream from the burning boat, Nathan crouched waist-deep in the placid water, waiting. His head was clearing. A single buckshot from Shep's second shot had furrowed his skull, knocking him down, stunning him momentarily. Two or three pellets had lodged in his right shoulder; one had splintered the boards that Yancey had bound around his arm. His plunge over the side had washed the blood out of his eyes, but it was coming again in a slow red curtain. His wounds did not hurt him much; a numb, burning sensation in his scalp, an inability to move his arm, that was all.

With his left arm he had pulled the shotgun out of the cockpit. Then he had floundered, half wading, half swimming, away from the searing heat, away from the explosion he expected momentarily. But there had been no explosion. The fire seemed to be burning itself out.

A screen of tangled roots, slippery with river mud, was in front of him. He had balanced the muzzle of the twelve-gauge in a crotch so that it pointed toward the river. Both barrels were loaded; the safety was off. He felt the twin triggers under the fingers of his left hand, cold and wet, curving and smooth. They would be coming for him, he knew. Well, let them come.

He had been startled when the thunderclaps of sound came from the bridge, when the orange streaks of flame pointed at him like accusing fingers out of the dark. Startled, but not surprised. He had known they would get him, sooner or later, that flight was futile, escape hopeless. He had known it, really, ever since Bubber's hand had closed on his wrist, and the bone had snapped like a green stick breaking.

He had chosen to run because they all wanted him to run—Yancey, and his mother, and the white girl. They thought it was important for him not to be caught, to vanish, to get away. Well, he was caught now. In a little while, it would be over. He was not sorry. It might have been worse.

He put his face in the cool water and moved his head to and fro, washing the blood away. He remembered, suddenly, what his Aunt Cele had said. He saw the stern old face creased with love and misery. He saw the tablecloth and the soup tureen and heard her voice, hoarse with pleading: "They'll kill you, boy, just like they killed the others . . . one man ain't no good against that system down there."

Well, she was right. Aunt Cele was right. But that didn't change anything. What was done was done. Would he do it over again? The white man had asked him that. Probably. There was no choice, really; a man did what he had to do. So he'd do it again, just the same—except that he'd use a gun, not a knife, on Bubber Aycock. . . .

He raised his dripping face suddenly. His eyes flew open. Somewhere in the back of his brain a warning bell was ringing. He had heard nothing; he could see nothing. But they were coming for him. Now. He knew it.

The crackling sound the fire had made was dying; a few low flames still flickered. Nathan raised his body slightly. His eyes swept the unruffled surface of the river. Something glinted out in the darkness. He watched it. It winked again. Metal. Firelight or moonlight on metal. There was no sound. He curled his forefinger stiffly around the first trigger. His heart was hammering, matching the sullen throbbing in his head. He moved his gun barrels to the left until they covered the area where he had seen something. Slowly an outline took shape. Black, low. Something floating. Metal on top. Behind it a rounded silhouette that could be a man's head. Coming in, slowly, steadily. Closer. Closer. Twenty-five yards. Twenty.

Nathan shifted slightly so that the twin barrels bore directly on the target. One blast would blow the swimmer's protection away; a second would smash him, helpless in the water. Who is he? Nathan thought. Whoever he is, he's brave. You can kill him, if you want to. But even if you get him, then what? Behind him will come the others, some of them also brave. Lydia, he said achingly inside the throbbing ivory box of his skull. Fifteen yards. Twelve.

He watched the thing approaching. He saw it clearly now. A crosstie, with a gun on top and a man swimming behind. He saw it stop as the swimmer's feet touched bottom. He saw a white hand lift the gun; the metal winked again.

Shep stood up. He pushed the crosstie aside. Crouching low, he charged for the shore. From behind the dripping branches the twelve-gauge shattered the night with its stunning blast of sound.

Back on the embankment, Matson stood motionless, torn

with indecision. He waited for more shots. When they did not come, he ran frantically back to the pile of crossties and flattened himself behind it, pistol ready. He looked once down the track, to see if help was coming. The gleaming rails lost themselves in the distance, blank and empty. "Jesus!" he muttered to himself. "Jesus!"

He heard Shep calling him.

His relief was so great that he felt weak. He came out from behind his barricade. He shouted at the top of his voice, "You get the son of a bitch?"

Shep's voice came back faintly. "He got himself."

"Wait," Matson called, full of a sudden energy. "I'm comin'!" He thrust his pistol into its holster, let the hammer down carefully, and scrambled down the embankment. He plunged into the reeds, unmindful of the mud that sucked at his feet, the branches that lashed his face. He blundered forward furiously; twice he fell and came up covered with mud. He swore constantly, spitting the slime out of his mouth. The thought of snakes came to him unpleasantly and he moved inland a few yards, to higher ground. He staggered down the low bluff, finally, where the embers of the fire still glowed red. Shep was sitting on the tilted gunwale of the speedboat, his feet in the water. His wet clothes were plastered against his body. His shoulders drooped. "Got a cigarette?" he said to Matson.

The Police Chief gave him one and lit it for him. "Where is he?"

Shep motioned with his head. "I put him in the boat."

Matson bent forward and peered down at the figure huddled on the floor of the cockpit. The face was turned upward; it was unmarked; the eyes were closed. There were dark smears on the boards beneath it. "How'd he do it? Put the muzzle in his mouth?"

"Evidently." Shep drew hard on the cigarette and flung it

[309]

away. It made a tiny hissing sound in the black water. "He wasn't where I thought he was at all. He could have shot me. Easily."

Matson swung his thin legs into the boat. "Turned yeller, huh?"

"No. After all he's done, I don't think you could call him that."

Matson prodded the body with his foot. "Murderin' black bastard. Orta feed him to the catfish."

Shep lifted his dripping feet over the gunwale. "No. We'll take him back."

"Aw, leave him till mornin'," Matson said. "I'll send some men . . ."

"No." Shep stooped down and slid one arm around Nathan's shoulders, the other under his knees. "We'll take him back."

Matson watched in silence. When he spoke, his voice showed his distaste. "You'll have his God-damn blood all over you."

Shep stepped out into the water. "I know that," he said.

He kept moving through the reeds and the mud until he reached high ground. The body felt heavy in his arms. He glanced down at it once; the dead face looked peaceful in the moonlight. After that he kept his eyes fixed on the bridge, black and rigid against the glow in the sky that marked the lights of Hainesville.

ABOUT THE AUTHOR

ARTHUR GORDON *was born thirty-seven years ago in Savannah, Georgia. His family background, medical on one side, mercantile-military on the other, is completely Southern. His maternal grandfather was Stonewall Jackson's surgeon; his paternal great-grandfather was the first Georgian to graduate from West Point.*

Educated at Yale and Oxford (Rhodes Scholar from Georgia), he came to New York in 1936 to start a magazine-writing-and-editing career. At the time of Pearl Harbor, he was managing editor of Good Housekeeping.

He went overseas in 1942 as a lieutenant assigned to the Eighth Air Force, came out a major in 1945. During the war, with Major Richard Thruelsen, he wrote Target: Germany, *the official story of the VIII Bomber Command, which sold close to a million copies here and in England.*

After the war he became editor-in-chief of Cosmopolitan, *a post he held until mid-1948. Then he went back to Georgia to write* Reprisal.

He now lives in Princeton, New Jersey, with his wife and small daughter. He has written many magazine stories and articles, but this is his first novel.